Beverley Harper died of cancer on 9 August 2002.
She rests at peace in the Africa she so loved.

Her ashes lie by the Boteti River in Botswana,
below a lodge called Leroo-la-Tau. It means *Footprints of Lion*.

It is a special place.

This simple plaque marks her passing:

BEVERLEY ANN HARPER
AUTHOR, WIFE, MOTHER AND FRIEND
SET OFF ON HER GREATEST SAFARI

AUGUST 9TH 2002
AGED ONLY 58

SHE LEAVES LASTING FOOTPRINTS
AND A LONG SHADOW

"TSAMAYA SENTLE TATTY HEAD"

Also by Beverley Harper

FOOTPRINTS
of LION

BEVERLEY
HARPER

PAN
Pan Macmillan Australia

First published 2004 in Macmillan by Pan Macmillan Australia Pty Limited
This Pan edition published 2005 by Pan Macmillan Australia Pty Limited
St Martins Tower, 31 Market Street, Sydney

National Library of Australia
cataloguing-in-publication data:

Harper, Beverley.
Footprints of lion.

ISBN 0 330 42205 7.

I. Title.

A823.3

Cartographic art by Laurie Whiddon, Map Illustrations
Typeset in 11.5/13pt Bembo by Post Pre-press Group
Printed in Australia by McPherson's Printing Group

This novel is a work of fiction. Names and characters are the product of
the author's imagination or are used fictitiously and any resemblance to
actual persons, living or dead, is entirely coincidental.

Papers used by Pan Macmillan Australia Pty Ltd are natural,
recyclable products made from wood grown in sustainable forests. The
manufacturing processes conform to the environmental regulations of the
country of origin.

In completing this story I have drawn freely on many real people who, for better or worse, played their part in the ever-changing saga which is Africa. Some influenced events far beyond the shores of that continent. While it is not my intention to stand in judgment over the pages of history – or in any way distort documented fact – Africa is full of surprises. Should apparent coincidence or the suggested actions of any such individuals blur the fine line between fact and fiction, then I am well satisfied. The intention is simply to entertain.

My thanks to those people, living or long dead, who played their part in the rich tapestry which is Zululand. Their names are too numerous to mention individually but each and every one of them contributed to the magic.

And to the animals of Africa – wild, often persecuted, yet somehow adapting to the relentless pressures of change. They survive with uncompromising dignity.

As always, to Piers, Miles and Adam – sons of Africa. May you smile at the memories.

To Heidi and Steve in Botswana. Milestones in my life.

To Cate Paterson and Selwa Anthony, for believing. Sarina Rowell and Jo Jarrah – editors extraordinary.

Also Lindsay Christison in Pietermaritzburg, source of reference material on matters past and present. To Ian and Anne, keyboard wizards.

And especially to Peter Watt, friend, raconteur and kindred spirit, without whose input you would not be turning these pages.

That said, this is Beverley's story – she was Africa – where it all began. I miss her.

To all of you, *hamba kahle*.

Robert Harper
Barooga, 2004

RHODESIA

Okavango Delta △   △ Nxai Pan
                       △ Baines' Baobabs
        Lake Ngami △   ● Xhumaga
                        Lake Xau

GERMAN
SOUTH WEST
AFRICA   BECHUANALAND

                        Pietersborg ●
                    Transvaal
                        ● Pretoria
        Marekong ●
                Orange Free   Swaziland
                    State
    Bloemfontein ●   ● Natal
                   Basutoland ● Durban

    Cape Colony

                            Indian
                             Ocean

                    ● East London
Cape Town ●   ● Port Elizabeth

T R A N

PRETORIA ◉

Magaliesberg   ▲ *Diamond
                         Hill*

JOHANNESBURG

Doornkop ▲   ◉

                        ● Heidelberg

        River

Roodewal ●   ● Heilbron

                ● Kroonstad

                        ● Lindley

O R A N G E   F R E E   S T A T E

                    Brandwater Basin
                Fouriesburg ●

KIMBERLEY ◉

    Modder   River
    ● Paardeberg

        ◉ BLOEMFONTEIN

                        BASUTOL

Vaal

SCALE
0   Miles   100

ONE

Choking dust billowed from beneath the sweat-streaked horse as it bore down relentlessly on a fleeing steer. The young Zebu ox swerved back and forth in a desperate bid to escape but its pursuer was more than a match, keeping up with each twist and turn, effortlessly gaining on the animal. It veered away as the rider slipped from his saddle and launched himself at the ox. Legs planted astride the beast, he grasped the small horns, pulled back and twisted, the straining cords standing out on his arms and neck a sign of physical exertion as the animal fought back. Slowly but surely the Zebu steer's head turned sideways. Still the pressure remained, forcing it to look backwards, over one shoulder. Finally, the steer lost balance, toppling, bringing its tormenter down with it.

'Shite.' The crack had been audible, even above the bellowing of other spooked beasts. 'I've broken my bloody leg.'

Anxious eyes stared down at the man who lay immobile, obviously in agony. The steer scrambled up and escaped, stamping on the fractured limb in its panic to get away. 'Get help.' The words were squeezed out between clenched teeth.

He heard a horse galloping away. Everything went black.

The verandah ran wide around all four sides of a low, solid stone house, providing welcome shade against the fierce afternoon sun. It was late April, yet approaching winter had, so far, provided nothing more than a slight cooling of temperature at night and in the early mornings. The days remained consistently hot, though most of the humidity had dissipated, taking with it the infection-heavy air which laid low both cattle and man. Disease-carrying mosquitoes were still active but nowhere near as bad as in summer. All in all, it was usually a pleasant time, a four-month respite from the norm, an opportunity for rejuvenation, for taking stock, catching up with the small jobs for which there was no time during most of the year.

The man sitting in a cane chair on the front verandah laid aside a much-read copy of *King Solomon's Mines* and found himself wondering if the hero – Allan Quatermain – really had been based on his old friend Fred Selous. Making a mental note to ask him, he sourly eyed his left leg, which was propped on the riempie stool in front of him. A once-white plaster-of-Paris casing, frayed and grimy, stretched the woven strips of leather on which it lay. He couldn't wait to have the thing removed. It was heavy and cumbersome, the skin underneath itched terribly, and he was bored with enforced inactivity.

Six weeks. It had been a clean break, thank God. The plaster was due to come off tomorrow and, although the doctor warned him against trying to do too much too soon, Dallas Granger-Acheson was impatient to get on with his life without the restrictions of a leg that wouldn't bend.

'You're lucky to be so fit,' the doctor had told him. 'A person your age doesn't usually heal as quickly.'

Dallas had grunted and glowered at the man. At forty-nine, he did not appreciate being reminded of encroaching age. The farm kept him busy and he was as capable of putting in as full a day's work as any of his sons. Age had not added too many extra pounds to his body – he remained a fine figure of a man. Despite grey flecks in his dark, curly hair, it was glossy with no sign of thinning. Clear eyes still shone with inner amusement or could glow with desire for the only woman he had ever loved, his wife, Lorna. Laughter lines stretched out from the corners of his eyes and two horizontal furrows sat above them on his forehead – so far, the only creases on a deeply suntanned face. No aches and pains prevented him from joining his children in a game of tennis, or a fast and furious race on horseback. The fact he'd broken a leg whilst trying to prove to his eldest son that he could still wrestle a steer to the ground for branding was put down to bad luck rather than brittle bones.

Lorna stepped out onto the verandah. 'Thought you might like tea out here. The house is like an oven.'

Dallas caught his breath. She still had that effect on him, even after so many years. Sunlight captured the honey gold of her hair. It had once been pale blonde but the colour had deepened with age and, now Lorna was nearly forty-five, glowed rich and silken whenever she let it down over her shoulders. Usually, like today, it was pinned up, leaving tendrils to float around her face. Six children had thickened her waistline slightly – a fact that caused Lorna much annoyance – but the rest was still as slender as the girl he'd known when they were growing up together in Edinburgh. Slightly tanned skin remained wrinkle free although a few fine lines had begun to appear during the past couple of years. Eyes the colour of cornflowers had lost none of their lustre. Dallas loved Lorna now as much as ever.

Enforced inactivity over the past six weeks had left Dallas with little to do. There was a limit to how many books could be read and he quickly grew bored with writing letters. Even the farm accounts were up to date. In a reflective moment he found himself looking back over his life, to the early days in Zululand and the reasons why he'd come here. Lorna had, on more than one occasion, accused him of brooding. Now she did it again.

'I am not,' Dallas replied. 'I'm just remembering.'

She smiled, bent and kissed his hair, then returned inside, leaving him to reflect.

He'd been twenty-one when circumstances forced him to leave Scotland. The reason still caused Dallas – Lord Acheson – some pangs of guilt. Young, anxious to experience life and all it had to offer – a fact not lost on Lady Alison de Iongh. She was Lorna's mother and the affair had come abruptly to an end when she and Dallas were caught *in flagrante delicto* by her husband, Lorna's father. To save her own reputation, Alison accused Dallas of forcing himself on her, leaving Lord de Iongh no option other than to accuse the young man of rape. Dallas had two choices. Stay and face the real possibility of a hangman's rope, or flee. He chose the latter, changing his name to Dallas Granger, escaping from Britain and ultimately settling in Africa.

As if that wasn't a bad enough legacy to leave behind, his relationship with Alison de Iongh had become complicated by Lorna. Dallas had fallen in love with her but circumstance forbade the two young people from considering marriage. As fourth son of the Earl and Countess of Dalrymple, he had no prospects to offer a young lady of quality. Lorna, who had no say in the matter, found herself engaged to the Marquis of Dumfries, a man older than her own father.

For as long as she could remember, Lorna had adored Dallas. Although resigned to a future without him, she was determined that the Marquis would not be the first man to touch her. A few months after her seventeenth birthday, she declared her feelings to Dallas. This was too much for a young man who felt the same way and they became lovers.

Dallas knew that what he was doing was wrong.

Time and again he tried to stop seeing Lorna's mother but the older woman managed to maintain his much-divided attention. For two months he continued seeing both of them. He had placed himself in a hopeless situation, and it was only a matter of time before Dallas's world blew up in his face. When it did, Lorna was carrying their child.

Dallas moved his leg to a more comfortable position, remembering the despair he'd felt at having to leave Scotland and, in particular, Lorna. He'd believed he would never see her again. Trying to forget, he fell into a brief, though pleasurable, dalliance with a Danish woman onboard the ship taking them to Africa. Jette Petersen satisfied some of Dallas's needs, but she was not Lorna. When Jette jumped ship in Morocco, stealing a small fortune in jewellery belonging to Dallas, he was unable to do anything about her deception. Worst of all, Lady Dalrymple, his mother, in a last-minute confession before he left home, had told him that the gems once belonged to his real father, a man by the name of Jonathan Fellowes. Although Dallas loved and respected Lord Dalrymple, whom he had always known as his father, he was devastated at losing the only link he had with his natural father.

Arriving in Durban under the assumed name of Granger, and having few funds remaining, Dallas realised that he had to find something to do, and quickly. He teamed up with two men, trader Will Green and Logan Burton, elephant hunter. They worked the Thukela River valley, trading with the

Zulus and gathering ivory. From their first event-filled trip, Dallas became fascinated with Zulu culture, learning as much as possible about their traditions and lifestyle from his driver, mission-educated Mister David.

Along the way, Dallas rescued two fellow travellers, Jack Walsh and his daughter, Caroline, from a swollen Mngeni River which threatened to sweep their wagon over the Howick Falls. A second girl, Sarah, niece of Jack Walsh, remained stranded on the north bank and Dallas was charged with Sarah's safe return to her parents' home in Colenso.

Five months later, on arriving back in Durban, he was horrified to discover that Sarah had named him father of the illegitimate child she now carried. Her bullying, reputation-conscious father, William Wilcox, demanded that Dallas marry his daughter. At first he refused; he hadn't laid a finger on Sarah. But when Wilcox announced that he knew Dallas's real identity, was aware of the charges laid against him in Scotland, and threatened to contact the police unless Dallas made an honest woman of Sarah, he had no option but to comply.

Lorna, despite everything, still remained at the forefront of Dallas's mind. Married he might be, but in name only. When Sarah gave birth, the truth could no longer be hidden – the father had been African. To avoid a scandal, the child was sent to him and word put out that it had died. Wilcox still refused to consider his daughter giving Dallas a divorce. Outraged at the blackmailing tactics which forced him to remain in a loveless marriage,

Dallas walked out, returning to the boarding house he'd stayed at when he first arrived in Durban. There he found Lorna and their son, Cameron.

Lorna's husband had died, leaving her wealthy. Feisty and determined to be with Dallas at any cost, she defied convention and made her own way to Africa in search of him. There were many obstacles that might have come between them but Lorna had brushed them all aside. The two set up house together, living as man and wife.

At last, it seemed that Dallas's life had fallen into place but there was still one cloud on the horizon. More than anything, he wanted to be free of Sarah, free to marry Lorna. That, he believed, would complete his happiness. As it happened, fate hadn't finished with Dallas. In Durban, he unexpectedly encountered the Danish thief, Jette, who introduced him to Torben, also his son, the result of their liaison onboard ship. Jette told Dallas she expected nothing from him with regard to their offspring.

Surprisingly, she still had the stolen jewellery and opted to return it, keeping only one piece. In order to explain the sudden appearance of such obviously valuable items, Dallas had to confess the affair to Lorna. She'd already forgiven him his involvement with her mother and the fact that he married Sarah. Now she had to accept that he had a son with another woman.

Love between them was strong enough for Lorna to stay. Then, one day while Dallas was away, Jette arrived at their house, bringing Torben with her. She was, she claimed, being threatened by a powerful sultan for whom she had worked after disappearing from the ship in Morocco. She had also stolen from him. Jette told Lorna that the sultan would stop at nothing to get his revenge and she feared for her son's safety. Lorna agreed to look after the boy and Torben Petersen became part of their lives. All so long ago. So much had happened since then.

Dallas and Lorna were granted the use of land in Zululand by Cetshwayo, fourth king of the Zulus. Both the British and the Boers had their eyes on this richly fertile part of Africa. War was the inevitable outcome, which forced Dallas to choose sides. Using his considerable knowledge of the country and its people, Dallas scouted and fought for the British. Not that he wanted to; he was given no choice.

The pressure on Dallas to remain married to Sarah had continued until Lorna's mother died of tuberculosis in 1879. Lord de Iongh, released from the moral obligation to stand by his wife, dropped all charges against him. Sarah's father could no longer threaten Dallas, and after an uncontested divorce he and Lorna were finally free to marry.

Although the Zulu War had ended, the family were unable to return to their original farm. Cetshwayo had been captured, Britain controlled his kingdom, and unlike in the old days when the king allowed use of land as and when he saw fit, permission to acquire a farm was now at the discretion of Britain's administrators, who gave preference to those willing to grow sugar cane. So Dallas and Lorna secured two thousand acres in Zululand, establishing a property they named *Morningside*. Dallas did plant some cane, on the lower coastal flats, but cattle were his main interest and the majority of their farm was given over to raising beef stock, with a small but growing herd of Zebu cattle, bred for their disease and heat resistance.

During a disastrous outbreak of rinderpest in 1897, which destroyed over eighty percent of Zulu cattle, Dallas made extensive use of a newly developed vaccine and constructed miles of fencing to quarantine his land. It worked, and despite dramatic fluctuations in the price of sugar and beef, the farm flourished.

So did the children. Six in total were born to Lorna and Dallas, which meant there were seven in the family, including Torben. Cameron, or Cam, and Torben were only a few months apart in age. Now grown men, both nearly twenty-seven, their lives had taken very different paths. In fact, when Dallas thought about it, not one of the children resembled another. Their interests and personalities were all different. Lorna was largely responsible for this, allowing each to grow within the boundaries, or lack of them, as personality dictated. She had tutored the girls at home but all four of the boys spent time away at boarding school near Pietermaritzburg.

A tomboy herself as a child, she had vivid memories of growing up feeling constricted. Probably for that reason the more extrovert of their children were encouraged to be so; the retiring respected for their need of privacy. As a result, with one exception, the family were a well-adjusted, adequately educated and contented lot.

Torben was that exception. A brooding child, temperamental youth and secretive adult, he caused more worry for Lorna and Dallas than the rest put together. It seemed there was a self-destructive aspect to his nature. Given two choices, Torben could always be relied on to take the one no-one else would. Lorna said it was because he felt his mother had abandoned him and he was constantly trying to prove his worth. Dallas took a more simplistic view – that Torben was a lot like Jette. Whatever the cause may have been, the boy, and later the man, had moments that seemed to result from nothing more than a desire to disrupt the rest of his family. At other times, he was a pleasure to know. The trouble was, moods of varying kinds came and went with no warning.

Lorna, followed by Mister David, now their cook of several years, came onto the verandah, the latter bearing a silver tray heaped with scones, butter, jam, cream, home-baked biscuits and cakes, tea, slices of lemon and, especially for Dallas, a selection of savoury delicacies.

'Whew! When is winter coming?' Lorna sat down and fanned herself with a napkin. Her face was flushed from being in the kitchen. The sleeves of her blouse were already rolled up and, once Mister David had disappeared inside again, she hiked up her skirt in a most unladylike manner, causing Dallas to grin spontaneously.

'Just the two of us this afternoon,' she commented, gazing away over the rolling hills. 'Even Meggie has deserted us.'

Meggie. Their youngest. Bright as a button, the apple of her father's eye and, at sixteen, already a beauty. Not that she would have agreed with that. Meggie was the daughter most like Lorna – a tomboy, a rebel, outspoken to the point of causing embarrassment, and not at all fussed about feminine trappings. Early the previous year, when her breasts finally began to develop, both parents felt it necessary to convince her that, even if it were only around the house, wearing nothing more on top than one of Dallas's old vests was not a terribly good idea. Meggie glanced down at herself. 'Oh these.' She dismissed the two pointed buds with a wave of her hand. 'It's only flesh. Besides, I dress properly when I go out.'

'It's not out that worries me,' Dallas had said rather selfconsciously. Discussing his daughter's sexual attributes, particularly as she seemed so unaware of their significance, made him quite uncomfortable.

Lorna came to his rescue. 'I know, dear. But you are growing up. A little modesty wouldn't hurt.'

They'd never lied to her. Meggie took the advice good-naturedly and conformed. A little. She continued to go barefooted, skirts tucked into her knickers when playing tennis or games on the lawn. She was, Lorna once declared, the most free-spirited human being she'd ever known.

'That's just it,' Dallas had worried. 'She seems so completely unconcerned about how others view her. Young men . . . well, will they understand, do you think?'

'That's years away,' Lorna replied complacently.

'Yes, but the boys have friends over. You never know what . . .'

'I'll speak to her,' Lorna promised.

And she had. Although refusing to go into details Lorna told him that the conversation had been frank. Dallas didn't want a word-for-word report, all he needed to know was that his Meggie would not send out the wrong signals and ruin her reputation. The hypocritical nature of this wish had occurred to him but he didn't care. This was Meggie.

Her body safely confined in what could only be described as practical attire – she completely shunned soft and feminine dresses, preferring either loose-fitting shifts or pinafores with the skirt cut into trousers as her mother had always worn when in the bush – Meggie's acquiescence was confined to her clothes. There was nothing either parent could do about her mouth. Meggie spoke her mind and saw no reason not to.

Dallas shook his head and came back to the present. A storm was rolling in from the sea. Until the wilder weather stopped, winter would not fully arrive. He felt Lorna's hand on his thigh, warm and affectionate. 'Tomorrow,' she reminded him. 'One more day.'

'I can't wait,' Dallas stated the obvious. 'This leg is driving me mad.'

'What were you remembering?'

'Oh, this and that. Us. The early days.'

'Only me, I hope.'

'Only you.' At a disbelieving look from Lorna, he added with a smile, 'I skimmed the rest.'

She laughed and patted his leg.

They had grown into middle age together and neither of them had noticed. The passion of the early years had matured into love, respect and liking. They were the best of friends, partners in everything, lovers, and each trusted the other implicitly. Perhaps it was growing up together in Scotland – Lorna's brother had been Dallas's best friend and his sister, Charlotte, and Lorna were once inseparable – that meant that there was no pretence between them. Unencumbered by any need to impress, when they had finally been able to spend time together as man and woman, both simply picked up where they had left off. The flames of desire were strong, earlier ties and memories dispensing with formality.

Lorna's outspokenness constantly delighted Dallas. She threw false modesty back in the faces of those who pretended it. Her obvious breeding, and the fact that before she married Dallas she had been the Marchioness of Dumfries, allowed her to get away with this. People were usually intimidated by her manner and criticism was only expressed well out of her hearing. The few close friends they had were, of necessity, square pegs in round holes.

That suited both Lorna and Dallas, who needed no others to make their life fulfilling and enjoyable.

She was topping a jam-smeared scone with a liberal amount of cream. 'I suppose you'll go charging back to the fields once that plaster comes off.'

'What else would I do? You've seen me for the past six weeks. I hate being housebound.'

'I've actually enjoyed having you around,' she told him, laying a hand back on his leg.

His hand covered hers. 'Bad temper and all?'

'You haven't been that bad. A bit pensive, perhaps. The rest has probably been good for you.'

'Don't you start. The doctor keeps reminding me of my age. The bloody man treats me like an octogenarian.'

'You're not so young anymore.'

'Forty-nine. I keep fit and active. Just because I'll be fifty next year . . .' The forbidden word slipped out. Dallas had been conscientiously avoiding it for the past couple of years. To him, it marked the beginning of a downward spiral and he dreaded it. 'Where did the years disappear to?' he asked.

Lorna smiled wickedly. 'So your mind is going too, is it?'

He tried to lunge and tickle her, swore at his rigid leg and collapsed back into the chair, eyes closed in frustration. 'You,' he told her in mock outrage, 'are asking for trouble.'

'Good.' She clapped her hands together, eyes shining with mischief. 'Would that be taking the form of domination in the bedroom, because I'm sick of doing all the work.'

Dallas burst out laughing. 'Work, is it? You're a bad lady,' he joked with great affection.

She grinned and rose. 'Finished?'

'Tea, yes.'

She swiped gently at the top of his head. 'Now who's being bad?'

Mister David appeared at the door. 'I may take the tray?'

'Yes, please.' Lorna turned to Dallas. 'I'll be in the kitchen. We're trying something new this evening in honour of Torben's visit. Will you be all right here?'

'What am I?' he grouched. 'An invalid? Anyway, Suza and I have some fine conversations.'

The battle-scarred boxer lying sprawled beside his chair was stone deaf but still had a keen sense of smell. This was quite surprising as he always appeared oblivious to the general reaction to his frequent and often noisy releases of putrid air, after which he had been named. Born on the farm, his fourteen action-packed years had witnessed many a confrontation with fruit-stealing baboons, not to mention the odd leopard with a liking for chickens. Suza had a sister, Saba, but she was Cameron's constant companion. Alert eyes watched the Zulu's retreating back. It was too hot for any other movement.

Mister David's timing had been, as usual, impeccable. There were occasions when Dallas wondered if his long-term mentor lurked behind the lace curtains, waiting for tea to finish. He wouldn't put it past him. Mister David was part of the family, a fact which he was quick to remind anyone and everyone if the occasion warranted. He'd been with Dallas from the beginning – as a wagon driver on his trading trips down the Thukela, becoming *induna* at the first farm and then this one. As the years rolled by and Mister David became less able to do hard physical work, he, at his own request, was being trained by Lorna as cook. The Zulu had taken to her kitchen as though born to it.

It had been Mister David who taught Dallas so much about Zulu culture, customs and language. When the children arrived, he'd also tutored them. As a result, most had spoken Zulu before mastering English. Again, the exception was Torben, who refused point-blank to speak a language he claimed was made up mainly of stupid clicks and grunts.

Grey now peppered Mister David's hair and his back had bent slightly with age. Bright eyes still twinkling with fun, he constantly corrected everyone's pronunciation of Zulu words and would tell any of them when he thought they were wrong about something. Dallas regarded the man more as a friend than an employee. When the children were growing up, if any of them became ill Mister David could be relied on to arrive bearing a collection of roots, leaves, bark, and sometimes items which didn't invite investigation in case their origins became known. These he would boil up, strain, pulverise or whatever was needed so that the patient could be treated with traditional Zulu *muthi*. More often than not, his bush medicine was far better than anything the family's English doctor could recommend.

Dallas often thought how different his life had become from the one for which he was originally destined. As Lord Acheson, his future had been decidedly boring. Thomas, the eldest brother, inherited everything – estates and their late father's title. Boyd went into the army; Glendon, the church. It was all as expected. Which left Dallas with little more than a courtesy title, a small allowance, an excellent education and breeding. Had he stayed in Scotland, Dallas and Lorna might have married after her husband died and he would have been well within his rights to run the considerable estates owned by the Marquis. But only until Lorna's son came of age. Although Cam was actually Dallas's child, this fact remained unknown to anyone else. It was thought the Marquis had suffered a stroke in the act of begetting him. In truth, the seizure which rendered him helpless occurred before his marriage had been consummated. So, although not the natural heir, Cameron was entitled to inherit the Marquis's estate in its entirety. Any involvement by Dallas would have been nothing more than a caretaking role. While prepared to put up with most things in order to be with Lorna, the thought of living off her inheritance was quite unpalatable and he wondered how long it would have been before resentment set in.

As it was, fate intervened, forcing him to leave the land of his birth. Dallas quickly discovered that in the dark continent of Africa life was lived to the full, a man judged by deed rather than lineage, and opportunities abounded for all. Yes, Lorna's wealth certainly smoothed a path for which others had to work hard. But Dallas paid back every penny and was now extremely well off in his own right.

A sudden breeze ruffled his hair as the approaching storm flirted between sea and land. It would stay out over the ocean. Circling seagulls, wheeling white against clouds laden with rain, showed no interest in seeking shelter inland. He took a deep breath, smelling the salty tang released by an uneasy surf as it blended with the dirt dry scent of land. Back from the coast, cattle grazed contentedly. Dallas shifted his gaze down towards the unfenced stands of waving cane. Despite the British government's insistence that any sale of land be dependent on a commitment to growing sugar, the area he planted had changed little over the years. Dallas had no interest in crops. They were far more vulnerable to disease and weather than cattle.

He heard boots on the verandah. Cameron. Suza noticed nothing and dozed on.

'Father?'

'Here,' Dallas called.

Saba appeared first, then Cameron rounded the corner. Tall and blond, deep blue eyes, skin the colour of bronze, a ready smile. He had been beautiful as a little boy and time had turned him into a strikingly handsome man. He flung himself into the empty chair beside his father. 'I did it.' Suza opened a questioning eye as Saba seemed to whisper something in her deaf sibling's ear.

'And?'

'She said yes.'

Dallas stretched out a hand and Cameron clasped it, shaking firmly, a grin so wide it nearly split his face in two.

'Congratulations, son. Have you spoken to her father?'

'Of course.'

'Told your mother?'

'Just about to.'

'She'll be pleased. So am I. Virginia is so right for you.'

'Ja.'

'Yes,' Dallas corrected absently. All his children had picked up what was rapidly becoming a South African way of speaking. A mixture of English and Afrikaans with some Zulu thrown in for good measure. The young claimed it was a way to ensure an amicable blending of the cultures. Dallas wasn't so sure. Each clung possessively to their own very different protocols and customs.

'I'll go find her.' Cameron slapped his thighs, rose to his feet, told Saba to 'stay' and added, 'I can only hope our marriage will be as happy as yours.' With that he left his father, who wore a faint smile of satisfaction.

Virginia Waring-Jones. Dallas couldn't have dreamed up a better match for his eldest son. She was twenty-four, educated mainly in England, loved Zululand and its lifestyle, was gentle yet possessed a quiet strength, and she'd kept the lad waiting for five years before saying yes. Dallas didn't blame her. Cameron had a reputation that sometimes included other women. He also had a wild streak – nothing terrible – and an affinity for the Zulu people which occasionally took him beyond the boundaries of conventional behaviour. He was an intelligent man though not academically inclined, preferring his two years' practical work with the Cedara agricultural facility to those spent at Hilton College. Although Cameron could read and write perfectly well, do sums, and knew most of what there was to know about cattle, it would have been pointless asking him to recite Robbie Burns or Elizabeth Barrett Browning. Charm meant he got away with things others could never hope to.

Virginia and Cameron had known each other most of their lives. If anyone understood what was underneath his carefree exterior, it was her. When she was nineteen and he first proposed marriage, she realised that Cameron was still too immature for commitment. At twenty-one, she again said no. Both times, Cameron had disappeared from her life to lick his wounds, finding solace in the arms of women seeking nothing more than a night's pleasure, going on extended hunting trips with friends or just plain ignoring her. During the past couple of years, however, Dallas and Lorna could see that Cameron had matured considerably. Obviously Virginia thought so too.

A grand addition to the family. Lorna adored

the girl. Virginia had been best friends with Kate, Dallas and Lorna's second daughter. Like their own children, she spoke fluent Zulu, and was Zululand through and through. She wasn't beautiful in the chocolate-box sense, but was strikingly good-looking and possessed a natural style and a directness that set her apart.

Mother and son burst onto the verandah, arms around each other. 'Isn't it wonderful?' Lorna's happiness was completely genuine.

As for Cameron, he stood next to her, a stupefied smile on his face saying he couldn't quite believe his luck.

Yes, Dallas thought, sharing their joy. Suddenly his look turned serious. 'I hope you've done with philandering, young man. Virginia won't stand for it.'

Cameron shook his head. 'I wouldn't dare,' he replied in genuine amazement, as though he'd never strayed in his life. 'She'd kill me.'

She would too, and rightly so. Dallas prayed that Cameron meant what he said. You didn't mess with the affections of the Virginias of this world.

Once Cameron had gone back to work and Lorna exhausted herself talking about a ring, the wedding, getting garden and house ready, where the young couple would live and all the other female practicalities that men never think about, Dallas was, once again, left to his own devices. Suza hadn't moved.

He asked himself the same question he'd put to Lorna earlier: 'Where did all the years go?' It seemed like only yesterday that she had introduced him to Cameron as a nine-month-old baby. Although aware Lorna was pregnant when he fled Scotland, he'd had no contact with her since then and assumed she must have hated him for the affair with her mother. Lorna was out of his life and he'd attempted to come to terms with that. The instantaneous feeling of love and desire to protect which flooded through him when he first saw Cameron had been joyfully grasped and held. Dallas loved his son instinctively and it seemed the feeling was immediately reciprocated.

Cameron had been told at an early age that Dallas was his real father. He also grew up knowing that he stood to inherit a title and huge estates should he choose to acknowledge the Marquis of Dumfries as his own flesh and blood. A child of Africa, he had grown to be a man of that continent too. Despite several trips back to Scotland with the family, Cameron could not relate to the formality, bad weather and what he considered to be the stupid rules and regulations of Britain's upper class. Above all, he loved and respected Dallas.

At twenty-one, when he was entitled to take over responsibility for his Scottish inheritance, Cameron had to make a decision. The only guidance his parents gave him was that, whatever he chose to do, it would be for the rest of his life. If he elected to inherit the Marquis of Dumfries's title and fortune, history would forever regard him as that man's son. If not, there was no point in ruing his decision later. Although christened Cameron

Keith Adair Kingholm, he never used that surname, preferring instead the Granger-Acheson which his true parents had adopted at the time of their marriage.

As usual if a dilemma arose, Cameron sought an answer in Zulu beliefs. It was no contest, really. A young man's first loyalty was to his king, second to his chief and third to his father. Cameron didn't have a king – Queen Victoria still ruled Britain's empire – and anyway, he felt no allegiance to the British monarchy. The head of the Marquis's Scottish clan, whoever that might be, would certainly constitute a chief but again, he felt no connection. For that matter, he had no idea which clan it was. What did strike Cameron, for the first time, was a strange similarity between the family clans of Scotland and tribal affiliations among the Zulus. What it boiled down to was that Dallas remained his father and Cameron had absolutely no intention of masquerading as another man's son in order to gain property and title in a land in which he had no interest in living. The Granger-Acheson family were happy and better off than most so the prospect of greater wealth held little or no attraction. As for titles, Cameron was too practical to find them even remotely desirable.

The decision took him two hours and that was only because he felt his parents would expect careful consideration of his answer. Cameron knew what he wanted almost before the choice was put to him.

'I'm staying here,' he announced with no preamble, walking into the room where his parents were sitting. 'Do what you wish with my inheritance, Mother, I've no interest in it.'

'Fine.' She'd smiled up at him. 'I'll write to my lawyers in the morning. Charles has had his eye on that land for the last three years, ever since he sold his estates in Perthshire to pay the death duties on your grandfather's estate. Anyway, since he and Charlotte now live there, selling it to them makes sense.'

Almost six years on and Cameron had never once regretted that decision. On the rare occasions he thought about it, it was with relief at choosing the path he had. Lorna had shown no disappointment and Dallas knew she felt none. In fact, the smile she'd given their son held a touch of deliverance, as if she'd been dreading an affirmative response.

Dallas heard the clip-clop of ponies and a crunch of wheels coming up the drive. Their trap was back from the Thukela railhead, a good forty miles away. 'Lorna,' he called. 'Torben's here.'

TWO

Lorna came out onto the verandah just as the horses stopped. 'Hello, you two,' she greeted Dallas's son, and the plump, blonde young woman at his side. 'Did you have a good trip?'

'The road is as bad as ever.' Torben jumped down and looked up at Lorna. 'You're looking radiant, if I may say.'

Lorna's laugh tinkled. 'You were here a few months ago. What did you expect, an old woman?'

Torben grinned; then, at a sharp word from the girl in the buggy, went to help her down. The two of them came back to the verandah, Torben going to his father and his wife greeting Lorna.

'Hello, Ma.'

'Gerda, darling. How well you look.'

Dallas smothered a smile. Lorna hated being called Ma.

'What have you done to your leg?' Torben asked.

'Broke it. Damned steer fell on it.'

'Where was Cam?'

'He was there,' Dallas said lightly, though the implied criticism irritated him. Torben was always

quick to find fault with Cameron. 'I was just showing him what not to do.'

Torben raised his eyebrows.

'It's a clean break,' Dallas went on. 'The plaster
comes off tomorrow.'

Out of the corner of an eye he saw his
daughter-in-law bearing down on him. She
looked, he thought sourly, like a Dutch doll. Ging-
ham dress with puffed sleeves and a ridiculously
matching bonnet. All that was missing were the
clogs. 'Poppie.' Gerda was bending to kiss his
cheek, her near-white plaits swinging forwards and
brushing his face.

Dallas resisted the urge to push them away. Try
as he might, he had never taken to Gerda and just
about everything she did annoyed him. Lorna tried
hard but she too found it difficult to establish any
kind of common ground with the girl.

'How lovely you're here.' Lorna used the bright
tone she always resorted to with people she didn't
particularly like but to whom she was obliged to
be friendly. 'Come, Gerda, we've done up the spare
room since your last visit. I think you'll find it most
comfortable.'

Gerda followed her mother-in-law into the
house. As he knew she would, Dallas heard the girl
commenting on anything new and asking the
inevitable question, 'How much did it cost?' This
was a major sticking point with Lorna, who found
the question vulgar.

'You've had rain,' Torben commented, sitting
next to his father. 'The last five miles were rather

27

boggy. When do they expect to finish the bridge at Bond's Drift?'

Dallas braced himself. Whenever Torben prefaced a question with comment on the weather it meant he was working up to something else altogether. Last time, he'd wanted his father to invest in a harebrained scheme to grow roses commercially. He would not listen to reason – that the coastal climate was unsuitable. The visit ended with Torben cutting short his stay by three days.

'It'll be two or three years at best before the railway reaches Empangeni. As for rain, well, it certainly does nothing for the garden at this time of year,' Dallas replied, pointing deliberately to some past-their-prime rose bushes.

Torben ignored the comment.

Dallas persisted. 'Any further developments with the nursery business?'

'No. It had to be near a market and when I investigated the potential in Durban it became obvious that humidity brought too many pests and diseases. Frankly, it was too risky to guarantee a profitable return on any investment.' Conveniently, Torben ignored the fact that he was repeating his father's sentiments. 'But there is something else I wish to discuss with you. Perhaps after dinner?'

'Certainly,' Dallas murmured, dreading the prospect and the inevitable argument which would follow.

'Excellent.' Rising, Torben excused himself. 'I'll give Gerda a hand. Then I might ride out to find Cameron and Duncan.'

'Duncan has gone to the stock sales. He won't be back for a few hours yet.'

Torben nodded, smiled vaguely, looked at his fob watch, nodded again and went inside.

Dallas shook his head. Torben was, without doubt, the strangest man he'd ever known. He seemed to strive desperately for respectability. Perhaps the fact that he was illegitimate accounted for that. He had found it hard to accept that Dallas, his real father, had not married Jette. It wasn't until his mother came back for him – in dubious company and obviously down on her luck – that the boy had begun to regard Lorna with any kind of acceptance.

Or maybe it was the manner in which his mother had died that caused his concern for outward appearances. He was too young to remember his mother when she had handed him over to Lorna and Dallas for safekeeping. The only memory he had of her was the wreck of a one-time beautiful woman who returned unexpectedly, eight years later, to try to take him back.

Jealous of their past association, and the subsequent connection between Jette and Dallas through their son, the man with her – Jeremy Hardcastle, once first officer on the steamship *Marie Clare* which carried them to Africa – had been adamant that Torben be returned to his mother. He wanted the boy with them so that, through him, he could exercise control over Jette. In the argument that followed, Jette was struck by a bullet meant for Dallas. Torben had witnessed the whole distressing scene.

Dallas acknowledged that such a memory would have a lasting effect on anyone. Added to that, the mother Torben fantasised about had been beautiful, rich, clever, stylish and respectable. The woman who returned for him was none of these things. Thinking Jette had been killed in West Africa, Lorna and Dallas had kept the truth about her from Torben – that his mother had no scruples and was, in fact, a professional thief. The harsh reality of her reappearance could well explain his need for social acceptance.

There was more of Jette Petersen in Torben than first impressions would indicate. After leaving Hilton College at the earliest possible opportunity, his involvement in get-rich-quick schemes invariably led to him owing money. Dallas learned, to his horror, that repaying a debt was not something Torben regarded as essential. He owed large sums to a great many people, influential people, who were not impressed with his 'When this project is up and running I'll pay back every penny'. Dallas covered his debts on numerous occasions – something Torben had come to take for granted.

Then there was Gerda, an Afrikaner. With Boer and British relations becoming more strained by the day over possession of land within South Africa, intermarriages were rare. Gerda's parents had forbidden her to see Torben. Lorna and Dallas tried to convince their son that a full-scale war between the Boers and English-speaking South

Africans was likely and that Gerda, not to mention her family, could well end up as enemies. The young couple's answer to both arguments was to elope and marry. Torben had been twenty-two; Gerda, just sixteen. They were shunned by English and Afrikaners alike.

It wasn't only her lack of years, or the fact that she was of Dutch descent, which made her difficult to accept. Gerda's siblings were decidedly *déclassés*. One brother was in prison for murder – he'd taken a *sjambok* to a supposed friend during a drunken brawl and killed the man. A sister was reputed to be selling her favours to visiting sailors. Lorna tried hard to convince both herself and Dallas that Gerda's family was not the girl's fault. But her lack of social graces was made worse by the fact that she affected airs which only made the shortcomings more noticeable. Lorna once suggested to Dallas that Torben had married someone like Gerda so he could feel superior. It made sense in a strange kind of way.

For whatever reason, Torben appeared not to notice his wife's behaviour. He continued to run up bills he couldn't afford to pay and was constantly looking for new ways to make a fortune. The money left to him by his mother had long gone, frittered away on luxuries and ill-fated enterprises. Torben then assumed that his father would finance future ideas. When Dallas refused assistance for the rose scheme, he also warned his son that any further requests for monetary help might, or might not, be successful. If they were, the sum involved would be deducted from Torben's inheritance. That's where they had left it. And now, here he was, back with what was likely to be another madcap scheme and plea for backing.

Dallas was reasonably certain that it was not Torben's intention to cheat. He was obsessed by the need to make money – lots of money – which inevitably blinded him to obvious impracticalities. That, plus the fact he was not partial to the idea of a day's work, made him unreliable. Torben wanted the good things in life and he wanted them now. Gerda seemed to share his ambitions.

In the spare bedroom, Lorna was ready to scream.

'Oh, I do so love the new carpet. How much was it? Where did you get it? We're thinking of recarpeting.' Gerda held up a dress. 'Do you like it? It cost nearly ten pounds.'

'Does it fit?' Lorna eyed the slinky blue garment with ill-disguised disbelief. Low cut with a tiny waistline, a girl of Gerda's proportions would look as if she'd been poured into it.

'Of course it does, Ma. The things you say. I'll wear it tonight. It goes so well with the sapphire necklace Torben bought me. Have you seen it? No matter, I'll wear the necklace as well. I do so like to dress for dinner.'

Torben appeared at the doorway and Lorna thankfully escaped, saying something about checking on Mister David. She went briefly to the verandah. 'Prepare to be amazed,' she told her husband. 'Gerda's latest outfit will drive you insane with lust.' She grinned at his expression and disappeared back inside.

Mister David appeared beside Dallas carrying a bowl of mealie meal for Suza. The dog rose, stretched, broke wind, and moved off to where he knew his meal was going. 'It is time for you to come inside,' Mister David told his employer, in a tone that implied a negative response would not be tolerated.

Dallas gave him one anyway. 'Soon.'

'Now, if you please. The air is cooling and your leg will know it.'

Dallas had no argument against that logic. 'Oh, very well. Help me up.'

Mister David moved forwards. 'That is why I am here,' he said simply, slipping an arm behind Dallas and bringing him to his feet. 'Pick up your stick.'

'Bully.' Dallas could not keep the asperity from his voice.

His cook and long-time friend heard it and smiled. They walked slowly to the western corner of the verandah. 'You see the sun?'

'Yes.' Dallas knew what was coming but would never deprive Mister David of his delight in dispensing his unique brand of wisdom.

'It will set without your help.'

'I know, old friend. It is not pride that makes my temper short. It's . . . it's . . .'

'The cow is in the field but the bull is kept at the kraal. He knows what he wants to do but is unable to do it. You are like that bull.'

Dallas laughed. Frustration was the word he'd

been searching for. How like Mister David to put it so well.

Inside, they encountered Gerda. 'Poppie.' She swept up to him. 'Let me help.'

'I'm fine,' he said sharply. 'Mister David knows what to do.'

Gerda's eyes flicked to the Zulu. 'But he is a Kaffir.'

This derision was typical of her race, Dallas thought. It made his blood boil the way she spoke of Mister David or other servants, often in front of them, with no regard for their feelings. He'd taken her to task about it once but the attitude was so deeply entrenched she'd paid no heed. 'I'm fine, Gerda,' he told her. 'Why don't you see if Lorna needs a hand with anything?'

As she left in search of Lorna, Dallas favoured Mister David with raised eyebrows and a wry smile. 'As usual, I find myself apologising for my daughter-in-law.'

'I have told you many times, *nkosi*,' Mister David said, helping Dallas to his armchair, 'the Zulu way is patience. For as long as we allow misunderstanding to continue, we remain empty. Emptiness brings abuse. It is not her fault, nor yours. It is ours.'

'Patience, in your case, my friend, could be construed as defiance. You tried that once,' Dallas said, referring to the Zulu War. 'Look where it got you.'

'That is different.'

'So you say.'

Mister David smiled. 'We can be very patient. In

34

the end, it will win the respect of all white people. In the meantime, we can respect ourselves.' He gently placed Dallas's leg on a footstool. 'Do not feel bad about Master Torben's wife. She is guilty of ignorance, nothing more.'

Dinner that night was indeed an amazing experience. Gerda was bursting out of her slinky blue dress with sequined bodice, set off by a sapphire necklace which would not have been out of place at a ball, and had tried to complement the outfit with earrings, shoes and a shawl, none of which were of the same blue, nor indeed came anywhere near it. Torben glowed with pride when his wife joined them for drinks in the drawing room. 'Blue suits you, darling,' he told her.

By comparison, Lorna's practical cream-patterned tea gown, plain buckle-up soft leather shoes and caramel-coloured shawl were all delightfully understated. As a last-minute kindness to her daughter-in-law, she had pinned a small pearl brooch to the collar of her gown and added tiny matching drop-earrings. The gesture went unappreciated. 'You're wearing pearls, Ma. They're a little plain for me.'

'Each to his own,' Lorna murmured, head bent so Gerda could not see her flare of amusement.

Conversation was stilted until Cameron, and then Duncan, put in an appearance. Both had hastily washed and dressed – Cameron still had water dripping onto his collar.

'So, little brother,' Torben addressed Duncan.

'Where is that young filly I hear you've been sporting around?'

Duncan frowned at Cameron, who shrugged. 'Not me, old boy.'

'My fault,' Lorna owned up. 'I was telling Torben about the Taylors' new venture with sisal and it sort of slipped out.'

'No matter,' Duncan said lightly. He turned to Torben. 'Though I don't sport her around. Tat is a friend.'

'Still call her that, do you? I gather she scrubs up quite nicely these days.' Torben's crude response bordered on jealousy.

Tanith Anita Taylor was one of the most beautiful girls in the district and her affection for Duncan was well known. At twenty-two, Duncan believed he was too young for commitment but, when he was ready, she would be the one.

'Where are the others?' Torben asked, suddenly peevish. 'I don't come here often. You'd think they might be around to say hello.'

'Ellie is in Durban, as you well know,' Cameron told him.

Torben nodded impatiently. 'I meant Frazer and Meggie.'

Lorna cut in. 'Frazer is picking up some birds' eggs from Will Green in Swaziland. We had a letter from Mister Selous, in Germany, saying he would greatly appreciate some *Iseme* eggs for his collection. Will has kindly offered to give him a couple.'

Dallas did not condone the popular practice of bird nesting but, as it was for his friend's research, he said nothing, even though he knew the huge kori bustard was considered royal game by the Zulus. Subtly, he changed the subject: 'When Fred was here some years ago, looking for nyala, he saw some of your brother's bird sketches. Frazer was away at school but his work impressed Selous so much that he wrote to him. The two of them have kept in touch ever since. I think Frazer might be asked to illustrate one of his books.'

That information silenced even Torben. Frederick Courteney Selous had become a legend within his own lifetime. Arriving in South Africa in 1871 at the age of twenty, the short-statured Englishman started hunting and guiding to make ends meet. Respect for the animals and people of Africa soon overtook a basic desire for adventure and his interests developed into more scientific areas, although this didn't stop Cecil Rhodes's British South Africa Company from employing the young man to lead four hundred British pioneers into Mashonaland, ostensibly to thwart Portuguese slavers.

Through his writing, Selous was now financing his own travels and was recognised by the world-wide hunting brotherhood as the greatest outdoorsman of his time. He was also accepted as an expert on game lore through meticulous research in the field and years spent collating information about each and every animal he encountered. He much admired the Bushmen of southern and central Africa for their extraordinary tracking and bushcraft skills. And while the avaricious nature of the Matabele bothered him, their courage and skill earned his greatest respect.

Though Selous was not overly enamoured of the Boers – on one occasion writing to his mother, 'mentally they are the most ignorant and stupid of all white races and have not one-tenth the courage of the Zulus' – he did admire many aspects of their culture, publicly criticising Britain's apparent misunderstanding of their motivation. Selous once said to Dallas: 'How can you judge others unless you live with them and speak their language?' It was an observation Dallas had never forgotten.

The new revelation stunned Torben, who immediately felt his own talents should be recognised in a similar fashion. 'Does Selous need help with the writing?' he asked.

'I think Fred can manage that on his own,' Dallas asserted. 'It's what he does best, these days.'

Torben nodded, though his expression remained thoughtful. 'And Meggie?' he asked, changing the subject.

'She'll be home in the morning. Tanith is having a pyjama party.' Lorna smiled at Torben's look. 'It's all the rage.'

'What on earth is that?' Gerda sniffed in derision.

'A girls' get-together,' Lorna explained. 'They sit around and talk about things. Sounds like fun to me. I wish we'd had something like it when I was their age.'

'They stay out all night? In their sleeping clothes?' Gerda was scandalised.

'No, silly goose,' Lorna said, showing some exasperation. 'The party is at the Taylors' house.'

'Even so, it's quite unseemly, don't you think so, darling?'

Darling was too busy making up his mind to actually answer.

'Why?' Lorna challenged.

Dallas braced himself with a look towards Cameron and Duncan.

'Well,' Gerda blustered. 'In their sleeping clothes?'

Lorna ticked off points on her long, tapered fingers. 'Slippers, peignoirs, neck-to-ankle nightdresses, nightcaps. What on earth is your objection? They sit in Tanith's room, eat cakes and giggle about things they can't speak of anywhere else.'

'Perhaps there's a good reason for that,' Gerda opined. 'Some things are best left unsaid.'

'Rubbish!' Lorna cried, with a despairing look at her husband.

Dallas was out of his depth but Duncan leapt into the fray. 'I think it's harmless enough, Gerda.'

'You would. Nothing shocks you.'

Duncan left it. The truth was that he had been Gerda's first love. At sixteen, when he was eighteen, she'd confessed that whilst fond of Torben, her heart belonged to Duncan. This revelation frightened the wits out of him. Gerda was, Duncan thought, deceitful, full of family-learned prejudice, and likely to turn into a shrew in later years – a prediction which was becoming apparent even though she was only twenty.

The rest of the family assumed the tendency for these two to bicker was a result of their similarity in ages plus the fact that Gerda often appeared to pick on Duncan. He, just as obstinately, would react in kind. Only a few months ago, Cameron had come close to guessing the real reason. 'Anyone would think the two of you were married, the way you go at each other,' he said.

'Don't be stupid,' Duncan had snapped back more harshly than he intended. 'She irritates the hell out of me, that's all.'

Cameron had thrown up his hands and walked away, chuckling at his brother's momentary loss of composure. But the remark had stayed with him. Duncan was now more careful than ever around his sister-in-law.

It was a mercy that, at that moment, Mister David rang the bell for dinner. Knowing Gerda expected the full courtesy treatment, Dallas offered her his arm. Torben took Lorna's, leaving Cameron and Duncan to ham it up behind them with grotesque mincing steps, mimicking Gerda's swaying rear-end. Mister David's look as they entered the dining room was enough to stop their play-acting.

For all her disapproval of the pyjama party, Gerda was not bothered about generously display-ing her cleavage during the meal. As she bent forwards towards Duncan more often than neces-sary, Dallas wondered if a nipple would end up in the guinea-fowl soup. By some miracle, both stayed put.

After dinner, Gerda and Lorna retired to sit by

a fire in the other room, leaving all four men around the table with port and cigars.

'Now, son, what is it you wished to discuss?' Dallas figured they might as well get it over with.

Torben looked uncomfortable. 'I rather wished to speak to you about it in private, Father.'

'It affects us all.' Dallas felt his chin go out. He couldn't help it, Torben made him defensive.

Faced with three sets of inquisitive eyes, Torben backed down. 'It can wait.'

'It can,' Dallas agreed. 'But you'll still have to speak to all of us. I told you before, son, any more financial assistance from me is at the expense of your inheritance. I'm not a bloody bank and I will not allow you to treat this family as though I am.'

'I . . .'

'If you cannot speak of it now, then my heart tells me you are not committed. I'm not interested in hearing about another half-baked idea. Spit it out, boy, or stay quiet. It's up to you.'

He knew he was putting Torben on the spot. A sense of fair play towards the rest of the family was his prime consideration. The lad had to learn that money did not grow on trees – not even the metaphoric ones so often used by Mister David to illustrate a story or Zulu belief.

'No . . . now is not the time. You're right, Father, I'm having second thoughts. I can see a few flaws in the plan.'

Dallas noted the change of tack. Torben was still thinking about Frederick Selous and book writing.

His next words confirmed it. 'When is Frazer due back?'

'I've no idea, but if you're thinking of what we spoke of before dinner – remember, this is his opportunity.'

'He's my brother,' Torben protested. 'I just want to see him.'

Cameron had been unusually quiet but now spoke up. 'Really, Torben, this is too much. You use people with no regard for their own good. Let Frazer be. This could make him successful. Be happy for him and leave it at that.'

'I resent your tone,' Torben flared. 'It's all right for you, sitting on the fat of the land. What about me?'

'What about you? All you ever do is complain, connive and make excuses.' Cameron was winding up. 'The rest of us work like hell.'

'Boys!' Dallas held up his hands. 'Enough. Let us have at least one family gathering where we don't fight.' Trying to ease the tension, he smiled across at Cameron. 'Have you told Torben your news?'

But Cameron had risen. 'I don't imagine my engagement to Virginia will be of any interest to Torben – there's nothing in it for him.'

Torben stared up at him. 'Virginia! Well, well! I gave her credit for more sense.' Greedy eyes bored into his brother's. 'Where did you get the ring?'

'Same as you.'

'Which one did you choose?'

Cameron shook his head and left the room.

'Why must you always do that?' Duncan asked.

'Do what? I merely posed a question.'

'It wasn't so much the question as the way you asked it.'

'Don't be ridiculous.'

Dallas was fed up. 'Actually, it was one of mine. Now, if one of you would be good enough to give me a hand, I think we should join your mother and Gerda.'

'Yes, Father, why not?' Torben answered. 'Let us, as usual, allow the women in this family to diffuse anything potentially unpleasant. An excellent solution.'

God! What drove the boy? Dallas had no idea. He said as much to Lorna as they made ready for bed.

'We've been through that one time and again. I have no idea,' Lorna admitted. 'I'm bloody sick of it and I'm bloody sick of Gerda and, yes, Cameron may well have been given a ring with more stones than the one Torben wanted but only because it was the one Gerda asked for, and I'm sick of that subject too. Dammit, Dallas, those two make my blood boil sometimes.'

He wrapped his arms round Lorna's waist and hugged her into his body. 'I hesitate to say it but the main thing is they're happy.'

'Yes.' She breathed in the smell of him, loving it. 'It's the only thing preventing me from doing something drastic.'

'You?' He grinned and kissed her. 'Never.'

They laughed together.

In the room next door, Torben heard them. 'Listen to that. They're like newlyweds.'

'It's disgusting,' Gerda told him. 'We won't be like that.'

This had not been what he meant and her response worried him. He let it go.

THREE

Meggie crossed her legs and made herself more comfortable on the sofa in Tanith Taylor's spacious bedroom. Despite generous proportions, the room seemed cluttered with five girls and their accumulated belongings – bags containing all manner of night creams, chocolate snacks normally denied to them, magazines showing the latest London fashions and, wonder of wonders, Tanith had managed to place her hands on a publication devoted to women's hairstyles.

'This one.' She held up an illustration. 'What do you think?'

Four pairs of eyes regarded the page, turned to Tanith's perfectly oval face, then back. They all agreed. 'Mmm. Looks good. It would suit you. Who could cut it?'

The question was rhetorical. The girls ranged in age from sixteen to eighteen and their mothers still had the last say on anything they wore or adopted.

Meggie grinned at her best friend. 'You could ask Madame le Penn,' she suggested wickedly, as the others collapsed into giggles. The said Madame le Penn was a borderline hairstylist-cum-lady of the night and, as such, mention of her name was banned in polite society.

Tanith tossed her luxurious brown hair. 'Think I won't?'

The response came as a chorus: 'Yes.'

Their hostess, older than the next by nearly a full year, looked crestfallen. She liked to think of herself as the leader of these girls. However, Meggie, the youngest, was – more than likely – wiser than any of them.

'Have you set a date for coming out, Tanny?'

This subject kept them busy for a long time. Where, when, gowns, hair, food, music, men they admired – all needed to be dissected minutely and discussed seriously. Tanith had deliberately delayed her public passage into womanhood, citing her education – which had been lengthened by a year due to a fall from a horse – as the reason. In truth, Tanith wanted Duncan to realise she had no interest in declaring herself available to other suitors. Nothing seemed to work, however. Meggie's brother appeared determined to treat her as no more than a friend, which didn't stop him dallying with others' feminine delights. So she waited, knowing he liked and respected her, patiently believing that he would be hers in the long run.

Tanith had a special rapport with Meggie. Despite an almost two-year gap in their ages, a large difference so early in life, she found the younger girl to have more common sense in one finger than most of her friends had in their entire body. She was refreshingly outspoken as well, something Tanith appreciated.

Meggie took after her mother in many ways but appearance wasn't one of them. She was the spitting image of her father. Curly black hair had a life of its own whichever way she wore it. Up, and bits tumbled around her face; down, it swirled between her shoulderblades; caught back, it was a wild and bushy cascade. Meggie had the kind of face often described as cherubic when she was younger – a perfect rosebud mouth, small straight nose and dark, almost black, eyes that could burn when hurt or shine with happiness. As she matured, the innocence of youth was being replaced by a delicate grace, but she still resembled a young colt, long-legged and ready to bolt. The tomboy in her was merely an added diversion in a long list of attributes still coming together to make up the whole person – a process which fascinated both her parents.

There was already so much more to Meggie than met the eye. On the surface, she might have gone through life as one of the privileged few blessed with good looks, charm and breeding. But as she grew older, her emotions deepened and she was overtaken by a desire to help others. This may well have stemmed from the family's one true tragedy – the death of Kate. Seven years older than Meggie, Kate's passing left a gaping void in everyone's lives. Meggie took it upon herself, young as she was, to try to bridge that gap.

Kate had been seventeen and happily anticipating her own coming-out party. Gentle and beautiful Katie. Wouldn't-hurt-a-fly Katie. The black mamba that bit her remained indifferent to the life it snuffed out. Kate was human and, as such, an enemy: one who had come too close to its nest. Rearing up behind her as she passed, all Kate felt was a sudden impact on her shoulder. It had been so lightning fast that she thought the snake had missed her – until the pain started. The quick-acting neurotoxic poison had over two hours in which to work before Kate could reach professional medical care. Black mamba venom can kill within that time and it was too late. She died of heart failure as her respiratory system deteriorated and finally collapsed, deep-purple disfigurement and two near-invisible puncture marks the only external evidence of a concerned mother protecting her young.

Kate, who took on the ills and pains of every member of the family, was helpless to save herself. She left this world with tears rolling down her cheeks, a quiet smile of inevitability written on her shiny, sweat-soaked face. The family had been devastated. Katie was their little angel – the one they took their woes to; the girl who listened; the sister they trusted with intimate secrets; the daughter who filled her parents with a glow of special pride. It was Kate to whom Cameron first confessed his love for Virginia. Meggie would snuggle against her and whisper girlish hopes and dreams. She was the only one who could draw Torben out of his often secretive self. Even Lorna relied on her pragmatic wisdom and Dallas . . .

well, because she was physically a mirror of Lorna, Katie could do no wrong in his eyes.

With a legacy of sorrow burning in her heart, Meggie stepped into the void. She was ten years old. Somehow, no-one knew how, she managed to remain sunny, young, yet mature beyond her years. Without exception, the family let her take over from Kate, and Meggie flourished under the unexpected and uninvited extra responsibility. Which was why she became close to Tanith Taylor. Mentally her equal, although physically far behind, Meggie wasn't in the least bit interested in boys, although she good-naturedly accepted that could always change.

The pyjama party was hugely successful. Tanith's coming out dominated conversation but the girls managed to discuss all manner of other, hitherto prohibited, subjects, albeit in a whisper in case parents overheard. Three drifted off to sleep where they sat or sprawled, leaving Meggie and Tanith to sort out what was left of the world.

'Won't Torben be disappointed you're not there?'

Meggie looked disturbed for a moment. 'He has to get used to the idea that we're not at his beck and call. He treats us as if we're . . .' She threw out her hands. 'Oh, I don't know. Sometimes he acts as if he's the only one who counts.' She gave a half-apologetic smile. 'I feel guilty about not being there but, at the same time, I'd regret it if I weren't here.'

Tanith laughed. 'Poor Meggie.'

The comment was taken seriously. 'Not really.

Poor Torben, more like. I can't help feeling that we're all going to let him down at some stage or another.'

'Let him down?' Tanith was sensitive, yet outspoken in her criticism of Torben. 'Your family has done nothing but prop him up.'

'You know what I mean. In his eyes, it's no more than he deserves.'

'Mmm. Egged on by that wife of his, no doubt.' Tanith and Meggie had no secrets between them.

'Don't say that. Gerda isn't too bad. She just needs encouraging.' At a questioning look from her friend, Meggie laughed. 'In the nicest possible way, of course.'

Tanith nibbled another chocolate. 'I'm going to be sick.'

'Put it down.'

'Can't.'

'Pig.'

She threw a pillow, which Meggie ducked.

'What's Duncan doing tonight?'

'Having dinner at home.'

'Do you think . . .'

'Yes, I do, and you know better than to ask.'

The subject was usually taboo between them. Tanith was desperate for inside information on the love of her life. Meggie was just as keen to preserve Duncan's privacy whilst, at the same time, understanding the need in her friend. The only way to deal with it was to avoid the issue.

'I want to shake him sometimes,' Tanith confessed, tossing her hair.

Meggie smiled and they dropped the subject.

★

In the morning, when Meggie returned to *Morningside*, Gerda, then Torben, freely expressed their disapproval of the pyjama party, although each for very different reasons.

'I thought you might have given some thought to your reputation,' Gerda sniffed. 'Running around in night attire is hardly fitting for someone of our standing.'

Meggie heard the collective term and let it go.

'After all,' Gerda went on remorselessly, 'what if you'd been seen?'

'By whom?' Meggie asked quietly. 'We were in Tanith's room, inside the house. Her parents and brothers were all at home.'

'Mmm.' Gerda had her lips pressed together. 'Try to remember, my dear, you are not the only one in this family. Your actions impact on everyone.'

Meggie came close to a sarcastic response. Watching her sister-in-law sway back into the house, wearing an ice-green gown more suited to dinner than breakfast, Meggie had an overwhelming and completely alien desire to grab a flaxen plait and rip it from Gerda's head.

Torben, with impeccable timing, found Meggie on the verandah, still trying to calm herself. 'Missed you last night, little one,' he said, bending to kiss her cheek. 'You'd desert your brother for a mere acquaintance?'

'Sorry.' She couldn't help herself. Torben had a way about him that made her want to apologise. 'The party had been planned for weeks.'

'Understood.' He spoke lightly, somehow

emphasising the hurt at her perceived betrayal. 'As it happened, you missed nothing more than a family argument. Oh, and I hear that Cam has finally persuaded Virginia to marry him. She's not pregnant, is she?'

'Torben! How could you even think such a thing?'

'In that case she must have had her eye on Mother's jewellery.'

'Sometimes I don't understand you, Torben. Why can't you just be happy for them like everybody else?'

'I am, little sister, I am. And that goes for Gerda as well. We're both delighted.'

'Fine. Now, how about a game of croquet after lunch?' Meggie deliberately changed the subject.

'Good idea. Father is having his plaster removed this morning. Perhaps he'll be able to join us.'

'I doubt it, but we'll see.'

At that moment, they heard the pony trap belonging to their doctor from Empangeni. 'Here comes old sawbones,' Torben said. 'Pity Ellie isn't here. She could have saved him the trip.'

They waited while Doctor Roger Parry, who was also a family friend, alighted, collected his bag and joined them. 'How's the patient?' he asked, not waiting for a reply. 'I'll need some assistance, young lady. Someone to hold that damned father of yours.'

'Will it hurt when you take the plaster off?'

'Only his pride. Otherwise, not at all.'

'I can help, if you like,' Torben offered.

Roger Parry hadn't trusted Torben since the boy bit him, years ago, while he was trying to remove an acacia thorn that had turned septic. 'Thank you, Torben. Meggie knows what to do.'

Another rejection. Torben's face showed his reaction. 'Very well. I'll see you later.'

Parry watched Torben's retreating back for a second but all he said was, 'Let's get this over with.'

They found Dallas sitting in the parlour, a look of mutiny on his face. The doctor plonked his bag down and stood, hands on hips, looking at his patient. 'Bedroom,' he barked suddenly.

'No. Here.'

Mister David was hovering. He bent down and spoke quietly to Dallas, who nodded reluctantly and allowed himself to be helped from the room. When Mister David returned, Parry asked how he'd managed that. 'I told him you were an old man with a sore back and that he must make allowances for it,' was the Zulu's bland reply, leaving the doctor spluttering with indignation. He was a good ten years younger than Dallas. Shaking his head, Doctor Parry picked up his bag and indicated that Meggie should lead the way.

Dallas had no argument about accepting his daughter's assistance, much as he'd have liked one. He didn't enjoy the fact that one of his children was seeing him in less-than-perfect physical condition. With quick, precise movements, Parry cut through the plaster. All Meggie had to do was lay a hand lightly on her father's shoulder. For once,

Dallas behaved like a lamb, so pleased was he to have the restrictive covering removed.

The skin underneath had a puckered and grey appearance. 'That will soon change,' Parry said.

He gently manipulated the leg back and forth, paying special attention to the tibia, which had suffered the break, and the severely strained, perhaps even cracked, kneecap. 'That hurt?' he asked.

Dallas gritted his teeth. 'No.'

Parry grinned. 'Liar!' He produced a crepe bandage.

'What's that for?' Dallas growled suspiciously.

'To wrap around your leg.'

'Why?'

'Why do you think?'

'Oh, very well. When can I ride again?'

'Try next month,' Parry told him without a trace of sympathy.

Dallas closed his eyes and Meggie's met the doctor's with a grin.

Lorna chose that moment to look in. 'How is he?'

'Fine,' Doctor Parry said.

'Bloody awful,' Dallas chipped in. 'I still can't ride.'

'Oh, do shut up,' Lorna said, trying to hide her amusement. 'At least the plaster is off.'

'What *can* I do?' he asked in despair.

'Heal.' Parry's voice showed his exasperation.

Lorna added, 'Boss us around. You're good at that.'

'Get out of here,' Dallas told them all, smiling in spite of himself.

When he reappeared in the parlour it was in knee-length shorts. 'Might as well get some sun on the bloody thing,' he announced defiantly, fully expecting a negative from the doctor.

'Good idea,' Parry agreed, preparing to leave. 'Although it will have its work cut out getting through that bandage. Come and see me next week. Friday morning is relatively free. We may be able to do without it by then.'

'Wonderful,' Dallas said with irony. 'In the meantime, if you don't mind, I have to engage in some serious contemplation.' He stomped outside, refusing to wince as each step reminded him that his leg still had some complaining to do.

Torben cornered Lorna in the kitchen. 'I need to speak with you.'

'If it's about the discussion with your father last evening, I'd prefer it if you spoke to him.'

'No, no.' Torben was hasty with his denial. 'It has nothing to do with that.'

Lorna turned to him, smiling, wiping flour from her hands. 'Very well.'

'Why are you cooking?' Torben asked suddenly. 'Where's Mister David?'

'Mister David has other things to do and, anyway, I like to cook. Is this what you wish to discuss?'

'Don't be silly.'

She turned back towards the workbench. 'Then what is it?'

'Cam's engagement.'

Lorna nodded, pushing hair back from her forehead with the back of a hand. Now she knew what to expect.

'What ring did he get?'

'Is that any of your business, my dear?'

'I believe so.'

'I don't see why. We have many pieces of jewellery, as you know. Some belong to your father, some to me. I can't possibly wear it all. It gives us pleasure to give away a few items as and when we see fit. Gerda, if you recall, chose the ring she now wears. Cameron made his selection for Virginia. That's all there is to it. You'll just have to wait and see which one it is.'

Torben said tightly, 'Gerda chose that ring because I warned her not to be greedy. I really don't see why your more valuable belongings should be purloined.'

She glanced over her shoulder at him. 'Before your father and I are dead, you mean?'

'If you insist.'

'Don't be so prudish, Torben. Gerda could have had anything she liked and you know it.'

'Well, she feels that you and Father prefer Virginia. The ring proves it.'

As she sometimes could, Lorna momentarily lost her self-control, slamming both hands down on the bench. 'How would you know? You haven't even seen it yet. Damn it, Torben, a piece of jewellery proves nothing. Take another if it makes you happy. I'm sick to death of your petty

56

jealousies. No-one prefers anyone in this house. Each of us has good and bad sides, none of us is perfect. Take another bloody ring. Take the whole bloody lot if it makes you feel better.' With that his stepmother sailed from the kitchen, cursing herself for allowing Torben to get under her skin yet again.

Taken aback by the outburst, Torben rubbed a hand over his head. He hadn't meant to make her angry. Truth be known, he loved Lorna very much, appreciated her honesty and outspoken ways, and, as far as he was concerned, her only fault was the unconventional manner in which she approached so many things.

'*Moi cherub.*' It was Gerda, doing her best imitation of French, an affectation with which Torben really wished she wouldn't bother. 'What is it?'

'Nothing. I was just looking for you.'

She went to him, humming a little under her breath, one plump hand extended to soothe the frown from his brow. 'Something is bothering you, my dearest.'

Torben relaxed. His wife's lavish attention to his well-being was the one thing guaranteed to make him feel better. She seemed to know exactly when he needed it and when he wanted to be left alone. Sitting on a kitchen stool he pulled her onto his lap. 'I love you.'

'Mmm, mmm, mmmmm,' she hummed in the special way she did when trying to pacify him.

Gerda was too heavy to stay on his lap and, as soon as he shifted to a more comfortable position, she quickly rose. 'Come and choose a luncheon gown for me.'

Torben stood as well. Control over his wife's clothing made him feel good. He did most of the buying and knew exactly what her wardrobe comprised. 'Did you bring the cream silk? Mother seems determined to be drab. You don't have to follow suit. I thought you might try it with the amethyst pendant and that red scarf.'

'Not too daring?' Gerda smiled and dimpled.

'Daring!' Torben laughed. 'Not for you, my darling. You wear everything with such style.'

They went off arm in arm towards the guest bedroom. Torben still felt short-changed by his wife's engagement ring but Gerda had managed to take his mind off it.

Once the kitchen was clear, Mister David, who had been polishing silver in the dining room while waiting to reclaim his domain, returned. He could easily have prepared the pastry needed for lunch but understood why Lorna had volunteered. It was to get away from Gerda, who took every opportunity she could to avoid housework. The kitchen was a refuge where Lorna spent an inordinate amount of time during Torben's infrequent visits.

Mister David sympathised. Lorna's behaviour was typical of any Zulu mother who did not particularly like her daughter-in-law. Although she usually stopped short of outright rudeness, anyone who knew Lorna understood how she felt about Torben's wife.

On one occasion, taking matters into his own

hands, Mister David had put a mixture of unde-tectable herbs onto Gerda's food. Not enough to cause harm, simply enough to render her off-colour and consigned to bed, safely out of Lorna's way. Lorna had said nothing about it, though the knowing glare on her face had told him he'd over-stepped the mark. He didn't try it again, afraid a repeat performance might mean he could end up out of work. Mister David needn't have worried. That same evening he had overheard Lorna telling Dallas of her suspicions. She'd seemed more amused than angry.

Working quietly and efficiently in the kitchen, Mister David pondered the family he'd known for nearly thirty years. Dallas had aged, but otherwise was largely unchanged. He spoke Zulu as well as a native, understood their ways, loved the country he'd come to regard as his own (there'd been a few discussions between them on that subject, which neither man had won) and, apart from recent frus-trations over a leg which restricted his freedom, remained fair and free-minded. The Zulus on the farm respected and liked their employer. His family adored him. Dallas, in turn, lived for them.

He was a good farmer, a great cattleman, respected African customs regarding the working and keeping of his beasts and made sure he took care of the land, which in turn took care of the cat-tle, which in turn took care of everything else. The way it should be.

Lorna, too, remained much the same. She car-ried herself proud and tall, and continued to shock all and sundry with a dress-sense that was, to say the least, unusual. True friends sought her company. Those looking for the thrill of saying they knew her – not many had the opportunity of meeting an ex-marchioness – were quick to gossip about what they gleaned. Lorna was just as fast to see through such people and snubbed them with indecent haste. She remained her own woman, with one exception – Dallas. With him, Lorna was like putty.

If Mister David had a firm favourite among the children, it was Cameron. As a little boy he had carved a place in the Zulu's heart which, irrespective of any future bad behaviour on Cameron's part, would never be erased. Watching Cameron grow through boyhood to puberty and then manhood filled the elderly man with a pride equalled only by watching his own boys.

Dallas's firstborn responded in kind, with love and respect that far exceeded anything outside most family units. Mister David was his mentor, friend, second father, confidant and brother. He was the man Cam looked to for guidance in all matters Zulu. When Kate died, it was in Mister David's company that Cameron cried out his loss and listened to words of wisdom about ancestors and death. It was to the Zulu he turned when trying to find the courage to propose, yet again, to Virginia, and it was to Mister David that the tidings of success were first brought.

For Ellie, he reserved the kind of respect usually accorded a *sangoma*, or spiritual healer. The girl was clever – educated at home, an avid reader and now studying medicine in Durban – with knowledge only very few whites were privileged to attain. Ellie's fascination with injuries and disease had never diminished. Encouraged by her parents, and fortunately able to stay with family friends in Durban, she was already in her third year of training at Addington Hospital.

Ellie had slotted easily into life with Cecily and Stephen. They were two of Lorna and Dallas's dearest friends. Living outside formal marriage vows, their behaviour scandalised others, as had that of Lorna and Dallas so many years before. In each case, the woman of the couple had the connections and influence to make their choice possible. Cecily, now a self-confessed sixty-three, was cousin to the widow of Lord Randolph Churchill, the high-profile British politician who had died of syphilis in 1895, unrepentant in his widely publicised hatred of ugly women and the Boers. Cecily was as rare as Lorna. In a world of rules and regulations the two had gravitated together as naturally as bees to pollen.

Lorna and Dallas's eldest daughter loved her studies and work, devoted long hours to both, and regularly offered herself for extra duties when the hospital was short-staffed, which was not an uncommon situation. At eighteen, Ellie had reluctantly become a debutante, declaring her availability to the opposite sex, something in which she had little or no interest. Men were no mystery to her. They breathed air, swallowed bile, spoke, saw, heard, felt. Males of the species became ill just as easily as females, injured themselves or healed just as well and, as far as Ellie could see, were no different physically, apart from one or two additions and subtractions. These she treated as perfectly normal appendages.

Emotionally, members of the opposite sex had as many challenges as women. Mentally, Ellie had these nicely grouped into various categories. Crying was one. Anyone who believed men didn't feel enough to cry hadn't watched one by a dying wife's or child's bedside. Against colleagues' advice, Ellie actively encouraged men to show their emotions. In this regard she was way ahead of her time. The number of male patients who had come into the hospital nearly insane with suppressed grief and left again feeling able to cope were testament to the fact that she was on the right track.

So it came as something of a surprise to everyone, particularly Ellie, when she finally fell in love. She complained to Lorna that it had 'sneaked up on her'.

Her mother smiled. 'Men do that.'

'And I'm older than him.'

'Cecily is older than Stephen.'

'True.' Ellie stared off into the distance.

'He won't get in the way of your studies, not if he wants to be a doctor too.'

'Lindsay wants to get out there and be a missionary. I don't know, Mother; I'm more interested in mending people's bodies than saving their souls.'

'You can combine both. In fact, it's perfect.'

'That's what Lindsay says.' Ellie sighed and turned to Lorna. 'Have you been speaking to him?'

'No. It makes sense, though.' Lorna watched her daughter and thought, she has no idea of her beauty.

It was true. Ellie, at twenty-five, was not everybody's idea of beautiful. She wore unglamorous oval glasses – thanks to burning the midnight oil over too many nights of study – perched atop a tip-tilted nose which gave her a bird-like look. Behind the glasses, though, large and vibrant in colour, flecked with gold and rimmed perfectly with mauve, were two of the most delightfully blue eyes anyone could imagine. Framed by thick gold lashes, dark arches of amber above and crowned by a mop of short-cropped blonde hair which, despite Ellie's best efforts, insisted on curling, she had the look of a fresh-faced tomboy. Her wide, smiling mouth seemed to invite a similar response. Lindsay, the man who had captured her heart, found the combination irresistible.

For her part, the somewhat large yet naturally kind younger man – Lorna did try to tell her daughter that six months was neither here nor there – with friendly eyes, warm hands and the gentlest kiss in the world, had turned her life upside-down. Lindsay and Ellie became lovers – a fact she omitted from frank and free conversations with her mother. A body was a body and it was there to function in whichever way God designed. In matters sexual, it was no different from anything else.

★

With deft, expert movements, Mister David swung pastry over the pie, slit it perfectly, and thumbed down around the edges, frowning with concentration as he worked. Dallas liked his strudel stuffed full of apple and liberally covered with sugar, so that the cooking fruit could flow from each gash in the crust making a gooey mess as it mixed with the sweetener. Lorna preferred everything in moderation, including strudel. Cameron took after his father. Torben picked at food. His wife ate anything put in front of her; Duncan and Meggie tended to do the same. Catering for such a range of preferences made life interesting but the outcome was usually a foregone conclusion. Dallas and Cameron won hands down.

When life picked up the Granger-Acheson family and placed them at *Morningside*, Mister David had carried on his duties as *induna*. For this reason he missed a lot of the two youngest boys' growing-up. Duncan and Frazer, now twenty-two and nineteen respectively, had a close though unusual relationship. They were as different as chalk and cheese – Duncan sometimes bordering on wild, Frazer quiet and artistic. Where Duncan had a vociferous temper, Frazer preferred to solve problems with calmer words. Everything about them was so directly opposite that even Lorna and Dallas wondered how the two managed to get along so well together.

Duncan's bedroom, for example, was a mess of boys' stuff – cricket bats, tennis racquets, balls, discarded clothes, projects started and never finished.

Frayed pennants, sepia team photographs from Hilton College and silver trophies confirmed his prowess at sport. Duncan regarded the accolades as normal. What was on the floor stayed on the floor until a maid cleared it away. He never bothered to ask where anything went, assuming he'd find whatever he wanted in a drawer if and when it was needed.

Duncan rarely bothered to pull curtains, close windows, tidy cupboards or check his clothes for spiders, scorpions, snakes or just plain muck. He was, as his mother once said, 'a noise with dirt on it'. Duncan was born making loud sounds. His love of tearing paper ended abruptly, only to be replaced by a fascination with seeing how things worked. He nearly killed himself on several occasions – the most notable being the day he tried to dismantle one of Dallas's old wagons, which fell on his leg, pinning him underneath. A jagged scar was evidence of that episode but it didn't stop him. Duncan went on from there to tinker with farm machinery until, at eight, he was banned from the workshop – and also barred from playing with anything mechanical, such as the laundry mangle into which he had nearly fed a cat's tail. No malice was intended; he simply had a desire to see what would happen. Duncan was no bully or brute. He had sensitivity where others of similar nature had none. The cat's tail notwithstanding, Duncan's temper would be sure to flare if he perceived obvious injustice or cruelty. Like his mother, Duncan verbalised displeasure. He rarely resorted to physical violence, quick to back off as if alarmed by the possible consequences.

Frazer, on the other hand, was neat to the point of obsession. His room had a place for everything and, if an overzealous maid put something back in the wrong position, Frazer would quietly return it to where it belonged. His walls were adorned with drawings of African animals – mainly his own, though he had managed to acquire some fine pieces from elsewhere. Art was Frazer's passion – crayon and pencil drawings, watercolours and, more recently, an experimental foray into oil painting. His work ranged from expansive vistas which captured the very essence of Africa to amazingly detailed studies of its fauna. Portraits and the like he left to those for whom nature held no fascination.

Being the two youngest boys, Duncan and Frazer played a lot of games together, most of which they made up. Some included Zulu children of similar ages, like Mister David's eldest son, Henry, who introduced them to the art of spear throwing. Tests of skill were keenly contested but when Duncan and Henry went off to prove their prowess, seeking out small buck or giant rats in the stands of sugar cane, Frazer always found something else he had to do. Despite his dislike of hunting for hunting's sake, Frazer was no wet blanket. In stature he was solidly built, tall with a broad chest, tapering waist and slim hips. Blond like Lorna, he resembled Ellie facially, with one exception: her glasses. Frazer had excellent eyesight.

Both boys enjoyed more than a passing interest in the opposite sex. Surprisingly, it was Frazer who would normally find favour, soft words and gentle eyes winning hands down over the swashbuckling bravado to which his brother resorted. Older by two years, Duncan took these setbacks philosophically, secretly pleased for his younger sibling.

When Frazer went away, as he had now, Duncan missed him. It was strange not having a head popping around the corner of his bedroom door with a quiet 'Got a minute?'. The five-year gap between himself and Cameron was the difference between an adult and a fledgling. He loved his older brother but felt very much the junior. Torben was never part of the equation, being as distant from Duncan as the years had made Katie.

Pie finished, Mister David popped it into the oven. The rest was easy: cold meats and salad. Dallas would grumble but the strudel should more than make up for that. Served with fresh cream and wild honey from the farm, it would bring a gleam to his employer's eye.

FOUR

Two hundred and fifty miles more or less due west of *Morningside*, another family also sat down to lunch. Compared to the Granger-Achesons, their manners were atrocious.

A relative youngster had chanced upon the meal. He hadn't even been looking for one. Out for a walk to stretch his youthful limbs, lethargic from inactivity in the spot he'd chosen for a morning nap, the two and a bit year old lion virtually stumbled over it. As a young male he was nearing his last days with the pride. Soon they would kick him out to fend for himself. He was learning to do just that and, an opportunist by nature, wasted no time securing his share, more if he could, of such a windfall.

The victim stared skywards, unseeing. Two hours earlier, he had been a strapping sixteen year old boy out in search of a buck of some kind so that his mother would have venison to cook later that week. The fact that he was on someone else's land was of no concern to him. He was Danny Reese. His father owned nearly ten thousand morgen – about twenty thousand acres – around their house and the best herd of Afrikander cattle in the Orange Free State. Danny could do what he liked, or so he thought. Now he was dead, a bullet hole in the middle of his chest the apparent cause. And the reason? A twenty year old feud between his father and the perpetrator's.

Ripping into soft groin flesh, the lion made rapid inroads, tearing out both stomach and bowel to reach more favoured morsels, and was soon breaking his way up through the rib cage. Hungry, he was not at all bothered to be eating his only real predator. This one could not harm him. As still-warm intestines spilled onto sunbaked ground, the distinctive aroma brought others who, using their status and strength within the pride, soon swiped and snarled him off the feast. Before long, the boy's body was surrounded by gorging, mannerless lions.

'Pa, Pa, Pa!' The terror and excitement in Erich Gil's voice alerted his parents that something serious was bothering the usually taciturn youngster. The boy was fourteen, big for his age, with bushy tow-coloured hair and pale grey-blue eyes which rarely registered emotion. His long nose was noticeably crooked, broken years ago in a scuffle with an African boy. He had a mouth that hardly ever smiled and, when it did, seemed shy and uncertain. Erich's head was too large for his body, which was in turn too large for his arms and legs. God had bestowed on him huge hands and feet in an attempt to compensate but all these gave him was a misshapen appearance, clumsy movements and a tendency to try to hide both features by sitting on them.

Erich Gil was, according to their neighbour and his father's longstanding enemy, 'a fuck-up'. But the fuck-up had just done something he'd never forget – killed that very neighbour's pride and joy; his son, Danny. As the entire Gil family were well aware, holier-than-thou Wallace Reese did not forget or forgive anything, especially a direct challenge and particularly where it involved his only son. In this case the deed had been carried out – on the surface, anyway – for no other reason than simple trespass.

'What is it, boy?' Erich's father, Roth Gil, hurried outside.

'Come, come, you come quickly.' Erich turned to run.

Roth grabbed his arm. 'Whoa. What is wrong?'

Erich's mother joined them, followed by a string of younger children, each no more than a year apart in age. 'The boy is scared, Roth.'

'I can see that, Selma.' He turned back to Erich. 'Come inside, son. Tell us.' Roth led his trembling eldest into the house.

'Danny,' the boy managed, grasping a tumbler of brandy forced on him by his mother – her cure-all for everything from a mild cold to severe trauma.

Roth scowled. 'Do not mention that family in this house, boy. How many times must you be told?'

'But, Pa –'

'Never,' his father shouted. 'May God strike them all down.'

Selma interrupted timidly. 'Let him speak, Roth. Something has happened. I think he should tell us what it is.'

For all his bluster, Roth Gil was a reasonable man and could see the extent of his son's distress. 'Very well. Just this once.'

'He's dead.'

'Wha–' Roth hadn't been expecting news of this kind. 'How?'

'I shot him, Pa.'

Roth Gil slumped into a chair opposite his son. 'You what?' His staring eyes widened in disbelief.

Erich dropped his oversized head into huge hands and nodded. Looking up again, his father saw fear and tears. 'Will I go to prison, Pa?'

'Not if I can help it,' Roth growled. He tapped Erich on one knee: 'Drink that dop and tell us what happened.' He waited patiently as his son sipped sparingly on the fiery liquid, pulled a face and set it aside.

'I was trying to find the old bull when I saw him. Danny was on our land, Pa, trespassing like he owned it. He had a gun and was looking for something to shoot. I challenged him.'

'Rightly so.' Roth was proud of his brave son. Two years younger than the bullying Englishman's cub, though more than a match for him physically, Erich had the dual disadvantage of age and confidence. Yet, right was on his side in questioning what Danny Reese might be doing on their property.

'So, he pointed the gun at you, did he?'

Erich dropped his head again. 'I can't remember, Pa. I think so but I can't remember. All I can see in my mind is him falling over backwards.'

Selma held the knuckles of one hand between her teeth. 'The police,' she whispered, drawing one of the younger children closer as her words caused him to whimper.

Roth waved a dismissive hand. 'Pah! They hate Reese and that son of his as much as we do.'

'But, Roth. This is murder.'

He rounded on her. 'Don't say that. Not now, not ever. How do you know Erich wasn't in danger and fired to defend himself? That's what we'll tell the police.' Roth stood. 'Come, son. You'd better show us where.'

By the time they reached the spot where Danny Reese had been shot, the lions had dragged his body some yards away. The carcass, with its telltale bullet hole, had already been crushed beyond recognition. One full-maned male was still feeding. A hyena, several black-backed jackals and a growing number of vultures waited patiently. Of the pride, only their footprints remained.

Roth smiled at Erich. 'Perfect, ja. We have an alibi. It couldn't be better. Let the law make sense of this. By the time they get here, there'll be nothing left. Come, use this branch to clear the area of our signs. Leave everything else as it is. Make haste. The *Engelsman* may come looking for his precious son.'

The incident, unrecorded and remarked on by

any but immediate family and friends, was typical of the depth of dislike which had built up between Boer and British settlers for more than half a century. Hatred fed on hatred until a line – blurred at the best of times with emotion rather than reason – was no longer visible. It was simply there. Acts like those committed by young Erich Gil were applauded by Afrikaners, bringing howls of protest and threats of reciprocal action from the British. By the time a full-scale Anglo-Boer war erupted, such incidents were so commonplace that no-one noticed an escalation in the atrocities. All they saw was the natural extension of a loathing which had fuelled distrust between the two races for so many years. Some, like Erich Gil, even Erich's and Danny's parents, knew of no other way to live.

The pride of lions, existing on slim pickings in the harsh veld of the Orange Free State, had long since learned to capitalise on opportunity in what would soon prove to be a land of plenty. It was as well they were prepared. Feasting in such barren conditions was virtually unheard of.

Sated and sleepy, the pride found shade and resumed their slumbers. Wallace Reese considered shooting the lot. In the end he left them alone. Danny had been born and brought up in the bush and, as such, took his chances along with everyone else, including the animals. He would not have found it necessary to kill those who killed him. His fate was at one with the continent on which he lived.

Not suspecting foul play, there was, nevertheless, an inevitability about the incident that left an incredibly bitter taste in the Englishman's mouth.

Erich and Danny might have been friends except for the ongoing distrust between their respective families. Wallace's wife often commented on what a shame it was that, in such desolate surroundings, their son remained ostracised because of his background, growing up lonely and friendless. His parents had tried sending Danny to boarding school. That proved a disaster. The boy would not conform to discipline, made no attempt to fit in and was ultimately asked to leave after deliberately smashing a stained-glass window in the school chapel. Elizabeth Wallace knew their only son was socially flawed but always made excuses for him. In truth, Danny Wallace was arrogant, sneaky and often dishonest. Despite her husband's unnecessarily insulting description of Erich Gil, Elizabeth found the Afrikaner a nice enough lad: polite, well-mannered, helpful and open.

Although it didn't consciously occur to Elizabeth that deep-seated tensions between British and Boer could have been responsible for Danny's death, at the back of her mind she must have suspected something. She was English, married to an Englishman, and it was right that her family's loyalties and duty should stand squarely behind Queen and country. Yet somewhere deep inside lurked the sad certainty that Danny might still be alive if Britain's insatiable greed for land, power and mineral wealth could be contained. It was a very big *if*. Elizabeth doubted that such a thing would ever be possible.

Totally unaware of the unfolding drama so far away, the Granger-Achesons continued yet another squabbling lunch. A stranger to the household might have come to the conclusion that this was their way, but under normal circumstances, Dallas and his family enjoyed their meals together. They used the time to catch up with each other, talk of new ideas, memories, ambitions or whatever subjects occurred to them. Torben inevitably brought dissension – it was as though he couldn't help himself.

Gerda – dressed in cream silk and, contrary to Torben's advice, bright-green accessories – started the ball rolling, complaining she had no jewellery to wear with her ensemble.

'I swear, darling, you'd make a wonderful lawyer,' Lorna commented.

'What do you mean?' Unsure if she was being criticised or not, Gerda frowned.

'Simply that you don't drop anything until you've shaken every last crumb from it.'

Silence followed. Lorna seldom came so close to outright censure.

Torben came to his wife's defence. 'Gerda isn't complaining, Mother.' She was. 'It was nothing more than a comment about her wardrobe.' It wasn't. 'She packed the wrong things, didn't you, darling?'

'Of course.' Gerda sprayed laughter and a little lime juice cordial across the table, fanning herself with a chubby hand. 'Don't think for one moment, Ma, that I'm not grateful for all you've given me.'

'Good.' Lorna was being very brisk and Dallas glanced at her, wondering what was wrong.

Cameron tried to deflect the black mood he saw developing on Torben's face. 'Coming out to the cattle this afternoon? We've got some new calves you might be interested in. Good stock, nice and deep in the chest.'

Torben threw down his napkin. 'No, of course I'm not. I couldn't be less interested in the bloody cattle. That's what you all believe and it's fine with me.'

'Come on, Torben,' Dallas intervened. 'This is still a family business. They're as much yours as anybody's.'

'A fact you all tend to forget,' Torben snapped.

'Rubbish!' Dallas had been sucked in, wondering how a simple conversation concerning jewellery and cattle could have become so complicated. 'We can only try to make you interested. If you're not, you're not.'

'I am,' Torben said through gritted teeth, his anger rising fast. 'But for some reason, you seem to be picking on Gerda and that I won't stand for.'

'Nobody is picking on her,' Duncan tried to calm his older brother.

'Meggie?' Torben asked, ignoring him.

She shook her head. 'No. Sorry, Torben, I really can't see how having nothing to match a dress has anything to do with criticism.' Although it was unlike Meggie, she added a reprimand. 'And I don't think it's fair that you ask me to take sides.' She turned to her sister-in-law. 'I have a malachite necklace which you're more than welcome to.'

Most women would have backed down at such an offer. Gerda's eyes lit up. 'Really? I'd like to see it. After lunch perhaps?'

'Darling.' Lorna's eyes warned Meggie against such generosity. 'That was given to you by Frazer. He made it himself. I don't think –'

'If she wishes to give it away, it's hers to give,' Torben said sarcastically.

'Yes, but I still don't think –'

'Gerda would love it.'

Cameron, Duncan and Meggie glanced at each other in surprise. Torben rarely spoke to his parents in such proprietorial tones.

'She may well,' Dallas said curtly. 'However, I forbid Meggie to give away a gift from her brother, something that has great sentimental value, out of nothing more than the softness of a big heart. You should be ashamed of yourselves for assuming she would.' His glance took in Gerda. 'Both of you.'

Gerda went red and pouted. 'Very well, Poppie. If that is your wish, I'll go without.'

'Why should she?' Torben wasn't to be silenced. 'Gerda always goes without. Can't any of you see that?'

'Enough,' Lorna exploded. 'This conversation is too penny-pinching for words. In case it's missed your attention, you two, it's customary to wait until someone dies before fighting over the spoils. No more handouts. Your greed has just ruined things for everybody. That can't be helped.' She removed her napkin, dabbed a slightly moist mouth and rose. 'Excuse me.' Lorna strode from the room, going outside to the garden – a place where she sought refuge whenever her feathers were ruffled.

Dallas found his wife staring at the black marble headstone which marked Katie's grave. He laid a hand on her shoulder. 'What brought that on?'

'Them.'

He gave a half-smile. 'You don't normally react quite so violently.'

She dropped her head on his chest. 'I know. Sorry. I'm tired and cranky. It's all just too much. Who cares if the silly little girl has no green jewellery? She can out-drip most in diamonds and sapphires. God, I hate this, Dallas. Can't Torben see through her?'

'Obviously not.'

'Don't you dare be reasonable.'

'Who, me?'

She snuggled closer. 'How's the leg holding up?'

'Come inside and I'll show you.'

She shoved a hand against his chest and he pretended to stagger backwards. 'I hate you.'

'No you don't.'

'You're right.'

'Make up your mind.'

She smiled, then giggled.

'That's better. Now . . .' He took her hand and they walked slowly to a garden seat. Shaded from the early afternoon sun by an ancient fig tree, it afforded the best panoramic views of *Morningside*.

'Something's the matter. If I didn't know better I'd say you were with child.'

She sat very still for a moment, then turned to him, a look of absolute horror on her face. 'Dallas, that's it.'

'You're pregnant?' He wore the same expression.

'No, silly. I'm forty-five in a few weeks. I've been wondering . . . well, I've had some hot flushes lately and been tired. It's the menopause, Dallas, don't you see? That's why I'm like a bear with a sore head.' Lorna put the palms of her hands against her cheeks. 'Oh, my God. I'm going through the change of life.'

'So what's wrong with that?'

'I'm old. Finished. Dried up. Dallas, you won't stop loving me, will you?'

He threw back his head and laughed. 'Just how do you think I could ever do that? I love you with every bone in my body. I'll love you till the cows come home. I —'

'Yes, yes,' she said impatiently. 'Don't get carried away.'

'That's my girl.'

Reason and order restored, they returned to the house, where Lorna apologised and explained her lapse into irritability.

'Oh, Ma,' Gerda tinkled out a relieved laugh, her pride restored. 'I thought you'd gone through the change ages ago. My mother did.'

The comparison with that odious woman very nearly drove Lorna over the edge again.

After lunch, the entire family made a short trip

to an enclosed quarantine pen where the cows and calves bought by Duncan were being held. Mindful of Zulu tradition, Lorna, Meggie and Gerda remained outside while the men went to examine the recent arrivals. They were joined by Mister David's eldest son, Henry, who, at eighteen, was shaping up nicely to replace his father. The acting *induna* had made it plain that his longer term interests lay in Durban. He was a son of Tobacco, one of Dallas's earliest employees in his trading days; after Tobacco failed to return from the Zulu War, Dallas had semi-adopted him.

Henry had been born on the farm and loved it like his own. He had a worried look on his face. 'That one, *nkosi,* "little wide head", he is not drinking well and already grows weak.'

'Is his mother rejecting him?'

'No. She has walked over an *inkomfe* plant. We must rub her calf with *ubuVimba,*' he said, referring to a small berry-bearing shrub, the root of which, when mixed with hippopotamus fat and licked off by a cow, was said to induce milk. Dallas knew this was something normally done to foster acceptance of an orphan, but saw how the same method could be applied to the present situation.

'It's worth a try,' he agreed.

'If this does not work, we will use bottles,' Henry said flatly, a dislike for anything other than traditional methods clear from his tone.

'So we have two ways to deal with the calf. Good.'

'When does Master Dallas return to work?'

Henry wanted to know, pointing at the cane on which Dallas leaned heavily.

'As soon as possible.'

'That is good.'

'Cameron and Duncan are here,' Dallas reminded him.

'Yes, this thing is true. And cattle know who is the boss man.'

'Like the damned steer that broke my leg?'

Both laughed.

'Your father sends this.' Dallas handed Henry a brown paper bag. 'And leave some for Sabani.'

Lorna's homemade cake and biscuits had long been a favourite on the farm. Now Mister David's creations were becoming equally popular.

'Is it allowed?'

'Most certainly. Though I doubt a dentist would agree.'

'Pah! Our teeth are strong.'

Dallas didn't doubt that for a moment. Zulus were meticulous about their teeth, keeping them clean using powdered ash and a small stick chewed at one end. All the youngsters, including his own, seemed to have an insatiable appetite for sweet things. They would even eat rock-hard sticks of raw sugar cane, extracting every last drop of juice before spitting out the fibrous residue.

Cameron was showing Torben his latest innovation – a self-regulating feed bin that allowed cattle to control their intake. The container swung on a central spindle making it easy for animals to reach the bottom. 'You should patent this,' Torben commented. 'It's a good idea.'

'Not mine to protect,' Cam replied lightly. 'Most of the farmers around here have something similar. Mine isn't that different.'

'Even so, you should get in first.'

'I don't think so.' He shook his head. 'It would be resented.'

'So what? Just because nobody else wants to make money from it?'

'It's more than that. We share ideas – that's how it works. Can you imagine how many other innovations I'd miss out on by capitalising on what is basically a communal idea? The rest would clam up and we'd be excluded. No. Far better to share and keep the status quo.'

'I'll look into it.' Torben would not be put off. His commercial mind had leapt ahead, grasping the profit aspect and completely ignoring practicalities.

Cameron wasn't bothered. He knew that in a few days his brother's scheming would focus on something else, self-regulating feed bins forgotten.

Erich Gil got away with murder. When the police finally arrived – a Boer sergeant who spoke no English and two African constables – most of the evidence had disappeared. The lions were gone too, leaving Africa's ever efficient clean-up service – hyenas, jackals, vultures and ants, among others – to tidy up any loose ends.

Everybody knew that a pride of lions lived in the area. Young Danny Reese should have been more careful. Surprising, though, that he didn't see the attack coming. A boy from the land should have been more aware. Perhaps he provoked them. Perhaps he'd had a fall, twisted an ankle. Nobody would ever know. Whatever the cause, it had cost him his life.

One constable suggested that they hunt down the lions.

'What's the point?' his sergeant said. 'These boys and girls have given us no trouble.'

So the pride was left in peace. Man was not a favourite meal. Lingering smells – tobacco in particular – the taste of soap and a diet other than grass, their strange hairless bodies; all made the mighty carnivores uneasy. But the knowledge remained that their only predator was undoubtedly edible.

FIVE

An outer door banged and four sets of eyes swivelled, waiting. The man who stepped into the inner sanctum instantly grabbed and held everyone's attention. Outside that room he was almost unheard of. His stature certainly did nothing to indicate any glimmer of potential in terms of the role he would play in the turbulent future of South Africa.

Born Paul Jooste, died Paul Jooste. The years between would always seem quite unremarkable. He was a pharmacist – a skilled professional well known only to the specialised chemist fraternity – and this was the one thing that set him apart. No-one seemed to know anything about him. The true value of his significant fortune was a closely guarded secret. He did not dress, speak or act like a wealthy man. No fancy carriages – Jooste travelled in a plain pony trap. No smart attire – he wore the seams out of his clothes before being coerced into anything new. The man's rough appearance and accent never failed to shock those to whom status and social standing mattered. His wife, a plain, well-rounded woman who sweated profusely, ate copiously and hankered after the high life with as much enthusiasm, or lack of it, as her husband, was perfectly suited to Paul Jooste's simplistic view of life. To Paul, she represented stability – meals on time, well-behaved children, house in order. He never once had any desire to stray from her side, despite the occasional invitation from those young and beautiful women who, despite his every precaution, whiffed the scent of money and imagined how it would look translated into fine clothes, houses, carriages and jewellery.

No-one had a clue about the fires that threatened to engulf the man. Not one person, not even his wife, had any idea of the lengths he might go in order to achieve his lifelong ambition. Jooste ached for order. He could see the way things were going in South Africa and knew that his people had to have policies in place which could control those changes when the time came. To Paul, he lived in the land of milk and honey. Anything thwarting his country's potential was a threat which had to be dealt with. Not harshly, for that was not his way. But by stealth. Paul Jooste was a forewarning of things to come. Secretive he had to be, fully aware that his ideas were well ahead of their time. If he wished to establish the foundations for a safe South Africa, heaven on earth for his *volk*, he had to move carefully.

To this end, Jooste floated his proposals past some of the most high-profile men in his adopted country. They listened, liked what they heard, and in turn passed them on to their own colleagues.

And so was born the first spark of what was to become the most powerful organisation ever to exist in South Africa – the *Broederbond*. The Brotherhood, as it became known in English, would ultimately embrace twelve thousand members. White, influential, male, protestant Afrikaners, men who would come to dominate and direct the lives of millions. Through infiltration, commitment and secrecy, the *Broederbond* would, come its day, secure absolute control of South African society – military, media, church, education, police and government, prime ministers, state presidents and members of cabinet joining the select group until it stood supreme, virtually untouchable.

'Good evening, gentlemen.' Jooste's raspy voice hung in the smoke-filled air. He looked into the faces of each man seated around the table and scowled. 'Where's Venter?'

'Sends regrets. His son is unwell. Again.'

Jooste frowned. 'His son should not take precedence over his country.'

An uneasy stirring greeted the comment. Jooste was fanatical in his convictions: patriotism at the cost of all else. However, each of the four others knew that Venter, the absentee, doted on his only child, with nothing being more important to him than the sickly little boy who'd had the misfortune to be born with a rare skin disorder known as Quincke's disease. Venter had spent a fortune on various treatments. But as nothing seemed to work he compensated by staying close to his son's bedside whenever the lad became afflicted by another symptomatic outbreak of giant hives.

Colonel Schuyler van Deventer scowled at the criticism. 'Do not speak ill of the man behind his back, Jooste. Venter's loyalty to his son is to be admired.' Van Deventer was the only one in the room who would dare express censure. He held a position of authority, was generally acknowledged as being privy to secrets unknown to the others and had earned respect as a significant power in the land. 'Without family where are we?' the colonel growled.

Paul Jooste held up both hands in surrender. 'Agreed. Sorry, gentlemen, a man gets carried away.' What passed for a smile crossed his craggy features. Where many a younger man's lack of good looks were enhanced by firmer features later in life, Jooste had missed out. He had simply become uglier, with moles and lumps emphasising a decade or so of acne and blackheads, the scars still visible on his nose and forehead. The man's lips looked bloodless – another area that the Almighty had ignored. Thin brown hair, badly dyed, remained his one vanity, scraped back in tortured straight lines. Little or nothing could be done about his eyebrows. Despite liberal applications of wax they sprouted at all angles. The eyes themselves were Jooste's only redeeming feature, large and square-shaped, rimmed by long dark lashes, each iris, nearly black, a fathomless depth in which burned the fierce fire of patriotism. There was something fanatically intense about them which gave an indication that beyond the poker-faced exterior lay life.

Jooste entered the room, carefully closing the door behind him. He did everything slowly, methodically, much as a larger man might. Paul Jooste was only five feet ten inches tall and the care with which he moved was odd, almost as though he were trying to avoid attention.

Aware of the effect he had on his audience, he hesitated, enjoying the moment. Fame he may have avoided, but power was in his veins and he thrived on being able to jerk the lives of others more influential than himself, bending them to his will. Money, he knew, was the key. These men needed his and more, now that the ideas put forward had been accepted.

'That incident on the Reese farm. Anyone hear what happened?'

Three heads shook. Colonel van Deventer nodded. 'His son got taken by lions.'

'So they say.' Jooste drew up a chair and joined the seated men. 'I've heard it different.'

'What do you mean?'

'Murder, man.'

'Serves him right, whichever it was. *Engelsmen* have no place in the Free State. All they do is cause trouble.'

'Agreed. Anyway, the matter has been taken care of. Seems like a neighbour's boy found young Reese on their land and shot him.'

'How do you know this?'

'I make it my business to know.'

Van Deventer nodded again. Paul Jooste left nothing to chance and was often the bearer of what, at least on first hearing, appeared to be useless information. 'Does this affect us in any way?'

'Not directly, though we might make use of it later.'

It happened. Remember. Don't write it down. Only use it if needs be. Van Deventer nodded a third time then stopped, suddenly feeling self-conscious. 'Reliable?' he asked.

'As can be. The killer's father is a friend of mine.'

'Then may I suggest you refrain from using the word "killer".'

'The investigating officer is also a comrade.'

Van Deventer threw back his head and roared with laughter – a raucous and infectious sound with which the others quickly joined in.

'To business, gentlemen,' Jooste said finally, wiping his eyes. 'A dop, Schuyler, if you please.' He waited while the colonel poured a generous glass of brandy and pushed it across the table. 'We must decide tonight on certain policies which, if adopted, will form the backbone of our organisation. I cannot stress the importance of this too strongly. We want a peaceful yet powerful Brotherhood which will unite us all. There can be no contentious issues left to chance. I have six points to make and we will examine each individually. Now, gentlemen, let us begin.'

Patiently, Jooste took his audience through what he perceived to be fundamental principles for the *Broederbond*'s future role in South Africa: 'Naturally, our responsibility comes first. I see this being to foster the unity and direction of South Africa. Not just among our own members but in all aspects of the community, from backward Kaffirs to those in positions of power who are unwilling or unable to openly join with us.'

Heads reacted with reflective agreement. It crossed van Deventer's mind that Jooste needed only to open his mouth and those listening had but one collective response. His rhetoric could sometimes be stirring, though more often than not the man merely stated the obvious.

One of those at the table had a four-point plan he wished to discuss. Jooste heard him out in silence, agreeing, objecting, accepting – each with small movements of his hands or head.

Then he moved on. 'Our press must become involved. It's essential we have them on side,' Jooste said, switching to the *Broederbond*'s second basic requirement.

No-one disagreed. To gain the attention of twenty-five thousand potential sympathisers would not be easy, and to annex their hearts and minds even more difficult. They needed all the help they could get.

Afrikaner cultural organisations came next, specifically the problems faced in promoting their activities and ensuring the widest possible recognition.

Being a deeply religious race, the philosophical needed airing as well. They discussed, at length, the burgeoning emphasis on humanism, communism and liberalism – and possible means to combat them. All agreed that such matters were a threat to the spirit of South Africa.

Jooste was warming to the subject he felt strongest about. 'The *Engelsmen* who rule business want economic integration. Few, if any, accept the term "separate development". They are so set in their ways that the apartheid of which we speak does not appeal to them. We must continue to strive for it – South Africa cannot move forward while our *volk* are relegated to subordinate positions. God help us, the British will soon be suggesting we bring blacks into our businesses.'

This comment was greeted nervously. It had occurred to each man in the room that, at some stage in the future, integration was a distinct possibility. None was comfortable with the thought. God, there were so many of them. The blacks would cream off what was rightfully due to the Afrikaners and where would that lead? After lengthy discussion on the subject, Jooste moved to his final point.

'Education, gentlemen. Do we educate the niggers or not? Do we want them running around telling us what to do because they know as much as us? I say to you, no. I say to you, let's keep them ignorant. Ignorant men work for less pay and don't know any different than to be happy with it. To hell with education. This country can't afford the cost.'

There was no argument. To the last man, the idea of educated Africans was abhorrent.

Jooste sat back satisfied yet parched. He'd been speaking for the best part of three hours and was quite wrung out with emotion. It had gone well, as he'd known it would. These men had been hand-picked for the likelihood they would agree with him and for their known influence over others. Soon the word would spread. Only the *Broederbond* could take care of the Afrikaners. Nothing else would.

Paul Jooste was not only ahead of his time, he proved to be prophetic as well. Sixty years later, his six points were still being bandied about by a different set of men, still under the same organisation's banner. Van Deventer handed him another dop. 'Thank you.' Jooste downed the drink with uncharacteristic haste, then turned to one of the others. 'I take it you will see that Venter is completely briefed on tonight's developments?'

'*Ja, meneer.*'

'English, if you please,' Jooste warned. It was the language he insisted they use. In his mind there was little doubt that English would become the lingua franca used in South African politics. He wanted his normally Afrikaans-speaking *Broederbond* ready and able to use it.

Torben and Gerda's visit ended on a high note. For some reason, Torben's tendency to find fault with everything melted away on the last day, revealing a different character altogether. When he wished, he could be totally charming, very funny and a good companion. His wife took her cue from him, dropping any affectations, showing genuine interest in others and proving she too could be excellent company.

Virginia arrived for dinner sporting a diamond engagement ring which had been part of Dallas's inheritance from his real father, Jonathan Fellowes. The entire family knew of this and Torben's only comment was one of congratulations. After all, Gerda had expressed a love of sapphires. In any case, there was plenty left to adjust any imbalance at some future date.

Gerda and Virginia enjoyed a cordial relationship, seeing each other infrequently enough to be able to do so. Gerda teased Cameron for dancing attention on his new fiancée. Virginia smiled winningly, Torben indulgently. Duncan remained wary, lest she start on him. He needn't have worried. Gerda had nothing more than a light-hearted evening on her mind, which was just as well since Tanith, who was also a guest that evening, openly loathed the plump Afrikaner.

Dallas poured wine and before sitting proposed a toast: 'To the women in our lives, gentlemen. Without them, we are nothing.' His eyes met Lorna's and he was wickedly pleased to see her surprise at such an open display of affection. He liked to catch her out sometimes. Dallas watched as laughter lines lengthened around her eyes and she smiled in private acknowledgement.

Christ, he was a lucky bastard! He wouldn't change a moment he'd spent in her company. When Katie had died and their blackest hour was upon them, Lorna and Dallas sought and found the most incredible strength in each other. She could bring him to his knees with laughter or despair, lift him from depression with love and understanding.

His wife was thinking similar things. Lorna still wanted and needed Dallas physically – sometimes as desperately as when they were younger, full of forbidden desires and unfulfilled dreams. He was her rock in the sand dunes of time. The children were pebbles, not solid as stone, because, despite their having grown up, they were still her babies. In one way or another each of them depended on her. Lorna could only provide that stability because she enjoyed the same and more from Dallas.

Katie was lost to them forever. Frazer would soon be making his own life, probably in Britain, and Ellie's chosen work kept her away. How long before Meggie flew the coop as well? Torben was settled in Durban. Of their seven children, perhaps only Cameron and Duncan were destined to stay. That was fine; families everywhere faced the same defection. Children had to make their own way, not rely on parental protection.

Lorna's eyes found Torben. Such a handsome young man, sitting proud and tall next to his wife. Ah, God, the wife! No matter. Virginia was all she could hope for and more in a daughter-in-law and, if Tanith eventually became part of Duncan's future, the same would apply to her. Lindsay and Ellie seemed happy, even if the girl was fooling herself thinking her mother didn't know the two of them were sleeping together. It was so obvious.

Did Dallas know? He liked Lindsay though he had his doubts – that the man was too academic, with not enough get up and go. But Lorna saw a strength in him. He had Ellie's best interests at heart. And Frazer? Oh-so-meticulous Frazer. Artistic, gentle Frazer. A lover. Good combination. Lorna had heard rumours . . . It didn't matter.

Good grief! The soup was finished. Lorna gathered her wits and rang the bell to summon their second course.

Zululand was no longer a British protectorate. In 1897 it had become part of Natal, opening the way for an influx of European settlement. For the Zulu people, leaderless since their king – Dinuzulu – had been exiled to the island of St Helena, this was not the only difficulty they faced. In the last three years plagues of locusts had decimated food crops and then, when all looked well again, the spring rains failed and cattle began dying of a mysterious disease.

Britain's answer to the growing rumblings of discontent was to bring back Dinuzulu. He set up his kraal at Nongoma, thirty miles from Cetshwayo's one time royal residence at Ulundi, but with no power or authority, found himself little more than an advisor.

Mister David had a problem. To speak or not to speak. His information had been passed on as confidential and that meant tribal loyalties were brought into play. It was not only allegiance to his chief that kept Mister David silent. The Zulus were being placed in a difficult position by both Boer and British. A likely confrontation between the two might well be made worse if certain gossip were repeated.

The Boers had made cautious advances to a number of chiefs. They sounded innocuous enough – would the Zulus be prepared to perform certain important duties should there be an outbreak of hostilities with the British over land issues? This was a very real problem. Zulu, Basuto and Tswana tribes tended to sympathise with Britain while Swazis seemed to favour the Boers. Now, despite deeply held differences, individual chiefs were once again vacillating, as they had done for centuries, trying to broker the best deal they could without compromising the uneasy truce that had held, more or less intact, since the great Zulu War.

It was obvious to some, Mister David included, that the supposedly innocent requests meant much more than was stated. The Boers wanted intelligence gatherers and claimed to have ten thousand blacks who, whilst working as cattle herders, cooks, domestic servants, transport drivers and such, would listen and report back on employers, who were invariably less than cautious in their servants' hearing.

The British were well aware of this. They also knew that using Africans to gain access to intelligence was fraught with danger. Generally polite, most tended to deliver information they thought the recipient would like to hear rather than the truth. Misinformation was the inevitable outcome and Britain had learned from the Zulu War how costly such a thing could be. Confrontation with the Boers was increasingly regarded as inevitable. To this end, the British were bolstering troop numbers by redeploying regiments already serving in India – their responsibilities being taken over by locals. The timing conveniently coincided with a decision to do away with that colony's military administration.

What worried Mister David was whether Dallas knew just how advanced negotiations were between the Boers and Zulu chiefs. The rhetorical outpourings of a man called Jooste in Johannesburg had, until recently, caused some mirth in British ranks. At least they were aware of him and his ambitions. What Britain didn't know was that the tone had changed from 'what if' to 'when'. Dallas's long-term friend wondered at what point he should advise his employer of the changed status quo. The more he thought about it, the more Mister David realised it must be soon. Dallas had played a not insubstantial role in the Zulu War and it was right that he be appraised of the subtle switch in affiliation that was taking place. The Boers were planning something and Britain had to be made aware of it. And he, Mister David, had the means to do precisely that.

The dining-room bell rang and Mister David sighed, his dilemma not completely resolved. He sent two girls to clear the last course. Dessert, then cheese and biscuits would follow. Perhaps he'd find a chance to speak with Dallas after Torben had gone back to Durban. It would be unwise to do so before this. As everyone knew, Torben's loyalties were to himself alone.

News of Danny Reese's death reached them about a week after it happened. Lorna and Dallas knew the family, largely through Lorna's longstanding friendship with Elizabeth, Danny's mother.

'I must write to her,' Lorna said. 'She'll be devastated.'

'Danny was Wallace's pride and joy,' Dallas added. 'When you write, please send them my condolences too.'

'Of course.'

'Funny, though.'

'Funny?' Lorna raised her eyebrows.

'Two things don't add up . . . the lad knew that land like the back of his hand and, in my experience, lions seldom attack people unless provoked.'

'What do you mean?'

'I mean,' Dallas said quietly, 'that something stinks.'

'Don't make it worse,' Lorna warned. 'It might be as they say – an unfortunate accident.'

'Do you believe that?'

'Not particularly.'

Dallas pulled a face. 'Twenty years ago I warned Wallace about settling there. He's surrounded by Afrikaners. Not a good idea.'

'Each to his own, you mean?'

'Something like that.'

'I disagree,' Lorna argued. 'To achieve a united

South Africa we must move away from this separate development nonsense the Afrikaners keep going on about. It's dangerous talk, Dallas. It won't work.'

'True, but is there any point in sticking yourself right under their noses? They resent it. They feel it's an intrusion and, in a way, it is. Slowly, slowly. Change can't happen overnight.'

'We're off the subject,' Lorna said briskly. 'Young Danny is dead, whether by fair means or foul, and that has to be the most important thing now.'

'You are right, as usual, my darling.'

She lifted her eyes lazily and Dallas instinctively ducked the flying ball of wool. She hated to be patronised. Laughing, though the boy's death was far from a joke, he left Lorna's sewing room.

Dallas couldn't get the image of young Danny Reese from his mind. The boy was a first-class pain in the arse, a fact that no doubt stemmed from isolation and more than a degree of adulation by both parents. As an only son – the Reese family consisted of four daughters before Danny was born – he had been indulged from birth. The fact he felt comfortable doing a little trespassing would indicate that, although he should have known better, Danny believed himself above challenge.

Something else bothered Dallas. He'd met the Gil family, devout Afrikaners and the Reeses' nearest neighbours. He'd once heard Wallace refer to young Erich Gil as a 'fuck-up', a comment carelessly made within earshot of both the boy and his father. If anything were designed to promote antagonism, it was a senseless, downright cruel remark like that. Erich Gil, as Dallas remembered from their one and only meeting, was a pleasant enough young man who happened to have been born with a number of unfortunate defects, and he was selfconscious to the point of agonising shyness. What if Erich had come across Danny and decided to take revenge? Who could blame him? Erich had to be slightly dysfunctional, living with such obvious physical deficiencies.

If Boer and British hatred came that close to the surface in a predominantly Afrikaans-speaking Orange Free State, at what point would it spill over? How far? How badly? How quickly? Dallas had no doubt that the escalating conflict was edging towards all-out war. He'd been there before, though this time would be different. No lopsided struggle between guns and *assegais*. A full-scale white man's war would destroy everything that had been started. No. Not quite true. The Afrikaners would never allow that. But who would emerge as winners? Ahead, and looming fast, all Dallas could see was trouble.

In a determined frame of mind, he decided that now was as good a time as any to get back onto his horse. Fortunately for him, the animal was of a quiet disposition and more than happy to stand still. Mister David was also on hand.

'You're a cook, not a bloody watchdog,' Dallas muttered in frustration. 'Go and do something useful in the kitchen.'

'When you are safe.'

'I'm fine. Go on, get out of here.'

'I am fine also, *baba*. And I will stay.'

'Stubborn old man.'

'Then send me home.'

'Never. You are so stubborn you would only go if the king called.'

Mister David smiled. Dallas's reference was a direct comment on his loyalty and it touched the Zulu deeply. In the old days – and Dallas included himself in those – when the king called his regiments, any man too old would be sought out and 'sent home'. Being too old to fight rendered a warrior useless and, depending on past brave deeds, he would be killed kindly or clubbed to death. Whichever way he died, the job was done by his own people and always with the individual's interests at heart.

'Besides,' Dallas continued, 'who would make my cheese straws and bread-and-butter pudding the way you do?'

'No-one,' Mister David acknowledged. 'And you'd better remember that. Now, put your foot in my hands and pull yourself up.'

There were only two people Dallas would allow to boss him around. The other was Lorna. On his horse at last, he looked down into the familiar kindness of Mister David's face. 'Thank you.'

'How does it feel?'

'Good.' He stopped. 'A bit stiff, if you must know.'

Lorna joined them. 'Dallas! What are you doing?'

'What does it look like?'

Her tone brought Cameron and Meggie from the house. 'Father! Get off that damned horse.'

'No. Are either of you coming with me?'

'Where to?'

'Nowhere. Just a ride, I promise. Nothing strenuous.'

'How did you get up there?'

Dallas looked guilty. Mister David moved quietly backwards, his look conscience-stricken.

'I made him help me.' The distortion of truth on behalf of his old friend they accepted as being typical of their father.

Meggie rounded on the cook. 'Really, Mister David, I thought you had more sense.'

'Does it make sense to smother a man with reason?' the Zulu countered. 'Will he thank you? I think not. He will blame you for his boredom.'

'And what if something goes wrong?'

'How often does this thing happen?'

Meggie had no answer. Rarely, she knew that.

Reluctantly, Cameron joined his father and the two set off at a sedate pace. Within minutes Dallas's laughter carried back on the light breeze.

'Listen to him,' Lorna said to Meggie, an arm around her daughter's waist.

'You indulge him too much, Mother.'

'And why not?' Lorna asked gently.

Meggie smiled. 'I hope I find the kind of love you have.'

'You will. Just be patient.'

SIX

I n Durban, ten days or so later, fate played a
hand nobody could have anticipated.

Ellie arrived at the hospital early one morning to find she had an unexpected and very badly
injured patient on her hands. As a third-year intern,
she was entitled to some degree of autonomy in
her ministrations – dealing with broken bodies was
not unusual. This one had been damaged in just
about every place possible. The police were
involved, believing the incident to have been a
professional beating rather than an act of God or
providence. They had brought the victim to
Addington and would be back later, hopefully to
get some answers.

The man had been found lying next to the railway tracks near Durban harbour – not a salubrious
part of town at the best of times. Bruised and battered beyond recognition, he barely breathed, yet
there was still a faint pulse. After cleaning him up
as best she could, Ellie examined each and every
injury. She was not helped by her patient remaining unconscious and thereby unable to shed any
light on what had happened. Judging by his

clothes, he was a man more used to the bush than the dubious delights of Durban. A trader or hunter, he certainly wasn't new to the shores of Africa. Ellie, through her father, had met many such characters. This one she failed to recognise. It was hardly surprising. A blow to the man's right sphenoid bone had caused such severe swelling that his face was puffed out of all proportion. His upper and lower jaw also evidenced attention from a very solid object. Teeth were missing, lips split, gums laid bare to the bone.

The head was clean-shaven, leaving little clue as to hair colour. The man's brows and beard were stone grey. He was probably in his early sixties.

Ellie's summary of likely bone damage read like the pages of an anatomy textbook: right clavicle, lower left ribs, thoracic vertebrae, lumbar vertebrae, sacrum. The man's knees and ankles had taken a severe beating while his right arm and most of the fingers on that hand were either broken or lacerated, no doubt from trying to fend off his attackers. Luckily, there was no evidence of internal bleeding.

On a superficial level, scratches, bruises and cuts covered most of the man's face, torso, arms and legs. He'd put up one hell of a fight.

'He's coming round,' a nurse said.

'Poor devil.'

'Morphine, doctor?'

'Not yet. Let's see if he can talk.'

He couldn't. The patient was unable to make more than a nasal moaning sound, due to the injuries to his mouth and jaw. It wasn't long before kindness dictated that Ellie administer an injection of the opium-based drug.

Something bothered her about this man. He seemed familiar, and yet was not. She made him as comfortable as possible, wrote up his notes, then – leaving instructions that she be called if there were any change – left to join Lindsay on his rounds.

The penny dropped for Ellie only minutes before the police returned. She was standing by her patient's bedside, wondering what the hell had happened to him, when he suddenly mumbled, 'Ellie, s'me, ill. Hata tell Dallas.' At least, that's what it sounded like.

'Will? Will Green?' She moved closer. 'My God, is that really you? What happened? What are you doing in Durban?'

'Ngyah.'

An uncharacteristic welling of panic rose briefly but she quickly pushed it away. 'Lie still, Will. Don't try to talk.'

'Ngyah.'

Ellie was uncertain whether that was negative or affirmative. Gently she took Will's leathery left hand between hers. 'Squeeze once for yes, twice for no.'

A squeeze.

'Do you know who did this to you?'

A squeeze.

'How many were there, Will? One?'

Two faint squeezes.

'Two?'

Two more squeezes.

'Three?'

A squeeze.

Three against one elderly and slightly built man. *What a world of heroes we live in*, she thought. 'Was it robbery?

Two squeezes.

'Do you know why?'

A squeeze.

'You owe them money?'

Ellie knew her man! She received a couple of hard contractions and grinned. Will might have been badly beaten but he still had his pride.

Lindsay joined her by the bedside. 'How is he?'

'Down though not out. He's in a lot of pain but seems to be improving. I know him. He's fighting back.'

Lindsay squinted at her. 'You know him?'

'Yes. He's an old friend of Father's. Cam's god-father, actually.'

'Ah!'

She smiled up at him. 'Explains everything, does it?'

'Sort of. Your father does have some . . . er . . . interesting acquaintances.'

'Will is special. Back in the early days he and Dad hunted and traded through the Thukela Valley. They fought together during the Zulu War. Will lives in Swaziland, with Lord knows how many wives. He runs a trading store at Nsoko. Do you mind, Lindsay? I'd like to stay with him. The police will be back any minute.'

'Not at all, darling. Take as much time as you need.'

Ellie didn't answer. She was checking Will's eyes for signs of concussion. Knowing the patient had added a personal dimension to her concern. She was taking no chances.

'Ngyah.'

Ellie picked up Will's hand. 'Would you recognise them, Will?'

Two squeezes.

'Who were they?' Bother, she thought, I can't ask him that way. 'Forget that. Were they white?'

A squeeze.

'English?'

Two squeezes.

'Afrikaners?'

A squeeze.

'Had you insulted them?' She knew he was capable of running off at the mouth about Boers, particularly when it came to their attitude towards any black African.

One squeeze, two squeezes, a shrug, a moan. Will's grip eased, his head lolled to one side and he was back in the cotton-wool calm of morphine.

When the police returned, Will was deeply asleep.

'How is he?' the sergeant asked.

'As you can see. Sleeping.'

'Not unconscious?'

'No. His system has taken over. It's the best

thing for him. I'd prefer it if any questions could wait until tomorrow. He needs to rest.'

The sergeant eyed Will dubiously. 'I'd say he needs more than just rest. Never seen such a mess.'

'He's tougher than he looks.'

'Know him, do you?'

Ellie nodded and told the policeman what little she'd been able to learn from Will.

'Bloody Boers. Not too many of them around here. Could be some of the traders. Shouldn't be too difficult to find. Drunk, I'll bet. Silly buggers.'

Ellie was convinced that Will had information he'd been unable or unwilling to communicate. What was it he wanted to tell her father? She'd deliberately made no mention of that to the police.

Will's distinctive black Basuto pony had been found grazing contentedly along the Esplanade. Nothing seemed to be missing from the saddlebags and Ellie managed to arrange stabling at the racecourse.

'There's more to this than meets the eye,' she said later to Lindsay. 'Why attack Will so viciously? I mean, I know he's quite objectionable at times but surely a punch or two would have been just as effective. Why half kill him?'

'I don't know.'

She looked reflective. 'It's happening more and more, Lindsay. Apparently isolated acts of extreme violence, even murder. What about that young girl we saw last week, the one who'd been raped by three assailants?'

Lindsay nodded but didn't interrupt.

'They were white too. She was English. Said her attackers spoke Afrikaans. The police still haven't found them. In fact, they've had very little success in finding any of the bastards who seem to be committing these crimes. It's almost as if Durban is being targeted.'

'Planned attacks, you mean?'

'Something like that.'

'It's a frightening thought. Look, I'm a bit busy right now. What say we treat ourselves to dinner this evening and talk about it some more?'

They ate at the Royal Hotel in its recently refurbished restaurant. Will Green's condition had continued to improve and, after another hectic day, neither Ellie nor Lindsay felt like returning to their earlier conversation.

'How are Cecily and Stephen?' Lindsay asked. 'I haven't managed to catch up with them lately.'

'Fine. Didn't I tell you? They're leaving next week for Bechuanaland. Going to see Lake Ngami and that inland delta where a whole river disappears into the Kalahari.'

'The Okavango. Rather them than me. According to Livingstone and Oswell the whole place is rife with sleeping sickness. You can't even eat the meat of animals struck down by it.'

'Who would want to? Cecily once told me about Randolph Churchill's method of stopping horses succumbing to tsetse fly. Apparently he used to brush the inside of their nostrils with tar, give them copious quantities of gin, then force them to inhale the fumes of burning sulphur mixed with enough quinine to cover a shilling.'

'That's barbaric. So much for modern medicine.'

Ellie inclined her head. 'Then there would be plenty of work for both of us?'

'Medical missionaries, you might say! It's a nice idea but with this blessed war looming we'll probably be of more use closer to home.'

Their food arrived. Traditional beef curry and rice, spicy hot, complemented with sambals of coconut, tomato and onion, coriander, cucumber and sour cream, all served in separate side dishes. A large plate of poppadoms accompanied the meal, which they washed down with tankards of cold ale.

'Dessert?' Lindsay asked some time later, mopping at his perspiring brow. 'Damn, that was good!'

'Mmm. Silly not to.'

They settled for rich and sticky – Ellie tucked into *koeksisters* dripping with syrup, Lindsay opted for plum pudding and hot custard. Observers must have wondered how the young couple kept such trim figures. Coffee followed.

'I couldn't live anywhere else,' Ellie said, apropos of absolutely nothing. 'This place is where I belong. I'm so glad Father chose to settle in Natal. By the way, Torben says his plaster is off but he's still hobbling around. Cranky as a caged lion, apparently.' Both laughed, feeling no guilt at the shared enjoyment of what they knew would be an absolute frustration to someone so active. 'Poor Mother,' Ellie went on. 'I suppose she bears the brunt of it.'

'I doubt it. Knowing your father, one look at her and he's jelly.'

Dinner over, they strolled together to where Lindsay's driver, Ezekiel, waited patiently for them. It was cold for Durban, a good excuse to cuddle close on the short journey to Cecily and Stephen's house near the racecourse. After making sure Ellie was safely inside, Lindsay had Ezekiel take him back to Addington. The observations made by Ellie earlier in the day were still preying on his mind.

Will Green swam in and out of sleep, hazy images alternating between fear and peace. He should have known better than to speak in front of his second wife, whose father was that deceitful dog, Mafula. Will was well aware that the man's sympathies tended towards the Boers. While welcome to entertain any fantasy the old fool wished regarding the future of South Africa, Mafula should have kept his nose out of Will's affairs.

In the best tradition of African marriages, Will had beaten his wife for indiscreet talk but the damage was already done. Mafula took his daughter's words – repeated verbatim from a conversation overheard between her husband and a young visitor from Zululand – straight to a Boer commander in the area, reporting that Will Green and Dallas Granger-Acheson were two individuals who would actively resist any Boer aggression. When the time came to take up arms, they would make dangerous enemies. Although that alone wasn't enough to warrant drastic action, Will would certainly be watched. For now, there was not much that could be done about the Zululand farmer. The *Broederbond* were not yet ready to show their hand.

Then came a new development. Will had heard of Danny Reese's tragic death. Like many, he did not swallow the lion story. There was something too pat about it. His suspicions were confirmed when a passing trader who'd had too much to drink boasted: 'If you *rooinecks* stand in our way and try to stop separate development you will all end up like the Reese boy.' It told Will two things. One, that the killing had been no accident. And two, that something secret was being planned by the Boers.

Will lived in Swaziland, a kingdom quite independent of South Africa. Yet he had to do something. Dallas was the only person he could think of who might set some kind of enquiry in motion. He knew his former partner well enough to be sure no stone would be left unturned in getting to the bottom of both matters, particularly since the Reese family were old friends. The biggest risk was that Dallas himself could become a target. Caution was called for. Will couldn't go straight to *Morningside* but, as he made regular visits to Durban, another trip south wouldn't seem suspicious to those he knew were keeping an eye on him. And so, the well-worn cogs of Will's brain strained and creaked until he decided that the least dangerous way to reach Dallas had to be through one of his children.

Torben was in Durban but Will didn't trust him. Cameron, Duncan and Frazer would be at *Morningside.* That ruled them out. It would have to be Ellie. God, he hadn't seen her for years. Will found himself remembering the fair-minded little girl who had always wanted to be a doctor. He knew she was at Addington Hospital. Finding her would not be difficult.

That dog. That mange-ridden jackal, Mafula. That . . . that . . . Will was at a loss to think of suitably insulting metaphors. Somehow the interfering old goat must have learned of the drunken trader's revelations. It wouldn't have been difficult. Will now had seven Swazi wives, which meant seven sets of in-laws. And in-laws being in-laws, intrigue was never far from the surface. Hell, Mafula's intelligence could have come from anywhere – from another damned father-in-law even. Wherever, whatever, however, the Boers had decided it was time to teach Will a lesson. His trip to Durban provided them with the ideal opportunity.

'Take him close to the edge,' had been the brief. They'd done that right enough. As fists, an iron bar, a hippo-hide *sjambok* and boots hammered their message home, Will believed his last hour had come. He fought back, remained defiant, but to no avail. All it achieved was a worse beating than had been ordered.

Panic welled in him. Was he safe? Where was he? The silhouette of a nurse who sat beside his bed, reading a book, drifted into focus. Hospital. How he got there didn't matter. He'd made it, found Ellie. Good girl, Ellie. Must tell her. Warn Dallas. 'Ngyah.'

The nurse rose immediately and, acting on Ellie's instructions, took Will's less damaged left hand in hers. 'Water?'

One squeeze.

When she returned, Will had lapsed back into sleep.

Next morning the police were, after a fashion, able to question Will. Though he didn't say much, they quickly came to the conclusion that robbery had not been the motive. The man had been warned off something. Exactly what, remained a mystery. Now that he had been identified, not one of the policemen was inclined to take the incident too seriously. Will's reputation for being an unreliable rogue even made them doubt whether his attackers had been white and Afrikaans-speaking. Surely the Boers wouldn't dare infiltrate so deeply into British-controlled territory?

Blissfully unaware of Will's problems and how Ellie had been caught up in his well-intended scheming, Lorna did what she could to help Dallas overcome the weeks of enforced inactivity which seemed to have rendered his leg more immobile than either of them had anticipated. It would give way at unexpected moments, sometimes causing him to lurch dangerously and grab for support.

In desperation, Dallas had Mister David take him to see Roger Parry in Empangeni. 'Age, I'm afraid. Nothing more to it than that.' The comment did nothing to help.

'What the hell do you mean? I'm not even fifty, for God's sake.'

'You're forty-nine. Same difference.'

'The leg will get better, won't it?' Dallas experienced a shiver of apprehension.

'Of course. But not while you persist in charging around like a wounded buffalo. It needs time. The muscle has wasted a little, that's all.'

'You wouldn't lie to me?'

'Only if I thought it might help.'

Dallas pulled a face.

Roger laughed. 'Relax. I watched you get down from the carriage. There's nothing wrong, nothing that time won't fix.' The doctor opened a drawer. 'Good thing you popped in, though. This arrived yesterday from Ellie.' He handed over an 'OHMS' envelope bearing the return address of Addington Hospital.

Dallas took it. 'Thanks.' If something important came up Ellie often communicated in this manner. Medical correspondence had a way of arriving more quickly than ordinary mail. 'Wonder why the urgency? I'm not expecting anything.'

'You won't know until you open it. Which reminds me, I'm a busy man. Unless you have any other problems . . .'

'No. Thanks, Roger, I appreciate this.'

'Out. My waiting room is filling up.'

Back in the carriage, Dallas ripped open the envelope and read the contents. As he did so his eyes widened in shocked disbelief. 'Jesus!'

'I do not think this communication is from

Him,' Mister David admonished. 'Is it bad news?'

'Yes, it's Will. He's in hospital. He was attacked in Durban.' Swiftly, Dallas summarised the relevant parts of Ellie's letter and detailed the injuries suffered by his one-time partner.

'This is a bad thing. Is Miss Ellie looking after him?'

'Yes.'

'Then he is in the best hands possible.'

Dallas turned to Mister David, heartened yet surprised by the comment. 'You astonish me. What happened to "We have *muthi* for such things"?'

The Zulu felt he had to justify his remark. 'Why do you doubt me? For broken bones we have no cures that are better than yours. Miss Ellie is a very good *inyanga*. She can do this thing. His arm will mend in the same way as your leg. It is easy.'

'Easy! You would bury it in clay and lift his body until everything inside clicks back into place.'

'It works.'

'So it does. It also hurts like hell.'

'A man does not feel such pain,' Mister David said contemptuously. 'But Master Will cannot be made well in this way. If what you read is true, too many of his bones are broken, ones that are not possible to reach. For this we would need a *sangoma*, or Miss Ellie.'

'I shall tell her. When Will is well enough to travel he must come and spend some time at *Morningside*.'

'His wives will wish to be with him.'

'According to what he's told Ellie, one certainly won't.'

116

Mister David shrugged. 'She has probably been punished. It is enough. She was not to blame.'

Dallas supposed this to be true. The poor woman's loyalties must have been dragged hither and thither – between a father to whom she owed allegiance, and her husband. Damned if she did, damned if she didn't. She'd been in an impossible situation. Anyway, that was the least of Will's immediate problems. He had to recover first and, from the sound of Ellie's letter, that could take months.

SEVEN

June, 1899. While the balmy winter weather did much to quell a growing suspicion that events were moving inexorably towards war, there were many players, too many ambitions and far too many differing agendas for good to come from any of it.

Will improved slowly, bones knitting, body fighting back. The swelling of his face had been enlivened by multi-coloured bruises. Nurses nicknamed him 'Compote' after the stewed fruit they regularly served for dessert. An oral surgeon, working with wire and infinite patience, had done his best to reset Will's teeth and jaw. The results to date had him looking something like a mule, particularly since he insisted his head remained shaved. Ellie begged Will to regrow his straggly red hair but he steadfastly refused, citing tribal custom as the reason. Nits were probably closer to the truth. Whatever, no-one, least of all Will, had been aware that he had such long and pointy ears.

'Impish,' he called himself, ignoring the mess of his mouth.

'More like an aging elf,' Ellie said, folding her arms and staring at him.

'That's not very nice,' Will almost whined.

'It's the truth,' Ellie told him shortly. 'Let's face it, Will, totally bald is not exactly a popular look.'

'You're just saying that.'

Ellie threw out her hands and spun round to leave, winking at a nurse. 'If he wants his crotch shaved, cut the whole bloody lot off.'

The nurse giggled, quite used to Ellie's colourful language. 'Yes, doctor.'

'Hey!' Will objected. 'That's enough from you, young lady.' He was still unable to speak clearly and it came out something like, 'Ay. Tha anuf a oo ya laddy.' All three burst out laughing until Will held up a hand begging them to stop. Many of their conversations ended the same way.

Dallas, prompted by Ellie's urgent note, opted to ignore his own doctor's advice. He and Lorna made the hundred-mile trip to Durban, both determined that when Will was well enough to travel, he come and recuperate at the farm. Though he gratefully accepted the invitation, Will warned that until then they should keep contact to a minimum. The beating he had taken made him even more determined to protect Dallas and his family.

'Give me one good reason,' Dallas prompted, hoping to find out more.

'They'll know I've told you. You'll be in danger.'

Dallas shook his head. 'Told me what? What's wrong with old friends getting together, especially when one of them has been hurt? Do me a favour, Will. Stop all this cloak-and-dagger stuff.'

Will refused to elaborate on who had put him into hospital, or why. Dallas respected his wishes and did not press for further information. Later in the day, alone with Lorna, he raised his concerns. 'It's not like Will. Usually he can't wait to talk if he knows something you don't.'

'He'll tell you when he's ready,' Lorna replied.

'Are you aware of what it might be?'

'Apparently Will told Ellie that Danny Reese's death was no accident. He seems to have some bee in his bonnet about a *Broederbond* conspiracy, even mentioned that Cecil Rhodes might be involved, though for the life of me I can't see how. The man's ambition to paint this continent British red from the Cape to Cairo puts him and his capitalist cronies in the Cape parliament well and truly at odds with Afrikaner nationalism. How it all ties together, don't ask me. Suffice to say, Will thinks something big and very secretive is going on.'

It crossed Dallas's mind that some of Logan Burton's canny perception – rather than the surprisingly erudite conclusions coming from Will – wouldn't have gone astray. He could not believe that the old scoundrel had ever read a newspaper, let alone made a study of politics, so whatever it was must have come from listening to others. His long-dead partner would no doubt have put a finger right on the pulse, so to speak.

'Ellie believes that Will has stumbled onto

something significant and was beaten up to stop him talking, more than likely to you.'

'Why me?' Dallas shook his head impatiently. 'Damn it! I wish I knew what was bothering the man.'

Lorna sympathised with his frustration. 'You have contacts in this country. He doesn't. Let's hypothesise for a moment.'

'I'm all ears.'

'As I see it, Rhodes may have failed with his scheming to take over the Transvaal goldfields but, even before the Jameson raid, Paul Kruger was worried by the growing number of foreigners try-ing to grab a slice of his cake.'

'I won't argue with that. Go on.'

'So, legislation aside, what if Kruger decides enough is enough or even goes on the offensive? He uses the Brotherhood to ensure secrecy and seeks support from Steyn in the Free State. From there it's a hop and a skip across the border to . . .'

'Kimberley,' Dallas finished Lorna's sentence.

'Precisely, and all Mr Rhodes's precious diamonds.'

Dallas sighed. 'It would also explain why we keep reading about more British troops coming to Natal and the Cape.'

'And that's something else which seems to be upsetting *Oom Paul*.'

Both lapsed into silence, each contemplating the inevitable consequences of a full-scale war. They were curled into chairs at Cecily and Stephen's house, their hosts having left for Bechuanaland with no idea of a return date. It was much more convenient to stay in Durban than use the family's beach cottage further up the coast at Umdhloti. Their original house, high on the Berea, had been sold more than a decade before.

Lorna knew Dallas had little patience when it came to man-made uncertainties. In truth, he was not a political animal, preferring to deal with obvious right or wrong than anything complex, especially when the dilemma was devised by politicians for the sole purpose of securing power, profit or territorial gain. Their inherent duplicity irritated her husband to such an extent that Lorna sometimes wondered why he bothered to become involved. On this occasion his conclusion was deliberately vague: 'I suppose we must all look to the future.'

Lorna shook her head. 'You do that anyway, my darling.'

'Not far enough,' Dallas reluctantly admitted.

'Is Lindsay coming for dinner?' Lorna asked as Ellie came into the room. It was as good a time as any to change the topic of conversation.

'If that's all right with you.'

'Of course.'

Ellie's eyes turned to her father. 'Dad?'

'Don't you start,' he grouched. 'It's bad enough when Meggie calls me that.'

'Sometimes you're so old-fashioned,' Ellie said, laughing, her eyes sparkling with affection.

Dallas grinned at her. Like all his children, barring one, Ellie could do no wrong.

★

Dallas and Lorna spent almost six weeks in Durban. They were regular visitors to the hospital but their spare time gave them an opportunity to see just how much the city had grown.

In the first week of July they attended a race day at Greyville, accompanied by Torben and Gerda. It seemed as if the whole of Durban had turned out, with ladies' fashions just as much in competition off the track as the horses were on it.

The atmosphere and excitement reminded Dallas of another day at the races, five years earlier, as a guest of John Dunn. It was to be the last time he would see Logan Burton's closest friend and his own mentor of fourteen years, the one-time Englishman who introduced him to Zulu king Cetshwayo and helped negotiate a royal grant of land in Zululand. That had been the beginning. Sadly, John had died the following year, aged sixty-one, leaving forty-nine wives and a hundred and nineteen children. Dallas shook his head and smiled at the thought.

Torben had a singularly successful afternoon using tips he kept very much to himself. Dallas had no such luck, his gut-feel selections running last in all but the main race, in which a horse called Early Mist came from behind less than a furlong out to win by half a length. The twenty-to-one outsider belonged to a C. Hammond of Dargle. Dallas didn't bother going to the winners' enclosure. Instead, he ordered a well-chilled bottle of Bollinger.

★

Will was eventually released into the care of Dallas and Lorna just before the middle of July. They had an uneventful if long trip back to *Morningside*, Will's pony secured behind the carriage and obviously happy to be back on the road.

Installed in the guest suite, Will enjoyed the luxury of a bedroom, his own sitting-room, a cosy courtyard and private bathing facilities. Dallas suggested sending a messenger to Will's trading store in Swaziland with news of his whereabouts. Will wouldn't hear of it. He gave the excuse that his wives would then want to come and see him and, for now at least, their attentions were the last thing he needed. Will's body still ached and, quite simply, all he wanted was rest. In part that might have been true, though Dallas suspected it had more to do with whatever was not being said.

Finally, Will spoke of what was troubling him. The two men were sitting up late, a decanter of Scotch between them on the verandah. Mister David hovered, not really part of the conversation until Will asked him to join them, seeming to need the Zulu's comments on what he was about to say. He also suggested they move to the parlour. Winter was raw and it was too cold to stay outside. Besides, as Will pointed out, they stood less chance of being overheard.

Dallas poured drinks for himself and Will, raising an enquiring eyebrow at his cook. At times like this, Mister David was more a friend than an employee. As a Zulu he would imbibe in private – beer served by one of his wives – though he seldom, if ever, drank in the company of white men, unless it was a festive occasion. The offer was refused.

Will hunched forwards. 'It's Rhodes,' he said succinctly. 'He's up to something again.'

'So, what else is new?'

Will glowered at Dallas but said nothing about the interruption. 'It would appear that this time he and that gold-bug Alfred Beit have prevailed on Milner to put pressure on Kruger and try to force some kind of retaliation.'

Nobody commented, so Will went on. 'In the last few years Johannesburg has become the richest and most highly populated place in South Africa. Gold has sucked in fortune hunters from all over the world, so many that the Boers feel threatened by people they see as outsiders. "Uitlanders", they call them.'

'Making the Afrikaners strangers in their own country?'

'Something like that.' Will glanced at Mister David. 'You'd know all about that.'

The Zulu nodded slowly. 'We lick our wounds and move forwards in silence, unlike the Boers who whine and complain yet do little else.'

'Not so, my friend,' Dallas was quick to point out. 'It was Kruger himself who brought in the Dutch, Germans and Cape Afrikaners to run his administration. There are even some Americans.'

'And what a mixed-up mess it all is,' Will added. 'The Boers may mouth off about losing control of their gold but I don't hear them objecting to its rewards. Fifteen million pounds is what they expect from the Witwatersrand this year alone. On top of that, the Uitlanders are taxed, denied political involvement and generally regarded as inferior. Damn it. They're treating them almost as badly as the blacks who dig their bloody mines for them.'

'Kruger's government hasn't trusted any Uitlander since the Jameson raid,' Dallas said, referring to a scheme devised by Cecil Rhodes to exploit their discontent and take over the Transvaal goldfields. His friend and colleague Dr Leander Starr Jameson, along with five hundred Rhodesian mounted police, had waited on the Bechuanaland border for word of a promised uprising. Nothing happened. Prevaricating between Britain's Union Jack and the Transvaal *Vierkleur*, not to mention being distrustful of Rhodes himself, the Uitlanders dithered to a point where any opportunity was lost.

Backing Rhodes's plan had been Britain's newly appointed Colonial Secretary, Joseph Chamberlain. When no revolt occurred he distanced himself from the plot by threatening to void the British South Africa Company's charter to administer Rhodesia unless invasion plans were stopped once and for all. Rhodes was forced to agree but late in December 1895, Jameson, acting on his own, went ahead and entered the Transvaal. The Uitlanders – instead of providing support – opted for negotiations with Kruger. The raid was an ill-conceived, unqualified disaster.

Will was nodding at Dallas's observation. 'Yes, that's where it started.'

Jameson had been captured. He, along with five of his officers, was sent for trial in England and later imprisoned. Rhodes was forced to resign as Cape premier. The sympathies of Cape Afrikaners and those in the Orange Free State – who had kept well out of the whole fiasco – lay entirely with Kruger, uniting them in a common condemnation of Britain. The whole of South Africa had become brittle, like granite – rock hard yet easy to split. Chamberlain's answer to the deteriorating situation had been to appoint a proven administrator, Sir Alfred Milner, as Governor of the Cape Colony and British High Commissioner for South Africa.

'What have you heard?' Dallas asked quietly, dreading the answer.

'Milner is working up a new crisis. He's insisting that the Uitlanders be allowed a number of major concessions, threatening force if they're not implemented. By demanding the impossible the man's hoping for a military confrontation which will give Britain an excuse to reunify South Africa and, in doing so, gain control of the Transvaal goldfields. Kruger has been pushed too far. It's only a matter of time before he forges an Afrikaner alliance with the Free State to attack the Cape Colony and Natal.'

'Jesus!' It exploded from Dallas in a shocked rush of breath. 'They could do it too. We don't have anything like enough men to defend both.'

Will went on: 'As I understand it, we have ten thousand regular troops spread between here and the Cape. Kruger and Steyn have ready access to at least fifty thousand men of military age and several thousand others would probably join up too. We need another forty thousand, maybe more. Britain is talking about sending five thousand – ten at best – and even that could take months to finalise. It's to be war, Dallas. Lose, as we're likely to, and Britain can kiss this continent goodbye. Win, an unlikely event as I'm sure you'll agree, and the Union Jack will fly from Cape Town to the Zambezi.'

Dallas rose and replenished their glasses. 'You're a dark horse, Will Green. Are you sure of all this? I've never heard you speak of such things before. How do you know so much? You live in Swaziland, well away from all this political manoeuvring.'

'Do I? Do you really think Kruger will stop at the Zululand border? No, my friend, Swaziland has its gold too. This war's going to be all or nothing.'

In the silence that followed, Dallas realised how close Lorna had come to working out what was going on. Gold or diamonds, it didn't matter. Both sides coveted southern Africa's mineral wealth and, it would appear, were more than willing to fight for its control.

Mister David's hooded eyes reflected the flickering fire, now burnt low in the grate. 'War,' he intoned in his deep voice, 'is a devil which devours all in its path.'

'Man is the devil, David,' Dallas said, dropping the 'Mister' as he usually did on such occasions. 'Though this time, it will not be your war.'

Will it not, Mister David wondered. 'Why then do I have a feeling that, once again, the tribes of my country will pay a heavy price? I have listened to the words of my chief, who repeats those of others. We will be drawn into your war whether we like it or not.'

Dallas had no answer.

'I'm positive my information is correct,' Will insisted. 'The more I think about it, the more I believe those bastards in Durban meant to kill me. It's the only way they could be sure I'd keep my mouth shut.'

'They? Who were they?'

'Names, I do not know. Their language, their actions, both suggested the *Broederbond*.'

'That's supposed to be a peaceful organisation.'

'And the Pope is supposedly religious.'

'Do you think they'll try again?'

'Most probably. It depends on how ready they are.'

'What will you do?'

Will gave a half-smirk. 'Die, I suppose.'

'Not funny, my friend.'

Will looked serious for a moment. 'Indeed it is not, and the very fact that I am here places you and your family in just as much danger.'

Paul Jooste's eyes swivelled around the room until he located Venter. He nodded at the man. 'How's your boy?'

'Recovering.'

'Hardly a boy anymore.'

It was a criticism and Venter knew it. 'He's still my son and I hate to see him suffer.'

'Quite.' Jooste lost interest. There were other fish to fry this evening. He waited until the room had quietened. Nine were present, including himself. 'Gentlemen, to order.' The everyday business was quickly concluded – a by-election to fill an Orange Free State vacancy; changes to the department responsible for the inclusion of English in schools; consideration of membership for leaders in the newspaper industry; suggestions to attract younger members . . . all were anxious to hear what their leader had to say next.

Finally, Jooste folded both hands over the agenda and looked around the table, a fond expression on his lumpy, crinkled face. 'As you know,' he intoned, 'I am stepping down.'

The murmur of regret sounded louder than it was after the carefully calculated pause.

'I do so of my own free will. My work here is done. The *Broederbond* needs a high-profile leader, someone who can command attention and keep it. Ballot papers will be available on Saturday. You have thirty-six hours to vote and return them. It has given me great pleasure, gentlemen, to participate in the formation of what I believe will become the most powerful organisation in the history of this country. I am proud to be associated with it. Not only does the *Broederbond* represent power, it shows a way this can be achieved without violence.'

A subtle stirring around the table was not lost on Paul Jooste. 'Rumours are just that. There are forces beyond our present limitations which would undermine the great efforts made to date. God willing, these can no longer harm us. We are too far advanced, too trusted, to let would-be thugs ruin the reputation we've strived so hard to achieve.'

Colonel Schuyler van Deventer interrupted: 'It is said that recent incidents of violence in Natal were perpetrated by us.' He was still the only man in the room prepared to query their leader openly.

'And that is precisely why we need more support from the newspapers,' Jooste explained patiently. 'They can create the truth.'

'I don't like it, Paul. Deceit could tarnish our image and I for one cannot risk my reputation.'

Jooste responded harshly. 'Your reputation, sir, is like Venter's son. It should be secondary to all else. Do not be so foolish, man. Your shining image is untouchable.'

Van Deventer flushed brick red with anger. 'I didn't mean –'

'I know what you meant,' Jooste went on more quietly. 'Our organisation is watertight. We do not resort to standover tactics – everyone knows that.'

'So what of the man who was nearly killed in Durban?' van Deventer continued remorselessly.

'Deplorable.' Jooste threw out his hands in a gesture of implied transparency. 'What else can I say? It wasn't us.'

'Who then?'

'I have no idea.'

Paul Jooste and his peaceful policies had changed. Those round the table knew he was capable of ordering – in fact, knew that he had ordered

– similar warnings to others. A small-time trader by the name of Will Green was hardly a threat to their plans and yet he'd been viciously targeted by a few thugs only too willing to throw some weight around. Those men were now back inside the Transvaal where the Durban police couldn't touch them. Uitlanders – Dutch on this occasion – easy to recruit for money, would always put up their hands for a job, keep their mouths shut and quietly drink or gamble away the meagre reward.

Jooste, the figurehead who wielded such power, was the first to admit that he had outlived his usefulness. The money flowed in, a seemingly never-ending stream of it. The *Broederbond* was well capitalised and, unless some unforeseen financial crisis arose, there would be no further need of his personal resources. It was time to move on.

Another man spoke, anxious to conclude the evening's business. 'Formalities, Paul.' He smiled sympathetically. 'Sorry, they're your rules.'

Laughter, tinged with nervousness, greeted the unnecessary prompting.

Paul smiled. 'Quite right.' He rose and raised his drink. 'To the *Broederbond*, my friends. Long may it last.' Swallowing the brandy in one gulp, Jooste banged his glass down on the table with a satisfied 'Ah!' Then, catching the eyes of each man in the room, he said in a loud voice, 'With regret, gentlemen, I hereby tender my resignation.'

It was recorded in the minutes, seconded and signed.

A cheer for Paul Jooste broke any tension and

the room rang with congratulations. More drinks followed and the meeting relaxed into a party atmosphere. Paul wondered, looking around at the men, what any of them would think if they knew just how damaging Will Green's information could have been. It was no longer a worry. Jooste had been reliably informed that the man would not survive his injuries. The woman doctor tending him was apparently the daughter of Dallas Granger-Acheson, an influential – and pro British – Zululand farmer. That could still prove a problem. If either of them learned the truth, further action would be needed. A pity, but sometimes these things had to be done.

EIGHT

Will's information turned out to be surprisingly accurate. On Monday 9 October 1899, President Kruger delivered an ultimatum to the British Agent in Pretoria demanding that Britain cease all interference in the Transvaal Republic, withdraw troops from the border and turn round others known to be in transit. Failure to comply within forty-eight hours would be taken as a formal declaration of war. The Johannesburg goldmines came to a virtual standstill as over thirty thousand fearful Uitlanders and unemployed black miners fled south to Natal and the Cape Colony.

It was Sunday 15 October, four days after the Boers' ultimatum expired and three since fifteen thousand mounted Transvaal burghers under Commandant-General Piet Joubert invaded Natal from the north and east, linking up with six thousand more from the Orange Free State in an attempt to cut off British forces at Dundee and Ladysmith.

The Granger-Acheson family and close friends were gathered at *Morningside*. 'This is serious,' Dallas announced. 'It's decision time for the men.'

'And women,' Ellie interrupted, correcting her father. 'Those who can help, at least. Lindsay and I will be joining the Natal Volunteer Medical Corps.'

'I thought you might,' Lorna said quietly. 'As I see it, we can all play our part.'

Dallas leaned sideways and covered her hands with one of his own. 'That's exactly what I was trying to tell you,' he said. 'I too have decided to enlist.'

A stunned silence followed his words and he felt the sudden tension in Lorna's clasped hands. For some unknown reason, Dallas had not recovered from his broken leg quite as quickly as might have been expected. He still limped and in colder weather often complained of bad circulation.

'Darling, you're too –' Lorna quickly bit off her words. 'When?'

'Not right away,' he reassured her.

'Better hurry up, Father,' Cam joked, trying to lighten the moment. 'Fifteen to fifty is the official call-up.'

'I'm only forty-nine,' Dallas pointed out. 'That gives me a good couple of years. Anyway, this thing won't last that long.'

Cameron said nothing, just smiled and shook his head.

'I'm fit enough.' Dallas needed to justify his decision. 'If this damned leg would heal, I'd be as right as rain.' Or possibly to divert attention. 'What say you, Will?' His friend of almost thirty years had not yet returned to Swaziland and, even at sixty-something years of age, knew exactly what had to be done. Before he could answer, a chorus of concern rose from several throats.

Will set his jaw, which gave him a more mulish look than ever. 'No-one tells me what to do! That's what I say.'

Ellie glanced at Lindsay in silent appeal. 'Will! You sit around most of the time or hobble along with a wrecked spine. One hand doesn't work properly. Anyway, you're definitely too old. Lindsay, please tell him.'

Lindsay found himself the centre of attention. 'Um . . . she's right, old chap. I hate to put it this way but, right now, you'd be more of a hindrance than a help.'

'Says who? I'm as ready as I'll ever be.'

Dallas suddenly understood what drove Will – his loyalty to the family was far greater than any to the British monarchy. Having put him on the spot, Dallas now sought to provide him with a way out. 'Will won't do anything he feels is beyond him. Am I right, Will?' Dallas's eyes pleaded with his friend to agree.

Will nodded. 'Of course.'

That drama aside, at least for the present, Dallas found himself back in the family's firing line. 'It's a fine thing,' he grumbled out loud. 'A man does all he can to protect his children and then, when it's time to stand up and be counted, finds that they feel obliged to protect him. I'm young enough and fit enough. Damn it, General Buller is ten years older than I am and he's due in Cape Town in a couple of weeks. I know the man. If he comes to Natal I, for one, will be joining him. If not, I'll offer my services to a volunteer unit.'

'Times have changed, Father. The Zulu War was twenty years ago. You can't expect things to be the same.' Cameron's point was well made.

'I can still make myself useful.'

'This is different. Things are more organised.'

'You could have fooled me,' Dallas nearly shouted in frustration. 'For God's sake, man, all I ask is that they put my knowledge and experience to good use.'

Cam backed down. He knew a man who knew a man who, with any luck, would make sure his father was kept in the background. As for himself, however . . . 'Well, I've already put my name forward. The 2nd Gordon Highlanders have just arrived from India and are recruiting scouts who speak Zulu. I'm in. Sir George White is at Ladysmith and I expect to be sent there before the month's end.'

Lorna's face was ash white as she turned to Virginia and saw the same disbelief reflected in her features. Cameron's announcement had been completely unexpected.

'Infantry,' Torben sniffed. 'Why not cavalry?'

'What's the difference?'

'A horse, you damned fool.' Duncan tried to lighten the moment and failed dismally.

'Cam,' Virginia stammered, 'you didn't say anything about this to me.'

'No, my darling, and look what's happening now that I have. It will be fine, Ginnie. Trust me. As soon as Natal is secure our chaps in the Cape will quickly have Bloemfontein and Pretoria in their sights.'

Frazer wasn't so sure. 'Rumour has it the Boers have already cut off Mafeking and Kimberley. I hear the "Lion of the Empire" is actually trapped in his den.'

'Serves him right,' Torben said scathingly. 'Rhodes is a fool. All he thinks of is money.'

'And you don't?' murmured Cameron.

'De Beers's diamond production will soon be worth more than five million pounds a year. I'd say that was well worth thinking about!'

'Well, I hope he's got plenty of Champagne on ice. Apparently the man drinks nothing else.'

'Except tea.' Torben had to have the last word.

Virginia tried to remain composed but the sparkle of tears let her down. 'If anything happens to you . . .'

Cameron crossed to where she sat, crouched until their faces were level and took her hands in his. 'Nothing will, you'll see.' Still in the same position he looked across the room at Torben and asked the question that had been on all their minds. 'How about you?'

Torben's eyes shifted to his wife. Gerda was an Afrikaner and proud of it, while he made no apologies for being self-motivated. Money could be made from this war, lots of money, though now was neither the time nor the place to go into that.

'I'm sure you can all appreciate what a difficult decision this is for me. In deference to my wife's family, we must consider their feelings. I believe it would be prudent to refrain from making any decision until I absolutely have to.'

'And then?' Cameron would not allow him off the hook that easily.

'Then . . . ' Torben spread his arms, turning his hands up in a helpless gesture. 'Then I'll let you know.'

Gerda intervened, placing a hand on her husband's leg. 'Torben is very considerate that way. My parents understand what he is going through.'

'So do we, young lady,' Dallas reminded her. 'This war won't go away.'

She nodded, serious for once. 'Then leave him to make his own decision. Being badgered left and right is no help when it comes to conscientious deliberation.'

Lorna's eyes flashed to Dallas in obvious surprise. Such genuine understanding was not what either of them expected from their daughter-in-law. Her choice of words aside, hysterics, tears, blackmail or even a threatened breakdown of the marriage would have been more in character. Instead they had received a calm rebuke, delivered straight from the heart. Mention of her family had been made with no underlying motive – she was simply stating the fact that they appreciated Torben's dilemma.

'I think you're quite right,' Lorna said sincerely. 'It can't be easy for your parents either.

Living in Durban, they must feel quite ostracised at times.'

'They do,' Gerda agreed quietly. 'They're used to it. My mother says it's born of ignorance.' She tittered suddenly, sounding more like the usual Gerda. 'Must we speak of the war? It's so depressing.'

'I'm afraid we must.' Dallas tried not to sound aggressive.

Torben patted his wife's hand. 'Not for much longer, my darling. Then you can show us your new dress.'

The brief truce of cultures was over.

Ellie and Lindsay were clear about their own roles. Doctors would be needed – in the field as well as hospitals far from the front line. Lindsay had tried to convince Ellie she should stay in Durban. She disagreed. 'It will be immediate attention that matters most,' she said. 'I'm nearly qualified. I should be out there.'

Lorna suddenly saw her entire family at risk. 'But you're a woman.'

The comment was met by an outburst of derision. 'That's never stopped you, Mother!' was Meggie's immediate reaction.

'So what?' said Ellie.

'I know,' Lorna capitulated. 'Call me a hypocrite, I probably am. This is my family I'm talking about.' She turned to Frazer.

A loud and very eloquent silence met her questioning expression.

'No, darling. Not you too?'

'I must, I'm twenty next month, Mother.'

She could see he was right. 'What will you do? Do you know where?'

'Thought I might tag along and take care of the old man.' Frazer grinned at his father's outraged expression. 'See if all those stories he tells us are true – give him a chance to prove himself.'

Dallas's eyes had narrowed to slits. 'You little shit' began a string of expletives which would have caused a sailor to blush.

'Have you quite finished?' Frazer asked as the rest of them sat spellbound. Not even Gerda had blinked.

'Quite.'

'So that's settled then.'

Dallas turned to Lorna in mock despair. 'Speak to the boy.'

She pulled a face but it didn't hide her tears.

In the silence that followed, Meggie tried to sound positive. 'I'll stay with you, Mother. We can make bandages and splints, things like that.'

'That would be lovely, darling,' Lorna murmured, frustrated that she and Meggie could do little more than behind-the-scenes bits and pieces. Still, someone had to knit all those useless little scarves, gloves and hats which held water, ripped at the slightest hint of barbed wire and more often than not became lost in the bottom of kitbags.

Tanith quickly declared her decision to help and turned a questioning look at Duncan, as though they'd already discussed what he would do. Resigned to hearing his decision, Lorna made the unspoken a question: 'Well?'

'Thorneycroft's lot, most likely. Too much spit and polish for me in the regular army.'

Dallas tapped out his pipe – smoking had become a habit he increasingly enjoyed of late. 'You might not be given an option.'

'I'll find out when the time comes.'

'I think it's here already, Duncan, more's the pity.'

'So.' Lorna's practical nature needed to sum up. It also stopped her worrying too much about the future. 'Between the lot of us we can muster four women to help wherever – I'm assuming you'll be with us, Ginnie – two medics, a scout for the infantry, three, possibly four, mounted volunteers to do as directed and two abstentions delaying any decision for cultural or conscience considerations. That's not bad going. I'd say Buller should have nothing to complain about from here, wouldn't you?' The question may have been directed at nobody in particular but Dallas sensed a bitterness in her words. Lorna resented the inevitable intrusion of imposed politics, just as she had when the Zulu War came into their lives.

'I wonder if Boyd will come out?' Cameron speculated, referring to an uncle on his father's side who had spent his entire working life in the army.

'He's retired,' Dallas reminded him, not wishing to discuss his older brother, who had fought in the Zulu War while managing to remain totally ignorant of the enemy and their culture.

Torben chose to take Lorna's words as an accusation. 'It's not my fault, Mother.'

'No-one said it was,' Dallas cut back crossly.

'Yes, but –'

'But nothing. Gerda put it as well as anyone might.'

Still feeling surprised by his daughter-in-law's succinct understanding of Torben's problem, Dallas turned to Gerda. 'I think it's time to get ready for dinner. Torben said something about a new dress, my dear. We're all dying to see it. Why don't we meet for drinks in, say, an hour?'

It was the first time Dallas had picked her out for special attention and she glowed in the limelight of his approval. 'Of course, Poppie.' Gerda dimpled at Torben. 'We have some welcome news for you all but will save it for then.'

'Welcome news,' Lorna grumbled in the privacy of their bedroom, secure in the knowledge that with Will using the adjoining guest suite Gerda and Torben were out of earshot. 'Sounds as if the damned woman is pregnant. What on earth made you invite the fashion parade?'

'I don't know.'

'On your head be it. Whatever she wears, you'll have to enthuse.'

'I can do that. Watch me.'

It wasn't easy, pink not being one of Dallas's favourite colours, and the explosion of green stars at the front and back of the skirt certainly didn't help. Dallas tried his best. 'Where did you find such a gown?' The back of the dress trailed on the floor and he winced inwardly, knowing that Suza had just performed a vigorous flea-scratching routine on the very spot where the train was resting.

Gerda draped herself on one end of the sofa. 'Do you like it?' She adjusted a strap with a none-too-gentle heave. Dallas waited in anticipation of disaster, but it held.

Nobody noticed his lack of response. 'You two said something about welcome news? Come on, out with it.'

The interested twinkle in Dallas's eyes dulled immediately Torben spoke. 'Gerda is with child.'

Everyone knew they'd been trying. Gerda glanced modestly at the floor. Torben, expecting immediate cigars and congratulations, frowned. 'No-one has anything to say?'

'Con . . . gratulations,' Lorna managed, thinking only Torben could complicate matters by announcing an impending family in the very week war breaks out.

'Hell's teeth.' Dallas strove to achieve a light-hearted atmosphere. 'That's wonderful news.' He crossed to Torben, shook his hand firmly and thumped him on the shoulder. 'Congratulations, son. Took a while but, I say, this is terrific news. Our first grandchild. Think of it, Lorna, our first grandchild.'

Dallas's posturing had given her time to recover. Gliding elegantly to Gerda, Lorna bent and kissed the girl's cheeks. 'Thank you for the news, darlings. I couldn't be more pleased.' She clapped her hands together. 'Oh, what fun. A baby is just what this family needs.'

Torben, looking a little happier, turned in expectation to Cameron, only to hear what they had all been thinking. 'There's a war on, Torben. We all knew it was coming. Couldn't you have waited?'

Gerda, buoyed by Dallas and Lorna's reaction, responded for him. 'A baby waits for no-one, Cam. It's a blessing from God and should never be refused.'

Cameron turned away, rolling his eyes at Virginia.

'Duncan?' Gerda asked.

'Wonderful.' He shrugged. 'I look forward to being an uncle.'

Meggie was enthusiastic and genuine. 'Oh, Gerda, how thrilling. You must promise to visit us more often.'

This was more to Torben's liking. 'Will you deliver the baby?' he asked Ellie. 'We'd prefer a woman doctor, wouldn't we, darling?'

'It would be my pleasure,' Ellie responded. 'Though, please realise that family members are restricted with the medical help they can offer. If there's any complication, someone else would have to take over.'

'There'll be no problem,' Gerda promised. 'I'm as healthy as anything.'

Frazer was quietly happy for his older brother. Life had to go on despite the war. Tanith and Virginia also refrained from comment. A baby was good news. The timing certainly wasn't. Still, it was on the way and nothing could be done about that.

Will hadn't joined the family that evening, as a more pressing matter demanded his attention. Late in August he had reluctantly allowed Dallas to send a message to his trading store in Swaziland. It said simply that Will had been very sick but would soon be well enough to return home. And that was how they had found him.

When Will's wives started turning up at *Morningside* they insisted on looking after him but refused to enter the main house. Dallas solved that problem by allowing them to construct two traditional beehive *rondavels* a short distance down the hillside. He also agreed with Will that no more than four family members would be present at any one time. It had worked well for a few short weeks but now Will had the unenviable task of telling whichever relatives were currently in residence that they would have to return home the following morning. He would not be returning with them, a decision taken in view of Will's determination to play his part in the war, and Swaziland's growing sympathy for the Boers.

The following weeks passed quickly. Ellie and Lindsay joined the Natal Volunteer Medical Corps. A paperwork mix-up gave Cameron a commission in the South African Light Horse while Dallas, Duncan and Frazer found themselves destined for another newly formed group, the Fairfax Scouts. Both units comprised Natal volunteers as well as refugee Transvaal Uitlanders funded largely by Cecil Rhodes's multi-millionaire business associate, Alfred Beit. They were part of a dozen or so divisions that made up the Natal Cavalry's 3rd Mounted Brigade commanded by Dallas's one-time schoolboy friend Douglas Cochrane, now a highly experienced and decorated Major-General and the Earl of Dundonald.

Virginia, much to Cameron's displeasure, opted to drive an ambulance wagon. 'I'll be closer to you,' she told her fiancé. 'It's not dangerous work. All I have to do is pick up wounded soldiers from whichever railway station they arrive at and transport them to the nearest hospital.'

'And make a nice target for Boer snipers,' he pointed out.

'Don't be silly. We'll be well away from any fighting.'

Cameron knew she was right and realised he was probably being overprotective.

Lorna, Meggie and Tanith signed on as hospital assistants in Empangeni.

Before being posted – they were unable to say where – Ellie and Lindsay managed one more trip to *Morningside*, bringing with them a rather strange present.

Dallas lifted down the heavy wooden crate, clearly marked 'CASTOR OIL – MEDICINAL PURPOSES ONLY'.

'Why on earth would we need this?' he asked, puzzled by Ellie's look of amusement.

'Better be careful with that, Father.'

'Here, let me give you a hand,' Lindsay offered. 'Where should I put it?'

'Leave it on the verandah, there's a dear,' said Lorna. 'I'll take it to the hospital tomorrow.'

'Not a good idea, Mother. I suggest you open it.'

Intrigued, Dallas levered off the lid and, with a look of astonishment on his face, extracted a magnum of French Champagne.

'Two cases were delivered to Addington. We don't know where they came from or who they were meant for.' With a twinkle in her eye Ellie added, 'And all of us were far too busy to try to find out.'

Dallas laughed. 'Then we'd better open it this evening – just to see how well it travelled.'

The immediate British plan was to secure Natal, assemble the Army Corps in Cape Town, then push north to take the Boer capitals of Bloemfontein and Pretoria, relieving Kimberley and Mafeking along the way.

Late in the third week of October mixed messages and rumours started coming through from the Natal front. There had been a victory, of sorts, at Talana Hill, near the British forward position in Dundee. Unfortunately, losses included the death of Major-General Sir William Penn Symons, garrison commander, and the ignominious surrender of cavalry sent out to cut off Boer retreat.

The 2nd Gordon Highlanders, along with Dragoon Guard cavalry and the largely Uitlander-recruited Imperial Light Horse, had routed the enemy at Elandslaagte. Using bayonets and lances – weapons the Boers refused to adopt – they had all but annihilated an entire *komando*.

The news was mixed. Under heavy artillery fire, British troops had evacuated Dundee and fallen back forty miles along the railway line to Ladysmith, leaving behind two field hospitals, all the wounded and provisions for a force of five thousand.

On 30 October, a day that became known as 'Mournful Monday', at places hitherto unknown – Modderspruit and Nicholson's Neck – over twelve hundred British soldiers were lost, killed or forced to surrender as a direct result of tactical inflexibility and Boer mobility. A new type of warfare was emerging. Three days later Boer forces cut railway and telegraph lines to the south of Ladysmith. The garrison, and almost all the troops who were supposed to defend Natal, found themselves under siege.

Ellie and Lindsay had been posted to the rapidly reinforced British garrison at Estcourt in the Natal midlands where, quite coincidentally, they were introduced to a newspaper reporter by the name of Winston Churchill. He was the same age as Ellie and she had often heard of him, his mother being a cousin of her American mentor, Cecily Jerome. 'Small world,' Ellie said later to Lindsay, little imagining what fate had in store for the young Englishman.

On 15 November an armoured reconnaissance train set out north along the railway line towards Colenso and the Thukela River. On its return journey a Boer ambush derailed the three troop-carrying trucks, pinning down their occupants with artillery and rifle fire. Over seventy men were killed, wounded or captured – Winston being one of the latter – and a muzzle-loading ship's gun lost to the enemy.

Closer to home, Tanith and Meggie found

themselves emptying hospital bedpans, spooning food to those too badly injured to feed themselves, applying dressings, mopping floors – in fact, anything to relieve pressure on the qualified nursing staff. Lorna helped too, as and when the running of *Morningside* would allow. All three women worked at home as well, turning out handcrafted cushion covers, quilted eiderdowns, crocheted blankets and the like, all donated as raffle prizes to raise money for vital medical supplies.

With the situation in Natal looking far from encouraging, Sir Redvers Buller had been forced to split the Army Corps in Cape Town and send reinforcements by sea to Durban. Two weeks later he personally took command and established his headquarters at Frere, north of Estcourt, only twelve miles from where Boer forces had blown up the railway bridge at Colenso and dug into an elaborate network of trenches and gun emplacements along the Thukela River.

The South African Light Horse, which Cameron had joined early in November, waited for Buller's arrival. Will was also at Frere. Much to his disgust, the only duty offered – and this grudgingly – had been as a noncombatant to help with the horses, many of which were out of condition, still recovering after their long sea voyage from England and not yet acclimatised to the debilitating heat of an African summer.

'At least you can keep an eye on your godson,' Dallas said, trying to cheer up his friend the day he and Cameron left the farm.

'*Ja*,' Will agreed. 'I can make sure his horse has a leg at each corner too!' He was not a happy man.

Duncan, Frazer and Dallas, the latter's leg now back to normal except for an occasional twinge, were finally called up just after the middle of November. They left *Morningside* on Frazer's twentieth birthday.

NINE

Felton Fairfax had two hundred men under his command. Their task was to slip past the main Boer forces in Natal and move west, across the Orange Free State, gathering information on enemy troop movements and disrupting them where possible. This was of particular importance to Lieutenant-General Lord Methuen, who, with eight thousand regular soldiers, waited on the Orange River for a push north to relieve Kimberley. The lack of information on Boer deployment was Methuen's greatest concern.

Fairfax and his men were camped deep in enemy territory on the top of a small, flat-topped kopje near Lindley, some two hundred miles to the east of Kimberley. Dallas knew that the Reese farm was not far off and wondered if the family were still in residence. Unfortunately, now was not the time to find out.

It was hot, what clouds there were bleached white by a relentless summer sun and offering little or no likelihood of rain. Even the airless nights brought scant relief. Felton Fairfax seemed oblivious of the conditions, not allowing the weather to affect him or his men.

Dallas instinctively liked their leader. Fairfax wasn't out to impress and was not too proud to seek advice. He was tall, almost stick-like in stature, with blond haystack hair, obvious cataract damage in his left eye and a mouth which once fell foul of a childhood game of cowboys and Indians. A wayward tomahawk had nearly removed his top lip, leaving a line so perfect that sometimes people blinked on meeting him, just to be certain they weren't seeing double. Fairfax – for all his apparent frailness – had a deep, gravelly voice which had many wondering about the size of his testicles. The man positively growled when he spoke. In complete contrast, his almost feminine hands, with their long tapering fingers, looked like those of a concert pianist. Not so. Felton Fairfax was tone deaf – a fact that became painfully evident to any who heard his attempts at song. As for playing a musical instrument, he restricted his efforts to a mouth organ and only when others helped him hold the tune.

As his name implied, he was a fair man, regularly displaying understanding and good humour. His oft-repeated motto, 'Blaming others doesn't help – we're here to fix the problem', made him popular with the men, who had been quick to give him the affectionate nickname 'Fairy'.

In the company of other commanders – men from military backgrounds, aristocrats or black sheep in search of adventure – Fairy Fairfax stuck out like dogs' balls. Unashamedly. Once described as being 'rough as a bear's backside', he wore no uniform or insignia of rank yet those he led carried out his orders without question. He had yet to prove himself in the field and once admitted to Dallas, 'There's too many would-be heroes running this show. I sometimes feel that I'm up to my arse in bloody crocodiles and the water level is rising.'

Most of the volunteers were equally untried and so it was to those with experience – men like Dallas – that their leader would turn for company and occasional advice. At the end of a day, with sentries posted, the sounds and smells of the bush became more noticeable, reminding them all that while their circumstances might be different, the country for which they fought was unchanged.

One evening Dallas relaxed with his back against a still-warm rock, watching a blood-red summer sun lose its glare in the dust-laden distance of an invisible horizon. It seemed to move more quickly, as if eager to be somewhere else, now that the day's job was done. Even the light breeze held its breath in awe. The kopje was small, easily climbed and extended their view by a good ten miles in every direction. Rock, scrub and parched earth are rarely pretty but Dallas loved the African bush. Stunted acacias dotted the veld, their two-inch needle-like thorns stark white and clearly visible in the fast-fading light. Far to the east, a deep-purple mist seemed to be rolling towards them. Night was near. A lone jackal trotted busily away and disappeared into it. Otherwise, nothing stirred.

Fairfax trudged wearily towards him, a bottle and two tin mugs in hand. Dallas moved over to allow the man a share of his backrest. 'Dop?' the younger of the two queried.

'Please.'

Fairy sat and poured generous helpings of warm brandy into each mug. 'Pretend it's crystal.'

'This is fine.'

'Would be nice, though.'

'What?' Dallas hadn't really been listening.

'Crystal. Drinking fine brandy from a glass which sparkles with elegance and fire.'

Dallas glanced at him. 'What's got into you this evening?'

'Ah! Don't mind me, man. The Boers are watching us. Have you seen them?'

'Yes. About three miles out. They'll leave us alone.'

'What makes you so sure?'

'They usually do. More than likely doing what we're doing. Gathering information. It's only a local *komando*. They won't risk confrontation.'

'Wish I had your confidence.'

'You're young.' Dallas smiled. 'Though, believe me, age has its drawbacks as well.'

Fairfax smiled too and relaxed. He was thirty-eight, a farmer with no fighting experience. His main attribute was a natural ability to lead others, a competence that came from controlling his family's business. They ran beef cattle, employing hundreds of Africans and a handful of Europeans on two farms, each of which was over five thousand acres, in the currently Boer-controlled Natal midlands.

'You're from around Colenso. Do you know a man there by the name of Wilcox?' Dallas asked idly, not really caring if Fairy did or didn't.

'Who doesn't? William's a bloody pain in the arse.' Fairfax turned his head quickly. 'Hope you don't take offence at that.'

Dallas grinned. 'I'd take offence at anything less.'

'Ah, I see! Most seem to run up against him if they spend any time in our fine little town. How is it that you've had the pleasure?'

'I was once married to his daughter. Not by choice, I hasten to add.' That part of his life had come to an end many years ago and Dallas didn't mind speaking of it.

Fairfax blinked at his outspokenness. 'Then why?'

'Blackmail,' Dallas replied flatly. 'Bloody man accused me of getting her pregnant.'

The whole of Natal knew the scandal of Sarah, Dallas and Lorna. The fact that Fairfax didn't was probably a result of his relative youth. 'What happened?'

'Sure you're interested?'

'It has to be better than sitting here discussing this damned war.' He held up the brandy bottle and Dallas raised his mug for a refill, beginning to wish he'd said nothing.

'I came out here as a remittance man,' he began. 'Back in Scotland I'd been accused of a crime I didn't commit. Wilcox found out and because of

156

circumstances which I won't bore you with he forced me to marry his pregnant daughter. When the truth finally emerged, he did everything possible to stop me from leaving.'

'So how did you get out of it?'

'Walked away. Simple as that. The baby wasn't mine and I had no intention of remaining married to a girl I didn't love, trust or even like.'

'And the woman who is now your wife? She came out from Scotland, I believe. Lorna, isn't it?'

At the mention of her name Dallas's face – although he wasn't aware of it – softened. 'From the moment she arrived, there was no decision to be made.'

'Bit of an awkward one, though,' Fairfax offered. 'Back then, well . . . these things were rather frowned on, weren't they?'

Dallas laughed out loud. 'I'll say. You'd think the Scots had just declared war on England the way people carried on. Luckily for me, Lorna didn't let it worry her. She's one in a million.'

'I've heard of your wife. People even talk of her in Colenso. You were a trader back in the early days, were you not? She travelled with you. Made quite an impression, as I hear. Sounds like a pretty amazing lady.'

'Thank you,' Dallas said, his mind recalling many months spent on the road and how well Lorna had taken to the life, learning, listening, loving every moment of it. And the day they so nearly lost Cam. She and Will turning a herd of stampeding elephants with little more than a peashooter.

157

That was also the day an enraged elephant had killed his friend and business partner, the inimitable hunter Logan Burton. One memory led to another until a question brought him back to the present.

'You have two sons riding with us.' Fairfax lit himself a cigar. 'Are they your eldest?'

'My youngest, actually. Apparently they want to keep an eye on their old man.' Dallas grinned. 'They're welcome to try.'

'And others?'

'One with the South African Light Horse and another in Durban, married to an Afrikaner.'

'Ouch!'

'I know. So far he's kept out of things.'

'Wise man.'

Dallas let the comment go.

'Daughters?'

'Two. We had three but . . . a snake. She was seventeen.'

'I'm sorry.'

Fairfax rose suddenly. 'What are those damned fools up to?' In the distance he had noticed movement, several men making their way stealthily from tree to tree, rock to rock, towards the kopje. 'Pah!' he said in disgust, fortified by the brandy. 'They're playing games. Lion cubs, testing their strength. Pass me your telescope.'

Dallas handed him the spyglass he always carried, a relic of many hours spent searching for the ultimate stag – a 'Royal' – in the Scottish highlands.

Fairfax focused on the approaching Boers.

There was just enough light to observe them. 'As I thought. Youngsters flexing their muscles. Cheeky buggers, they're waving at us. Get them killed one day.'

Dallas was reminded of young Danny Reese. He had been killed around here, also flexing his muscles. In a matter of months the myth of Lindley's man-eating lions had been exaggerated to epidemic proportions. Out here, raw recruits – Uitlanders in particular – were spooked by the slightest sounds, not to mention the idea of being savaged while they slept. Old Africa hands wrote off the stories for what they were: rumours. Whichever way you looked at it, the death of Danny Reese unnerved most who passed this way. The Boers even capitalised on it, trying to scare their enemies with good imitations of lions roaring during the hours of darkness. As it transpired, not all the sounds were man-made.

Before either of them heard the shot, a bullet slammed into the rock where, seconds earlier, Fairfax had been sitting. Both men instantly dropped and rolled in search of cover. 'Bloody snipers. A thousand yards is nothing for those new Mausers,' complained Fairfax. 'Can't even see smoke now they're using cordite instead of black powder.' There was a crackle of random return fire along the hilltop but nothing more from below. Both men waited until it was fully dark before moving.

In the Boer camp, the commanding officer was bright red with rage. 'What do you think you're doing, you young fools?' he roared at his grinning would-be invaders of the British position. 'This is no game.'

Kaptein Hanson Wentzell had not one iota of the understanding or humour that Fairy Fairfax displayed. He was a Cape rebel who hated the British, hated the war and hated the way others disobeyed orders, particularly as he was the man giving them. He especially hated knowing that, although the Boers were winning most confrontations, it could only be a matter of time before that changed. The enemy appeared to have an unlimited supply of troops, food and ammunition, while the Boers were already scraping the bottom of the barrel. If he could, Wentzell would have walked away and returned to his farm, far off in the Hottentots' Holland Mountains where, as he delighted in telling anyone who would listen, his forefathers had hunted the mighty Cape lion to extinction. In his mind they were twice as big and ferocious as the kittens out there now. He didn't see how even the Kaffirs could like this godforsaken place.

'Sorry, sir,' the sniper said, seeking to get his reprimand over and done with as quickly as possible.

'Sorry! You young skellum. I'll make you sorry. Double guard duty. Get to it. Now!'

Grumbling, the young man turned away, making no pretence at contrition.

Wentzell dismissed the others and turned to his adjutant. 'I've a good mind to show this lot how it's done.'

'Why don't you, sir? That would teach them all a lesson.'

A smile spread over the officer's face. 'I might just do that. Show them an old dog has no need of new tricks, eh?'

'Sir?' The man was suddenly nervous. 'I didn't mean –'

'I know what you meant, man,' Wentzell rasped. 'This war won't be won with words. *Lekker slaap.*' With that he stomped off towards his makeshift sleeping shelter. Having as good as committed himself, he couldn't back down now. *Damn!* Wentzell was already regretting his bravado. The last thing he needed that night was more physical exertion. His body craved sleep, nothing else. Every part of him ached. Despite a life spent out of doors, and being extremely fit, half a century of hard manual work had slowed him down. He wanted nothing more than to curl up in his favourite arm-chair, look fondly at his wife, Magda, and do precisely nothing.

Bugger it, he thought, *they can think of me as they wish. I'm getting some sleep.*

At that moment, a shot rang out.

'What the hell . . .?' Fairfax actually jumped, the unexpected noise had been so close.

'Sorry, sir. It just went off. I was only cleaning it. I didn't touch the trigger, honest.'

Fairy believed him – it had happened before. Luckily nobody had been hurt. 'Okay, son. No harm done. You've learned your lesson. Next time, make sure it's not loaded. Right now, I suggest you get some sleep.'

Wentzell took the sound personally. It was as intrusive as it was offensive. 'That's it, you limey bastard,' he growled, using the British navy's version of 'Pom', which had been adopted by the Boers. 'One of you will die before we move out in the morning.' Hanson had no intention of spoiling his sleep over some soon-to-be-dead enemy. Tomorrow would come quickly enough.

Dallas had a deep feeling of unease. That shot should have drawn a response. None came. No retaliation. *Why?* Fairfax expressed the same concern. 'Could be they're up to something. We'll post extra guards just in case.'

Frazer drew the dawn watch: 0400 to 0800 hours. A none-too-gentle hand shook him awake. 'Umph!' Frazer groaned, taking a second to realise where he was before rolling from his blanket, standing unsteadily and rubbing a grimy hand over an equally grimy face.

'Morning, sunshine,' a cheery voice greeted him. 'Grab some tea and get moving. All's quiet.'

'Do you have to sound so damned chirpy?' Frazer grouched.

'Silly not to. This is probably going to be the highlight of me bleedin' day.'

Frazer gave what passed for a laugh. 'Piss off, Trevor.'

'Temper, temper.' The unit clown clapped his

hands against his cheeks in a gesture of mock surprise.

As did others, Trevor had believed there might be something quirky about this lad's sexuality, but it was something none of them talked about. Frazer's father would not stand for such speculation, his retribution likely to be swift and inventive. Besides, Trevor genuinely liked the lad and knew from talking to him that, despite his love of sketching and art, he was no different to anyone else when it came to more basic instincts.

Frazer picked up his Lee Metford carbine, checked it had a full magazine, stumbled to the fire and poured himself a mug of sweet stewed tea. Turning from the glowing embers he let his eyes adjust to the dwindling darkness before moving off towards a rocky depression on the east-facing slope, just below the skyline. Looking out at the coming dawn, Frazer marvelled at the magic of nature. He recalled a Zulu belief that one great chief – the sun – travelled the sky by day passing under the sea at night only to set off again each new morning. Perhaps they were right.

The land below remained quiet, shadows lay long in the early light. It was not yet six and the sun had already signalled its challenge to a new day, wrapping itself round each tree, shrub and rock, turning everything golden brown. As he watched, the sky changed from deep dark blue to purple to rich red. Morning had come and with it a chorus of new sounds. Clearly heard, not always seen, animal and bird alike heralded the new day with gusto.

Frazer scanned the surrounding country. There was no movement from the Boer camp. Last night's fires had burned out. He found himself thinking how the wildlife must be suffering, not only from prolonged drought but also as a result of the Boers' ceaseless struggle for sustenance. Frazer didn't blame the Afrikaners. Though birds, bucks, even rats and snakes fell to the guns of their expert marksmen, the men had to live.

A discordant noise down and to his left had Frazer turn towards it, weapon at the ready. Squinting straight into the low sun, he saw nothing yet remained alert, listening, watching. Boers could move like shadows, leaving footprints and little else. The sound was not repeated and after some minutes he relaxed.

Dallas woke from sleep, immediately alert. The sun told him it had to be around six. Frazer would be halfway through his watch. For some unknown reason, alarm bells rang and Dallas scrambled to his feet. Hunching over, he snatched up his weapon and set off towards the edge of the kopje, anxious to make sure all was well with his youngest son. Looking down, Dallas was just in time to see a bandolier-strapped figure, carrying a carbine and jumping from one rock to another, about to disappear into the thorny bush below.

Heart beating wildly, he registered that there was no sign of Frazer. The intruder was moving fast, sure footed and agile, his back broad, strong arms held out for balance, bull neck bulging with muscle. 'Stop!' Dallas yelled, working the bolt and squeezing off a shot without waiting for the Boer's response. He still couldn't see Frazer.

The man dropped from sight. Dallas instinctively fed a new round into the chamber and cautiously made his way down the slope. Stifling a most terrible fear, he reached the scrub line and stopped to listen. Where was Frazer? There was movement ahead and the stranger rose unsteadily to his feet, a dark red stain spreading from just below his left shoulder. Dallas raised his rifle, finger already on the trigger. The Boer took one staggering step backwards, steadied himself and smiled humourlessly. 'Lucky shot, *Engelsman*,' he said, discarding the stolen Lee Metford in exaggerated disgust.

Dallas stared at him. The wild weather-beaten face, lined and smeared with dirt. Fatigue circles under each eye. Hair and beard unkempt, grey and frizzy. His clothing filthy. One arm dangled uselessly, flesh and shattered bone exposed. Well-worn boots, seams gaping and stuffed with dry grass, promised scant protection from the elements. But it was the man's voice that captured Dallas's attention. He recognised it.

'Wentzell?' he rasped, throat dry and scratchy.

'*Ja*. Who wants to know?'

'Granger. Dallas Granger. We met thirty years ago on the *Marie Clare*.'

'So we did. And I liked you no better then.' Hanson Wentzell gave a tortured laugh despite his obvious pain. 'Got water?'

'Not here.'

The Boer grunted. 'Neither did the kid up there.'

Dallas felt his stomach churn. 'What kid? Where?'

Wentzell nodded in the direction from which Dallas had come. 'No water, no food – nice clean carbine, though. Little bugger was half asleep.'

Frazer!

Hanson Wentzell was talking again, his right hand suddenly holding a long-bladed Bowie knife. 'Do we settle this my way or yours? Have you got the guts?'

'The boy?' Dallas managed. 'What did you do to him?'

Wentzell drew an imaginary line across his own throat with the knife and grinned obscenely. 'Jerked around a bit, made it tougher on himself than it might have been.'

Ice cold now, Dallas tightened his trigger finger. Hanson Wentzell flew backwards, dead before he hit the ground.

Back up the hill, Dallas knew what he'd find. It didn't stop him hoping, praying.

Frazer. His youngest son. The one who should never have joined this crazy war. Too gentle, too sensitive, too damned nice to be in a world of death, destruction, hate and anger. Too intelligent to believe the potent propaganda dished out in defence of what amounted to nothing more than man-made greed.

'Dear God, let him be alive.'

Frazer lay on his back, one leg kicked out sideways, arms above his head where they'd fallen. Across his neck, a jagged line that had gushed blood so fiercely its dark red stain drenched his chest and the ground around him. Eyes wide and staring, seeing nothing. Mouth open, frozen in a silent scream of protest.

'Nooooooo!' The cry rang out from Dallas, deep from somewhere far beyond his control. Dropping on both knees he pulled the bloodied body of his son close and cradled the lifeless shell. It was still warm. 'I'm sorry, son. I'm so, so sorry.'

Tears ran unchecked down Dallas's face. He'd promised Lorna to keep this one safe, this son with whom she shared a bond somehow deeper than that she had with the others. She loved all their children but Frazer and Lorna were connected in a way no-one fully understood. Soulmates, she called it. They were so attuned to each other that one would often answer a question before the other asked it. Frazer's death would destroy Lorna. 'Forgive me, darling.'

Duncan found them there. 'Father!' His eyes took in the scene and he stood, staring, unable to hold back the emotion that shook him from head to foot. 'Dear God,' he managed, 'not Frazer.'

Father and son sat in silence next to the uncovered body. It seemed as though others on the hilltop, possibly even those below, shared in their grief. Silence surrounded everything, wrapped it in a cocoon of sympathy. They had all lost something that morning, and for what?

Frazer had been popular. Always willing, always smiling. His death was like losing the unit's good-luck charm.

Finally, Duncan broke the unnatural quiet. 'I'll come with you.' He understood what his father had to do.

'No, son.' Dallas shook his head. 'Better you stay with Fairfax. I'll break the news to your mother, get word to the others and be back as soon as I can.' He reached over and gripped Duncan's shoulder so hard the boy nearly gasped with pain. 'Stay safe. That's all I ask.'

He was the one who would have to tell Lorna. An impersonal telegram from the war office? No. Dallas had to break the devastating news himself. There was no choice.

Fairfax assumed both shots had been directed at the enemy and quickly ordered back-up. Moments later he heard Dallas's anguished cry of grief.

The burial detail made its way quietly to where Dallas and Duncan still sat in reflective silence. With no unnecessary conversation, they began digging. It was hard, hot work and took them the best part of an hour to make the hole deep enough. Reluctantly, Dallas allowed them to pre-pare Frazer and place his body in the shallow grave.

'What about him?' one of the men asked, nod-ding down the hill to where Hanson Wentzell lay sprawled on the ground.

'Leave him to the lions,' Dallas said in a hard voice. 'And leave me with my sons.'

Later, on a white wooden cross bearing Frazer's

name and the dates of his birth and death, he carved the words *hamba kahle*, Zulu for 'go well', carefully colouring each letter with a burnt stick.

Fairfax waited for a couple of hours before intruding on Dallas's grief. 'I'm afraid we have to move on. You can stay or come with us. The choice is yours.'

'Thank you. I have to tell Lorna. Then I'll be back. Duncan will go on with you.'

'As you wish. I'm sorry about your loss. If I can help in any other way?'

Dallas sat still, head bowed. He nodded acknowledgement. 'Nobody can.'

Without further words, Fairfax turned and left.

A few minutes later, Dallas rose, rested his hands briefly on Duncan, then went in search of his horse. He'd need ammunition, water and food. All were in short supply. Turning, he looked back to Duncan and the fresh grave. They seemed so small and insignificant against the sun-scorched back-drop of nondescript bush, dotted here and there with flat-topped kopjes. 'Goodbye, my son,' he whispered, committing the place to memory. The hill looked identical to so many others, but when this war was over Lorna would wish to visit Frazer's grave. He would never forget where it was.

On reaching the horses, Dallas found that his mount was already saddled. Someone had filled both his wet skin waterbags, packed rations and extra ammunition. 'We couldn't spare much,' an apologetic Fairfax told him.

'This will be fine. Just look after Duncan.' Dallas mounted, checked his stirrups, raised a hand in silent farewell and set off down the steep escarpment, not once looking back. He and Lorna had faced heartaches, hardship and despair over the past twenty-seven years. There'd been good times as well as bad, but telling his wife about Frazer's death would be the most difficult thing Dallas had ever done.

TEN

S he was in her prime – sleek and largely free of the scars which, in later years, would bear witness to her struggle for survival. Pregnant with a first litter, unexpected sounds of danger caused the lioness to remain hidden whilst the drama of men unfolded. The blood smell told her that a meal awaited. Patience was required.

The Boers were well aware of the lions. They had heard them during the night and, when dawn came, found fresh pug marks within yards of the camp. It was of little concern until the new day also revealed that their *kaptein* had disappeared.

Sentries saw nothing, but two shots from the kopje had all twenty-nine men of the Reitz *Komando* awake and alert. There was movement on the slope above. They too watched, waiting. Before long, with the sun well up, what appeared to be a burial detail came into sight.

Wentzell's adjutant feared the worst and when, by ten o'clock, there was still no sign of their leader, a decision was taken to leave and report the incident.

She watched, waiting, the blood scent still there.

So were the men above. One had already gone but she knew there were more, many more. Eventually they appeared, moving carefully down the slope, turning south-west and urging their horses to pick up speed. Silence returned, yet she waited. Caution had much to do with it, though, in truth, it was too damned hot. The meal would have to wait.

Hanson Wentzell had been a victim of war – one of many – and few of his men spared further thought for their sometimes cranky, often unfair and more than a little brutal *kaptein*. As a Cape rebel, he had not been popular with his Free State *Komando*. Arrogant – to him, the enviable enthusiasm of youth was no substitute for age and experience – Wentzell flaunted success and ignored failure. He drank to excess – as did most of his men – but brandy made him loud and brash. Quite simply, nobody liked him.

Under cover of darkness, the lioness overcame her lethargy and succumbed to the craving for food. She sniffed the dried blood and took a tentative lick with her rasp-like tongue. Mixed with salty sweat, the taste was not altogether unpleasant. By now she was hungry. Soon others would find this meal and the father of her unborn cubs would more than likely chase her off. The lioness lowered her head and began to eat.

It was the same pride that had devoured Danny Reese. Vague memories of that unexpected meal, decidedly edible and putting up no resistance, told her all was well. It also encouraged the others to partake of a free feed. Led by smell and sound, the rest of the pride loped in uninvited. Food was a rare and precious thing. It could be snatched from them at any moment. Made nervous by the lingering smells of man – fires, tobacco and the dreadful and out-of-place odour that their noisy stick-like weapons left – they ate hurriedly and disappeared into the darkness.

And so war added to legend, or was it legend to war? Myths exaggerated out of all proportion. A ferocious pride, stalking the veld, waiting to prey on any unfortunate enough to cross their path. Stories grew until what had been, and still was, a hard-pressed group of carnivores facing drought and the ravages of man turned into marauders of indefensible savagery. The Lindley Lions, as they were now known, became larger, stronger and more cunning, able to appear and disappear at will. Their reputation demanded extreme caution from those finding themselves within thirty miles of the place. Word spread, much as it had the previous year when work was stopped on a section of the Uganda railway near Tsavo in east Africa, because of the horrific cost of human life wreaked by a pride of man-eating lions.

A few, Dallas and Duncan included, ignored the stories, sticking to what they knew of the animals' behaviour. The Lindley Lions had long learned to be cautious. They remained hidden during the day, instinctively aware that although the presence of people meant danger, come darkness, it brought the promise of food. Despite usually sparse pickings, starving animals would willingly risk injury just to lick the inside of an old bully-beef tin or snatch a few discarded bones. There was no more to it than that.

When Dallas left to break the devastating news of Frazer's death to Lorna, he knew he was being watched, not only by lions, but also by a handful of Boers whose task it was to clear any signs of the *komando*'s presence. The others had gone. Such was Dallas's misery that morning, he cared little for either. He'd heard the pride last night, even seen one of them that morning. The lions would leave him be.

What Hanson Wentzell had done was a deed of bravado, one man acting on his own, probably out to impress or prove something to the others. And that made Frazer's death even harder to bear. The boy had been no match for Wentzell, who must have known it. This was no act of war – it smacked of murder, the same thing Dallas was now feeling in his heart. If Wentzell weren't already dead, he would have killed him again.

Although dreading the task ahead, Dallas took what he thought would be the shortest route home. From Lindley he rode due east, back into Boer-occupied northern Natal, skirting Dundee and turning south to Greytown, then east again through Eshowe before dropping towards the Mhlathuze River. The journey, through nearly three hundred and fifty miles of rugged country, travelling dawn to dusk – more if light and conditions allowed – took him four full days. For the first time since coming to Africa, Dallas remained unmoved by the wild beauty around him. The country was harsh and unforgiving, the weather terrible, and he was tempted to hate both. But in his heart, he knew that neither had changed. Dallas pressed on, realising, probably for the first time, that by choosing to live here he had accepted a way of life which no mere mortal could ever hope to control.

By the time he reached *Morningside*, his horse sagging with fatigue, Dallas still had no idea how he would break the news to Lorna. His unexpected arrival, unwashed, unshaven, clothes stinking and still stained with blood, would immediately tell her that something had gone seriously wrong.

There was no-one home. Doors and windows stood wide open though not a single servant was in evidence. Only the dogs, Saba and Suza, deigned to see who had arrived. Dallas greeted them and, after some suspicious sniffing, both wagged stumpy docked tails and licked his hands in slobbery welcome. Although he had been away for only a few short weeks the dogs seemed older. A year ago they'd have bounded all over him. Soon servants started appearing, so Dallas gave instructions to look after his horse and bring hot water for a bath. Despite dreading what lay ahead, there was nothing he could do but clean up and wait. More relaxed due to a long, luxurious soak and clean clothes, Dallas sat on the verandah to await his family's return.

Having fallen asleep, he heard them before he saw the carriage. Lorna's voice, pleased for some soldier who'd had bandages removed that morning and was able to see. Meggie's delight at a doctor's praise and Mister David's calm voice bringing the horses to rest. Tanith was with them too.

'There's someone here,' Lorna said. 'Hello, the house,' she called. 'Who's there?'

'It's Master Dallas,' Mister David told her, although it was near dark and he had no way of seeing who it might be.

'Dallas!' Lorna was out of the carriage before it stopped. She ran up the steps and straight into his arms. 'Darling.' He held her tightly and to his horror felt himself start to shake with uncontrollable emotion. Lorna would need his strength, not weakness.

With a supreme effort, Dallas drew breath and regained his composure.

'Something's happened!' Meggie came up the steps, closely followed by Tanith.

Over the heads of the women Dallas's eyes met those of Mister David. 'I see you, my friend.'

'And I you,' the Zulu responded, nodding. He knew.

'Come inside, all of you. I have bad news.'

Lorna wouldn't wait. 'Frazer!' Hysteria was close. 'It's him, isn't it?'

'Be strong, my darling. Yes, I'm afraid it is.'

'No.' She pulled away. 'No. You promised me, Dallas. You promised to keep him safe. I'd have known. Go back and look for him. He's alive, I'm sure of it.'

Inside, the few lamps that had already been lit threw a gloomy light. Mister David hurried to brighten the room.

Dallas stood in front of Lorna, who had collapsed into a chair and was looking up at him with desperate hope. 'I'm sorry, dearest. We buried him four days ago.'

'No, it can't be.' Lorna refused to accept what she was hearing. 'Not Frazer. Not . . . I . . .' Suddenly her face crumpled and she buried it in both hands, as if hiding from the truth.

Dallas sank to his knees and reached out. She shook herself free. 'Look at me, Lorna.'

Slowly, reluctantly, she did so.

'Frazer knew the risks. We all did. It was his choice to be there. None of us could have stopped him.'

'But why him?' Lorna moaned. 'He was just twenty, for God's sake.' Then, inexplicably, she gave a brittle smile. 'Oh well . . . if the good Lord demands sacrifices, somebody should tell him we've made two. Let's hope he's satisfied. I'll let the rest of the family know. Can't trust anyone else to do that.'

'Lorna?' Her changed attitude concerned him greatly. Shock he'd expected, grief obviously, even blame, but this? 'I can only stay a few days.'

'No. No need for that. We'll be fine. You just run back to your little war and get on with it. The sooner somebody wins, the better for all of us.'

Dallas had never seen Lorna like this. 'I'm staying,' he said firmly.

Much to his relief, a surprisingly composed Meggie stepped in to try to help. 'Come, Mother, I'll take care of supper. It might be best if you lie down for a while.'

Lorna turned savagely on her youngest. 'What do you think I am, a bloody invalid?' she snapped. 'Leave me alone, all of you.' She rose and strode from the room, slamming the solid wooden door behind her.

Meggie looked shattered and burst into tears, burying her face in Dallas's chest.

'I will take Miss Taylor home,' Mister David offered.

Tanith touched Meggie's shoulder in sympathy and turned a questioning look to Dallas.

'Duncan's fine,' he said, and she went without a word, leaving Dallas to console his daughter. They could both hear Lorna's keening but knew it was best to leave her be. She'd meant what she said. She needed to be alone.

Food, without Lorna, was barely picked-at leftovers. Meggie and Dallas spoke in fits and starts, mainly about Frazer. She asked after Duncan, said there had been a letter from Cam. He and Will were well. Neither had news of Ellie and Lindsay. Ginnie was now at the field hospital outside Mooi River. Inevitably, their conversation kept coming back to Frazer.

'There was nothing anyone could have done to save your brother.' Dallas needed Meggie to understand what had happened. 'He was deliberately targeted.'

'Why Frazer?' she asked quietly. 'Did he suffer?'

'I think not.' Dallas didn't intend to go into details. 'I killed the man who did it, Meggie. I couldn't stop myself.'

'Good.' She reached out and found one of his hands. 'Even that sits hard with you, doesn't it, Father?'

'Surprisingly not.' Dallas shook his head. 'He deserved to die. That Boer bastard committed murder. His action was cold and calculating, nothing to do with the heat of battle – that would have been different.'

'How? War is war. Dead is dead.'

'I know but, believe me, there is a difference.'

'If you say so.'

'Strange thing is, I knew the man.'

'Does that matter? Who cares?' Meggie seemed to be asking herself the questions, a dreamy quality creeping into her voice. She was being forced to think about Frazer's death and the shock had just begun to penetrate. Her father's words sounded as if he were speaking under water. She had to face the loss of a brother; he, that of a son. One hurt as much as the other but both knew it was Lorna who had lost the most.

When Dallas went to bed, Lorna, who had not bothered to undress, turned away from his touch. They had always found solace in each other, no matter what the situation. Now both were facing a pain that was almost insurmountable. 'I understand, my darling,' Dallas whispered in the dark. 'I do. It hurts me too. Please come here.'

She rolled into him, letting his arms enfold her, and the tears came; hot, unchecked, in great heaving sobs. 'Why Frazer? Why him?'

'Could you choose, really?' he asked.

'No,' Lorna admitted, bringing herself under control. 'Forgive me, Dallas. It's just that . . .'

'I know, my darling. You don't have to say it. I'm the same with Meggie.'

And there it was, out in the open. Favourites . . .

'I must apologise to Meggie in the morning. She'll be terribly hurt.'

'She understands.'

'Oh, Dallas. How self-obsessed I am! Meggie is far too young to face this on her own.'

'Our baby is more mature than you give her credit for. Meggie is resilient. She'll be there when you need her. I only wish I could stay longer.'

They lay in the darkness, holding hands, speaking of their youngest son with fondness. Some memories brought smiles, others tears. Dallas was relieved when Lorna started to talk of things to do with the farm, of her work at the hospital, as well as that of Meggie and Tanith. She told him more about the letter. It appeared that Will had ruffled feathers left, right and centre in an effort to secure his choice of mount for Cameron. He'd won the confrontation.

General the Right Honourable Sir Redvers Buller, overall commander of British and colonial troops in South Africa, had arrived in Natal to take charge of the Ladysmith offensive. Apparently he remembered Will and Dallas from Hlobane and

Kambula Hill during the Zulu War. He still spoke of the tenacity they'd shown when sent to reconnoitre enemy positions the night before his troops attacked. Buller recalled that both men brought with them a deep love of Zululand and a great respect for the Zulus. It was knowledge he had put to good use.

On discovering that Cameron was Dallas's son he hoped to do the same again and grudgingly went along with Will's belligerent demands. Perhaps, some said, he'd met a man who could match him in the stubbornness stakes. In any event, Will's mule-like personality – not to mention appearance – both amused and impressed him. The two men were of a similar age.

Despite their crushing personal grief, Lorna and Dallas found themselves smiling at a mental image of Will squaring up to the pugnacious Buller.

Three days after Dallas arrived home they held an intimate memorial gathering for Frazer. Torben and Gerda had responded quickly to Lorna's telegram but no word came back from Cameron, Ellie or Virginia. Family and friends – women in the main – rallied round. With no coffin, no physical evidence, it was difficult to find the right words of farewell. Unexpected and unplanned, Zulu servants and other farm employees gathered close by, women ululating in a haunting display of grief while the men stood silent as a mark of respect. Lorna, standing ramrod straight, showed no sign of the terrible grief she felt inside. She had dug deeply into her past and called on the 'stiff upper lip' of the British nobility to sustain her through those awful first few days.

Glowingly pregnant, Gerda's robust good health appeared almost obscene and, after expressing token condolence, seemed to be all she could talk about. Gerda had hardly known Frazer, but Dallas thought this shouldn't have stopped her from respecting how others in the family felt.

Torben blamed everyone and everything for his brother's death yet was careful not to generalise about Afrikaans-speaking people. Lorna deliberately ignored his rantings while Dallas just wished he'd shut up. As Fairy Fairfax would have said, 'blaming others doesn't help'.

A cairn of limewashed rocks had been erected next to Katie's grave. Standing beside it after the ceremony, an arm around his wife, Dallas said quietly, 'We'll bring him home, my darling. That I promise you.'

She laid a hand on his comforting arm. 'That would be nice.' Her voice had the same dreamy quality Dallas had heard in Meggie's the day he arrived back. She was in a private world, one of her own making, and he decided it was best not to intrude.

Returning to the house, reality hit hard. Soon he would have to leave, even though Lorna still needed him. Once again, Meggie showed wisdom beyond her years. 'Don't worry, Father. I'll make sure she's all right.'

Dallas sighed. 'I know. The thing is, my dearest girl, you shouldn't have to.'

182

'She is my mother, Daddy.' Meggie deliberately used an affection-filled version of the parental endearment she knew he hated.

Realising what his daughter was doing, Dallas smiled at her. 'You always could get around me, young lady. Never stop.'

They hugged and she clung to him, his child, a woman so young yet so certain of her role in the family – Meggie of the dancing black eyes and free spirit. Dreading his daughter's uncaptured soul would buckle under the weight of such responsibility, he held her close. 'Don't ever let this madness get you down. I'm there if you need me. I'll desert if I have to.'

She drew back, knuckling tears from her cheeks. 'Thank you.'

It was all either of them needed to say. Dallas understood how it must be for Lorna. Her special child – her soulmate – had been snatched away. She loved the others, all of them, loved them fiercely and honestly, but there was not the same invisible bond that had existed between her and Frazer.

Ellie did arrive, after dark that same evening. She looked exhausted, half sliding, half falling from the saddle of a borrowed army horse. 'Sorry I'm a bit late. Couldn't get away until yesterday. Spent last night in Durban. Lindsay had to stay. Sends condolences, of course. Hello, Torben, Gerda. I trust all is well with the pregnancy? Who else is here?' She was babbling and knew it. The next second – safe in her father's arms – she broke down, sobbing. 'God, this bloody war. Where will it all end?'

They stood like that for several minutes, then Dallas said, 'Food and bed for you, my girl. Your mother and Meggie are already asleep. Anything else can wait until the morning.'

She gave him an affectionate squeeze. 'You'll hear no argument from me. Right now it's just good to be home.' Ellie and Frazer had always been close. Medicine was in its own way an art, so she completely understood and respected her brother's passion for his. He had a talent that few possessed, an understanding of form. In Ellie it was human; in Frazer, animal. As far as she was concerned, there was little difference.

The next day, having had her first good night's sleep in weeks, Ellie rose to find the house empty but breakfast laid and waiting. No sooner had she finished the already prepared pawpaw – bittersweet from the fresh lemon juice squeezed over it – than Mister David appeared from the kitchen with a bowl of hot cereal. He fussed around her, explaining that Lorna, Dallas and Meggie were in Empangeni while Torben and his wife had had to leave early for Durban. After asking about Lindsay and telling her where to find Frazer's cairn, Mister David respectfully withdrew. Welcoming the peace, Ellie found she couldn't face her favourite mealie meal porridge and took herself outside to the mound of white rocks. She sat on the neatly swept grass, curled up both legs, and rested her head against the cold black marble of her sister's headstone. Ellie wanted to think, to lose herself in memories. She was soon speaking to her siblings.

'So young. Both of you were so very young.' Ellie felt calm, as if the unseen hand of God rested on her shoulder. 'Soon you'll be together, if you aren't already. Stay close, Katie. Be ready to help your brother. Wherever you are, whatever wonderful place, he needs you now.'

She patted the cairn. 'We'll bring you back, dear friend. One day you too will rest here, in the shade of this tree. Remember the first one we planted? You were only five and decided to climb it.' Ellie gave a soft laugh. 'Broke it off, right at the base, you did. Mother was furious. The roots of that tree had been specially soaked in a mixture made from pulped *kaempferia*, mealie meal and corn seed. You were too young to know that but Mother and Father wanted it to grow quickly. Mister David said that his *muthi* would help by warding off the effects of drought and heat. Because of you, we had to go through the process all over again. It worked, though. Look how big this tree is now.' Ellie pointed upwards into the leafy branches of the flowering cassia, covered with spikes of brilliant yellow buttercup-shaped flowers. 'In winter it will lose most of its leaves so that the sun can reach you. It's such an obliging tree.' She smiled, wondering if Mister David would use some simile to give it more meaning.

Ellie tilted back her head, testing a sudden breeze for the scent of summer blossoms. 'I have to leave tomorrow. Others need my help. Lindsay especially. He's a good man. I think I'm going to marry him.' The silence which greeted her statement was a friendly one and she smiled. 'Yes, I knew you'd approve. He's a very special person. Did either of you know I was sleeping with him? Do you think the good Lord would approve? It feels natural enough though sometimes I think I'm committing a sin. It says in the Bible to wait for the sanctity of marriage. Why? What difference can a ceremony and a piece of paper make? Other animals don't need them, why us?' She laughed, a happy sound, yet one that confirmed her confusion. 'Bet you never thought your big sister, the calm and collected doctor, would be at a loss over anything so simple.'

The feathery leaves moved overhead. 'That you, Frazer?' She looked up. 'Bet it is. Can't wait for the family to bring you home, eh?' Ellie had been speaking directly to Frazer, but also for the benefit of Katie. Her clinical mind wondered if she was being just a little too calm. Her emotional one responded – *what the hell!* Ellie knew that they could both hear her and, quite simply, it felt right.

Time slipped into the afternoon until her thoughts were interrupted by the sound of somebody arriving. Reluctantly returning to the house Ellie was delighted to see Cameron's fiancée standing on the verandah.

'Ginnie. You made it. What a wonderful surprise. Is Cam with you?'

'No. No he's not.' The girl burst into tears.

'What is it? Tell me. Whatever is wrong? Not Cameron. Please God, tell me it's not Cameron.'

'It's Kevin. I wanted to be here for Frazer but my brother . . .' She sobbed, tears streaking a dust-encrusted face.

'Oh no, Ginnie. Not him too.'

Virginia shook her head. 'Wounded, though he may as well be dead – shrapnel – both kneecaps. His legs are useless.' She took a shuddering breath. 'I brought him back to Empangeni because it's close to home. He's at the hospital. I haven't been to the house yet. I just wanted to . . .'

'To talk.' Ellie understood Virginia's emotional state and gently led her towards two well-worn leather chairs on the verandah.

'Who's his doctor?'

'Parry. He's already seen him.'

Ellie nodded. 'That's good. He knows Kevin.'

'Yes, and the man he once was. Oh, Ellie, what can any doctor do?'

The professional in Ellie said she mustn't allow this girl to wallow in pity. Virginia had to remain positive, if for no other reason than to help her brother. What Kevin would do was certainly a problem. Active and aggressive, he would not take kindly to the enforced lack of mobility. Kevin loved his family's farm. He was its future. He had walked every square inch of it, working, checking, observing it all – a young prince proud of everything within his father's realm, planning for the day he would be king. 'Others will return just as badly injured, if not worse.' She paused. 'Some not at all. You are fortunate.'

'I know.' Virginia rubbed two fingers over her eyes. 'I know it's selfish, Ellie, but all I can think of is Kevin. Do you think . . . you know . . . will he walk again?'

'It's perfectly possible.'

'You don't believe that for a moment.'

'I do, actually. I've seen it happen. We'll just have to wait and see what Roger has to say. Your brother mustn't give up. That's the worst thing he could do.'

Virginia rose tiredly. 'I must go. Thank you, Ellie. Give my condolences to your parents. I'll see them . . . phew! What is that smell?'

Suza winked but didn't move. Both women burst out laughing.

After Virginia had gone, Ellie sat thinking. Kevin might – just might – come right. Then again, if the man had serious damage to both kneecaps, it wasn't very likely. Life in a chair would be all he could expect. Kevin was older than his sister, though still only thirty-one. He had a young wife and baby. He'd want more from life than that. And where was Cameron? Did he know what had happened to Frazer and now Kevin?

Torben could easily have stayed but had been anxious to finalise his first foray into the arms business – to replace a naval 7-pounder which the Boers had made off with after ambushing an armoured reconnaissance train near Chieveley, south of Colenso. It was the third artillery piece the British had lost. They were desperate and their money was good. Concluding the deal was a far more attractive proposition than holding his stepmother's hand.

Having allowed Ellie to sleep in that morning, Lorna was eager to catch up on her daughter's news. Despite this, their conversation seemed almost strained and focused on the last couple of days rather than recent weeks. Lorna took the news of Kevin with no outward display of emotion and changed the subject to something quite unexpected: Virginia and Cameron's wedding plans. 'This war has shown both of them how unpredictable life can be.'

'So they're going to tie the knot sooner rather than later.' Ellie looked surprised. 'Ginnie didn't say anything about it when she was here, but I suppose there were more immediate things on her mind.'

Lorna went on without commenting. 'They're talking about a small private ceremony in Maritzburg. Later, if they want to, we'll do something here. A full family occasion. That's what your father and I did.' She hadn't once queried the fact there had been no word from Cameron or that he had not come home for the funeral.

Lorna's look and distant voice made it obvious her mind was meandering somewhere in the past rather than facing up to the present. Ellie decided now was not a good time to say anything about her own plans.

Outside on the lawn, Dallas and Meggie were having an almost whispered conversation. 'Your mother worries me. She's holding her emotions in check as if nothing has happened. There's no knowing how long she might stay like this. I hate having to leave again but there really is no choice. Are you sure you can cope? Will you be all right, Meggie?'

'I'll be fine, Father, and so will Mother. I spoke to Roger this morning. He's aware of the situation and has promised to keep an eye on her. We'll both be working at the hospital so it won't be difficult. Being busy and having people to take care of will be the best thing for her.'

Dallas agreed and together they walked arm in arm towards the house. Deep in his heart he knew that one more tragedy could tip his wife over the edge.

The following morning Dallas and Ellie left together, riding south towards the Thukela crossing and Durban. Lorna stood on the verandah to see them off, a beautiful though suddenly frail woman, hair wound up yet loose enough for strands to stray and soften her overall appearance. Head held proud and high, she could not control the quivering of her lips. Meggie stood with an arm around her mother's waist – a comforting, almost unnoticed presence.

Mister David had offered Dallas his own words of assurance. 'She is as my sister. Know that I will watch over her.'

'Thank you, David.'

'When the mourning period is over, we will sing for *nkosaan* Frazer.'

'That would be good.'

'It is possible that a wizard was responsible for Master Frazer's death. If you wish, I can summon a *sangoma*. Such a man will find the evil one.'

'No,' Dallas said hastily. Looking for a so-called wizard would not help. In the first place, he seriously doubted that anyone on the farm would mean his son harm. In the second, the smelling-out of wizards was done covertly, so the authorities didn't find out. Dallas knew it was still a part of Zulu tradition and was well aware of the severe penalties incurred by anyone caught performing such acts or even requesting them. The perpetrators were usually put to death. 'Thank you, David. Frazer's death was an act of our own God, nothing for which your people should feel responsible.'

Mister David looked so relieved it was obvious he held the same belief. 'Then at least I shall refrain from lying with my wife for two months.'

Dallas nodded solemnly. During a Zulu period of mourning – the duration of which depended on who within a family had died – no activity could be performed unless considered absolutely necessary. Immediate relatives did no work in the fields. No singing or dancing was permitted and no finery worn – only grass ornaments. Married men's hair was allowed to grow unshaven around the *isiCoco*, or headband. Women did not put ochre on their hair and no sexual intercourse took place. Mister David was according Frazer the status of family. It wouldn't bring him back but the honour somehow helped.

As he sat on his horse, trying to delay their moment of departure, Dallas remembered the day he first met Mister David. It was outside Cato's Store in Durban. Both his experienced partners – Will Green and Logan Burton – had warned against taking on a mission-educated 'smart Kaffir'. The fact that he was out of work and seeking employment along with all the others down on their luck was, to them, suspicious in the extreme. What had he done? The answer – provided by way of a reference from the respected hunter David Leslie – was nothing. Mister David's situation had arisen only because his previous employer had fallen ill. Dallas took him on as a wagon driver and endured months of doubtful comments before the others came to accept his true value.

However, the man had quickly proved his worth. He was totally honest, an invaluable mentor and, as demonstrated time and time again over the years, a true friend. He'd stood shoulder to shoulder beside Dallas during the elephant hunt that cost Logan his life. Instead of giving way to blind, blood-pumping panic, Mister David, with unhurried and precise movements, calmly reloaded Dallas's two double rifles, his safety dependent on an inexperienced young man in whom he had placed his trust. They had been on opposing sides during the 1879 Zulu War yet no personal animosity existed and once it was over, they found each other again. It was Mister David who kindled Dallas's fascination with Zululand and its people, taught him to speak the language like a Zulu and encouraged him to think like one. The end result – over and above Dallas's profound respect for most things Zulu – was an enduring friendship which had lasted nigh on three decades.

The words '*Hamba kahle*' cut through Dallas's thoughts. '*Sala kahle*' – stay well – he replied, turning his horse's head south towards Durban.

Dallas had never seen so many ships riding at anchor off the port. Ellie pointed out HMS *Powerful* and HMS *Terrible*. She laughed. 'Their names are hardly appropriate anymore.' Her father's puzzled look prompted an explanation. 'They've had their teeth pulled. Both have been stripped of guns and men to help with the defence of Ladysmith.'

Dallas nodded. He knew that Sir George White needed better artillery to counter the Boers' Long Tom, a monstrous gun which could lob ninety-four pounds of shrapnel-filled shell six miles or more. He'd had no idea even a partial solution had been found.

'Those other ships,' Ellie went on, 'they're transport vessels bringing in troops and supplies. Some have been converted to floating hospitals and take the seriously wounded back to Britain. They wanted to use others for holding prisoners of war but that idea has been scrapped. Well, for now at least.'

That night they stayed at the Royal Hotel and through talking to others learned that the Boers' leader in Natal, Piet Joubert, had been badly hurt when his horse was shot from under him. His second in command, Louis Botha, was now in charge and had pulled back to the Thukela River at Colenso. Ladysmith remained under siege. In the west, Lord Methuen had started his push north for Kimberley, winning costly confrontations against General 'Koos' de la Rey at Belmont, Graspan and Modder River. Although wounded himself, Methuen and his troops were less than twenty miles from Kimberley and able to communicate with the besieged garrison by shining a searchlight into the night sky.

Nobody had heard anything of the Fairfax Scouts.

ELEVEN

It was pleasant to be away from the coast. Traffic on the road inland from Durban was not nearly as congested as they had been led to believe. Troops and supplies arriving daily in Durban were being transported inland by rail, the carriages returning with those whose wounds were sufficiently serious to warrant a sea journey back to England. The ships were always full.

Estcourt was a muddy bustle of activity with men, horses and overloaded wagons on the move everywhere. Ellie threaded her way through the seemingly uncoordinated chaos, leading Dallas to the field hospital which had been home to her and Lindsay for over a month.

All seemed quiet in the tent that served as both operating theatre and, adjacent to it, their sleeping quarters. Lindsay was lying down, fully clothed, dozing. Dallas noticed that he and Ellie obviously shared the same accommodation, if on separate camp stretchers. He said nothing.

The medical facilities were spotless – gleaming surgical instruments laid out and ready beside two sheet-covered operating tables, the wooden duckboard floors recently scrubbed, a slight whiff of chloroform lingering in the air.

'Don't wake him,' Dallas said, but at the sound of voices Lindsay was quickly on his feet, perhaps too quickly, as he had to sit down again until his blood pressure knew what was going on. That aside there was no mistaking the look of love on his face as he reached out for Ellie's hands and allowed her to help him up.

'Good to have you back, little one.' He folded Ellie into an embrace, resting a cheek on her close-cropped blonde hair and breathing in its familiar scent. They stood like that for a few seconds before Lindsay seemed to realise that Dallas was there too. 'Sorry, sir.' He held out a hand. 'It's good to see you though I wish the circumstances were different. Please accept my heartfelt condolences – to you and your family. I know how much Frazer meant to all of you.'

'Thank you, Lindsay. These times are far from easy for any of us.'

'Will you be staying the night? I'm sure we can arrange a bed.'

'That's kind of you but being so close to Frere I'll press on. Cameron and Will should both be there, though there was no reply to Lorna's telegram telling them about the funeral. It could be neither of them yet know about Frazer.'

'The Light Horse have been scouting down as far as Lion's River. Perhaps Cameron's been away?'

'As long as that's all it is.'

'I'm sure it will be, Father.' Ellie sounded more confident than she felt.

Following the suspected sighting of a small Boer *komando* unit near Nottingham Road, Cameron had been part of an uneventful patrol through the Drakensberg foothills between Dargle and Lion's River. He knew that Virginia was driving an ambulance wagon at the Mooi River field hospital and had intended to pay her a surprise visit on the way back to Frere. She was not there, having left some days before to take her wounded brother, Kevin, back to Empangeni.

The telegram from Lorna was pinned to a noticeboard in the officers' mess. Cameron held the small, distinctly coloured envelope, so often the harbinger of tragic news, fearing yet needing to know its contents. Hesitantly he ripped it open and read: 'FRAZER KILLED. FUNERAL AT HOME DECEMBER 5TH. OTHERS NOTIFIED. TELL WILL.' The emotionless message was simply signed, 'MOTHER'. Cameron stood stunned. He had no idea of the date and grabbed a copy of that day's *Natal Mercury* to check. It was Friday 8 December. He'd missed the service at *Morningside* by three days.

The mess was buzzing with news received by heliograph from Ladysmith that a night raid by the Natal Carbineers and men of the Imperial Light Horse had successfully blown up not one but two Boer guns – including their Long Tom – on Lombard's Kop. Cameron couldn't have cared less. Clutching the telegram and uncertain what to do next, he blundered from the tent, almost colliding with his father and Will.

Dallas had already discovered that Cameron and Will knew nothing of Frazer's death. Having told his old friend where he had been and why, Dallas established that the scouting patrol had just returned and together they set off in search of Cameron.

The man who stood before them had tears streaming down his cheeks and was finding it difficult to talk. He shook the offending piece of paper as if the telegram itself were to blame for the tape message pasted to it. Without speaking Dallas and Cameron gripped each other's shoulders hard and stood, sharing a common bond of sorrow, until words finally came.

'What happened, Father?'

They walked and talked as Dallas told his eldest son and Will everything that had transpired during the last ten days.

'I promised your mother I'd take Frazer home when the war is over. Thinking about it now, I don't know if I could bring myself to disturb him. In spirit he's there already. I hope Lorna will understand.'

'Her telegram is so impersonal. It's as if she's talking about some casual acquaintance rather than family.'

'We are all dealing with this differently,' Dallas said. 'I bear the burden of having been there when it happened and in some ways your mother holds me responsible. You feel guilty for not knowing or being able to attend the funeral. These are things over which we have little control. Only time can make them less painful.'

Will had hardly said a word since learning of Frazer's death. He too had a special empathy with the artistic young man who had loved the African bush and was blessed with a God-given ability to capture its endless drama on paper or canvas. He found himself wondering if the birds' eggs Frazer had so recently collected from him in Swaziland had ever reached Dallas's friend, Fred Selous. Had anybody thought to tell him what had happened?

'Sorry to hear the news about Kevin.' Dallas was trying to change the subject. 'Ginnie called by the house but Ellie was the only one to see her. Your mother says that you two may get married in Maritzburg? Any idea when?'

Will had picketed Dallas's horse near the handlers' quarters. He left father and son deep in conversation, soon returning with a mess tin of steaming curry, three spoons, bread and a full bottle of Cape brandy. They sat under the stars, shared the food and talked, passing the bottle from hand to hand, toasting absent friends with the fiery liquid until it too was gone.

Cameron told Dallas and Will about the scouting trip from which he had just returned. 'Must be my Scottish blood. There'sh a place called Fort Nottingham. Between there and Dargle is some of the mosht magnificent country imagin . . . imaginable. You could be back in Scotland, Father. There's deer to be stalked, except they're eland and reedbuck; the rivers are an angler's paradise, not salmon but trout aplenty. Even managed to guddle a few the way you taught me.'

Will's snoring emphasised his interest in Cameron's observations. Dallas leaned over and held his nose, starving him of air until he turned to a more comfortable sleeping position and the intrusive noise ceased.

'There's a hill – looks like Arthur's Seat in Edinburgh. They call it the Inhluzan. Below it is a farm called *Wakefield*. It's for sale. I want Ginnie to see it.'

'Meaning?'

'Meaning, if she approves, I'd like to buy it.'

'And what about *Morningside*? It's not exactly next door. Anyway, how do you know this place is on the market?'

'She told me. That's how.'

'She?'

'Mishes Hammond. My horsh threw a shoe. We had no nails with us, just spare shoes. She fixed it.'

'Cameron, hold on. You're losing me.'

'Caroline breeds horses. Racehorses. That's what she does.'

'Caroline Hammond? The name is familiar. Tell me more.'

'She's about the same age as Mother. Her husband was killed six months ago. An accident. That's why the place is for sale. Loves her horses but the farm runs cattle as well. Even has a small dairy. They make their own butter and cheese. There are acres of mealies and a black wattle plantation. It'sh too much for one person to manage.'

'And how do you propose to make this purchase?'

Cameron hesitated. 'I thought you and Mother might help. Make it a family thing. Ginnie and I could run *Wakefield*. Duncan and . . . well, Duncan can help you at *Morningside*.'

'Shon,' – Dallas was also feeling the alcohol's effects – 'might I suggest that you seem to have positioned your proprietorial cart well and truly in front of Mishes Hammond's horses.' He belched, excused himself and went on: 'Let's see now. How many morgen are we talking about – acres, if you prefer?'

'Dunno.'

'What stock goes with the farm?'

'Dunno.'

'Are there outstanding mortgages?'

'Haven't a clue.'

'Must see the farm accounts. Last three years at least.'

'Why three?'

Dallas ignored the question. 'What's her labour force?'

'Dunno.'

'Fences?'

'Think so.'

'Have you seen the house, compound, any other buildings?'

'Of course.' At last Cameron had heard a question he could answer – at least in part. 'The house is wattle and daub. Thatched with a polished cow manure verandah. And there's water. Plenty of water. You forgot to ask about water. Frazer would love it.'

The silence that followed said it all. Frazer would never see *Wakefield*. Perhaps Dallas wouldn't either.

The next morning, early, head throbbing and mouth dry, the last thing Dallas felt like doing was setting off towards Lindley, a good hundred and fifty miles distant. His route would take him well to the west of Ladysmith, climbing to cross the Drakensberg through Van Reenen's Pass, leaving Natal and moving into enemy territory. At first he could travel cross-country, keeping the towering eleven-thousand-foot peak of Mont aux Sources out to his left. It was there that the Thukela, so much a part of his early life in South Africa, began its twisting two-hundred-mile journey to the distant Indian Ocean. Once into the Orange Free State, the going would get easier, though there would be the ever-present risk of running into an enemy *komando*. Dallas wore no uniform, but his military mount and Lee Metford carbine would not stand close scrutiny. His knowledge of Afrikaans was, to say the least, limited.

Will, who seemed none the worse for wear, had carefully checked and fed Dallas's horse, refilled both waterbags and deposited a fistful of biltong in his saddlebag. He neglected to say what it had been made from. Cameron, probably feeling no better than his father, promised to find out more about *Wakefield*.

The morning was already hot, clouds building

over the Berg promising rain later in the day. As the pain behind his eyes eased Dallas began to take in his surroundings. They were breathtakingly beautiful: once-volcanic basalt towering above time-weathered sandstone shaped by the elements over millions of years, mighty waterfalls – high rather than wide – calming to crystal-clear fossil-laden streams as their plunging descent finally eased. Scrub covered the south-facing slopes, becoming dense and heavily wooded in each kloof and krans. Leopard country, Dallas found himself thinking, as he heard the warning bark of baboons. High above, a tailless eagle soared with effortless grace, never once beating its wings.

All day Dallas climbed, instinctively becoming more alert, watching for unexplained movement, any signs of hidden danger, as his choice of ways over the pass became more and more limited. Dassies made each and every rock slide come alive with now-you-see-them, now-you-don't curiosity. Sure-footed klipspringer stood on tiptoe to watch his passing. Overhead, crowned plovers – *mbagaqwa*, the Zulus called them – twisted and turned, screeching their annoyance at his presence. Long-legged secretary birds ignored him completely, striding the veld in their ceaseless search for snakes or any other live prey.

The morning's promise of rain had not materialised and except for a slightly queasy stomach, Dallas was feeling considerably better. He had made good time and, with luck, would be well into the Free State before dark. Cresting the final rise he dismounted to find a spot where observation of the way ahead would not leave him silhouetted against the skyline. He hobbled his horse and cautiously moved forwards, looking for a suitable vantage point.

Sometimes, though not always, the lethargic and deadly puff adder issues a warning that intrusion will not be tolerated. Dallas hadn't noticed the coiled and well-camouflaged snake. His foot was hovering above it when a screeching hiss caused him to freeze. He had heard the sound before – once – and it was not a noise to be forgotten. A sidestep would expose his inner thighs and groin but Dallas managed to turn the movement into more of a twisting leap. The smashing open jaw connected with his left boot, venom-filled fangs failing to find purchase. Dallas rolled away in one direction, his attacker slithering off in the other.

It had been close – too close – bringing back a vivid memory of Katie, killed eight years earlier, not by a puff adder but by the lightning-fast strike of an eight-foot black mamba, a snake so quick many believed it could attack any bullet aimed at it. Certainly Dallas had seen one moving over the top of his sugar cane at a speed faster than a horse could gallop. He shook his head to clear the memory. It hurt. *Bloody brandy.*

Dallas decided to use all the hours of daylight before stopping for the night. The country was opening out, making it easier to avoid signs of habitation or others on the road. Turning due east he kept to the south of Harrismith, hoping to reach a shallow cave he had used before. Stick-figure hunting scenes depicted on its walls told him he was far from the first to do so. It was near Aberfeldy on the Wilge River, an area that was quite beautiful but nothing like the part of Scotland after which some homesick settler had probably named it.

The night had noises of its own. Gone was the continuous alarm call of crested barbets and the banter of arrow-marked babblers. In their place came the peaceful *prrrup* of a Scops owl and the yapping of a freckled nightjar somewhere on the rock-strewn slope. Stars – the backbone of the sky – became increasingly evident as he stared up into the heavens. With no moon the nightly display was at its finest, undistorted by humidity or the misty blending of land and sea temperatures. Best of all, it belonged to nobody. Katie and Frazer were out there, of that Dallas had no doubt.

The farm looked uninhabited. Gone was the Afrikander herd Wallace Reese had so painstakingly built up over the last twenty years. The gates stood wide open giving goats access to what had once been a well-tended garden. A few chickens scratched out an existence near the house, having probably been left alive to provide eggs for the Africans who were undoubtedly around but nowhere to be seen. Wooden shutters barred every window, the doors were locked and dust lay thick on the verandah. A skin-and-bone bitch of unknown breed, her nipples swollen and splayed, must have had her litter somewhere close by. She watched the stranger with cautious curiosity.

Where was the Reese family: Wallace, Elizabeth and the girls? What had happened? Did Danny's death make them move? Was it the war? By the look of things, nobody had been living here for months.

By now it would be known that a white stranger had arrived at the house. Nothing moved. Even the dog settled down, panting. It was hot.

Dallas checked the water tank. Low but not empty. He opened a once-polished brass tap and ran some murky brown liquid into the horse trough. His mount sniffed it and drank gratefully. Still having one full waterbag, Dallas didn't.

Cautious and unwilling to invite closer scrutiny he left everything as it was and moved on, taking the road towards Lindley and the kopje where Frazer was buried.

TWELVE

S he had given birth well away from the pride: three balls of cuddle-soft fur disguised with dark rosettes and weighing only a pound apiece, their infant eyes open if unable to focus.

Although a first-time mother, the lioness instinctively knew the danger they were in, not only from jackal, hyena and leopard, but also from her own kind. During the last ten days she had moved her family five times, picking up each cub in turn – velvet-soft jaws spread shoulder to shoulder across their backs – carrying them from one hiding place to another. Each move brought her cubs closer to the pride, though it would be four weeks at least before she could risk an intro-duction to their father. All had gone well, until that morning.

The constant strain of feeding herself, suckling her offspring and keeping them hidden made the lioness momentarily careless. So intent was she on moving her second cub that she didn't notice the hyena. An opportunist at the best of times he waited until she was out of sight before letting the faint mewing sound beneath a thorn-laden acacia bush lead him to the likely meal. His jaws were not as gentle as those of the helpless youngster's mother. They crushed the cub's head in a single bone-crunching snap. Keeping a clamp-like grip on the limp body he loped off out of harm's way to dine at his leisure.

On her return, the lioness heard no sound emanating from within the den. Senses suddenly alert, she gently released the cub she was carrying and called softly. The silence seemed deafening. She could smell it now, fresh blood, and the unfamiliar scent of the intruder. Somehow the mother in her knew it was too late. There was no need to check further.

It was just on dusk when she picked up the man smell and from deep in her throat gave a drawn-out rolling growl. Dallas instantly lost interest in finding somewhere to relieve his cramping stomach, courtesy of Will's highly suspect curry at Frere. The sound had come from a dense thicket to his left. It told him two things. The lion was protecting something, either a meal or cubs, and it was seriously contemplating aggression. He caught sight of a twitching tail, waving in agitation. Lioness. If it stopped he could expect a charge from which she would not swerve.

'Shite!' Dallas muttered under his breath. He had no desire to harm the animal. She was only doing what was natural, protecting that which was hers. Very slowly, he lowered his eyes and started backing away. The continued warning ended in a short snarl. He dared not turn his back to her, nor could he move any faster. Given the slightest excuse, she would attack. The clear sound of cubs reached him. Their little chirrups might have been endearing to anyone not where he was at that moment. A rustle. Was she moving forwards? His grip on the military issue carbine tightened as he continued to widen the gap between them.

Dallas was lucky. The lioness, encouraged by his backdown and not wishing to leave her remaining cubs, decided against any follow-through. Sweating – though it had nothing to do with the oppressive heat – Dallas reached his knee-haltered and highly agitated horse, quickly released the restraint and mounted. He heard one last threat from the lioness and, with a sigh of relief, turned away. There was movement out on the open veld, too far off for him to make out but definitely something to avoid. A Boer *komando*, probably.

The lioness also turned her attention to the distant dust. Excellent eyesight told her it was a small herd of springbok. She hadn't eaten in days and although the man smell meant food, their strange taste was not really to her liking. This was much better. Now she just might get lucky.

Cautiously cresting the small kopje, Dallas checked to make sure nobody else had made camp there. Its flat top was deserted, finally giving him the chance to unburden his distinctly rebellious bowel.

Frazer's grave was as he had left it. Dallas added a few more rocks to make sure it stayed that way. Of Hanson Wentzell he found no sign. Africa's scavengers had done a good job. After securing his horse for the night, Dallas dug his pipe and some biltong from a saddlebag and settled down to watch the sunset. The pain had gone.

It was late on the afternoon of Sunday 10 December when Dallas had encountered the lioness near Lindley. Two hundred miles to the south-east, unseasonal sleet-like rain blanketed the advance of Lord Methuen's troops. Led by Major-General Andrew Wauchope they were within three miles of the assumed Boer positions on Magersfontein Kopje, the last-but-one hurdle before Kimberley. An artillery barrage battered the as yet unseen enemy until nightfall, by which time the weather had deteriorated even further.

The Fairfax Scouts had reported significant Boer reinforcements being drawn from the blockade of Mafeking but had failed to discover General de la Rey's plan that Piet Cronje should dig in below – rather than on – the hill itself. There were now over eight thousand Boer burghers at Magersfontein and in six days a conscripted African labour force had miraculously managed to conceal them in twelve miles of newly dug defensive trenches.

When Dallas reached Lord Methuen's camp late on 12 December it was to discover the troops demoralised and in a state of total disarray. More than nine hundred men had been killed or wounded – among them Andrew Wauchope – while trying to take the near-invisible Boer positions. The advance on Kimberley had come to a costly and completely unexpected halt.

News from elsewhere in the Cape was no better. Two days earlier General Gatacre had lost nearly seven hundred men – most taken prisoner – at Stormberg, south of the Free State border. The war was not going well.

Fairfax and his scouts had the task of monitoring enemy troop movements to the north and east of Magersfontein. They were in constant contact with Lord Methuen so Dallas ascertained more or less where he would find them. Concealment wasn't easy in the almost featureless flat country but a sixth sense warned him he had been under observation for some time. Dallas was almost on top of the dry riverbed when a challenge rang out. It was in English. Seconds later Duncan rose to greet him.

That night, although fires were not possible, it was far from cold and a nearly full moon provided more than adequate visibility. Dallas gave Duncan the news from home, saying how badly Lorna had reacted to Frazer's death and how strong Meggie was being. He told him of Cameron not receiving the telegram and that Kevin, Virginia's brother, had been wounded and might not walk again.

Duncan spoke of Methuen's so-called success on the Modder where more than four hundred British soldiers had been killed or wounded before the Boers upped and rode away, leaving trenches thick with spent cartridge cases, their dead drifting in the river.

'It was only later we learned both General de la

Rey and his son, Adriaan, had been wounded. He has since died, but as far as we know his father is still away.'

'Mind if I join you?' Fairfax's gravelly voice cut into their conversation.

'By all means, Fairy. Come sit. Duncan and I are just catching up.'

'Thanks. Did he mention that Methuen's lot should be in Kimberley by now?'

Dallas was surprised, recalling what he had recently seen and heard of the failed attempts to take Magersfontein.

'The man sat on his backside for too bloody long after he crossed the Modder. It gave Cronje all the time in the world to take over and dig in where they are now. Apparently President Steyn came in person to rally his *komandos*. We didn't find out what was going on until it was too late.' Fairfax's frustration was obvious.

They talked for an hour, maybe more, before calling it a night. Dallas lay on his back wondering what the new day would bring. A spotted hyena seemed to find the situation amusing and gave voice to his opinion. Dallas was already asleep.

All day Lindsay kept up the pretence that he had forgotten. Ellie said nothing, which made him wonder if she even realised it was 13 December, her twenty-sixth birthday.

Everybody at the field hospital in Estcourt was aware Buller had been preparing to advance on Colenso. He had already moved his troops from

Frere up to Chieveley, halving the distance to their objective. That day, the distant sound of artillery announced that the long-range naval guns had commenced their barrage of the enemy's positions. It sounded like far-off thunder. And storm that day it did, rain closing in, turning the wagon-rutted ground into slippery, boot-clogging mud.

As it neared six in the evening Lindsay began to wonder if the plan he had so carefully conceived was going to work. Perhaps they couldn't get away, he worried. If they were coming, would the weather make a difference?

Precisely on the hour two dripping wet, turban-clad Indian stretcher-bearers arrived, their upturned trench-coat collars providing scant protection against the driving rain.

'Here we go,' Lindsay called to Ellie, who had been unpacking a crate of medical supplies.

Quickly she joined him as their latest patient was placed on the operating table. A pair of muddy boots stuck out from one end of the blanket which covered everything else on the stretcher.

Gently Ellie peeled back the sodden cloth. Beneath it lay the contents of a Fortnum and Mason food hamper, a bottle of Champagne, four glasses, a birthday cake and two boots connected to nothing.

She stared down in disbelief as three voices behind her blended – none too harmoniously – in an enthusiastic rendition of 'Happy Birthday'.

The mud darkening Cameron and Will's faces was streaked from the rain but both were grinning from ear to ear. 'Didn't think we'd forgotten, did you, little sister?'

Ellie's shriek of delight was spontaneous. She didn't know who to hug first.

'Lindsay is responsible for most of this lot. He's been planning it for weeks. The cake is a contribution from Will. It's his cooking so before you taste it, just remember it's the thought that counts.'

Ellie was bubbling with excitement. 'Thank you, Will. I'm sure it will be delicious.'

'Hope so, doc. I've got more to thank you for than most but it's like this: some of the ingredients aren't quite as they should be.'

Ellie was not sure what he meant so to prevent any embarrassment, changed the subject. 'Wherever did you get the turbans?'

'That was easy,' Lindsay laughed. 'One of the Indian orderlies helped us out.'

'Father left this with me last week.' Cameron produced an envelope. 'It's from everybody at home. Duncan couldn't sign it but he sends his love as well.'

'And here was I thinking you'd all forgotten. I hope the Champagne has been chilled.'

Later, when they were alone, Lindsay gave Ellie his real present: an 1859 first edition of Charles Darwin's controversial work *On the Origin of Species by Means of Natural Selection*.

'My God, do you know what this is?'

'Some old book I found in Maritzburg. The

man's theory may not meet with my approval but I hope you like it.'

'Like it? It's what life is all about. Thank you, my darling.' Ellie put down the pristine volume, reached her arms round Lindsay's neck and pressed her body hard against him. 'I love it,' she said.

Cameron and Will had left before ten pm.

'That cake you made was quite delicious,' Cameron commented as they rode back to Chieveley. The rain had stopped and he was feeling strangely relaxed, even happy, any thought of the coming confrontation far from his mind. 'You must give Ginnie the recipe.'

'That might not be such a good idea.' Will chuckled.

General Sir Redvers Buller was only too aware of the setbacks suffered at Stormberg and Magersfontein. He could not afford another mistake. Louis Botha's *komandos* held the high ground overlooking Colenso from both sides of the river but the Boer positions were easily within range of his 4.7-inch naval guns. They would plaster the enemy with fifty-pound lyddite- and shrapnel-packed percussion shells providing the prelude to a three-pronged attack across the deep and twisting Thukela.

What Buller's field intelligence division failed to find out was that for two weeks the Boers' African labour force had been digging lines of trenches much lower down, carefully concealed in thick scrub immediately opposite the river's few possible crossing points. They had also removed thousands of rocks from the drifts to make them deeper.

Before dawn on 15 December, after a two-day artillery bombardment which did little more than announce his intentions, Buller's advance from Chieveley began. Columns split into three and moved forwards with parade-ground precision. Those on the left quickly became lost, finding themselves surrounded on three sides by a loop of the river with no way out but back. Suddenly that too became impossible as shrapnel shells began bursting above the defenceless troops. Mauser fire and deadly impact-exploding bullets from quick-firing belt-fed Maxim 'pom-poms' tore into them from the Boers' near-invisible trenches only yards away across the Thukela.

Buller could see the chaos unfolding before him. The enemy were not where they should have been and neither were most of his men or artillery.

Twelve 15-pounders – supposedly preparing the way for a frontal attack by the second column – had been hauled too close to the river and detached from their limbers. They too were coming under concentrated fire from the other side. As he watched, the guns fell silent, abandoned by their teams who sought refuge behind a small fold in the ground. It was not yet 0700 hours.

Also south of the Thukela and less than two miles north-east of where Buller stood, the Boer positions on Mount Hlangwane were under attack by colonial volunteers commanded by the Earl of Dundonald. Rough terrain had already made it necessary for him to dismount his men, among them the South African Light Horse. Faced with more defenders than anticipated the advance was going nowhere.

Cameron carried back an urgent request for assistance, only to be told that the whole attack might have to be called off. Two of the twelve deserted 15-pounders had been recovered but with unacceptably heavy losses. Buller himself entered the fray – his first frontline action for fourteen years – and was wounded, though not seriously, by exploding shell fragments. Without artillery cover he could not commit his main second column. The only guns available to him were those now being used to try to extricate troops still pinned down to his left.

Before midday Buller realised he had no chance of taking Colenso and gave the order for a general withdrawal. Ten field guns and their ammunition carts lay abandoned. Nearly a thousand men were wounded or had been taken prisoner, but less than a hundred and fifty actually killed. The outcome could so easily have been a lot worse.

'Black Week', as it quickly became known, resulted in Redvers Buller being replaced as Commander-in-Chief of the British forces in South Africa. The man chosen to take over was Field-Marshal Earl Roberts of Kandahar VC, affectionately known as 'Bobs' or 'The Little Man' by those who had previously served with him in India and North Africa. He was in Ireland at the time of his appointment. Only days before, Buller had the unenviable task of writing to tell him that his only son, Freddie, had been killed in action, lost in a failed attempt to save the guns at Colenso.

Although he had retained responsibility for the campaign in Natal, there was not much for Buller to celebrate at the end of 1899. His losses rivalled those suffered by Britain in the Crimean war some forty years earlier.

Ellie and Lindsay had no way of knowing how bad the situation really was but, since Colenso, they'd seen their commander's confidence crumble to the extent that he seriously suggested that Sir George White, in the besieged Ladysmith garrison, fire off all his ordnance and surrender. Fortunately Lord Roberts had not agreed.

Morale in Estcourt desperately needed a boost. It came with the news that Winston Churchill had escaped Boer detention in Pretoria, miraculously making his way to Lourenço Marques in Portuguese East Africa. His arrival in Durban on the steam-ship *Induna* saw him portrayed by the press as a popular hero.

Ellie and Lindsay attended a Christmas Eve dinner in Estcourt, hosted by Sir Redvers Buller, where it was announced that Winston, in addition to his role as reporter for the *Morning Post*, had been commissioned a lieutenant in the South African Light Horse. Later that evening, with only their host and a few of his senior officers present, they heard how close Winston had come to being shot by the Boers for his civilian role in saving the locomotive and many lives during the armoured train incident, after which he and seventy others had been captured. As port and cigars mellowed the hour, Winston seemed happy to tell the full story. His audience listened in rapt silence as the ceiling of pungent, eye-watering smoke sank lower and lower.

The saga started with a sixty-mile march to the Boer railhead at Elandslaagte. From there they had been taken by train to Pretoria and held in officers' quarters at the State Model School. Winston's solo escape some three weeks later had been blessed by good fortune.

After scaling a wall and dropping into an adjoining garden, he managed to avoid detection by the Zarps – South African Republic police guards – and used the night-sky constellation of Orion to guide him south in search of the railway line to Portuguese East Africa, almost three hundred miles distant. Jumping a train proved easy though he left it before dawn and hid in the veld all the following day. The next night brought no rail traffic and walking the track in bright moonlight was fraught with danger, all halts and bridges being under guard.

Winston could not say what prompted him to seek assistance in a small mining community. As luck would have it the house he chose was that of the colliery manager, a naturalised burgher but originally English. His name was John Howard. He and two Scottish miners kept Winston hidden in the mine for three days, white rats his only companions, until they managed to secrete him in a railway wagon carrying bales of wool to Lourenço Marques. It was there that Winston read fictitious Boer newspaper reports of his capture and learned that a reward of twenty-five pounds had been posted for bringing him in, dead or alive.

Walking back to their quarters, Ellie took Lindsay's arm. 'What an enjoyable evening. He certainly likes the limelight, does our Winston.'

Lindsay nodded. 'And his cigars. I don't deny he's an entertaining raconteur but why mention names? As a journalist he should have known better. The people who helped him could be in serious trouble if word of their actions reached the wrong ears.' They fell silent, enjoying the clean, cool air. 'And another thing,' Lindsay suddenly went on.

'What's that?'

'Happy Christmas, my love. Let's hope this war is over by the next one.'

She smiled and looked up at him, squeezing his arm closer. 'Amen to that. And a happy Christmas to you, my darling. Do you think a private celebration might be in order?'

'Please God,' Lindsay said, stooping to kiss her. 'Let there be no patients.'

They burst out laughing, their leisurely pace forgotten.

THIRTEEN

The lioness was a good mother but her cubs were almost six weeks old and their natural curiosity made it impossible for her to leave them unattended for any length of time. Twice she had come back from her ceaseless search for food only to find them romping about in plain sight outside their latest hiding place. The time had come for her to do what she knew she must – seek their safety within the pride itself. Others as well as herself would suckle and babysit the cubs. She would regain strength, teach them to hunt and eat meat. Their father, the dominant dark-maned male, would take care of everything else. If he accepted his offspring.

Slowly and with extreme caution, testing his mood every few steps, the lioness brought the first of her two remaining cubs – the female – and placed it in front of him. The lion looked down, almost surprised. Last year's litter from another female romped up to see what this small, squeaky thing could be. The mother turned and snarled at them. They skittered away. He sniffed, licked the tiny head, sniffed again and then, with a paw large enough to crush the life from such a small creature, gently rolled her over. The lioness relaxed. Her cub had been accepted as his own. If rejected, the youngster would have been dead by now. Leaving her in his care, she ambled off to bring back his son.

They would grow into adults not averse to feeding on the flesh of man, a learned behaviour passed on within the family.

Since Lord Methuen's costly advance on Kimberley came to a grinding halt at Magersfontein, the Fairfax Scouts had been busy reporting on the movement of Boer *komandos* in the Orange Free State. They were now operating almost a hundred miles north of its capital, Bloemfontein, near the Zand River.

On 10 January Field-Marshal Lord Roberts and his Chief-of-Staff, Lord Kitchener, had arrived in Cape Town. Within forty-eight hours an African runner found Fairfax and his men. Stitched into the messenger's nondescript greatcoat were despatches from Lord Methuen outlining changes in command and saying the scouts should stay where they were pending receipt of further orders. The runner was also carrying a satchel of mail for the men.

Dallas had three letters – from Lorna, Meggie and Will – all written around the middle of December. Will spoke only of Cameron. The undated note, badly written but well meant, told of his godson's bravery in securing the release of a dozen British regulars captured by the Boers. *Buller thinks highly of the lad,* Will wrote. *I suspect he could be up for a medal. Gongs aside, fact is Cam brought back twelve of our boys before they could be sent by train to Pretoria. He's a bloody hero.*

No real details of Cameron's actions were included so Dallas could only imagine his son's efforts behind enemy lines, presumably in the company of many others. From what little Will was able to say, it certainly sounded as if Cameron had been the man who made it happen. There was no way of telling if Will's words had been penned before or after Buller's reverses at Colenso. Dallas could only assume that he would have heard by now had Cam or Will been wounded, captured or – heaven forbid – killed.

Thankfully the lad keeps well and shows no symptoms of the ills which plague this place. I ain't sayin he's perfect, mind. The cards is another matter. There's not many will sit down with him.

Dallas smiled at that. Cameron's wild streak included gambling, and when he did it he played hard, losses and wins taken in his stride – something those less committed found hard to emulate. Will's epistle ended with one complaint. He was finding it impossible to focus even a portion of his young charge's mind on matters religious. Dallas folded the note with another smile. On that score, Will could try until hell froze.

Meggie's letter was full of snippets about daily life at *Morningside*, her job at the hospital and Lorna's apparent acceptance of Frazer's death.

Schooling was on hold, but she had been making do by herself using books borrowed from a variety of sources. Things on the farm seemed to be going well although Tobacco's son had left and Henry was acting *induna*, ably assisted by his younger brother, Sabani. The cattle were thriving in a good rainy season, weaned calves sold and Lorna had bought a new bull. Dallas winced at the price. Even the acreage under sugar was expected to yield its highest ever tonnage. Quite surprisingly, Meggie's work at the hospital was proving so fulfilling that she talked of following in Ellie's footsteps, not as a doctor but by becoming a nurse. 'Well,' Dallas reflected. 'My little girl, another Florence Nightingale. She's grown up so fast.'

Mother worries me sometimes. The statement had Dallas read and reread the same paragraph. *There are days when I simply can't reach her yet others where everything seems perfectly normal. She spends a lot of time at Frazer's cairn, just speaking to him. I pray to God that you can bring him home for I hate to think what it would do to Mother if that were not possible.*

Lorna's letter showed him exactly what Meggie meant: *Don't laugh, dearest; I was talking to Frazer the other day and he said that the good Lord has no plans for the rest of you. I believe him. You will all return safe and sound. Frazer has promised me that.* Only a couple of paragraphs later: *I feel such despair sometimes. Will I ever see you again, my darling? What has happened to our loving family? Katie's gone. Now Frazer. Did we have these children so they could be snatched from us? There are times when I question*

God's intent. What are we supposed to learn from such grief?

'Indeed,' Dallas muttered. 'A good question, my love.'

When on the subject of volunteer work, Lorna was lucid, funny and caring. She seemed vague about what was happening on the farm, going into great detail instead about moving furniture around in the parlour, sitting-room and their bedroom. In all, Lorna seemed to bounce from subject to subject, saying nothing of importance, even contradicting herself midway through a paragraph. Normally a good correspondent, her usual lucidity had been replaced by a lack of coherence. Thankfully the work she was doing at Empangeni hospital seemed to be taking her mind off other matters to a degree. The last line of Lorna's letter was what bothered Dallas the most: *Do not worry, my darling. I know you are not responsible for what happened. My son's death was beyond your control.*

'Damn it,' Dallas muttered. 'Nobody was responsible.' The war had claimed Frazer and he was just as much Dallas's son as Lorna's.

In a postscript – an afterthought – she added, *Fred has a second son – Harold – born in October. Both the baby and Gladys are fine. He thanks Frazer for the birds' eggs.*

Duncan had received something similar, as well as a letter from Tanith. When he found Dallas his need-to-talk expression said it all.

'I know, son. It's not easy for any of us.'

'Mother sounds as if she's blaming you.'

'That she does.' Dallas rubbed a hand over his hair. 'It's natural enough, I suppose. After all, I was on the spot, so to speak. I don't know if Lorna will ever accept that Frazer's death had nothing to do with my negligence. Who's the other one from?' Dallas changed the subject, handing over his mail so they could share.

Duncan held one back. 'Tat.'

'I see.' Dallas grinned. 'Well, I wouldn't want to pry or anything like that.'

'That's good, because I wouldn't let you.'

'Listen to you! Defensive to offensive in so few words.'

'Sorry.' Duncan hesitated. 'Do you think I'm too young to get married?'

'Thanks to this bloody war, no-one is too young. You're nearly twenty-three. I was the same age when your mother and I began living together as husband and wife.'

'Tanith's only nineteen but her father has given his permission. I spoke to him before we left home.'

'My, but you are a dark horse. When do you intend asking her? She's a fine lassie.'

Duncan beamed his pleasure. 'Fact is, Dad . . . sorry, Father . . . I already did.' He held up the letter as if to emphasise his next words. 'She said yes.'

Dallas grinned as his son did an impromptu little foot-stomping dance. 'Congratulations,' he said, holding out a hand.

Fairfax looked up from reading his own mail to watch Duncan's antics. 'Good news, I take it?' he called.

'She said yes,' Duncan shouted back, waving the letter and wanting the whole world to see his happiness. 'It scares me, though.'

The two older men laughed. 'You don't sound all that frightened,' Dallas pointed out. 'In fact –'

Duncan seemed to spin backwards and fall before they even heard the shot. It was so unexpected that Dallas sat in stunned disbelief for several seconds before scrabbling to kneel beside his son. Blood welled from Duncan's upper arm and Dallas sounded a sigh of relief. 'Flesh wound.'

They heard return fire break out but it was impossible to tell where the single shot had come from. Luckily the bullet had been fairly small, probably a 7mm Mauser. It passed clean through the flesh and muscle of Duncan's upper arm, missing the bone and leaving a neat exit wound. A few inches further over and Duncan would have been very dead indeed.

'Bastards!' Dallas swore under his breath as he cleaned and dressed the wound. 'It could turn septic,' he warned. 'Only time will tell. Keep an eye on it. Your arm won't be much good for a bit.'

Fairfax stood looking down at Duncan, who was still pale from shock. 'Sorry it doesn't warrant a trip home to be with your fiancée.'

The morphine Dallas had given him was having its effect, and Duncan found it hard to stay awake. 'That was the furthest thing from my mind, sir,' he said drowsily, grinning at the first ever reference to his new status.

Fairfax chuckled. 'Bullshit! Get some rest.'

They all realised what a near miss it had been. 'Bit too close for comfort,' Fairy commented as he and Dallas moved out of earshot.

Dallas nodded. 'If he hadn't been leaping around like a loon it might have been a lot worse.'

They lit up – pipe and cigar – sitting in contemplative silence, each with his own thoughts. *Oh, Lorna*, Dallas worried. *Dare I mention this in a letter to you?* Knowing her current state of mind he decided against it, making a mental note to ensure that Duncan did the same.

'How do they leap?' Fairfax asked unexpectedly.

'Huh?'

'Loons. How do they leap?'

'Usual way. Up and down. It's a Scottish expression. Short for lunatic. Haven't you heard it before?'

'No. But I'd say we have plenty of them running this war.'

Dallas laughed. 'Fair enough.'

Silence returned. That was how it was with the two of them. Despite a ten-year gap in their ages, they had developed a firm friendship. Words weren't needed to keep it alive.

For a few days Meggie had been trying to decide what exactly she should say in another letter to her father. Christmas Day at *Morningside* had passed almost unnoticed. Lorna's fluctuating mood and bouts of depression were becoming more apparent by the day. Now Doctor Parry had commented on the situation, suggesting that action was required.

'I don't wish to alarm you, my dear, but I've known your mother for a long time. In my opinion she needs Dallas to be here, and a rest, in that order.'

'Last time we heard, Father was somewhere on the other side of Basutoland.'

'That's as may be. He's also a friend who would never forgive me if I failed in my duty to warn him.'

'Warn him? Warn him of what?' Meggie felt dread settle in the pit of her stomach.

'Your mother's mental state is of considerable concern. You can't be with her all the time, and left alone she could well do something silly.'

Panic welled in the girl's eyes.

Parry went on, 'For that matter, you're under severe strain as well. Is there anyone you could stay with if we can arrange for Dallas to come back and take Lorna away for a few weeks?'

'Yes. The Taylors. Their daughter and I grew up together. I know Tanith's parents almost as well as my own. I'm sure they wouldn't mind.'

'Would you like me to write a note for your father?'

Meggie nodded, her relief evident.

The doctor scribbled – almost illegibly – on the back of a prescription form. It was short and to the point:

My dear Dallas, both as a physician and your friend, it is my opinion that Lorna would benefit greatly from your presence, the more so if it were possible for you to spend a few weeks with her in relaxed surroundings. Her

*malady is more mental than physical and whilst I have
no wish to alarm you, she needs a rest. See what you can
do. Sincerely yours, Roger.*

That afternoon Meggie posted the note in
Empangeni, along with a letter from herself. She
had enclosed both in one of the hospital's official
OHMS envelopes, hoping that it would be given
priority. Having no address other than care of the
Fairfax Scouts, she wondered how long it would
take to reach her father – or if indeed it would.

In a matter of days, Duncan's flesh wound had
turned septic and become cause for serious concern. Infection and disease were an ever-present
problem, so when Dallas showed Fairfax the
unexpected communication – received via Lord
Methuen's headquarters – his commanding officer
wasted no time in coming to a decision. 'Take your
son and go. It looks like we will be sitting here for
some time.'

'Thank you, Fairy.'

Fairfax nodded. 'Godspeed, Dallas. I'm speaking
as a friend. Make sure your wife is all right and get
some proper attention for that boy's arm. I'll see
you both when I see you. Go well.'

They set off at first light the next morning.
Duncan was in some discomfort, his left arm in a
sling, swollen and of no practical use, though the
fact he'd soon be seeing Tanith buoyed his spirits to
such an extent that he ignored any pain and
inconvenience.

The journey took five days, finally striking the

coast south of Stangar, near Shaka's Kraal. As they travelled, Dallas hatched a plan. Years before, he and Lorna had bought a hideaway house north of Durban, near the mouth of the Umdhloti River. Simple in style and set back into the trees, it overlooked a small bay bordered by two rocky outcrops. There were four bedrooms, a large family-area-cum-kitchen and a raised verandah along the seaward side where the ground sloped away to the beach below. Behind the timber house were separate servants' quarters and stables. Lorna had fallen in love with the place at first sight. Of late, what with one thing and another, they hadn't spent as much time there as either of them would have liked. That would soon be remedied.

Duncan was all in favour of the idea and promised that in his parents' absence he'd make sure all was well with the farm. Dallas remained reasonably certain that such enthusiasm had more to do with the assistance Duncan would be calling on than his sense of family responsibility. He didn't blame the lad. Tanith Taylor was a lovely girl and spending time with her could only be a pleasure.

On the fifth day around three o'clock, an oppressively hot afternoon heavy with the promise of rain, they turned inland and were soon climbing towards the house. *Morningside* looked splendid. Waving stands of green sugar cane gave way to fenced fields dotted with cattle. Smoke rose lazily from the chimney. It had the solid, unshakable appearance of a successful enterprise quietly going about its business.

'Someone's there,' Duncan observed. 'They've just topped up the kitchen stove.'

It was such a common remark, so familiar and welcoming, something he might have said to Dallas in times before war and uncertainty entered their lives.

'Mister David probably,' Dallas agreed. 'He usually starts cooking around this hour. Come on, lad. Let's see who's home.'

It was Mister David who appeared from the house, showing no surprise at their unannounced arrival. Cameron's dog, Saba, barked in obvious excitement while Suza continued to sleep beside Dallas's usual chair on the verandah.

'I see you, *nkosi*,' the Zulu greeted Dallas before giving Duncan's arm a perfunctory glance. 'They sent you home for that? Pah.'

Duncan laughed at the derision. 'I see you too, *madala*. They wouldn't have if Father wasn't coming back too.'

Mister David's eyes clouded with concern as they turned questioningly to Dallas.

'I am fine,' he assured him. 'It's Lorna we're worried about. Meggie sent me a message from the doctor.'

'Ah! Then it is good that you are back so soon. All is not as it should be and there is nothing I can do for her sickness.'

Dallas was aware that the Zulus associated an unbalanced state of mind with that person being called by ancestors to become a healer. If Mister David could see the difference in Lorna he probably considered her beyond the reach of his own people's medicine men. In any event, Dallas didn't intend to waste time trying an assortment of treatments which would probably be useless. He had to take Lorna away, have her to himself. Being together, without any outside influence, would be a start.

'Who is at home?' Duncan asked as their horses were led off for a well-earned rest.

'Only your mother. She is lying down. Madam Lorna sleeps much these days. It is true that she is tired but it does not come from too much work.' Mister David thumped his chest. 'It is in here.' He indicated his heart. 'It is full of sadness.'

'I will be taking her to Umdhloti,' Dallas said. 'Can you spare Aminta?' he asked, referring to Mister David's daughter who worked with him in the kitchen and was shaping up nicely as a cook.

'It will be her honour,' the Zulu said gravely, pride evident that his eldest child's assistance had been requested. 'When is this to be?'

'I don't know. As soon as I can persuade Lorna to leave what she is doing here and come with me.'

'That will not be too hard. I have heard Madam Lorna speaking of it with Miss Meggie. She is sad not to go there more often.'

'Good. Then we will make my wife happy again.' Dallas slapped Mister David's shoulder. 'It's good to be home, old friend. Now, I am anxious to see her.'

Dallas was shocked by Lorna's appearance. Dark circles where her skin had once been fine and pale. Pain in eyes that no longer sparkled. Questioning fear in the suspicious smile that greeted him. He crossed to the bed and took her in his arms.

'It's all right, my darling.' Dallas suddenly realised just how close she was to emotional collapse. 'Duncan and I are both fine. He's waiting to see you.' Dallas felt her tension subside and they sat in silence for several minutes, drawing strength from each other's presence. 'Come; Duncan will be wondering what we're up to and I'm sure the boy would rather be somewhere else.'

Lorna smiled and seemed to regain some enthusiasm. 'Of course. Tanith. They're engaged. Such wonderful news and I completely forgot. Where is he?'

'In the parlour.'

The cry of horror when she saw his arm in a sling drove away all thought of congratulations. 'Oh God, your father didn't tell me.'

'It's all right, Mother. A flesh wound, that's all.'

'You don't come home for a flesh wound, Duncan,' she replied sharply. 'How bad is it?'

'Well now,' he said, slowly peeling off the bandage. 'Let's see what the nurse has to say.'

She examined the wound minutely, satisfied only after five minutes of searching for signs of trouble. 'Mmph!' she grumbled. 'Looks all right.'

'Actually, it's a lot better than it was. Father made up some special *muthi* – Lord knows what went into it – and has been changing the dressing every day. The swelling has gone down and it's stiff rather than sore. Anyway, don't you worry about me, Mother, it's this old codger you should be concerned about.'

Her eyes flicked anxiously to Dallas. 'Why? What's wrong?'

'You are. He misses his little lass. Poor diddums.' With that, Duncan turned towards the door, laughing and dodging the cushion Lorna threw at him. 'I'm going out for a bit. Be good children.'

Lorna laughed too, a genuine smile lighting up her face. 'Say hello to Tanith. I'm so pleased for you both.'

'Thanks, Mother. I'll see you later.'

Dallas took her in his arms. 'He's quite right, though. I do miss you terribly. We're bored out of our minds most of the time. Often it's so quiet you'd wonder whether there's a war going on at all. Fairfax has been damned decent letting us come home. We will have to go back but not for a couple of weeks.'

'Oh darling, how wonderful. What will you do?'

'What will *we* do, you mean. We're going away. Just the two of us.'

'Can we? Can we really? Where? Oh, do tell me, Dallas. Where?'

'How about Umdhloti?'

Lorna closed her eyes and snuggled into his chest. 'Bliss. When?'

'Tomorrow.'

It was as easy as that.

'Meggie has been quite worried about you,' Dallas said softly, breathing in the familiar fragrance of Lorna's hair. He deliberately omitted to mention the note she had forwarded from Roger Parry.

Lorna eased herself out of his arms and the moment was gone. 'And I worry about all of you. Tanith is concerned about Duncan. Cameron and Virginia no doubt worry about each other. Torben fears for Gerda. At least Ellie and Lindsay are together.'

'Wait a second. Why would Torben be worrying about Gerda?'

'The police are questioning Afrikaners in Durban. There's even talk of putting them in prison camps. Husbands, wives, children, servants, the lot. Maybe sending some out of the country.'

'That rumour has been going round for some time,' Dallas said.

'It's no rumour, my dear. Some have already been locked up.'

'I didn't know that. Why in Natal? Why Durban?' Lorna lapsed into silence. She had no answer.

'This is depressing talk, my darling. For the next couple of weeks, you and I will speak only of good things. Pact?'

'Pact.'

'Now, what's this I hear about you being tired?'

She smiled. 'A ploy, I'm ashamed to admit. It gives me time to myself.'

'No ploys at Umdhloti. Promise.'

'I promise.'

Meggie had failed to arrive home the night before. Lorna said it was not unusual for her to stay over at the hospital if things were busy. Dallas, although keen to be on the road as soon as possible, didn't want to head south without first seeing his daughter. He and Lorna needed to pick up supplies in Empangeni, so a quick visit to the hospital would be easy. The night's other absentee, Duncan, arrived back just as they were leaving, his sling no longer in evidence and an embarrassed grin from ear to ear.

The carriage was heavy with occupants, provisions and other essentials. Dallas handled the horses with practised ease. 'When this war is over we must get away more often.'

Lorna was quiet that morning. 'Good.'

'Is that it? Just good? Are you all right?'

'Of course. What makes you ask?'

'You're not exactly talkative.'

'I'm leaving Frazer.'

'No sad things, remember?'

'It's not sad,' she contradicted. 'Simply that I miss him.'

'He's with Katie. And Duncan will be at home to keep an eye on both of them.'

'I know.' Lorna adjusted her shawl. 'If he's not too busy doing other things.'

Dallas reached over and patted her hand, relieved to see that she was smiling.

The house at Umdhloti was maintained by a Zulu the family all knew as Nostril, the older brother of Tobacco. Lorna had saved the younger man's life when her husband's business partner, Logan Burton, was killed by elephants. From that day forward, Tobacco considered Lorna to be his sister and accepted a brother's responsibility to protect her son, Cameron, who could so easily have been killed as well. It was a relationship which had endured until the Zulu War, when Tobacco answered Cetshwayo's call to arms only to die in the fierce confrontation on Kambula Hill. That had been over twenty years ago but to Dallas, who had been there also, it seemed more like yesterday.

Nostril first appeared at *Morningside* after the war was over. Despite the loss of an arm, courtesy of a sabre slash by one of the King's Dragoon Guards at Ulundi, he bore no animosity and sought only to maintain the longstanding relationship his brother had established with Dallas and his family. Now the elderly Zulu looked after their holiday house. He kept the place immaculate, even raking the beach when nobody was in residence – not an easy task for a man with his physical disability. Other servants were brought in as and when required, but Nostril was very much the *induna*. On this occasion, Aminta would do the cooking and take responsibility for the kitchen; another girl, Fanny, had come along to act as housekeeper. Nostril supervised everything, taking personal responsibility for the horses, carriage and garden. It worked well and no other servants were needed.

As dusk slid quickly through its spectrum into darkness, an oversized full moon rose in majestic silence from the near-flat ocean. Lorna breathed in the warm salt air with obvious pleasure. 'Mmm. If it stays like this tomorrow, might I suggest crayfish for lunch?'

It had been many years since Dallas first tried catching the giant red-backed crustaceans with a homemade basket trap based on Scottish lobster pots. His design worked well and crayfish soon became a holiday favourite, along with mussels and oysters gathered off the rocks at low tide.

'Sounds good to me.'

Something happened to the family when they stayed at Umdhloti. Unconventional already, at least by society's standards, Lorna and Dallas had seen nothing wrong in allowing their children to play naked on the beach, tearing around in unrestrained exuberance. Although less ebullient than their offspring, both were quick to embrace each new fashion as it appeared, delighting in a growing freedom of dress and behaviour. To them, change meant that old attitudes were, at last, catching up with their mutually held belief in common sense.

Relaxing in canvas-backed deckchairs that evening, enjoying pre-dinner drinks – Champagne for Lorna; Dallas, his favourite Islay malt – they watched the waves break, surging up the beach only to be sucked back in a foam of shimmering phosphorescence. As the sea retreated towards low tide, hundreds of crabs performed a moonlit ballet while newly exposed rocks took on lithograph-sharp outlines of black against white. Both sight and sound combined to bring a sense of total tranquillity and Lorna soon fell under its spell. She was wearing an orange and white bathing suit of the very latest design. It covered her from neck to knee but was frilly, frothy and feminine with a cheeky slit from neck to cleavage and very short sleeves which ended above the elbow. Drawn in at the waist it ballooned out until caught by laces just under each kneecap. It might have been a clown's outfit except that, on Lorna, it was chic and ever so naughty. The matching look on her face showed that she loved it. A mobcap was supposed to top off the outfit but she'd decided against it, allowing her hair to spring free. Bare feet simply added an element of defiance.

It mattered little to Lorna that no-one other than Dallas and the servants was there to see her. Umdhloti was not frequented by many people and being mid-week, those fortunate enough to own property there were not in evidence. Lorna could cavort to her heart's content.

Earlier they had played a game of badminton and the hot flush on her cheeks had told Dallas that Lorna was determined to win. She had, though not by much. Dallas blamed it on his bad leg.

She swatted at him. 'Liar.'

The ships were still out there, dark silhouettes against a solid silver sea, constant reminders that the world and war were not far away.

Dallas sensed Lorna looking at him in the moonlight and turned towards her. He loved this woman so much, sometimes it threatened to engulf him. If he had a recurring nightmare, it was of losing Lorna.

'You've got that look on your face,' she told him.

'What look?'

'The one that tells me you're about to say something soppy.'

'Soppy! I take exception, Madame.'

'So you admit it.'

He chuckled. 'Guilty.'

He felt her fingers, warm against the skin of his forearm. 'Thank you,' she said softly. 'I was losing my way.'

Dallas picked up her hand, turned it palm up and kissed it gently. 'You will never do that, not for as long as I draw breath.'

She nodded acceptance. 'I know. And that's the most comforting feeling in this world.' Her eyes never left his face. 'I'm afraid there's still some distance to go.'

'Not as far as you might think. And I'm here to walk with you. Don't ever forget that.'

'Never.'

They ate steaks by candlelight, their own beef, cooked to rare perfection on an open fire and served without gravy or sauce of any kind. Salad was picked at with fingers. The same went for boiled new potatoes, swimming in butter and topped with a sprinkling of mint. At the coast the family preferred to keep life simple. No dressing up, no silver-set table, no formality of any kind. Lorna had found a few frangipani flowers and floated them in dishes on the table. Their fragrance wafted over them. For good measure, she placed another behind one ear. Looking at his love of almost thirty years in her orange and white outfit, hair hanging in unrestrained curls, the flowers, candles and casual way of eating, Dallas felt they might have been in a different world. The incessant mosquitoes didn't give a damn where they were.

They made love that night with the tenderness of newlyweds. 'I remember our first time,' he whispered later.

'Me too.' Lorna hesitated. 'Who was your first?'

Dallas propped himself on an elbow. 'You've never asked me that before.'

'I've never wanted to know.'

'Why now?'

She smiled and shook her head. 'No particular reason.' Shrugging, she went on. 'Curiosity.'

'The answer might disappoint you.'

'Tell me anyway.'

'It was in London. A brothel. Father took me.'

'The Earl?' Lorna appeared more amused than disappointed.

Dallas laughed. 'He said it was about time I found out about such things. It was all so matter-of-fact; the man might as well have been speaking about his cattle.'

Lorna gave a snort of mirth. 'Oh dear me, Dallas. How young you must have been.'

'I was seventeen and as green as they come,' he admitted.

'What happened?'

'I can barely recall. Terrified is a word that springs to mind. I stood in a lavishly furnished room, deep red it was, turning my hat round and round in my hands and not knowing what to do next.' He gave a self-deprecatory grin. 'Fortunately, one of the ladies took pity on me. Father went off with someone and left me to it. This woman . . . Constance, that was it, though for the life of me I don't know why I remember her name . . . Anyway, Constance took my hand and led me upstairs. It was a disaster.'

Lorna shook her head, laughing.

'What's so funny?' Dallas demanded.

'I just can't imagine you behaving like that.'

'I was young. The fact that my father instigated the experience was acutely embarrassing. I'd have preferred to keep that part of my life a secret.'

'My father did something similar for Charles.'

'Well, I most certainly didn't for Cameron.'

'He didn't need help.'

'How do you know?'

'People talk.'

'People! Like Duncan or Torben, perhaps?'

'Mmm.' She would not be drawn further, preferring the original subject. 'What do you mean it was a disaster?'

'Must we speak of this?'

'We most certainly must,' she said firmly. 'I'm enjoying every minute of it.'

Dallas hemmed and hawed for a while before accepting the inevitable. 'I was shaking like a leaf. Constance was very considerate. She took my hand, led me to the bed, even undressed me – and was kind enough not to remark on the fact that I didn't appear to be . . . er . . . ready.'

'Not a problem I've ever noticed.'

He hugged her in appreciation. 'No, thank God. Um . . . anyway, she was skilful and patient. Before long . . . well . . . once I got the idea –' Dallas broke off. 'For God's sake, Lorna, can we change the subject?'

She snuggled into him, stretching a possessive arm across his naked body. 'Yes.'

'What brought all that on?'

'I needed to know.'

The penny finally dropped, or at least he thought it did. Lorna was vulnerable and somehow it helped to embarrass him. She knew full well the reason he had been forced to leave Scotland. Dallas had been only twenty-one when his affair with Lorna's mother, a woman nearly twice his age, was discovered, and, to protect her reputation, Lady Alison de Iongh was forced to accuse him of rape – at the time a hanging offence. True, she had not provided Dallas with his first experience of the opposite sex but did Lorna know that? Even after so many years it was still a subject they never discussed.

Feeling slightly hurt – it was as though she didn't trust him – Dallas tried to understand. Slowly came the realisation that it had nothing to do with the past, or doubt. She simply needed to demonstrate her love for him by talking openly about subjects which had always been a closed book between them. It proved to be the key which unlocked much of the private sorrow still trapped within her.

They spoke for hours and by the time Lorna drifted into exhausted sleep, Dallas knew how deep was the abyss into which his wife had fallen. She was trying to climb back and with his being there was managing to make progress. Until that evening Dallas hadn't fully understood the way in which Frazer's death had affected Lorna. Surprised that he hadn't seen it before, realisation only dawned when he recalled his relationship with his own mother. Dallas had loved and respected his late father but Lady Pamela stood out as something more – a friend, the one person in this world who had known him inside out and loved him like no other. Although she had died five years earlier – at the age of sixty-nine – something quite strange suddenly occurred to him. The day was 21 January, her birthday. At that moment he knew it was no coincidence. Wherever she might be, Lady Pamela had just helped him understand the magnitude of Lorna's loss.

Cradling her in his arms, Dallas too succumbed to sleep. The healing had started.

FOURTEEN

Aware of Lord Roberts's imminent arrival in Cape Town, General Sir Redvers Buller decided to demonstrate his command of the situation in Natal by making a flanking movement to try to get behind the Boer forces besieging Ladysmith. He knew the garrison had been reduced to eating horse meat, though even that could not last more than a few weeks. The South African Light Horse made up a small part of the three thousand cavalry at Buller's disposal. They led the move west, followed by nineteen thousand infantry and some sixty artillery pieces.

Cameron was buoyed by the thought of action, the creak of saddle leather music to his ears as they left behind the stinking heat and boredom of Chieveley, their task to secure two possible crossings of the Thukela. This they did with ease, encountering no enemy resistance and setting up a base camp on Spearman's farm, near Mount Alice. There they waited for six days, until the main force finally caught up. With it came Will. His relief at finding Cameron fit and well was obvious, though he didn't much take to his godson's new-found

English friend, Winston Churchill, who seemed to have a better way of doing everything.

While Sir Charles Warren's infantry laid pontoon bridges and crossed the river, Dundonald's cavalry ranged north, towards Acton Homes, successfully ambushing a Boer *komando* and reaching open country behind General Botha's position. The back door to Ladysmith was well and truly open.

'I don't believe it,' Cameron commiserated with Winston when he heard they had been called back. 'If Buller thinks we're too spread out, why doesn't he close up on our position and split the enemy's defences? Dammit, man. Ladysmith is less than two days away.'

'He's worried about his supply line,' Winston pointed out. 'It's stretched already. If the Boers cut him off he could lose the entire army. It takes a ton of provisions each day to keep a hundred men in the field. Redvers has twenty thousand. A disaster like that could lose us this war.'

'Point taken, Winston. Would you take the chance?'

'Without a doubt.'

Lookout Hill, better known as Spion Kop, was to be the pivot point. On the night of 23 January, Lieutenant Colonel Alec Thorneycroft – wearing his all-too-familiar 'TMI' stencilled helmet – led two thousand men of General Woodgate's Lancashire Brigade as well as his own normally mounted infantry, in a night attack on the fourteen-hundred-foot outcrop of weathered rock. They gained what was thought to be the summit at 0400 hours, a final bayonet charge dispersing the few Boer defenders into an impenetrable blanket of morning mist.

The flat plateau was only as big as the area needed for a good game of cricket, and a shallow defensive trench was dug on the assumed crest. As a new day dissipated the mist it became clear that their only protection lay a good two hundred yards from where it should have been. Unbeknown to Buller – or General Warren, who waited below – the Boers had already withdrawn seven thousand men and twelve heavy guns from their siege of Ladysmith. Come the dawn they commenced pounding the exposed British positions with shrapnel shells and a hail of sniper fire from two higher kopjes which remained in their hands. General Woodgate was killed shortly after 0830 hours.

It was not long before General Botha's Carolina and Pretoria *komandos* reached the rim and added to the deadly barrage. In a heliograph message from below, Warren promoted Thorneycroft to Brigadier-General, giving him command of the hilltop. The summer sun beat down mercilessly. Still there were no reinforcements and it fell to Thorneycroft to rally the flagging morale of his men, some of whom opted for surrender and were taken prisoner before a white flag could be torn down by their new leader.

One of the Natal volunteers, Stanley King, led an attempt to reach a rocky outcrop on the plateau's edge, the place where their forward position was supposed to be. He and those who followed were cut to pieces by the pinpoint accuracy of enemy marksmen. Thorneycroft tried himself but fell, twisting his ankle – an accident which probably saved his life.

As the cloudless summer day wore on, casualties mounted on both sides. Confined to their meagre protection, without food, water or shelter, British losses were less obvious. It was a fact that seemed to demoralise the Boers, who quickly fell back when faced with a bayonet charge by Thorneycroft's long-awaited reinforcements. The advantage didn't last long.

With the Light Horse being held in reserve, Winston and Cameron decided to see for themselves what was happening on the plateau. There had been no news for hours. Leaving their mounts at the white-tented field hospital they cautiously climbed the hill and looked out on a scene of indescribable carnage. They saw the smashed heliograph and decided to report an immediate and critical need for further assistance. On General Warren's orders, Cameron rejoined his unit while Winston returned to the summit with a handwritten message for Thorneycroft telling him that the desperately awaited men and artillery were on their way.

It was now after dark, making it impossible to see that the Boers had abandoned their positions and retreated, leaving only the unnerving sounds made by the wounded or dying. Thorneycroft had no idea that he had won the day and by midnight – still without water or the promised support, low on ammunition and with half his men killed, wounded or taken prisoner – he chose to save those who remained.

Two days later, Spion Kop was reoccupied by the Boers and General Botha communicated a truce to clear the dead and wounded of both sides. The day passed in eerie silence as friend and foe sought out any who were still alive. The dead were buried where they had fallen. Nearly two hundred and fifty British soldiers lay in the trench alone. Half as many again had been lost by the Boers. As Indian doolie-bearers carried those unable to walk from the hill, the search for survivors went on and an ashen-faced photographer recorded the scene for posterity.

Cameron was carefully checking casualties who had fallen beside a rocky outcrop. Suddenly something moved against his ankle. Looking down he saw a huge blood-soaked hand flex, its owner almost hidden under two dead bodies. Gently Cameron rolled one aside, the man's sightless eyes staring accusingly back as if objecting to the intrusion. The second couldn't have cared less, his face torn to pieces by an impact-exploding pom-pom shell. It was impossible to tell which bits of bone or how much blood belonged to the one man left alive. He wore no khaki uniform – none of those surrounding Cameron did – meaning they were probably Natal volunteers from Thorneycroft's Mounted Infantry.

Cameron held up a hand to summon stretcher-bearers. 'Over here,' he yelled, dropping to his knees beside the wounded man, subconsciously muttering encouragement in Zulu.

The softly spoken sound brought a surprising response: one whispered word – '*Bayete*' – the Zulu war cry. This man was most certainly from Natal. His eyes flickered open for a second and in their dark-brown depths Cameron saw a spark of recognition.

Carefully the doolie-bearers lifted him onto a stretcher. He was big all right, obviously strong, probably in his mid to late thirties, and swarthy, with dark, receding hair. Cameron had no idea who the man might be or whether he would survive.

Buller blamed the fifty-nine year old Warren for his latest misfortune, one which left him no option but to pull back south of the Thukela.

On Spearman's farm, the anticipated arrival of more troops and artillery tempted Buller to wait where he was, then try to break through the Boer line slightly further east, this time at Vaal Krantz. The fresh faces included Winston's nineteen year old brother, Jack, for whom he had pulled strings to secure a commission in the South African Light Horse.

On 5 February the assault began. Long-range 4.7-inch quick-firing guns, borrowed from the navy, pounded Boer positions across the river, though the troops who did manage to cross the fast-flowing Thukela were soon forced to dig in and suffer a similar bombardment. For two days it went on. The Light Horse could do nothing but watch and wait. Unable to take the high ground and faced with what was far from ideal cavalry country, Buller once more decided to pull back. The failed attempt added more than three hundred casualties to his losses. In just over two weeks some eighteen hundred British troops had been killed, wounded or captured. Confidence in Buller himself was at an all-time low.

'Poor bugger,' Will muttered as their commander praised his men's efforts in a desperate attempt to boost morale.

'The key has turned, lads. I'll give you Ladysmith within the week.'

There was a murmur of approval but they all knew it would probably take that long just to return to Chieveley.

Will went on, 'Sir Reverse, they're calling him, Ferryman of the Thukela. It's hardly his fault that this war is unlike anything any of us have been in before. Nothing is decisive. The Boers seem to cut and run. Now you see 'em, now you don't.'

Cameron nodded. 'The country round here lends itself to that. Botha is using it well, though for the life of me I don't see how we can do the same. Buller needs a major victory, something clearly seen as such. He has to relieve Ladysmith and do it quickly.'

They had been at Umdhloti for almost a week, the days disappearing faster than either of them could believe. Lorna was thriving under Dallas's tender and loving attention. She admitted to blaming him for Frazer's death, though time and acceptance of the circumstances had at last combined to dispel her initial reaction. The house even heard sounds of laughter. There were quiet moments too, reflective times when they grieved together for their youngest son. Gone, however, were the torturous elements of doubt and accusation.

'I'd forgotten,' Dallas confessed one afternoon as they made their way up the beach carrying what they'd kept from the day's catch, 'that life could be so good.'

'Me too,' she said. 'It's another world.'

They dumped two still-snapping crayfish into the kitchen sink and Dallas set to work preparing a couple of dozen fresh oysters he had harvested from the rocks at low tide.

'What would you like with them?' Lorna asked. 'Something hot, or cold with salad?'

'Neither.' He turned his face towards her and whispered into their kiss. 'Just you.'

'Hot or cold?' Lorna giggled.

He grinned back. 'Hotter the better.'

Their kiss deepened, shellfish forgotten. Aminta and Fanny were told to take the rest of the day off. Lorna and Dallas lost all track of time, surfacing only when shadows stretched long across the beach below, disappearing into a deepening blue sea. Dinner was going to be late.

'Just like old times.' Lorna sighed luxuriously. 'I love you very much, you old rascal.'

He poked her in the ribs and she jumped. 'Not so much of the old,' he warned.

'Prove it,' Lorna challenged, inviting a repeat performance. Dinner was delayed still further.

An all too quick shower of rain had cooled the early evening air, tempting thousands of flying ants into the darkening sky in a brief celebration of life. Attracted to the lamplight, they landed everywhere, shed their wings and set off in search of sexual satisfaction. The swarm didn't last long, twenty minutes at most. Their wriggling sausage-like bodies – a Zulu delicacy with which Mister David had failed to tempt Dallas – soon disappeared, leaving only a gossamer carpet as evidence of their passing. Nostril was outside, eagerly gathering them up.

Lorna and Dallas carried plates loaded with seafood and salad out onto the verandah. Listening to the waves and smelling the salt air, they were at peace with the world and each other.

Sucking down an oyster sprinkled with lime juice and dipped in a concoction of her own making – onion, tomato and mushroom, fried with a little butter and chilli – Lorna voiced a reflective opinion on their family. 'I nearly lost sight of how fortunate we are, Dallas. Cameron and Virginia were meant to be, as are Duncan and Tanith. I'd love it if Ellie and Lindsay would, well, formalise their relationship – before a surprise of a different nature comes along.'

'Whatever do you mean?'

'Don't be silly. Even old you must have guessed.'

His brows drew together. 'I thought I made my point about disparaging remarks.'

Lorna's laugh tinkled out into the night air. 'Be serious, darling, Ellie's a grown woman.'

Dallas appeared not to believe what he was hearing. 'You mean to say . . .?'

'Exactly.'

'Under my roof?' He sounded outraged.

'Yes. Elsewhere as well, I'm sure.'

'And you didn't tell me?'

'No.'

'Why ever not?'

'Because you're a stuffy o–'

Dallas burst out laughing. 'Old hypocrite. I suppose I am, aren't I?'

'Most assuredly.'

'If you must know, I saw their sleeping quarters at Estcourt. Not that we didn't do the same thing!'

'Touché.'

'Well, good for them, I say.'

In spite of the darkness, Dallas noticed Lorna's eyes widen with surprise. 'You don't mind?' she queried.

He inclined his head. 'Not really. I've always liked Lindsay. Any other surprises?'

Lorna smiled wickedly. 'Meggie's quite fond of Sabani,' she said, dropping in the name of Mister David's younger son as she snapped a succulent crayfish leg and drew out the tender white flesh.

Dallas rose swiftly, gripped both sides of her chair and tipped it backwards. 'Tell me you're lying.'

She screamed in mock horror.

'Quick, woman. Tell me.'

'I am, I am. Please, Dallas. You're spilling my food. I'm only joking.'

'You'd better be. Promise?'

'I promise.' She laughed.

He righted the chair, laughing too.

'Got you going, though, didn't I?'

'Not at all. Was there a point to all that?'

Food back on her plate, dignity restored, Lorna answered. 'Meggie's special to you, that's all. Even if she is a bit young for us to be worrying about.'

'Then that leaves only the problem pair.'

'Precisely. Torben and Gerda. I can't help it, darling. That girl drives me crazy. Still,' Lorna shrugged, 'leaving aside Meggie, three out of four isn't bad. And Gerda's trying harder. Haven't you noticed?'

'When have I had the chance?'

'Well, she is, believe me, and deserves credit for it.'

'So you keep saying.'

'How very boring of me.' Her tone was so droll that Dallas laughed again.

As everything ends, so did the interlude at Umdhloti. Lorna and Dallas returned to *Morningside*, refreshed and relaxed. They had drawn on each other, used little things to rekindle a burning love from the embers of sorrow. So soon it had become time to face the real world again – one without Frazer, one of hardship and fear, one which both agreed could get worse before it got better.

Tanith was at *Morningside* when they arrived,

standing arm in arm with Duncan on the verandah. Mister David fussed around. The dogs dozed.
Of Meggie there was no sign.

It was the first time Dallas had seen Tanith since
she and Duncan became engaged. 'You two certainly make a fine picture. I'm very happy for you
both.' He gave Tanith an affectionate embrace and
said to his son: 'I see that arm doesn't seem to be
bothering you anymore.'

Duncan looked positively guilty.

'Where's Meggie?' Dallas asked.

'At the hospital. She'll be home for dinner.'

Lorna took Tanith's arm and together they went
to check on Frazer's cairn.

Inside, Duncan produced a three day old *Natal
Mercury* and showed it to his father. 'Spion Kop
looks like another bloody disaster.' The newspaper
carried images of Buller's orderly retreat across the
Thukela, its editorial ignoring British or Boer
losses while extolling the bravery of Thorneycroft's
Mounted Infantry and the decisive actions of Winston Churchill.

'So the Light Horse were there,' Dallas
observed. 'No word from Cameron, I suppose?'

'Not a dickybird. Some of the men who were
wounded are here at the hospital. One of them
told Meggie that they could have held the hill had
it not been for nonexistent communication and a
total lack of urgency by those sitting on their backsides down below.'

Dallas didn't doubt the observation. 'Have you
seen Virginia?'

'No. She's got her hands full at home helping with Kevin.'

Meggie was greatly relieved to see the improvement in her mother. That evening she took Dallas to one side and whispered, 'It's quite amazing. She's like a new woman.'

He merely grinned, prompting his daughter to roll her eyes and dig him in the ribs. There was a difference in Dallas too: a mischievous sparkle she had not noticed in months. Sometimes Meggie wondered about her parents' sex life. It might have surprised her to learn just how satisfying it really was. Meggie inwardly doubted she would ever find a love that could even come close to that shared by her parents.

'By the way, there's a man in the hospital who says he knows you. Stanley King. Arrived today. Apparently Cameron helped him after Spion Kop.'

Dallas sounded relieved. 'So Cam's all right. What a small world this is. Stan King keeps very much to himself. Runs cattle at Nkwalini. "*Ndlovu*", the Zulus call him.'

'Elephant. I can see why.' Meggie suddenly blushed and turned away.

Her embarrassment wasn't noticed. 'The man's size may well have something to do with it. More likely the fact that he used to spend most of his time chasing elephants in Bechuanaland. It was ivory that paid for his farm, *Kingsway*. Stan's still got the biggest pair of tusks I've ever seen. Well over a hundred pounds each.'

Meggie's whole face seemed to be on fire.

'Got badly mauled by a lion back in the mid eighties. Some mad Irishman saved his life. Get him to tell you the story. Is he badly hurt?'

'Nothing that won't mend.'

'That's good. Give him my regards.' Meggie's mention of Stan King started Dallas thinking.

Back in seventy-two he'd bought his Rawbone double rifle from one of the Kings – John, that was it. He had just taken over old man Bailes's business in Field Street. Came from Birmingham and wouldn't let you forget it. Best gunsmith in Durban, though. Funny the things you remember. They're in West Street now. His sons work with him. Stan's related to them in some way . . .

When Stanley King had arrived at the hospital in Empangeni, Meggie found herself with the task of changing his three-day-old dressings and giving him a bed bath. Everyday jobs, nothing complicated. The new arrival wore a woven bracelet on his right wrist, made from the thick tail-hair of an elephant. She wondered why.

'Dallas's youngest, if I'm not mistaken?' His unexpected words cut into her thoughts. 'Know your father.'

Meggie was staring. Not at this giant of a man's missing nipple or the recent stitches which crisscrossed his shaved chest. What she saw were the scars, deep and raking. Jagged puncture marks, badly healed tissue and distorted muscle on his right arm and shoulder. Old wounds.

'Sorry. Yes, I'm Margaret. No, Meggie.'

'King. Stanley King. Your family seem to be making a habit of looking after me.'

'What do you mean?'

He told her about Cameron finding him after Spion Kop and they talked easily as Meggie checked his wounds for any sign of infection. Nothing. Somebody had done a good job.

'Can you sit up?'

'I think so,' he said, wincing as damaged muscle took the strain.

'I'll be as quick as I can. Just lift your arms a little.'

Obediently he raised his arms, allowing Meggie to wrap a new dressing round his upper body. As she helped him into a clean pyjama top with buttons down the front, Meggie noticed that he couldn't straighten his right elbow. She didn't ask why.

'Right, you can lie back.' Meggie put an arm behind him, trying not to think of what had to be done next. 'Now we'll just wash the rest of you,' she said, peeling back the sheet which had been covering him from the waist down.

Her patient said nothing as Meggie quickly rinsed and dried his legs and genitals. No sign of any shaving there. She pretended not to notice as his penis became aroused. It had happened with others and she'd thought nothing of it. This time it was different. Stanley King was enormous. Meggie couldn't bring herself to look him in the eye. Pulling the sheet back over him she fussed around, straightening his pillow. 'Better get some rest now.' He was already asleep.

With a distinct feeling of relief, she was about to wheel away the privacy screen when a soft voice behind her said, 'Thank you, Meggie.'

She turned. His eyes were still closed. Perhaps she had imagined it.

Dallas and Duncan left *Morningside* three days later. A telegram to Torben had him join them for drinks at the Durban Club. As it was a men-only establishment, Gerda was not with him.

'We would have come to Umdhloti if anyone had taken the trouble to inform us that you and Mother were going to be there. Anyway, it's too late now. Gerda sends love and says if you see Ellie to tell her that all is going well. She'll understand.'

'Of course,' Dallas agreed, wondering why Torben wouldn't talk more openly about his wife's pregnancy.

'And as for my little brother, you don't look wounded to me. In fact, quite the opposite. Is there something I should know?'

'Tanith and I are engaged. Is it that obvious?'

'Not just good friends, eh? Gerda will be pleased.'

Duncan couldn't help but wonder if she would.

Although Torben seemed evasive when talking about his own activities, he became quite animated on the subject of Lord Kitchener's drastic proposal to burn out Boer farms, destroying the food supplies on which their *komandos* relied.

'And as for imprisoning innocent women and children, even African servants . . . it's a disgrace.

261

Not only that, with all the country's crops destroyed, how does he expect to feed them? It's nothing short of genocide.'

Their quickest route back to rejoin Fairfax in the Orange Free State took Dallas and Duncan inland, following the railway through Pietermaritzburg and on to Estcourt. Ellie was delighted to see them and learn of Duncan's engagement, though there was no disguising the strain she was under.

'Lindsay's not too good,' she said. 'He's through the worst. Thank God it wasn't enteric fever. The hospital at Intombi is losing a dozen or more patients every day. Typhoid and dysentery are killing more than the Boers. Dammit. If the siege goes on for much longer there'll be nobody left to defend Ladysmith. At least White has decided to stop feeding his useless cavalry horses and eat them. That might make some difference.'

Over a meal of corned beef and boiled potatoes Dallas brought Ellie up to date with news from home and passed on Torben's reference to Gerda's pregnancy. Duncan fell asleep.

Knowing that they wanted an early start Ellie organised beds and suggested that in the morning they go on to Chieveley then follow Buller's supply column west before cutting through the Drakensberg north of Basutoland.

That was what they did, reaching Buller's camp on Spearman's farm late the following afternoon. Clearly preparations were being made to move out – by the look of it, back to Chieveley. There was an overall air of despondency but what struck them most was the sheer size of the force. Dallas couldn't see how the Boers could possibly have beaten back so many men or stood up to the assembled artillery.

It was not difficult to find the South African Light Horse. Will's jaw dropped in amazement when he recognised Dallas and Duncan.

'Don't tell me the Fairfax Scouts are here too? Is there anybody who isn't?'

They dismounted and shook hands. 'No, Will. We're on our way back to join them. Duncan was wounded – not badly, as you can see – and Lorna needed me at home for a while. We've been in Zululand for the last ten days or so. How are you, old friend? Where's Cameron?'

'He's around. Can't keep an eye on him all the bloomin' time.'

'I heard Cam was at Spion Kop.'

'Yes. What a mess that was. Then the old man gave it another go at Vaal Krantz. It's too rough across the river for horses. Cam's just been sitting around for the last few days.'

'And now?'

'Back to Chieveley, it would appear.'

'Do you think there's any chance of seeing Buller?'

'Don't see why not. He could probably do with some cheering up. Ah, here's Cam now.'

'Well, well. This is a surprise. Hello, Father, Duncan. You two have lost some weight. What brings you here?'

Dallas had last seen his eldest son at Frere. There was much to catch up on. Both Cam and Will were delighted by Duncan's news, though his brother seemed sorry that neither he nor their father had found time to visit Virginia. It was almost three weeks since any mail had reached the men.

Dallas couldn't believe the change in Sir Redvers Buller. True, it had been a good twenty years since they fought together during the Zulu War, but this was not the man who had saved his life at the bloody battle of Kambula Hill, the man of courage and charisma, loved and respected by those who served under him.

'Good to see you again, sir.'

For a few moments the face that stared back showed no recognition then, quite suddenly, a smile of genuine warmth broke the burdens of time and command. 'You've changed a bit, Granger. Any idea how we might actually win this little war? The Boers seem to have everything going their way.'

They talked in private for well over an hour as the camp around them made ready for departure. 'My successor, Lord Roberts, is about to start his push for Bloemfontein. Only problem is, Methuen still can't get past Cronje at Magersfontein. Fairfax is scouting for Johnny French, who will have to outflank the Boers if he's to relieve Kimberley. Apparently Rhodes is kicking up quite a fuss about the delay in breaking them out. A chap called Kekewich runs the military garrison but, truth is, De Beers has more employees in the place than he has regular troops. There are ten thousand out-of-work blacks in the mine compounds alone and little or no food for any of them. Scurvy is rife. Newborn babies seldom survive. I only hope we can get them out before they're forced to surrender.'

There was something about Stanley King that flustered Meggie's usual calm. In all of her seventeen years not once had she been aware of boys as anything other than brothers – usually because they were able to do things a girl couldn't or, more correctly, shouldn't. She and her father had always been close – quite normal with a youngest child, Meggie told herself, especially a daughter. Dallas often said that her confident no-nonsense character reminded him of Lorna. Why then should a total stranger who was twice her age – she knew he was thirty-six, if only just, from the chart at the foot of his bed – disturb her so? Dallas had said that the man was reserved. Did that mean shy or was it because he didn't talk much about himself? *Nothing wrong with that*, she thought. Her father seldom spoke about his past.

The afternoon was hot and humid. Stan King dozed, his pyjama jacket unbuttoned and open to the waist, exposing the crisp white bandages wrapped tight around his chest. The single sheet was rumpled and Meggie felt compelled to straighten it. She had no idea what made her bend down and kiss the stitched scar where his left nipple had once been. The sleeping giant didn't stir.

FIFTEEN

It was three in the morning when a loud banging at the door woke Torben and Gerda. No servants slept in the house so Torben went downstairs. Gerda could hear him having a heated exchange with whoever stood outside. Strange male voices raised in authoritative demand mingled with her husband's infuriated responses. The irate confrontation struck terror into her heart. At just over six months pregnant, Gerda was already ungainly and clumsy. Clutching a gown too small to close completely around her, she came partway down the staircase and in a trembling voice called out, 'Who is it, dearest?'

'Military,' Torben barked. 'They say we have to go with them.' He turned back to the two men standing beyond the open front door. 'Why now? Surely tomorrow will do?'

'Sorry, sir. We have our orders –'

'And who might they be from, pray tell me?'

'Our commanding officer, sir. That's the way it works. You're not the only ones to be woken.'

'Indeed. And that's supposed to make me feel better? It's a bloody disgrace, if you ask me. An invasion of personal privacy. What's to be gained by dragging honest people from their beds at this hour?'

'We will give you and your good lady half an hour to dress, Mister Petersen.' Torben had retained his real mother's surname.

'Damned decent of you.' He slammed the door, debated whether or not to have a drink, decided against it, turned and took the stairs two at a time.

Gerda waited on the landing. 'Oh, Torben. What do they want? Have they come to take me away? I'm frightened.' Gerda's fear found its way through her fingers as she clutched his arm. Torben could both hear and feel his wife's panic. It angered him that two impersonal soldiers could invade their home in the middle of the night and disturb his wife to such an extent.

'Shh, my precious one. I won't allow any harm to befall you. I'll be right by your side.'

'What if they hurt the baby? What if . . .'

'Don't fret yourself, darling. It's not the fault of these men,' he tried to reassure her. 'They were quite courteous. They don't like being up at this time any more than we do. We'll be fine.'

And they were. Along with about twenty others, Torben and Gerda were individually inter-rogated and sent home. The questions they were asked sought to establish and clarify any connec-tion with Boer families, be they in *komando* units or not. The focus of attention was on brothers, fathers, uncles and male cousins, names and other details being meticulously jotted down. Gerda felt uncomfortable answering some of the queries, believing she was betraying her own *volk*. In truth, she, Torben and her parents had often discussed the coming of this time and all were well prepared. Their answers tallied to the satisfaction of the interrogators and by mid morning they found themselves being taken home.

Despite the hour, Torben poured himself a whisky. Gerda settled for a glass of cordial. 'Let's hope that's the end of it,' he said, his relief obvious.

'I still can't see why they wanted to question us,' Gerda persisted. 'Could it have something to do with Mark?' Her older brother had recently been released from prison where he had been since the *sjambok* killing of his supposed best friend. As he was drunk when it happened, the courts had decided his crime was not premeditated and waived the death penalty. Family pressure and a good lawyer had secured him an early release. The police hadn't been happy, though there was little more they could do. 'They've been watching his house, you know,' she went on. 'Waiting for him to put a foot wrong.'

Torben knew that Mark hadn't taken kindly to what he saw as 'the bloody English and their red tape', but he'd buckled down and behaved, much to the relief of his father and mother. The army did try to bluff him into becoming a spy. He saw through their threats and refused, leaving the British administration no choice but to respect his wishes. They did, however, warn him to keep well away from any more trouble. Mark had every intention of doing just that. His one experience of prison had been enough to last a lifetime.

Gerda's frightened eyes reminded Torben of a mesmerised rabbit, aware of danger yet too terrified to do anything about it. The incident only served to make him more protective. No-one would hurt her. No-one would take this woman from him. He'd make damned certain of that.

As it happened, military intelligence had not been worried about Gerda at all. It was Torben in whom they were interested or, more specifically, his arms-dealing business. Despite having family ties with the enemy, the man was good at what he did and had helped the army out on more than one occasion – a fact first demonstrated when he had been able to replace ten breech-loading 15-pounders lost to the Boers at Colenso. For that reason they had decided to let him be, at least for the time being. Rattling the man's cage was just to let him know they were watching. Torben Petersen could be useful again.

Dallas and Duncan finally found the Fairfax Scouts. As Buller had said, they were now reporting back to Major-General John French who, thanks to Cecil Rhodes's nonstop demands for action, had been ordered by Lord Roberts to relieve Kimberley.

'Roberts has forty thousand men, a hundred guns and five thousand cavalry about to cross the border but is refusing any assistance for Buller. He's determined to take Bloemfontein and believes Steyn will pull some of his Free State *komandos* out of Natal to help defend it.'

'Makes sense,' Dallas commented as he and Fairy discussed what had been going on in his absence.

'I agree. So you can see why Kimberley remains a thorn in his side. Last week the Boers brought up one of their Long Toms. It's done more damage in a matter of days than anything since the siege started. Rhodes expects worse is to come and has thrown open both De Beers's diamond mines to shelter women and children.'

'So you think French will try to break through this week?'

'Sooner the better. Before he gets caught up in Kitchener's supposedly simplified transport system. It's causing chaos, Dallas. Right now there are four thousand African drivers with Lord knows how many wagons, oxen and mules milling around in utter confusion near Ramdam.'

Delays were inevitable, and not helped by the fact that Lord Roberts had been forced to abandon two hundred wagons – containing almost a third of his food and supplies for the advance on Bloemfontein – after Christiaan de Wet found them outspanned north of the Riet River at Waterval Drift and succeeded in stampeding their peacefully grazing trek oxen – nearly three thousand of them.

It was not until Thursday the fifteenth that a way to Kimberley appeared to be open. The scouts had reported Boer activity on two ridges near Abon Dam and French decided on an all-out cavalry charge to smash his way past the last hurdle. Dallas watched as five thousand mounted men thundered across the parched veld and disappeared into a choking blanket of dust. He knew that most of the mounts had only been in the country for a matter of weeks and were not yet acclimatised to the stifling heat of Africa, the terrain or their riders. They were being pushed too hard. It was madness. He was not wrong. After only a few miles, hundreds of irreplaceable horses were either killed or so badly crippled as to be of no further use. Britain's only mobile force in the whole of South Africa had been devastated by one act of thoughtless folly.

After four months of siege, Kimberley was finally relieved. To those who had waited so long Cecil Rhodes became their hero. Dallas had not forgotten that the next day, 16 February, was his fiftieth birthday. Not being able to be with Lorna, Kimberley seemed as good a place as any to pass such an unwanted milestone in his life. He resolved to tell nobody, hoping that Duncan would become too caught up in more important celebrations to remember such an insignificant family event. As it transpired, that was exactly what happened.

By now the Boers were aware of Lord Roberts's intention to take Bloemfontein. With British troops now well to the north of his entrenched position at Magersfontein, Piet Cronje – 'The Fox', as he was known – deserted the trenches which had held Lord Methuen at bay for over two months and, during the night of 15 February, simply slipped away, taking his force of five thousand to help defend the Free State capital. Having to move fast, he was forced to abandon over seventy fully loaded supply wagons. The scouts found him heading east along the Modder, and French quickly closed in with what was left of his cavalry. Nobody expected The Fox to stop and dig in but that was what he did, north of the river at Paardeberg.

Thirty miles to the south, Christiaan de Wet heard of Cronje's predicament and undertook a desperate overnight dash to support the main Boer force, now faced with fifteen thousand troops under the command of Lord Kitchener, who, in a message to Lord Roberts, confidently predicted being in the enemy *laager* early the following morning. It was not to be. In a matter of hours, nearly thirteen hundred British officers and men were killed, wounded or captured and de Wet, against all odds, held a strategically vital kopje south of the river, offering Cronje a way out. All that night and into the following day de Wet's guns fired on the British positions.

Some did take the unexpected opportunity to escape. Most stayed. Cronje's remaining wagons and horses had been decimated by Kitchener's artillery though fewer than one hundred of his men were killed, with two hundred and fifty wounded. His request for an armistice to bury the dead was rejected by Lord Roberts, who arrived on the nineteenth, fearful that any further delay could cost him his main objective – Bloemfontein. Scouts had already reported the anticipated reinforcements moving in from Natal.

Further to the south, at Colesberg, recently arrived colonial troops – Australians, in the main – faced a superior force under 'The Lion of the West', General 'Koos' de la Rey. This posed a direct threat to Lord Roberts's line of supply. Sir Alfred Milner, Governor of the Cape Colony, was also showing concern about fresh outbreaks of rebel activity close to Cape Town.

After three days spent trying unsuccessfully to dislodge de Wet from his high ground, Roberts was on the verge of giving up. Fortunately, fate intervened. For no obvious reason, the Boers abandoned their positions and rode away.

Still Cronje held out. On the twenty-third heavy rain flooded his dug-in defences, a swollen Modder River carrying away the rotting, maggot-ridden corpses of both men and horses.

At 0600 hours on Tuesday 27 February, a white flag announced the surrender of General Piet Cronje and over four thousand Transvaal and Free State burghers – among them fifty women. Ironically, Lord Roberts's first significant victory of the war fell on the anniversary of Majuba Day when, nineteen years earlier, Paul Kruger defeated the British in a battle that gave the Transvaal Boers their independence.

Taking of the Thukela Heights and Ladysmith stumbled towards success though it had been a long and bloody time coming. Each new confrontation added to the toll of those wounded or killed. Winston Chuchill's younger brother, Jack, had been hit during his one and only contact with the enemy. Shot in the leg, he became the first patient of his mother's hospital ship, *Maine*, when it arrived in Durban harbour.

Places like Horse Shoe, Wynne's and Hart's hills were heard of for the first time as Buller's fourth attempt to relieve the siege of Ladysmith gathered momentum. The press were describing it as the biggest ever military undertaking in the southern hemisphere. On 19 February, Boer forces had deserted Colenso and retreated north of the Thukela, leaving the rail bridge a twisted mass of collapsed steel and sleepers, only its stone supports still standing.

Since the battle of Spion Kop just over a month earlier and Buller's subsequent repulse at Vaal Krantz, Ellie and Lindsay had never been so busy. Their field hospital was now at Colenso, even closer to the front line. Lindsay had recovered from his bout of dysentery and, with Ellie, was working up to eighteen hours a day, sometimes snatching no more than half an hour's rest between cutting off some soldier's beyond-repair limb, attending to horrific shrapnel wounds or patching up those too far gone to save. Fatigue invariably brought mistakes and some died as a result. Nobody pointed the finger of blame. Many more were saved. Officers and men alike knew how hard the medics had to work.

During one particularly messy amputation, the unfortunate patient woke during the process and, not surprisingly, screamed, thrashed and cried in pain. Lindsay solved the problem with a full bottle of brandy. On that occasion Ellie had been assisting. As they cleaned up in exhausted silence, a spluttering Tilley lamp highlighted the silver blonde of her short-cropped hair. Gold-rimmed glasses failed to hide dark shadows of fatigue as she stretched her back to relieve the strain of bending over an operating table for three concentration-filled hours. At that moment, Lindsay thought she was the most beautiful woman in the world.

On more than one occasion he had asked her to marry him. Ellie always said no, to try again when she had qualified as a doctor. Well, now she had, and Lindsay waited only for the right moment.

She looked up to see him watching her and smiled tiredly. 'Any more?'

'Not right now. Come, my girl, time to get your head down.'

Lindsay led her to a curtained-off area – basically a connecting tent – next to what passed for the operating theatre. After Ellie lay down on the canvas camp bed, he gently removed her glasses and covered her with a blanket. 'What about you?' she whispered, exhaustion clear on her face.

'I'll be right over there.' He nodded towards a second similar stretcher.

She watched him as he sat and scratched the itchy stubble of a week's beard. Boots still on he fell backwards and gave a grateful sigh.

'Lindsay?' Her voice was fading.

'Mmm?'

'Will you marry me?'

'Silly not to.'

'When?'

'Any time you like.'

'That's good.' Turning her back to him, she dropped into a deep sleep, leaving Lindsay staring towards the dark tent top, a beaming smile on his swarthy face. In the silence he quietly muttered, 'Thank you, Lord.' Ever since meeting Ellie, Lindsay had known she was the one for him. He loved everything about this woman – her single-minded determination; the dedication to her work; the satisfaction she found in caring for others; her near fanatical obsession with understanding the human body. For him, it summed up someone who had the makings of not just a good, but a great, doctor.

As if that wasn't enough, Lindsay had always been attracted to women with clean-cut, no-nonsense good looks. Ellie had such qualities in abundance, no matter what the occasion or how she dressed. The first time he saw her, Lindsay realised he'd found his idea of perfection. Then she spoke, and her accent – influenced by background and breeding – told him that whatever this woman had to say would be worth listening to; the subject mattered not. She aroused him in every way imaginable.

Sighing, Lindsay turned onto his side and settled into a more comfortable sleeping position. He had been just plain fortunate that she'd seen something in him as well. It was typical of her to propose. They both knew the time had come and for Ellie that meant no more messing around. He loved her for that as well.

A commotion outside told Lindsay that sleep would have to wait. Another patient was being brought in for attention. Surely this one could be dealt with by someone else? But no. The flap was flung back and he heard his name being called. In an instant he recognised the voice. Cam!

'Lindsay, Ellie.'

'Shh! Your sister's asleep. What is it?'

'Will. He's been shot.'

'Shit!' Lindsay swore softly. 'Coming.'

Blinking in the still-illuminated operating theatre, he quickly assessed the situation. Will lay on a stretcher, displaying no sign of life. Two bearers hovered, awaiting instructions. He recognised one – Mohandas Gandhi – and nodded a quick greeting.

'Help me get him onto the table.'

Exhaustion forgotten, Lindsay pushed Cam aside, cut away Will's blood-soaked shirt and carefully examined the wound. A bullet had hit just above his collarbone, chipping off a clearly visible fragment before exiting slightly lower down his back. It would not have been serious unless, as was the case with Will, there had been previous damage in that area. Cameron paced up and down in agitation.

Lindsay smiled at him reassuringly. 'It's not as bad as it looks. He'll be fine. A nurse can fix this up.'

'I . . . I just thought . . . well . . . you mean he's not going to . . .?'

'Far from it. In shock, I'd say. Will's no youngster. The wound needs to be cleaned and dressed, that's all. We may have to strap his arm but first things first.' Lindsay turned to an Indian orderly and indicated that he should take over. 'Then see if you can find him a place in one of the ward tents.'

'I'll stay for a bit, if that's all right with you?' Cameron was clearly bothered by Will's injury.

'As you wish, though I can't offer you a bed. It's been a madhouse here since that brief armistice yesterday afternoon. Anyway, tell me what happened.'

'We came under fire near Pieter's Hill. Didn't see the blighters. Damn it, Will wasn't even supposed to be there. The silly sod hung back to try and spot them. I turned just as he was hit. He passed out when I tried to lift him. I thought he was gone.'

'You were lucky, both of you.'

'Yes, I know. Will worries me. He's like my shadow. It's as if he feels an obligation to keep me safe.'

'Maybe he does.'

Cameron sank into a canvas chair and rubbed a grimy hand over the top of his head. 'Why? He owes me nothing.'

'Perhaps the debt is to your father?'

Cam went on as if Lindsay's comment hadn't registered. 'What with Will watching my back and me looking out for him it's dangerous for both of us. We should be taking care of ourselves, not each other.'

A groan from the operating table stilled their conversation. 'That you, Cam? You all right, boy?'

Cameron got quickly to his feet. 'Yes, Will, I'm fine.'

His sigh sounded heavy with relief. 'Good.'

'And so are you, *madala*.'

'Who's an old man? Stop fussing, will you?'

Cameron actually smiled. 'Only if you do.'

Will grinned up at him.

'I don't suppose either of you is interested in my news?' Lindsay had decided it was time to distract them.

Two sets of eyes turned to him in obvious surprise. Lindsay was known to offer information only when asked.

'Ellie has asked me to marry her.' He couldn't hide the pride in his voice.

Will propped himself up on his good elbow. 'Why not the other way round?'

'She didn't give me time.'

'Rubbish.' Will sank down again. 'You've had plenty of that.'

'True. Don't think I haven't tried. She always said no.'

'And what did you say?'

Lindsay smiled and yawned. 'I said yes.'

'Excellent.' Cameron extended his hand in congratulations. 'I don't care who asked. You were meant to be together. Mother and Father will be delighted.'

'Thank you,' Lindsay said. 'You two are the first to know.'

'When's the big day then?'

'I have no idea.'

'Why ever not?'

'Ellie fell asleep right after I accepted.'

All three were still laughing when the Indian orderly returned with two stretcher-bearers and proudly announced that he had managed to find a bed for the patient. Cameron, noticing Lindsay trying to stifle another yawn, left with them, promising to return to see his sister in the morning.

The following day, word came through of Lord Roberts's success at Paardeberg. Inside the town, Sir George White saw no reason to celebrate. Instead, he cut the defenders' already meagre bread ration by half.

The significance of Majuba Day was not lost on Buller's men and they redoubled their efforts to take revenge. Tactics learned the hard way had already paid off, securing two hills – Cingolo and Monte Cristo. The Boers still held Pieter's, Railway and Hart's but by coordinating artillery and infantry attacks it was only a question of time before they too were won.

Hart's and Railway fell first, the latter taken by Lord Kitchener's younger brother, Walter. By nightfall only one end of Pieter's remained in enemy hands. Come the dawn its defenders had disappeared.

On 28 February, after one hundred and eighteen days of siege, the garrison in Ladysmith could see a column of wagons and men wending their way north. The Boers were in retreat, already out of artillery range. White's two naval guns managed one farewell salvo before a summer thunderstorm closed in to cover Louis Botha's escape. The garrison had no cavalry horses to give chase (they had eaten most of them) and Buller's troops were too exhausted to pursue the departing enemy on foot.

Ladysmith was a scene of jubilation as Cameron listened to a frail and stooped Sir George White praise those who had been through so much. 'Thank God we kept the flag flying,' he said, talking more to Ladysmith's defenders than those who had come to their rescue. 'It cut me to the heart to reduce your rations as I did.' Faltering, he went on, 'I promise you, though, that I'll never do it again.' His words were met with laughter, cheers and applause.

The next day Cameron went with a column sent out in pursuit of the Boers. They reached Modder Spruit station only to discover that Botha must have had trains waiting to evacuate his men and their equipment. They were too late to stop them.

Buller made a formal entry into Ladysmith on 3 March, bringing with him much-needed food and medical supplies. It was his moment of triumph. Lord Roberts, Chamberlain and even Queen Victoria sent telegrams of congratulations. In gratitude, he praised his long-suffering troops, paying tribute to their tenacity with the award of a Special Army Order. Buller was fortunate that he remained popular with his men. Aside from the backslapping and congratulations there were officers on his staff – Sir George White included – who had been quick to make known their lack of confidence in his leadership.

'He'll survive,' Winston predicted as he and Cameron enjoyed cigars and Cognac after an unexpectedly excellent dinner at staff headquarters. 'This may be a twenty-acre patch of tin houses and bluegums but it's famous to the uttermost ends of the earth.'

'And Sir George?' Cameron queried. 'Roberts must know how invisible he became during the siege.'

'Now there you have a point. Bobs's friend he may be but I do believe High Command are unlikely to offer the man another posting.'

The following day Sir George White succumbed to a fever. It was the excuse needed to have him invalided back to Britain.

SIXTEEN

'It was a long time ago,' her favourite patient said, his eyes staring up at the ceiling. 'I can't have been much older than you are now.'

'I'm eighteen,' Meggie lied, then thought better of it. 'Nearly.'

He didn't seem to hear. 'Life was just waiting to be lived. Everybody expected me to join the business but I wanted to do something for myself. Young John and William have done well, though.'

Meggie had no interest in the other members of Stan King's family so didn't seek to find out more.

'Before they joined the firm, John senior had given me a much-used muzzle-loading 8-bore made by Isaac Hollis in Birmingham. We're all from Birmingham, you see.'

Meggie didn't.

'It was the best twenty-first present a young lad could have had. My only problem was where to shoot it.'

'What's an 8-bore?' Meggie asked. 'Is it very big?'

'Size isn't everything but it's big enough to

knock down an elephant. Eight balls of pure lead having the same bore as the barrel make up one pound in weight.'

'I see. So the two 4-bores that Mister Selous uses must be massive.'

'Quite so and very heavy. Twenty-five, maybe twenty-six pounds apiece.'

'Father has hunted elephants, you know. I wasn't even born then. He doesn't like talking about it, though.'

'In those days there were elephants in Zululand. By the late seventies they'd all gone. Finding good ivory in any quantity meant going to Bechuanaland.'

'But that's all desert.'

'Most of it is but once you get north of the Kalahari there are Mophane forests stretching for hundreds of miles, up to the Zambezi and beyond.'

'So you went there?'

'Not right away. Old John was like the father I never had. He took me under his wing. I remember him saying, "Just because somebody gives you a horse doesn't mean you know how to handle the thing or what to feed it. The same goes for guns".'

Meggie had grown up with guns so she'd never thought about people not knowing what to do with them. If she'd come out from some city in England it would probably have been different.

'He showed me how to cast bullets, adding just the right amount of tin to harden the lead. Temperature is important too. You must heat the mould before using it if you're going to turn out blemish-free balls.'

Meggie mentioned reading in one of Roualeyn Gordon Cumming's books, *The Lion Hunter in South Africa*, how he ran out of tin on one of his expeditions and ended up melting down pewter plates and mugs.

'It works but that mad Scotsman's story says to me that either he wasn't recovering the bullets from what he shot or the man missed more than he hit.'

'Probably the latter, according to Father.'

Stan nodded and glanced at the girl sitting beside his bed. The clinical uniform did nothing to detract from her beauty. Dark curly hair framed a face that was a little pale, though that only emphasised the twin pools of her black eyes that stared confidently back at him. She smiled and her button nose seemed to turn up even more. 'Do go on.'

'Where was I? Oh yes.' Stan shook his head as if that would make some sense of the fact that he was actually enjoying talking to this girl. He who never needed the company of others was being taken out of himself by a woman half his age. Come to think of it, she looked a lot like her father.

'With a bag full of balls – about fifty had passed muster and I was getting better at casting them – we set off for the Bluff and my next lesson.'

'And you still hadn't fired a shot?'

'No. I'd cut patches and poured a few tweasles. That was all.'

'Tweasles? What on earth are they?'

'That's what John called the twisted paper packets of powder which we made up at the shop.'

'Never heard them being called that before.'

'The ocean was very calm, as I remember. John bit the top off a tweasle and poured its contents down the barrel. At least, I thought he did. After putting a patch over the muzzle he placed a ball on top of it and used the ramrod to push them both as far into the barrel as they would go. "See the brass tip?" he asked. "Wouldn't do to have sparks in there, now would it?" With that he handed me the rifle.'

'What about the percussion cap?'

'Last thing. Always the last thing. I was quite nervous, easing back the hammer and placing a primer on the nipple. "Aim for the horizon," John advised as I held the rifle and looked out over an empty ocean. It was not a moment to be faint-hearted. Putting the butt to my shoulder I hung on as tightly as I could and pulled the trigger.'

'What happened?'

'Nothing. The primer went off but that was all. Load your own gun – that was his lesson.'

'Sometimes it's not possible.'

'You're thinking about Mister David loading for your father. Yes. There are times when you have to rely on somebody else. Then your life is in their hands.'

'In that situation it applies the other way round as well.'

'Indeed it does.'

'So you had to pull the ball out with that worm thing and reload before firing your first shot?'

'Correct, and this time I did it all myself. By the

end of that afternoon my shoulder was black and blue.'

A bit like when you first arrived here, Meggie thought to herself.

'Once I'd fired a few normal loads John had me double the charge. Black powder pushes you, it's not the sharp kick you'd get from a horse. Spun me round nevertheless. "That's going to happen too", was all he said.'

'At least he warned you.'

'Sadistic old sod that he was.'

'Could you see where the shots were landing?'

'No. Too much smoke.'

'I suppose you had quite an audience by then?'

'Of course. They wanted us to come and shoot a hippo in the harbour – for its meat. John refused and decided that was enough for one day. Back at the shop he had me scrub out the barrel with boiling water and wipe the gun down with pig fat to stop it rusting. Guns don't like life on the coast. It's different inland.'

'To be continued,' Meggie said, rising to her feet. 'Mother worries if I'm not home before dark and my shift finished hours ago.'

'Then *tsamaya sentle*, as they say in Bechuanaland. Go carefully. I've enjoyed this afternoon, Meggie. Thank you for listening to my ramblings.'

'I've enjoyed it too. *Sala kahle*, Mister King, and sleep well.'

Having decided that she and Lindsay should marry, Ellie had no intention of delaying matters until the

287

war ended and so running the risk of one or both of them being killed before the wedding had taken place. That was her story at least – it was not as if a simple piece of paper would make any difference to their lives.

Lindsay had to admit that he rather liked the idea. 'What about family?' he said when Ellie unexpectedly raised the subject. 'Your parents would want to be here, I'm sure.'

'As would yours, so it's better we tell nobody. Besides, my darling, I've no idea where Father and Duncan are. Mother can host a reception at *Morningside* when the war's over.'

'Who would give you away?'

'Cameron, with Will acting as witness.'

'Sounds good to me.'

'Oh, and I'd like Winston to be there. Did you know that he's taken leave from the Light Horse and intends joining Lord Roberts in the Free State? We may never see him again.'

'If the "little man" will have him. Word is that Roberts has refused his application.'

'Only because of the *Morning Post* article he wrote after Spion Kop.'

'The one questioning the role of army chaplains?'

'That as well as advocating a spirit of forgiveness towards the Boers in Natal. Let's not forget, though, Lord Roberts and Winston's late father were close friends. Pound to a penny the whole thing blows over. Winston just wants to be where the action is.'

'Is that the way he'll see our wedding?'

She laughed, punching him on the arm. 'Don't be silly, Lindsay. If you want a reason it's because he's related to Cecily. You know how important she and Stephen are to me. Anyway, I like the man. He gets things done. Do you mind?'

'Not at all, my darling, not at all.'

Ellie and Lindsay were married in the Ladysmith courthouse at eleven o'clock on the morning of 6 March 1900. 'I now pronounce you husband and wife. You may kiss the bride.'

Lindsay had waited so long to hear those words. He took her in his arms. 'I love you, Missus Mayer.'

Cameron stepped forwards, congratulating his new brother-in-law before giving Ellie a huge hug. Will, one arm still in a sling, used the other to wipe tears from his eyes. 'Not before time, if you ask me!'

Winston signed the register as witness. At no time did he or the Church of England army chaplain say one word to each other.

Boer *komandos* held a twenty-five mile line of kopjes along the Modder River but Lord Roberts was not yet ready to continue his advance on Paardeberg. Piet Cronje, the Boer general who had surrendered there, had been sent with his wife as prisoners of war to the remote Atlantic Ocean island of St Helena.

The Fairfax Scouts were reporting an estimated six thousand burghers – led by Christiaan de Wet – massed at a place called Poplar Grove. French's cavalry had been given the task of outflanking the main Boer force and preventing it from falling back to assist with the defence of Bloemfontein. What nobody had discovered was that the Transvaal's charismatic President Kruger was also there, urging, encouraging, stirring Afrikaner patriotism and promising the helping hand of God for his chosen *volk*. A distinct lack of urgency seemed to have pervaded the British ranks and a feeling was growing that the war was all but over. It was probably this lethargy that allowed de Wet and Kruger to evade capture.

At long last Bobs continued his advance on Bloemfontein. French fought one bloody encounter with de la Rey at Driefontein before the Boers melted away, evacuating the Free State capital and falling back on Kroonstad. Lord Roberts's main force occupied the city on 13 March, swelling its population from four thousand to nearly ten times that number and placing a severe strain on available services – in particular the water supply. Not realising how grave the situation would soon become, Lord Roberts anticipated an early end to the war and offered an amnesty to any Boers – other than their leaders – willing to hand in weapons, sign an oath of neutrality and return home. Six thousand did, though most of the guns surrendered were old. More modern Mausers had been buried or kept by those determined to fight on.

Sir Alfred Milner, Governor of the Cape Colony and British High Commissioner for South Africa, arrived in Bloemfontein suggesting further concessions in an attempt to end the war. What he feared most was that the Transvaal Boers would dynamite the Reef goldmines, destroying a significant part of Britain's real reason for taking on Kruger and Steyn in the first place.

Winston Churchill did join his late father's old friend and found himself attached, if briefly, to Lord Brabazon's much-maligned Imperial Yeomanry – recruited volunteers despised as amateurs by many regular officers and men. Their record of success certainly did nothing to justify such slander. Later Churchill would ride with French's cavalry.

The early autumn night was pleasantly cool. 'At least Cronje is out of the way,' Fairy said as he and Dallas enjoyed what had become their usual after-dinner smoke.

'Dinuzulu was held on that island for nine years,' Dallas responded, his thoughts turning to others who had suffered the same fate. 'Napoleon died there.'

'Yet the powers that be brought Dinuzulu back in ninety-eight and had him reinstated as fifth King of the Zulus.'

'True. But only because Britain thought it would help to stabilise their growing problems in Zululand. They gave the king an education, taught him to read, write and play the piano, then allowed the poor man no power and paid him five hundred pounds a year as an advisor to the government. What kind of king is that? Remember, Zululand was annexed to Natal in the previous year. Allocations of farmland for settlement by Europeans had reduced traditional areas to thirty percent of what they once were. From ninety-five to ninety-seven the Zulus faced three years of locust plagues and their cattle were decimated by rinderpest. Then the rains failed. Few could even afford the *lobola* to buy a bride.'

'You seem to have the wind in your sails this evening.'

'Sorry. All this sitting around must be getting to me. Do you believe that this thing is nearly over?'

'Far from it. The Little Man doesn't understand what he's really up against. It's not just numbers. This is about hearts and minds, the opportunity to achieve an Afrikaner identity. Politicians may have pushed them into it but winning a few battles won't make us the victors. This war has a long way to run.'

'You sound just like Fred Selous. He has no love for the Boers – largely because of the way they treat Africans – but he firmly believes that the British have never understood what actually motivates them.'

'In my opinion, he's quite right. We're actually fighting for two totally separate things. The Boers want no more than to control their own destiny. Whitehall, chivvied along by Rhodes, Beit and Milner, to name but a few, lusts after land and what lies beneath it. By sheer coincidence neither camp gives a damn about those who were here well before any white man set foot on the shores of

Africa. Dallas, you and I make our living from this land but we work with it, learn from its people and hopefully give back to both. That way it may still be here tomorrow, for our children and theirs, irrespective of colour, creed or nationality.'

'Now who's got his sails set?' Dallas quipped.

'So why are we here? Protecting this country and its people? I think not.'

'All I can say is, this is a war that had to happen. If you and I hasten its end then we have played our part.'

'You're probably right. As Jack Walsh would have said, "enough is enough".'

Dallas nearly dropped his pipe. 'Jack Walsh?'

'Yes. Now there was a character. We bought his farm in the early eighties. Back then it was called *Wakefield*. The daughter and her husband sold up after Jack died, though she insisted on keeping the name to use on another place. Sad, really. Poor chap drank himself to death. Bottle of gin a day man. Said it helped his breathing, would you believe? Blamed it on an *assegai* in the chest during the Zulu War. He was with Chelmsford at Ulundi. As I recall, his accent was very similar to yours. It's one thing you Scots never seem to lose. Did you know him?'

Dallas could feel the sudden lump in his throat. There was no point in explaining that Jack Walsh had been his father. 'Friend of the family. From Edinburgh,' he said, trying to keep emotion out of his voice. 'Just wondered what had become of him.'

It was over eighteen years since Dallas's late

mother had told him the name that her one-time lover, Jonathan Fellowes, had assumed since leaving Scotland to settle in South Africa. Dallas had met the man not long after he first arrived in Africa. Fate had brought them together during a near-disastrous crossing of the rain-swollen Mngeni River above Howick Falls. He had no idea if Jack Walsh ever found out about their relationship. Now he would never know.

The name *Wakefield* was certainly familiar. It was the farm near Dargle that Cameron wanted to buy. A good three months had passed since they drunkenly discussed it. Dallas had no idea if the place had now been sold.

As he glanced upwards a comet caught his eye, leaving its shimmering trail of stardust across the African night. He watched, wondering if some greater power was at work orchestrating the events of his life. Caroline Hammond – nee Walsh – had to be his half-sister.

'Why is it that nobody comes to visit you?'

'I doubt any of the family know I'm here. Besides, it's almost fifteen years since I left Durban. Let's just say we all went our separate ways. They're happy with the shop and I made enough money from ivory to buy a farm.'

Meggie noticed that he kept twisting the elephant hair bracelet on his right wrist. '*Kingsway*, I believe it's called.'

He wondered what else she knew about him.

'It's written on your chart,' she said in response to his questioning look.

'I thought your father might have told you.'

'Well, actually he did.'

'Did he also mention that rinderpest damned near put paid to us?'

'No. Who is "us"? I thought you were a crusty old confirmed bachelor.'

'That's as may be but the boys who work with me are as much a part of *Kingsway* as I am. Who do you think looks after the place while I'm trying to keep my bank manager happy?'

Meggie avoided his question. She had the answer she wanted. 'Do you still hunt?'

'Have to. The good Lord doesn't pay bills. Fences and restocking have cost me an arm and a leg, metaphorically speaking, of course.' She laughed. 'We're trying Afrikanders this time. You must come and see.'

'Thank you. I'd like that very much.'

'Your father has spent quite a lot of time at *Kingsway*. We have an unwritten understanding that if I ever choose to sell he'll have first refusal.'

'He's always interested in new ventures. Especially where cattle are concerned.'

'I think he saw me starting out in much the same way as he had done and couldn't resist lending a helping hand.'

'He told me about the tusks you have.'

'Those I won't sell. Ever.'

'Why not, if times get tough?'

Stanley was twisting the elephant hair bracelet again. 'Because they're not mine.'

'Whose are they then?'

'They belong to a man called Michael Duffy.'

'The Irishman?'

'None other. Somebody has certainly done her homework.'

'Father told me that a mad Irishman with an eye patch once saved your life. Was that when you got all those scars?'

He nodded, his mind drifting back fifteen years. 'It was in the winter of eighty-five. My first season in Bechuanaland. We had made camp by the Botletle River, near a village called Xhumaga. I'd never seen so many animals. Elephant, buffalo, zebra, wildebeest – you name it. All coming down from further north to find water. There must have been tens of thousands.'

'And with them came the predators, I suppose?'

'Lions mainly, but there was so much food for them they left us well alone. All those hours spent with John King were paying off at last. My stock-pile of ivory was steadily growing. The boys had plenty of meat and we hadn't lost a single horse to fly strike – *nagana*, they call it.'

'You're saying "we" again. Were there others with you?'

'Only the Africans. I prefer it that way. The day it all went wrong I'd gone off on my own towards Nxai Pan, trying to find a place they call the Sleeping Sisters. It's a group of baobabs that stands on the edge of a shallow depression off the route

Selous once used to reach his camp. Sometimes there's water there, sometimes there isn't. You can see the place for miles. Thomas Baines carved his initials on one of the trees when he did a painting of them back in 1860.'

'I've heard my father speak of him. What happened?'

'There was no track as such and the sand had become quite soft. Stupidly I dismounted. There were footprints of lion everywhere.'

'Where was your rifle?'

'Slung across my back – the way the Boers carry them – but I can assure you that it didn't stay there for long. My horse saw him before I did, sitting in the shade of a small scrub thorn with a look of bored indifference on his face.'

'*Ibhubesi*?'

'Well, it certainly wasn't Thomas Baines's long-lost puppy! The horse got such a fright that it decided to be anywhere else but there. Only problem was, I didn't appear to be on it. The lion and I locked eyes and he didn't like it one little bit. A big black-maned fellow he was, old and seriously scarred. It took him no time at all to cross the distance between us. He came low, ears flat against his head. I got a shot into him after he leapt but the bullet hit underneath and too far back, passing through his stomach before smashing the base of his spine. I didn't realise that at the time because four hundred and fifty pounds of angry lion had landed on top of me, sinking his stinking teeth into my right shoulder and ripping out wildly with both front paws. We went down together, his momentum somersaulting us over. I had lost the Hollis and was bleeding badly. At least he'd let go. It took me several seconds to realise that my attacker couldn't move. He was lying on the rifle glaring at me from a few feet away, snarling and trying to drag himself forwards. It was the most terrifying moment of my life. I knew I had to move – and fast – but that wasn't to be. The shock and loss of blood caused me to lose consciousness.'

'And there were other lions there too?'

'Plenty. I came round lying in the shade, my eyes slowly focusing on a face I'll never forget. The man was squatting beside me. A bearded apparition with long dark hair and this patch over one eye. He held out a canteen of water, saying, "And here's me thinkin' you was plannin' to do a perish out here! Take a wee drop o' this, laddie, and we'll be havin' a look at the mess old leo has made o' that arm". The next thing I remember is waking up beside a fire. It was dark but a full moon enabled me to make out my saviour. For a moment I thought it was Jesus Christ. He introduced himself. "Michael Duffy, at your service." I tried to move my right arm and couldn't. It seemed to be on fire. He'd cleaned me up as best he could but wanted to dress the damage with fresh milk and castor oil.

' "How far's your camp?" he asked, and I told him.

' "Then it's best we get moving. These things have a habit of turning nasty very quickly. The horses are ready. There's no sign of yours so the lions probably got him. Selous's horse, Bottle, was killed by *tau* not far from here".

'The horses turned out to be two wiry ponies, one of which had a more than adequate pair of tusks slung on each side of it. "Where's the lion?" I asked. "With his maker", Michael said. "The skin's a bit rough but it should fetch a bob or two. Listen and you'll hear the hyena tidying up". He helped me into the saddle. It was a type I didn't know but most comfortable.'

'What was it?'

'An Australian stock saddle. I've used them ever since. The front arch sits well clear of the withers and it's got a deep channel to keep pressure off your horse's backbone. The cantle is higher than usual and well padded so you tend to sit back against it. Most have long flaps, knee rolls and a double tongue girth, though I personally prefer a circingle.'

'You're digressing.'

'You asked. Michael walked, leading both ponies one behind the other, my rifle held by the barrel over his shoulder.'

'How old was he?'

'Mid to late forties, I suppose. Very fit and strong. He had this theory that if animals could hear you coming they would invariably move out of the way.'

'Meaning?'

'Michael talked or sang as he walked, alternating between what he called Australian bush poetry by some chap called Paterson and a variety of hymns. It took us over eight hours to get back and never once did he repeat himself.'

'Did Michael stay?'

'For a couple of weeks. He changed my dressings every day. Luckily we had plenty of fresh goat's milk and castor oil – though that was no guarantee the wounds wouldn't turn septic.'

'Mister Selous's remedy is to cauterise any wounds caused by a lion with carbolic acid.'

'Ouch. How on earth do you know that?'

'He's a friend of Father's.'

'Remind me never to hunt lions with Dallas.'

Meggie laughed. 'He also says that lions possess two requisites for terrestrial happiness – a good appetite and no conscience.'

Stanley laughed too.

'Obviously you survived.'

'Thanks entirely to one Michael Duffy.'

'That's quite a story. You must be good friends?'

'Sadly no. Michael would leave camp each morning and bring back meat for the boys. Either that or just get away on his own. One day he didn't come back.'

'What, never?'

'We waited for over a month but heard nothing. He'd simply disappeared, leaving behind a pony, one salted lion skin and two very fine tusks.'

'The ones that are now at *Kingsway*?'

'He'll come for them one day. Him or his son. But that's another story.'

★

Meggie and Tanith had few secrets from each other. Although older by two years, it was more often than not Tanith who sought a confidential ear – even advice – from her level-headed and seemingly unflappable best friend. She usually prefaced a need to talk by saying that her brothers simply wouldn't understand.

Because both girls worked at Empangeni hospital they saw quite a lot of each other and at least once each week Meggie would spend a night at the Taylors'. Lorna didn't mind being on her own at *Morningside* and was actually glad that her daughter had such a close friend to talk to. Meggie always made sure her mother knew when she wouldn't be home.

Meggie could hardly believe what she had just heard. 'Are you sure?'

'I'm never late, Meggie. You have to help me. What do I do?'

'And it's definitely Duncan's?'

'Of course. We . . . well, we didn't mean to. It only happened once. There was so much blood. Oh God, Meggie, what am I going to tell my parents? What will Duncan say?'

'What will Duncan do is probably more to the point.'

'Yes, but he isn't here and a letter will take weeks to reach him, if it ever does. He may be dead, Meggie. Right now he may be dead and he'll never know. All I'll have of him is his bastard child.'

'So you want this baby?'

'Yes. Well, yes and no. Oh hell, Meggie, what do you mean?'

'They say that a bottle of gin and a very hot bath . . .'

'Don't be so stupid.'

'Then face facts, Tanith. This must have happened at the end of January. At least you two are engaged. Simple solution. Get married.'

'I wish it were that easy. Duncan might be away for ages and you know what my father's like.'

'Then we'll just have to give everybody blindfolds.'

Tanith smiled, placing a hand on her stomach.

'Are you feeling sick in the mornings?'

'A bit.'

'That'll pass. If you're lucky, nothing will show for a few months. Write to Duncan. Do it now, tonight. Post the letter tomorrow morning. There's time. It'll be our secret. I've got something to tell you too. It's also a secret. Pact?'

'Pact.'

'You know that patient they brought to the hospital after Spion Kop?'

'The big man with dark hair?'

'That's the one. Stanley King is his name. He farms at Nkwalini.'

'Sister says he's lucky to be alive.'

'Apparently it was Cameron who saved him. He knows Father too.'

'I've noticed you talking to him.'

'Well, that's the man I'm going to marry.'

Her own situation suddenly forgotten, Tanith's

mouth fell open and she stared at her friend in shocked disbelief. 'But he's so . . . I mean, well . . .'

'Old, is that what you're trying to say?'

'Yes. Not that it matters, I suppose.'

'Tanith, he's so different. He talks to me, not at me. He's done so many exciting things.'

'That's hardly surprising at his age.'

'No, no. You don't understand. Apart from Father he's the only man I've ever met who goes out and actually makes things happen. He's had more than his fair share of setbacks but when something goes seriously wrong there seems to be an angel sitting on his shoulder. He and I were destined to meet. I can feel it.'

'Isn't he going home soon?'

'Yes, and he's asked me to go and see his farm. It's called *Kingsway*.'

'Will you go?'

'Of course.'

SEVENTEEN

Lord Roberts was ecstatic but little did he realise the war was about to change. While Bobs confidently consolidated his position in Bloemfontein before pressing on to Johannesburg and Pretoria, his adversaries – Kruger and Steyn – were holding a council of war in Kroonstad. Many Boers had become demoralised, worn down by the seemingly endless stream of fresh and better equipped troops being thrown against them. The British lion had mobilised significant colonies, bringing regular soldiers, idealistic volunteers, even noncombatants, from places as far away as Australia, Canada, New Zealand, India and the small island of Ceylon. Kruger realised that the many Uitlanders who fought alongside his Afrikaner *volk* were just that: outsiders. Although Germany and Holland maintained close links with Pretoria, their open intervention in the war was unlikely. Another solution had to be found.

It came from The Lion of the West, General Koos de la Rey, and veteran leader Christiaan de Wet. Together they advocated tactics which would capitalise on their *komandos'* better mobility to exploit the enemy's ever-extending lines of communication and supply: no wagons, waverers or camp followers, only those committed to the cause, each responsible for his own horse and provisions – hit-and-run flying columns. The proposal was adopted.

Serious problems were becoming evident in Bloemfontein itself. Water rationing had been introduced but many resorted to drinking from the Modder, a river heavily polluted by countless carcasses from earlier confrontations and the excrement of man and beast alike. The army-run hospital found itself unable to cope with four-and-a-half-thousand who succumbed to enteric fever – typhoid, as it was better known, would kill over a thousand in just four weeks.

To compound the problem, de Wet struck at Bloemfontein's waterworks, destroying the pumping station at Sannah's Post twenty miles to the east. While there he had a stroke of unexpected good fortune, ambushing Brigadier-General Broadwood's 2nd Cavalry column. An urgent SOS was sent to Lord Roberts, who, fearing an attack on Bloemfontein itself, did nothing. De Wet took over four hundred prisoners, capturing seven artillery pieces and a hundred and seventeen wagons. One of them contained mailbags, the contents of which were carefully checked before being burnt. The letter from Tanith to Duncan was of no interest to anyone.

★

Stanley King could probably have gone home sooner but he was in no rush. During his time in hospital he had received not a single visitor and only one letter, an official envelope containing his honourable discharge from active duty. Attached to it was notification that his bravery at Spion Kop had been Mentioned in Despatches.

Slowly his wounds healed, inside and out. He read newspapers and books – anything he could lay his hands on – often falling asleep in his own special chair which Meggie had placed outside on the shaded verandah. They talked a great deal about all manner of things and played games of chess which progressed a few moves at a time.

'It's not fair,' Meggie laughed, knocking over her white king. 'You have all day to think about your next move.'

'And thought about it I have. It's time I got back to the farm. Doctor Parry's little exercises are all very well but they're not getting anything done.'

'At least you won't be going back to Ladysmith.'

'Judging by the *Mercury*, Buller doesn't seem to be doing much either. He's got fifty-five thousand men sitting on their backsides and Roberts won't let him do a damned thing with them.'

'He thinks the war is nearly over but Buller doesn't agree.'

'And in my armchair editorial opinion, the man's quite right. Boers still control Van Reenen's Pass and the Biggarsberg. Even in Natal they're a long way from being beaten.'

'That reminds me: did you read in the paper that Piet Joubert died in Pretoria?'

'I saw that. He never fully recovered after falling from his horse. Louis Botha's taken over so that should shake things up a bit.'

'Right, Mister King, to more pressing matters. How do you intend getting home?'

'I thought you might like to take me. It would be a chance to see the place.'

'Somehow I don't think my mother would agree.'

'Not on your own, of course. I need supplies so if it were possible to borrow a wagon . . .?'

'I suppose Mister David could drive. It's a bit over thirty miles, isn't it?'

'Yes, but there and back in a day might not be possible. It will depend on the road.'

'Let's cross that bridge when we come to it. I'll speak to Mother.'

'Good.'

Meggie was surprised when Lorna readily agreed that Stanley King could borrow a wagon and use Mister David as driver for his return to Nkwalini. 'After all, he is an old friend of your father's,' her mother said.

'Then you won't mind if I go along too? Stan – Mister King has invited me to see his farm.' For one terrible moment Meggie thought that her mother might want to come too.

'Of course not, my dear. You'll like it up there. The country is quite different from here: much drier.' With that she changed the subject. 'Now, come and see what Aminta has been doing in the vegetable garden. We're going to try something new this year. Suza! Saba! Come on.' Only one dog followed.

Mister David and Meggie arrived at the hospital just after seven in the morning. Stanley was already sitting in his chair on the verandah, wearing a dressing gown over the only clothes he had: his hospital pyjamas.

'I think we forgot something,' he said as Meggie walked towards him.

'Try these. They're Duncan's. The boots might be a bit tight but it was the best I could do. See if they fit while I have a quick word with Matron.'

When she returned, Stanley was talking to Mister David. The borrowed shirt and trousers were obviously too small, a fact further emphasised by his bare feet.

'No luck with the boots, I'm afraid. David's put them in the wagon. Shall we go?' He didn't seem a bit embarrassed about his comical appearance.

They spent an hour at the Pioneer store, loading up with goods ranging from nails to mealie meal, potatoes, sugar and tea. The Zulus who were hanging around obviously knew him and Meggie heard the word *Ndlovu* on more than one occasion.

The journey to Nkwalini was uneventful yet it took nearly six hours, the lush coastal vegetation soon left behind as they followed the river valley then climbed into rolling hills covered with acacia scrub. Mister David pointed out a spiral-horned kudu motionless in the bush watching them, its colour and striped markings making it nearly invisible. Only the occasional twitch of an ear gave it away.

'*Tolo*, they're called in Bechuanaland,' Stan commented. 'Nice eating too.'

'Then it's a pity you haven't got your rifle or that would be dinner taken care of.' Meggie realised her words were a way of saying that she and Mister David wouldn't be leaving until the next day.

'I have no idea what we'll be eating tonight.' Stan had understood Meggie's meaning.

There was virtually no traffic on the rough road, though the Zulus they passed invariably raised a right hand, palm open in the traditional sign of friendship. Some even called out, welcoming *Ndlovu* or simply having a conversation with Mister David until they were out of earshot. This created a good feeling.

Kingsway seemed dry and dusty compared to *Morningside*. It was sprawling, with newly constructed fences and an extensive Zulu kraal of at least a dozen domed dwellings. The main house appeared surprisingly small, dominated by a huge ornately carved front door. There was no garden except for what looked like a few small sisal plants.

'Water can be a bit of a problem up here,' Stanley said, as if reading Meggie's thoughts. He greeted everybody from his *induna*, down to the smallest *abantwana*, calling each by name. Two babies had been born in his absence and these were proudly brought to him for inspection.

After making arrangements to unload and outspan the wagon, Stanley made sure that Mister David would be looked after before he and Meggie walked over to his house.

'Mustn't forget to give you back your brother's clothes. They'll be washed and dry by tomorrow.'

Standing before the huge front door Meggie realised just how thick and solid it was.

'Once belonged to David Livingstone,' Stan told her, pushing it open. 'I'll show you to your room and have some water brought in. Candles are by the bed.'

The house had one central room which the front door opened onto. Opposite was a large stone fireplace – big enough to sit in – with logs piled beside it. There were two doors in the right hand wall and one opposite.

'Your bedroom, my bedroom, kitchen,' Stan said, pointing out each in turn.

'Are those the tusks you were telling me about?' Meggie indicated two long narrow teeth on either side of the fireplace.

'No. Michael's are under my bed. They're much bigger.'

Meggie didn't ask to see them.

Stan excused himself to give instructions. On the table – which seemed to be used for everything – was a charcoal sketch held flat by four pieces of crystalline and gold rock. She lifted one, testing its weight. A corner of the drawing curled back.

'Unfortunately, it's only iron pyrite,' Stan's voice came from the open doorway. 'They call it fool's gold.'

Embarrassed at being caught snooping, Meggie almost dropped the heavy paperweight. 'Did you do the drawing?'

'A long time ago, before that damned east coast disease nearly wiped us out. I leave it there to remind me of what this house will look like one day.'

'It's good. I like it.'

'Come, let me show you round.'

There wasn't really much to see but Meggie loved every inch of it. The drawing was one man's dream that she knew would eventually become a reality.

They ate chicken peri-peri, spicy, hot and tough as old boots. 'Sorry about the food,' Stan said. 'Give me more warning next time and I'll come up with something better.'

'It was fine,' Meggie lied. 'Next time sounds good.'

They said goodnight, both aware that one word, one touch, was all that would be needed to change their relationship for ever.

'*Rabala sentle*,' Stan smiled. 'That's Setswana for "sleep well". And thank you.'

Meggie lay in the strange bed thinking about the picture and things she would one day add or change. How much of it was conscious thought and how much dreaming was impossible to tell.

Meggie and Mister David left at eight o'clock the following morning.

Eight weeks after Torben and Gerda had first been interrogated, a nervous maid announced the arrival of three official visitors. Gerda was, once again, terrified, so frightened in fact that the callers had to reassure the very pregnant lady of the house that their visit had nothing whatsoever to do with her. It was then that the penny dropped for Torben who, characteristically, exploded with anger before calming with the realisation that something important was sought of him, something which could prove significantly profitable.

All four men were comfortably seated in Torben's study. 'Mister Petersen,' the spokesman said without introducing himself, 'we understand you recently supplied General Buller with a number of artillery pieces to replace some that were unfortunately, shall we say, stolen near Colenso. May we ask from where you obtained such specialised items?'

Torben hesitated, reluctant to divulge his source of supply yet aware that if he didn't, collaboration with the enemy might be assumed.

'We understand your reticence and apologise for having to force the issue.'

A slightly younger man leaned forwards. 'Truth of the matter is, those guns were of the very highest quality. Most certainly not ours: the barrels were so much better. We think they came from Germany. As you can imagine, this could place us, and to some extent yourself, in a most awkward position.

The service you provide is not in question but your sources could prove embarrassing. Everything has to be above board, I'm sure you can see why.'

Torben nodded in agreement. He was well aware of the political dangers peculiar to his business.

The older man spoke again, this time more harshly. 'So. From where did they originate?'

'I'm simply the middle man, you understand.'

'We do.'

'They're shipped out of Copenhagen.'

'Denmark! That explains it.' All three sat back in obvious surprise.

'I have family connections.'

'That's excellent. And you can obtain more?'

'Most certainly.' Torben saw money floating before his eyes. Was this the chance he'd been waiting for? A couple of years earlier, when the trust fund established by his true mother became available to him, Torben had found the contact he needed in Europe. Jette Petersen's banker brother, Olaf. Albeit in different languages, both men had seen the same writing on the wall, though for them it was red map of British colonial Africa and it didn't take them long to work out an arrangement profitable to both parties, draw up an agreement and invest in stock.

'When?'

'I can provide five breech-loading 12-pounders right away. Anything else would need a little longer.'

Three sets of scheming eyes met in silent jubilation. 'And how long would that be?'

'Six to seven weeks.'

'That fast, eh? Very well, Mister Petersen, five it is. Same price, same terms. Cash. Fifty percent down, balance on delivery to the fort here in Durban.'

The third man, who up until now hadn't spoken, rose and extended a hand to conclude their deal. 'I don't need to mention that this is all very hush-hush.' Producing a key from his fob watch pocket he opened the brass latch locking a well-worn leather case.

'Say no more.' Torben rose, trying to conceal his excitement. 'Discretion is an essential part of my business.'

'Excellent.' The man glanced briefly at his companions. 'Howitzers?'

'Size?' Torben slipped into familiar territory.

'Five-inch, breech-loading.'

'How many?'

The man rubbed his chin. 'Let's say ten to start with.'

Visions of impending wealth were rushing around in Torben's head. Outwardly he remained calm. 'Within the week.'

'Where from? The original source, please.'

'Czechoslovakia.'

'Only the best.'

Business concluded, the three men shook his hand. 'We'll be in touch,' the youngest said as they departed.

Torben returned to the study and sat staring at the pile of money they had left on his desk. He was in. Now all he had to do was deliver.

Gerda appeared in the doorway, her frame almost blocking it. 'What did they want?' she asked, entering the room.

'Can't you see?' He picked up a bundle of Bank of England promissory notes and waved them in the air. 'They're hooked, my darling.' Reaching out an arm he eased her onto his lap. 'This is the break-through I've been waiting for. Gerda, this is where we get rich.' Torben was bubbling with excitement. 'You don't have to worry anymore. It's not you or your family they're interested in, it's guns, lots and lots of lovely guns. Long may the war continue.'

'Is it dangerous?'

He gently kissed her. 'Not at all, poppet. Queen Victoria wants what I sell. It's as simple as that. Didn't I tell you it was a perfect time to be in the arms business?'

'Does that mean we can buy a better house?'

'Patience, dearest. Wait a while and you can have whatever you like.'

'Oh, Torben. Something big, on the Berea, and a new carriage.' His happiness was infectious and spread through her. 'A shiny black one with leather seats. Lanice will be green with envy.' Gerda loved to lord it over her sister. 'Our baby will have noth-ing but the best.'

'Indeed,' Torben said, absent-mindedly stroking her arm. 'He or she will be blessed by our good fortune.'

'It's a boy, Torben. I can feel it.'

★

Lord Roberts was far from happy with the deteriorating situation around him. Despite the apparent success of his olive branch offer to a war-weary enemy, de Wet was still running riot, easily avoiding French and Colvile, who had been attempting to curtail his activities since the setback sustained at Sannah's Post. With only eight hundred hand-picked men, de Wet had surprised the British garrison at Reddersberg and in twenty-four hours forced its surrender. The Royal Irish Rifles lost nearly fifty officers and men, with over five hundred more taken prisoner and sent by train to Pretoria. Bobs took his anger out on the much-decorated veteran Lieutenant-General Gatacre, who soon found himself on a ship bound for home, replaced by Sir Archibald Hunter from Natal.

De Wet's flying column had since swung south, laying siege to a force three times its strength at Wepener. Doggedly, the largely colonial troops held on, digging in and beating back attack after attack until finally, sixteen days later, de Wet gave up and disappeared to the north, unwilling to engage an infantry relief column which was slowly plodding towards him.

Although Presidents Kruger and Steyn were seeing the success of changed tactics, they still believed that Lord Roberts's advance on Johannesburg and Pretoria could not be stopped solely by such an unconventional strategy. Time was running out.

★

Tanith was just over three months pregnant when Duncan first learned of her condition. Having received no word from home in more than six weeks he had no idea that she anxiously awaited his response to a letter posted in the middle of March.

She could hardly believe that her fiancé didn't care, but when the pregnancy could no longer be disguised, Tanith broke down and told Lorna. The reaction was not at all what she had expected.

'That's wonderful news, darling. Your mother and I were wondering when you were going to say something. Duncan must be delighted.'

Tanith shook her head in a mixture of amazement and relief. 'That's what I don't know,' she said. 'I told him in a letter weeks ago but he hasn't replied.'

Lorna took over. 'That boy never writes to me either, so I tell you what, we'll send a telegram to his father. That should shake things up a bit.'

Duncan stared at the telegraph message Dallas had handed to him. 'Congratulations, son. This might have raised a few eyebrows in Empangeni but, judging by the look on your face, that won't bother you one little bit. While we are here, might I suggest you allay the young lady's fears with a few well-chosen words in reply?'

Duncan pulled a blank form from the pad, found a pencil and wrote. His missive was considerably longer than private messages were allowed to be, but the operator had nothing else to do and turned a blind eye to regulations.

EIGHTEEN

The night had been bitterly cold and Cameron felt its pre-dawn bite through the thin army blanket. He lay in a foetal position trying not to move, one hand thrust between his legs for comfort and warmth. Dawn was touching the veld. Soft pink fringed the cloudless curtain of darkness as one by one the stars disappeared.

'Wake up, sir.' An out-of-place voice cut through cotton-wool thoughts of Ginnie. Fragments of a distant dream fled with the opening of his eyes, only to be replaced by the acne-scarred face of Sergeant-Major Mulligan hovering above him.

'Thank you, Sarn't-Major,' he said, rising to a sitting position, shivering and surveying a frost-covered landscape dotted with flat-topped kopjes. 'Anything to report from the sentries?'

'Nothing of consequence,' the older man replied, pressing a battered tin mug of steaming coffee into his commanding officer's hand. Cameron took a grateful sip of the strong black brew and raked a hand through his longer than usual hair. The detachment of specially selected men spoke softly as they went about their business preparing for another day in the saddle, hounding the retreating *komandos* of Steyn and de Wet.

Lord Roberts's stop-start advance through the Free State had taken Kroonstad and on 16 May Mahon's column moving north met up with Plumber's largely colonial force coming down from Rhodesia. Together they put to flight a two thousand strong *komando* under Koos de la Rey.

The following day, a predominantly Uitlander-comprised Imperial Light Horse had the honour of relieving Mafeking, where a deceptively small force commanded by Colonel Robert Baden-Powell had held out for an amazing two hundred and seventeen days. There was nothing of strategic importance about this northern Cape railway town but it had served to tie down significant Boer resources which might otherwise have been better deployed elsewhere.

At home, a war-hungry British public fed on the news as herald of an inevitable victory over the Boer republics. To entertain the middle class as it sat down to breakfast *The Times* ran stories lauding the garrison's ingenuity: 'The Wolf', a gun fabricated from four-inch steel pipe, capable of lobbing an eighteen-pound shell at targets over two miles distant; 'Lord Nelson', a 1770 naval cannon brought back into service for Queen and country; dynamite grenades made of empty bully-beef cans; an internal railway system fuelled by cow dung and coal. The British public lapped it up, believing that the war was as good as over. For the men fighting in South Africa, reality was another thing altogether.

Roberts's main army was about to cross the Vaal. He remained grudgingly respectful of the way de la Rey had kept intact his army of wagons, men and heavy guns, destroying the railway in his wake and burning tinder-dry winter grass to help his snipers pick off khaki uniforms against the blackened background.

In Natal, General Buller had at long last commenced his advance north from Ladysmith, pushing past Dundee to Newcastle, outflanking seven thousand Boers entrenched in the Biggarsberg and forcing their retreat. Again he stopped to consolidate his position.

It had been Cameron's oft-repeated acts of gallantry both during and after the siege of Ladysmith that had drawn attention in the right circles. Early in May, as part of Ian Hamilton's division, he had been transferred to Lord Roberts's army in the Free State. Now he found himself in command of his own troop. Given the rare opportunity to select men from the South African Light Horse, he had done so with specific criteria in mind, choosing mainly those with knowledge of and experience in the veld – farmers, former hunters and one-time traders – all in their own way pioneers of the few little-known places still left on the African continent. Most were Cameron's seniors and he knew that despite a reputation for success, he was yet to prove his worth as their leader. Out of respect for his age and safety, Will Green was not one of them.

Grudgingly, but with no choice in the matter, he remained with Buller in Natal.

Before the war, Sergeant-Major Mulligan had built railways, living rough and leading his own team of track layers. He was in his late thirties. The younger of his two subalterns, Lieutenant Grantley Christison, was a farmer from the Cape and so far seemed to know what he was doing. Two Zulus also rode with the troop, acting as trackers and messengers.

Cameron did not wear any sign of rank in the field, knowing from past experience that should there be any Boer sniper in the area, it would make him a prime target. He also scorned the wearing of a revolver – another sign of a commissioned rank – and carried a Lee Metford carbine, as did his men.

Rising to his feet, Cameron gulped down the remaining coffee before it cooled in the sub-zero temperatures. Rations were consumed cold. The only fire lit that morning had been carefully concealed behind blankets and used only to heat a blackened pot of coffee. Even that might have attracted unwanted attention. Hamilton himself had lost over sixty men in skirmishes since he had chased Steyn from his last provincial capital at Lindley.

The two section commanders came to Cameron as they did each morning before moving out. A winter sun had put in a wan but very welcome appearance and all three men squatted beside a map spread on the ground in front of them. After the briefing, Cameron took questions to clarify any points of doubt then, without fuss, the others returned to their men, who were already mounted and impatient to get going.

It was just another day for Captain Granger-Acheson. As he swung himself into the saddle of his big bay gelding, Cameron had no idea that he was within sight of the kopje where Frazer lay buried. Of the lions there had been no sign.

Torben rose that same day to a typical Durban winter's morning. It was chilly but not really cold and the kitchen range, which burned all night, warmed the whole house. He slipped from bed leaving Gerda in a deep sleep snuggled beneath a patchwork quilted eiderdown.

Shivering, Torben dressed and made his way downstairs where a pan of porridge bubbled on the hob and fresh paw-paw had been laid out for him. He ate quickly, the early hour's silence broken only by the soft tick-tock of a grandfather clock standing imperiously in one corner.

Torben removed a fob watch from his pocket and compared the time. It was nearly five-thirty – he had half an hour to catch the train. A note for Gerda would reassure her that his trip north would not put him in peril. Before going to his study he slipped into the nursery. The arrival of his daughter, Alice, a little over three weeks earlier, had been one of the most joyful events of his life. He smiled down at the peaceful sleeping face and adjusted a blanket to keep her warm. Alice had been born on the first day of May and Torben felt the date to be auspicious. In Europe it was the old pagan day of celebration, summoning an abundance of crops and wealth in the coming summer. The birth had been relatively easy for Gerda. She had strong, child-bearing hips – not to mention the determination of tough farming forebears who had smashed the Zulu *impis* at Blood River during the Great Trek away from British occupation in 1838.

Torben felt a lump in his chest as he stared down at his tiny daughter, who remained blissfully unaware of his presence and slept with her eyes tightly closed. 'Papa has to go away for a while, my precious, but when he returns, our lives may be very different. All being well, I will make you a true princess. One day you will wear diamonds and gold from the mines of this vast country. It is not without risk,' he added sadly. 'But to give you all that I was denied will be worth every moment of it.' He leaned forwards, gently kissing Alice on the forehead, smelling her milky scent, and a surge of love rushed through him. From that moment he knew that she had become his world.

Going quickly to the study, Torben scribbled a note explaining that he had been called away on urgent business and would be home in a few days. After stating his love, he blotted and folded the single sheet and left it in the drawing room for Gerda to find. Torben knew that had he attempted to discuss his trip into an area still in a state of war she would have raised objections. He was not willing to argue with his wife. With a newly born baby she would have plenty to occupy her during his short absence.

Unshaven, Torben closed the front door behind him and with little more than a small suitcase, had his waiting carriage take him to the railway station.

Cameron's day of riding the veld proved hot and dusty, a cloud of choking ash announcing the presence of his men to all and sundry as they plodded through what seemed endless miles of burnt grassland. The occasional farmhouse and outbuildings showed no signs of life. Cameron ensured that they skirted any obvious pockets of European habitation as they were well into what was still considered hostile territory. As far as he could ascertain, they had not been sighted by the enemy. If they had, their nondescript uniforms would have made them look like a Boer patrol – a *ruse de guerre* but one necessary to carry out their mission.

Cameron rode point, beside him his NCO, Sergeant-Major Mulligan. The others fanned out on either flank, cautiously moving forwards to spy out the country. At night the column would regroup and form a defensive *laager* until the following morning. The young captain realised that one of his key roles as their leader was to set an example. Although he often wished to call a halt, dismount and light fires in anticipation of the night ahead, he knew that the safety of his men demanded a stoic face which ignored any personal craving for comfort.

'We going to risk a fire tonight, Captain?' Mulligan asked, as if reading Cameron's thoughts.

'Only if we are well hidden from prying eyes,'

Cameron replied. 'Perhaps a gully with some dry camel thorn which will burn without giving away our position.'

The warrant officer merely nodded. He agreed with the decision, tough as it was. The Boers were just as careful. A fire on the open veld could cost men their lives. Mulligan was yet to see how his commanding officer would react to conflict. He was not a man who accepted reputations without verifying them for himself.

'Sir!'

Cameron turned to see the youngest member of his patrol pointing off to their right flank where a cloud of dust indicated a rider galloping towards them.

'I think we have something,' he said.

The breathless African pulled up his mount, steam snorting from the hard-ridden horse's nostrils. '*Nkosi*. Boer patrol. Seven men and one wagon over the next hill. They do not know we are here.'

'Sarn't-Major,' Cameron responded, 'call in the flankers. We might manage a prisoner or two.'

Mulligan wheeled away to signal the others while Cameron and the black messenger went back to the ridge, dismounted and crept forwards to observe the valley beyond. Sure enough, a small group of armed Boers were escorting an ox-wagon driven by an African. The enemy seemed quite relaxed, slouched in the saddle, rifles slung over their backs. They were moving slowly north and Cameron's patrol outnumbered them three to one.

Good odds for the young captain. He also had the element of surprise.

Cameron glanced over his shoulder and could see his men already grouped under the watchful eye of Sergeant-Major Mulligan. The two men moved back to where their horses were haltered a few yards behind the crest, mounted and rejoined the troop.

Cameron slid from his saddle and used a dusty boot to kick clear a patch of ground. The section commanders joined him in a huddle as he scratched a rough diagram in the dirt. 'Right. This is the rise up ahead.' Cameron pointed to the slight slope. 'We are here, and there are seven mounted Boers with a wagon moving in this direction.' Using the curved tip of his Bowie knife Cameron drew a mark. 'Sarn't-Major, I want you to take six men and move as quickly as possible along a parallel line. Here.' He made another scratch in the dust. 'Keep out of sight until you can cross in front of the enemy then turn in from the east and open fire from that position. Do you understand your orders?'

'Yes, sir,' Mulligan replied.

'Mister Christison,' Cameron said, looking up at his second in command. 'You are to hold back in reserve. Keep your men here, behind the ridge, and only engage the enemy on my direct order. Is that clear?'

'Sir.'

'Good,' Cameron grunted. 'The rest of the troop will follow me. We'll take up line abreast and advance right up their arse. Are there any questions?'

Silence was the answer. The orders were unambiguous, his troops ready for whatever lay ahead. Quickly, section commanders briefed those who would be going with them, then, with a wave to Cameron, Mulligan led his men out, keeping well to the west of their target. The others watched their comrades ride away, wondering what the next hour would bring. When the Zulu messengers reported everybody in place, Cameron had his remaining men mount up and form an extended line facing the slope.

'Walk,' came his next order. Carbines slipped from leather boots attached to their saddles as they moved slowly forwards, Cameron at the centre. Although his troop outnumbered the Boers, he had deliberately split it into three. Cameron had a sick feeling of apprehension. This was his first real command of men in action where he was solely responsible for the plan. In the past, as a junior officer, he had simply carried out orders, albeit with confidence and courage. Now it was all down to him. If things went wrong he would be held responsible.

Cameron checked to see that his reserve troops were in position. Although an officer, Lieutenant Christison was probably the most inexperienced member of his patrol, taken only on the condition that Cameron could select the rest of his troop. The young man came from an influential farming family near Grahamstown and his father had wrangled a commission with the South African Light Horse. The lad was likeable enough and keen to prove himself. Cameron could see that he had understood his orders and was holding his men just below the crest, out of sight of the Boers.

When Cameron's attack section reached the ridge, they saw the enemy in a state of confusion, milling around, pointing, not sure which way to turn. Mulligan's men had cut off the Boers' advance and now the way back was blocked too.

'Into them, boys,' Cameron whooped as his troop thundered down the dusty slope towards an enemy a mere half-mile distant. The fat-spitting crackle of carbines shattered a sleepy Sunday afternoon as the trap closed. Any attempt to fight back was quickly cut short by the scything crossfire. The oxen panicked but with two down in their traces, the wagon was going nowhere. For the Boers there was no possibility of escape as, to a man, they were swept from their saddles. Only the African driver escaped, leaping off the wagon to lie face down in the dirt, hands clasped over his head and ears.

'Bejesus!' Cameron heard one soldier swear beside him when they came to a halt next to the scattered bodies of dead or wounded enemy. 'So quick! Like a bloody surgeon cutting off a leg.'

Cameron knew what the man meant. The attack had started and finished in a matter of seconds. His first action as a commander of men – if only a small skirmish – had gone well, and glancing round he counted all six of the men who had ridden with him. The ambush had been a complete success.

Mulligan rode up and dismounted to check on the wounded. A young beardless boy, wearing dark farming attire and still clutching a Mauser rifle, had been hit through the thigh. He was around fifteen years old and lay on his back, blood pumping from a severed artery that had already soaked the upper part of his trousers with a sticky red stain. The boy's ashen face was filled with pain and he moaned.

'This one's still alive, sir,' Mulligan called, glancing up at Cameron. 'Poor bugger's just a kid. You want to try to talk to him?'

Cameron dismounted and knelt beside the boy, whose eyes were tightly closed. 'Do you speak English?' he asked in a gentle voice, registering the lad's peculiar appearance. His head seemed far too big for the young shoulders it rested on.

'*Ja*,' he answered through gritted teeth, opening grey-blue eyes which lacked any hint of emotion.

'What's your name, son?'

'Gil. Erich Gil. Where is my pa?'

Cameron looked questioningly at Mulligan, who silently shook his head. No others were left alive.

'His father is that one over there.' The African driver spoke in Zulu. His information escaped the rest of Cameron's patrol but not him. He nodded, rose and walked to a body lying face down by the wagon. Turning him over, Cameron saw the sightless eyes of Roth Gil staring back at him. The man's bottom jaw had been shattered, his thick beard already stiff with blood. Mulligan watched with a mix of curiosity and compassion as Cameron closed the dead man's eyes. Cameron knew there was no easy way to do what had to be done and, taking one of Erich Gil's huge hands in his, kept his words short and simple. 'I am sorry, Erich, but your father is dead.'

The boy closed his eyes as tears of despair poured down his cheeks. The life was draining from him. 'It is God's punishment,' he sobbed bitterly. 'Today is the Sabbath and God is punishing me for killing Danny Reese.'

Cameron thought the boy was rambling; he knew what had happened to Danny. 'A lion took Danny,' Cameron said gently, still holding the boy's cold hand.

'No, it was me. I shot him then left his body for the lions. Now God has punished me by taking my father. I don't want to die. I . . .' His voice fell to a whisper and with a strangled sigh Erich Gil slipped into a coma, soon to leave this world due to loss of blood.

Cameron suddenly felt a terrible cold deep inside his body. He had lost a brother to the war and now, whether Erich's confession was true or not, the Gil family would lose a father and son at his hands. The elation of such a small victory paled in the face of one so young dying in this lonely place on the vast veld of Africa. 'What a fuck-up,' Cameron muttered under his breath.

Mulligan had organised a search of the bodies for papers, to retrieve firearms and ascertain the wagon's cargo. As it transpired, there was little to be found. The wagon contained only empty ammunition boxes. Where the original contents might be was anybody's guess.

The two dead oxen were expertly butchered by Lieutenant Christison, who gave each man a piece of backstrap which he could hopefully cook before the meat went off. There was little point in trying to conceal their presence, so fires that night were more than likely.

Cameron intended to take with them the wagon and twelve remaining beasts of burden. The African driver stood off to one side. Cameron turned to him. 'What is a warrior of Dinuzulu doing working for those who treat him like a dog?' he asked in Zulu.

The man – in his mid thirties, Cameron estimated – answered in the same tongue. 'It was not by choice,' he said.

'Then you are free to return to your kraal,' Cameron replied. 'I will give you a blanket and *inyama* for your journey. *Hamba kahle.*'

The Zulu straightened and looked Cameron in the eye. 'You speak my language as one who was born among us. I see you, *ibhubesi. Sala kahle.*'

Cameron had a trooper provide meat and a blanket for the Zulu wagon driver, who accepted the gifts with dignified gratitude. The soldiers were amused to see the African strip off his European clothes, return to the wagon and from under the seat retrieve an *assegai*. Without another word he looked up to stare at the sky. For a moment he stood still, as if sniffing the air, then turned south-east and set off, jogging easily towards the distant Drakensberg.

Cameron watched him go and the transformation was not lost on him. 'We will not see many of his kind in the future, Sarn't-Major,' he said, swinging himself into the saddle. 'Theirs is a world that has not changed for the better.'

'If you say so, sir,' Mulligan replied noncommittally.

That night as he tried to find sleep under his blanket Cameron thought of those they had left behind for the scavengers of the veld. He wondered what would become of the Gil family, whoever and wherever they might be. It was a harsh land under any circumstances, but the death of a husband and son would make it even more demanding for any women and children they had left behind.

The name given to him by the young Zulu had not gone unnoticed. *Ibhubesi* – lion. Cameron liked it.

The journey had taken Torben longer than anticipated, due to the volume of military traffic transporting supplies to General Buller's forward position near Newcastle.

As instructed, he left the train at Glencoe junction only to learn that there was no regular service to the branch line railhead at Talana. Fortunately, a post-cart had been awaiting the train's arrival and Torben managed to bribe the African driver into giving him a highly illegal ride for the fifteen-mile journey.

Now he stood beside a jumble of railway huts and construction materials clutching the single small case, his other hand holding down a ridiculously out-of-place straw boater lest it be swept away by the winter wind that swirled around the desolate station.

Already Torben was regretting the mission and wondered why he had accepted the cryptic invitation to this out of the way place. Between him and the Transvaal capital lay General Buller's force of over ten thousand men. Soon they would be following the main line north towards the mining city of Johannesburg. Torben was still in Natal but close to the Transvaal border, with not a single soldier in sight.

Although he carried a derringer pistol for personal protection, it was not the most reassuring choice – should he actually have to use it. However, standing alone except for a handful of hungry natives lounging around the corrugated iron building that was the station, Torben was glad to have the weapon close at hand. They seemed to be eyeing him with undue interest considering how little he had. Turning his back to them he stared east, into the empty distance beyond the end of the tracks.

The note had said they would meet him on this day and at this place, he nervously reminded himself. Was it a trap? Perhaps they knew he had been procuring armaments for the British. Was the secretive letter smuggled to him from Johannesburg simply the bait to lure him into Boer territory and exact revenge for his role in supporting the hated English? Torben was feeling a chill from the inside and unconsciously patted the pistol in a pocket of his trousers. He turned, noticing that the Africans who had been lounging around the station were no longer there. Torben's fear turned to outright terror. 'Dear God,' he heard himself utter, 'protect me.'

Three riders leading a saddled horse had materialised in the distance. Torben could see that they were watching him with a spyglass. He was carrying the suitcase he had been instructed to purchase from a specific maker of portmanteaus at an address in New Germany. Placing the case between his feet he waited. The signal would be understood only by those who had made contact with him.

Obviously satisfied, the strangers cantered towards him. As they drew close, Torben judged from their appearance that they were Boers from the Transvaal.

'Your name, *Englesman*?' one of the bearded men asked menacingly, a Mauser carbine resting casually on his hip.

'Torben Petersen,' he replied, eyeing the three men with as much confidence as he could muster. 'My name is Danish, not English,' he added, hoping that identifying with his mother's family might help him in some small way.

'Get on the horse, Petersen,' the same man said without any sign of welcome, a fact which did nothing to allay Torben's growing regret at having accepted the curiously worded invitation. It was greed that had lured him to this desolate place and

put his life in the hands of these wild-looking individuals. 'You ride with us.'

And so, some hours later, Torben found himself
sitting in the book-lined library of a larger than
average farmhouse well beyond the Transvaal border, in his hand a crystal glass of fine Madeira
sherry. His unnamed host appraised him studiously
across a solid stinkwood desk. Torben's fears had
lessened somewhat with his more hospitable
reception and a second glass of the fortified wine.

The man spoke perfect English but with a slight
Afrikaans accent. He was in his mid to late fifties,
clean-shaven – unlike most Boer men – and well
groomed, dressed in an expensive European suit so
different from the usual apparel of his Afrikaner
kinfolk. Torben instinctively sensed a fellow not
unlike himself and took the mysterious man to be
a financier or banker.

'Cigar, Mister Petersen?' his host asked, pushing
a wooden box across the desk towards Torben, who
raised a hand politely declining the offer.

'You have my name, sir, but I do not know
yours,' he said.

'Names are of no consequence,' the man
responded, leaning back in his upholstered leather
chair. 'What is important is that I know all about
you and your dealings with our deceitful enemy.'

Torben felt the chill return as hairs on the back
of his neck seemed to rise of their own accord. His
initial fears had been confirmed.

'I can see that you look somewhat concerned at
my statement, Mister Petersen. Fear not. Your

proven success in the arms business is the very reason why we need your help. Having said that, I should provide you with some background as to why you were singled out with an invitation to come here.'

'That would certainly help,' Torben replied, sipping his excellent sherry in silence while his host trimmed, licked and lit a long Dutch cigar.

'Are you a reader of history, Mister Petersen?'

Torben shook his head. For him, reading was restricted to newspaper reports of stock markets and commodity prices.

'Well, I most certainly am and I suggest that we would do well to learn from the civil war which not so long ago divided the states of America. Man for man the Confederates were more God-fearing than their counterparts from the north but they still lost the war. The reason was simple. Defeat boiled down to basic economics. Lincoln's Yankees came from a strong industrial economy with unlimited resources of men, money and materials. Very much like those from the southern states, we Boers are mostly farmers and face the same problems. You see, Mister Petersen, I do not share the belief of my *volk* that we can beat the British lion on the battlefield. Queen Victoria has an empire to draw on and a navy quick to discourage any European nation from coming to our aid. At the moment we still hold Johannesburg and control what the British want most – our goldfields. It needs no crystal ball to know that the city will soon fall. In fact, the good Doctor Krause, who is in charge at the moment, has already concluded a deal with Lord Roberts to hand over everything without any damage to the Rand mines. By way of exchange, we will be allowed twenty-four hours in which to withdraw our *komandos*. We shall of course take much more than men, but the Little Man can have his victory parade through the streets.'

'Sir, I must ask why you should trust me with such information, or for that matter whatever else you have in mind?' Torben sensed that the answer was probably beyond his wildest imagination.

'Your father may be Scottish but you owe no allegiance to Queen Victoria and have a wife who is one of us.' The man leaned forwards, releasing a stream of blue cigar smoke that added to the eye-watering atmosphere of the dimly lit room. 'I also happen to know that Dallas Granger-Acheson is no longer willing to underwrite your more ambitious enterprises.'

'And you suppose such knowledge is sufficient to contract my loyalty?' Torben countered, suddenly feeling more confident.

'Certainly not, Mister Petersen. The future of your daughter – Alice, I believe – not to mention what I am about to place in your possession are much more persuasive reasons for assisting our cause. You are a man like me: a man who understands that the world of entrepreneurs does not know the meaning of national boundaries. When this war is over the true survivors will be those who profited from the stupidity of weaker men motivated by vague ideals of loyalty and causes which will soon be forgotten in the annals of history. We – the bankers of this world – have but one master. I have no doubt that you understand my meaning.'

Torben did indeed understand what this cultured Afrikaner was saying. Yes, he had suffered the ignominy of crawling to his family for money. The secret arms deals had given him an opportunity for future investment, but he always seemed to need more cash. Perhaps the answer lay in this smoke-filled room.

'I suspect that what you may propose will suit us both, sir.' Torben noticed the flicker of satisfaction on his host's face.

'In that case, Mister Petersen, I will tell you more – at least as much as you need to know to carry out our mutually beneficial mission. Have you ever heard of the *Broederbond*?'

'Rumours, but that is all,' Torben answered truthfully.

'It is much more than that, I can assure you. If we lose this war, as we are bound to do, it will be the most powerful force left to us in South Africa. Already it lies dormant at every level of our society ready to feed on the British concept of democracy and use it against them to establish an independent nation led by those chosen of the *volk*. As we know from the American civil war, success demands massive levels of finance. In the years ahead you can be one of those who establishes the means for us to achieve that objective.'

Stunned, Torben felt the blood drain from his face. This would be dangerous work and could easily be construed as treason. 'Am I to be a part of the Brotherhood?' he asked, almost whispering.

'No, Mister Petersen. It is best that you are not linked to us in any way at all. You will continue to run your own, most successful business while at the same time acting as our financial agent. A very simple arrangement with little or no risk attached. You are a man known to deliver what he promises. I refer to your arms dealing, of course.'

Torben wondered how much more this man knew.

'So you see, any transactions conducted by your companies would be above suspicion. Needless to say, should you be foolish enough to entertain any ideas of betrayal, we have the ability to reach out and destroy not only you but also those you hold dear.'

The quietly delivered threat was not doubted by Torben, who knew he would be making a pact with the devil. In his mind, reward outweighed the risk. 'Why would I jeopardise the goose with the golden egg?' he countered.

'Sometimes people get hungry,' the man replied. 'Your role in our sacred cause will become too valuable to tolerate failure. Do I have your word?'

After a slight hesitation, Torben leaned across the desk to take his host's hand. 'You do, sir, sworn on the life of my newborn baby.'

The gesture was accepted.

'We will be leaving the Transvaal's coffers all but empty. What the British will never know is how much we have spirited out of the country into international bank accounts. Gold is the universal pacifier and knows no loyalty other than greed.' The man reached into his desk and withdrew an envelope. 'This is a down payment on your first commission,' he said, sliding it over the highly polished surface.

Torben broke the wax seal and his eyes widened in shock. He dared not ask if the promissory note were real.

'One hundred and fifty thousand pounds drawn on the Bank of England,' his host said, delighting in Torben's avarice. 'I am sure that this will be the first of many payments if our trust in you is rewarded.'

Torben sat staring at the neatly written numbers. This was, indeed, far beyond his wildest expectations.

'Future instructions will be relayed by the man from whom you acquired your portmanteau. He will provide the necessary funds and tell you how they are to be disbursed. Do you have any questions?'

Torben shook his head.

'Then that is all. Food and a room have been prepared for you. Sleep well, Mister Petersen. At first light my brothers will take you back to the railhead at Talana.'

With the completion of their business the two men rose, shook hands and walked to the door. Waiting outside was an armed youth of no more than fifteen, his face scarred by some unidentifiable skin condition. He eyed Torben suspiciously before speaking in Afrikaans to the older man, who nodded and said, 'I am sure you understood most of that but it would appear Lord Roberts has annexed the Free State for his distant Queen and renamed it the Orange River Colony. A bit presumptuous of him, don't you think? *Lekker slaap, Meneer Petersen, Lekker slaap.*' With that he turned back into his study and closed the door.

'Come,' the boy said to Torben, indicating that he should follow. His room turned out to be small but comfortable. Brown bread smeared with dripping, cold *boerewors* and a glass of milk were set out by the bed. Torben hated the spicy Afrikaner sausage, hot or cold.

He lay awake in the sagging bed until an over-enthusiastic rooster shattered the pre-dawn silence. Torben fumbled to find the chamber pot, used it, then poured ice cold water into a basin and splashed his face. Dressed, he sat and waited. The door was locked.

No words were spoken as the four men rode back towards the Natal border. Of his host, Carl Johannes Venter, there had been no sign.

Torben was terrified lest he lose the envelope and regularly placed a hand in his pocket to reassure himself that the money was still there. He was already thinking of ways he would invest it for himself and Gerda. Oh yes, given the golden opportunity which the *Broederbond* had provided he could become the richest individual in South Africa. That the deal had made him a traitor to the

British crown was not a consideration. True entre-preneurs rose above petty conflicts. It was they who really ruled the world, and now he had been admitted to their ranks. Did not the bank cheque drawn on one of England's most prestigious insti-tutions prove that? A twinge of guilt touched the edge of Torben's conscience. By accepting the con-tract he was betraying a family who had given their all for Queen and country. Frazer – his half-brother – had died doing his duty. But all families had dark secrets, he consoled himself. His decision would have to become one of them.

What Torben had failed to grasp was that Pres-ident Kruger's deal with Lord Roberts would allow the unhindered evacuation of an army des-tined to wreak havoc on his occupying forces in the weeks and months ahead. The war was far from over.

Soon after Lord Roberts crossed the Vaal River on 24 May, the Fairfax Scouts reported that Louis Botha's *komandos*, chased by Buller from Natal, had joined forces with the ever-elusive Koos de la Rey and were entrenched in the hills south-west of Johannesburg.

While British infantry pressed forwards follow-ing the central railway, two cavalry brigades under Ian Hamilton were sent west to engage the enemy. This they did at Doornkop, the very place from where Doctor Leander Starr Jameson had launched his ill-fated attack on the Transvaal five years earlier. The success was costly but by 30 May, Johannesburg had been surrounded.

Cameron knew that Winston Churchill was with Hamilton, though their paths hadn't crossed. He heard that his friend from the Natal campaign had ridden a bicycle through the suburbs to inform Lord Roberts that the road ahead was now clear. Typical, he thought, wondering if the two men had patched up their differences.

As British troops triumphantly entered the city hauling two huge artillery pieces known as 'Jumping Ginger' and 'Pale Mable' – each drawn by thirty-two oxen – Boer *komandos*, led by Piet de Wet, attacked, and after a fierce fight, either killed or captured over five hundred Irish Yeomanry in supposedly safe territory near Lindley. Those not wounded were marched off to prison camps in the eastern Transvaal. That night, the lions enjoyed an unexpected meal of the bodies left behind.

It was another four days before a Union Jack flew over the Transvaal capital and British prisoners of war held in Pretoria could be released. President Kruger and his government were already gone, smuggled out of the city to Machadodorp, a hundred and forty miles to the east along the same railway line that Winston Churchill had made good his escape just over a year earlier.

Lord Roberts honoured his agreement allowing safe passage to Louis Botha and his men, still believing that the fall of Pretoria meant a virtual end to hostilities. He also extended amnesty to any rank-and-file burghers who would sign an oath of neutrality and return home. Eight thousand did but by then the Little Man realised he had been tricked. The Boer coffers were well and truly empty.

Despite a trail of men left to guard the central railway and other key installations, attacks on Lord Roberts's supply column were becoming serious. On 4 June Christiaan de Wet had pounced on a convoy near Heilbron, capturing fifty-six wagons and taking one hundred and sixty prisoners. Two days later he attacked Roodewal station, seizing a large quantity of ammunition and forcing the surrender of almost five hundred inexperienced militia before blowing up the railway bridge along with anything he couldn't carry away. All attempts to capture de Wet failed and the renamed Orange River Colony became a symbol of Boer resistance.

With renewed enthusiasm, Louis Botha used the British expectation of an unconditional surrender to form a new front sixteen miles east of Pretoria, centred on high ground near the railway at Diamond Hill. With him were over five thousand fighting men and twenty-three heavy guns, mainly the dreaded Maxim pom-poms.

Will Green had never been so bored in all his life. He was not a man to make friends easily and found his mind turning more and more to the trading store he owned near Nsoko in Swaziland. The war should have been a golden opportunity to make money – good money – but he very much doubted that his wives had done any more than maintain a supply of mealie meal and a few basic necessities. They would be brewing beer, of course, and providing the hospitality that traditionally went with its consumption.

These thoughts, together with a growing need to find sexual satisfaction, had led Will to one of the less reputable establishments in Newcastle, where very basic and age-old entertainment was provided to those willing to run the risk of gonorrhoea, syphilis or worse. Will didn't go there for sex alone; he also enjoyed drinking the gruel-like beer, consumed warm and more often than not while it was still fermenting. It was a place where nobody gave him orders or asked questions which might invade his personal privacy.

There was one girl he liked above all the others. Most were Sotho but Florence was a Swazi and spoke Zulu. She talked of her home near Piggs Peak and showed him a vulture's quill containing half a dozen shot-size pellets of gold which she said had been found there by her father. They were her only possession, a means of going home when men no longer wanted her body. Will was devastated when Florence was arrested and shot on charges of spying for the Boers. He never discovered what became of her gold.

Ellie didn't see much of Will but he and Lindsay shared a secret, something acutely embarrassing, about which he naively believed she knew nothing. The elderly trader's venereal disease, if left untreated, would undoubtedly have killed him. He had been very lucky.

★

General Sir Redvers Buller didn't resume his advance until 5 June, crossing onto the Transvaal a week later, taking Laing's Nek – the Gibraltar of Natal – and occupying Volksrust.

'Mark my words,' Winston said, 'this thing's going to drag on.' He and Cameron had almost collided with each other outside the officers' mess in Pretoria. 'Got time for a drink, old chap?'

Two hours later Cameron was warming to the effects of his fourth brandy and soda, though the cigar had made him feel quite sick.

'A whisky man myself but those Dutchies down in the Cape make a fine *brandewijn*, don't you think? I've had a dozen cases delivered to Mother onboard the *Maine*. Hope she knows they're mine and doesn't use them for cooking!' Both men laughed.

'Once we've pushed Botha's blighters back from Diamond Hill, I'm off. There's an election looming at home and, quite frankly, I can probably do more good there than sitting around here waiting for this blasted war to end. What are your plans, Cameron?'

They talked for another hour before Winston excused himself. 'Better not keep Bobs waiting. I'm supposed to be having dinner with him at staff HQ. Goodnight, old chap. So glad I caught up with you.' With that he was gone.

Cameron couldn't face the thought of food but a brisk walk in the bracing chill soon had him feeling better. He wondered what it was that Winston could do in England that couldn't be done where he was right now.

★

Diamond Hill proved to be one of the last set-piece battles of the war. It was a fragmented, two-day affair from which neither side could claim outright victory. British losses far outnumbered those of the Boers, and it was largely colonial troops from New South Wales and Western Australia that finally forced Botha to retreat, escaping eastwards under cover of darkness in a tactical withdrawal which once again saved the main Transvaal army.

During the days that followed, Roberts despatched his Chief-of-Staff, Lord Kitchener, to secure a still-vulnerable lifeline – the railway back to Bloemfontein – which was still coming under attack by Boer *komandos*. Garrisons were established throughout the Orange River Colony and a proclamation issued that any farm buildings found to be harbouring the enemy would be razed to the ground.

A new war had begun, one born of the twentieth century and soon to spawn the horror of concentration camps where men, women and children – irrespective of race – would be confined under woefully inadequate conditions and die in their thousands, more than were ever lost to conventional weapons of war. It was a time destined to haunt Britain for many years to come.

NINETEEN

Lord Roberts wasn't having an easy time of things. Far from it. He had pushed Botha east, away from Pretoria, but reports were coming in that a heavily armed force led by de la Rey and Jan Smuts was gathering in the Magaliesberg, a largely undefended range of hills to his north and west. Sending Kitchener to secure the Orange River Colony had severely depleted his defensive capability leaving no option but to pull Methuen back from the west and curtail French's cavalry pursuit of Louis Botha and his Transvaalers. On 11 July the Fairfax Scouts had narrowly avoided capture when de la Rey mounted three separate attacks, one taking nearly two hundred prisoners at Zilikat's Nek.

'That was a bit too close for my liking,' Fairy admitted to Dallas as they followed yet another change of orders and turned back towards Pretoria. 'I wonder what the Little Man wants of us this time?'

'Your guess is as good as mine. Please God it doesn't get in the way of Duncan's wedding. That's causing enough drama as it is.'

'Whatever do you mean?'

'Didn't I tell you? Tanith's pompous ass of a father has all but disowned the poor girl. Bloody stupid, if you ask me. What's done is done and there's no doubt the two of them love each other. Anyway, to cut a long story short, she's left home and is living on her own.'

'Whoops. Not easy.'

'Certainly isn't. Especially with Duncan so far away. Lorna has been helping where she can but Tanith's mother is in rather an awkward position.'

'I see what you mean. Will they be at the wedding?'

'Doesn't look like it. Apparently the minister is coming out to *Morningside*. I have no idea who will be giving the bride away. If there are half a dozen guests I'll be surprised.'

'What, no Champagne and speeches?'

'I honestly have no idea. August 20 is also Tanith's twentieth birthday, but so many of their friends are away.'

'With luck this war might be over by then.'

The two men just looked at each other. Both knew there was no chance of that.

'At least things might speed up a bit now the Natal line is back in operation. Come to think of it, Fairy, when was the last time you had a break? It would probably do you good.'

'True. Try telling that to our friend *Meneer* Botha. And while you're at it, ask him not to cut south and start a new front in Zululand. The way's wide open and he's got at least seven thousand tried and trusted men with him.'

'Heaven forbid.' Dallas knew it was a distinct possibility.

'Roberts really has no option but to deal with the man once and for all. My money's on our going to the eastern Transvaal.'

'That would seem logical. Should Steyn and de Wet manage to break out of the Brandwater basin, chances are they'll try to join forces with Botha.'

'I wouldn't bank on it. If they avoid Kitchener – and that's a mighty big *if* – it would make sense to move west and keep Bobs busy on two fronts.'

'Hadn't thought of that. And in the Cape?'

'That uprising seems to have fizzled out again. Support for the Boers' cause just isn't there.'

'So it's back to the good old Free State and Natal?'

'In my opinion, yes.' Changing the subject, Fairfax went on. 'Any word from your eldest son?'

'Cam was in Pretoria for a short time. Never saw him, though. Before that he and his troop were down near Lindley.'

The two men fell silent. A perfectly innocent question reminded them both of what had happened there so many months before.

'I told him how to find Frazer's grave. But I don't know if he got the letter.'

De Wet and President Steyn did manage to slip from Kitchener's clutches, taking with them two thousand five hundred loyal burghers and four hundred wagons. Four thousand men were left behind. More than half the entire Free State army had been trapped and forced to surrender at Fouriesburg, but not before setting fire to their entire arsenal of arms and ammunition.

For the next few weeks, de Wet left destroyed supply trains, tracks and telegraph lines in his wake. He headed north and crossed the Vaal, playing hide-and-seek with his pursuers for two hundred miles. Kitchener had a force of almost thirty thousand men out to get him. Eventually he was forced to abandon his wagons and rely on friendly farms for supplies and information. De Wet and his followers survived, slipping past Hamilton at Oliphant's Nek to join up with de la Rey in the Magaliesberg. Fairfax had been right and a furious Kitchener set about implementing Lord Roberts's farm-burning policy, rounding up the families of any Boers who had refused amnesty and carrying them off in cattle trucks to hastily improvised internment camps. It was just the beginning.

Sir Redvers Buller's advance through the Transvaal eventually reached Heidelberg, giving Lord Roberts the confidence he needed to leave Pretoria and resume his pursuit of Botha and Kruger. By 27 July he had taken Middelburg, pushing the Boers back along the railway line to Machadodorp. What he did not know was that President Steyn of the Free State had left the Magaliesberg, slipping past Pretoria to join Kruger and boost the flagging morale of Louis Botha's Transvaal *komandos*.

On 12 August Dallas and Duncan, taking their horses with them, boarded a train destined for Durban. The line was not totally secure but south of Heidelberg Buller had deployed a cavalry brigade and two divisions whose sole task it was to defend the track against de Wet and his marauding bands.

The journey south was slow and uneventful. Both men carried twenty-one-day passes and the heart of each was filled with nervous anticipation. For Duncan it was because of his impending marriage to a bride nearly seven months pregnant whom he hadn't seen since January. Dallas had a much more serious problem. He had completely forgotten Lorna's forty-sixth birthday in June and hoped that being home for their wedding anniversary on 15 August would, in some small measure, make up for it. That aside, there was one stop he had to make on the way back to *Morningside*. It was a mission long overdue. He and his horse left the train at Dargle Road.

The woman who looked down from a shaded verandah seemed strangely familiar. She was probably close to his own age, possibly a little younger, though it was difficult to tell. The burnt-brown skin of her face and arms stood testimony to a life spent out of doors, hair bleached by the sun, bunched and pinned clear of her neck. Her clothing was practical – a man's collarless white shirt, sleeves rolled up, skirt split for horse-riding, boots dusty and far from new. Turquoise blue eyes met his, a knowing smile softening her face.

'Mister Granger-Acheson, if I'm not mistaken.

I wondered when you'd finally get here. Some refreshment, perhaps?'

Dallas realised he was staring. 'That would be most agreeable, madam.' He dismounted. 'You were expecting me?'

'Indeed. Moses will see to your horse. Welcome to *Wakefield*.' She held out a hand, which Dallas took.

'Thank you. It's good to be here.'

Her grip was firm. 'Dallas, isn't it? Call me Caroline.'

'Thank you.'

'And do stop saying "thank you" to everything. If anybody should be grateful, it is I. Please, won't you sit down?'

'Tha—'

Caroline wagged an admonishing finger and they both burst out laughing. She shook a solid brass bell on the table beside her chair and in seconds a stooped Indian woman appeared carrying a wooden tray on which sat a jug of what looked like lemon cordial with sprigs of mint floating in it, two very ordinary glasses and a plate of shortbread. 'Thank you, Popeti. I hope you like *nimbo paani*. Popeti makes it. The limes are freshly squeezed. Help yourself.'

Dallas did, pouring a glass for each of them. He was not sure what to say next.

Caroline sprawled rather than sat, her long legs stretched wide apart in a most relaxed, if unladylike, manner. She spoke first: 'As the years pass, this world seems to become smaller and smaller, don't you think? We have met before, Dallas, all too briefly, I fear. When fate brought your son here not so very long ago I could hardly believe my eyes. They say that family likeness can skip a generation. That afternoon it was not Cameron who stood before me but my father, as a younger man – our father, Dallas – Jack Walsh.'

'Then he did know.' Dallas said it more to himself than Caroline, realising for the first time why his late mother – Lady Pamela Acheson, Countess Dalrymple – had always shown such an affinity for his eldest son. Cameron reminded her, more so even than Dallas himself, of the one-time lover who had been his true father. 'But you said nothing to Cameron.'

'What was there to say? From that moment I knew you would be coming.'

'So it was you with Jack and your mother on the wagon at Howick Falls?'

'Yes, and you who probably stopped all three of us from going over the edge.' She laughed, though at the time it had been far from funny. Dallas thought back to the day during his first trading expedition that he had encountered Jack Walsh with his wife and their daughter. Caroline had been a pretty, if spoilt, young woman determined that they should cross the raging Mngeni River so that she could get to Pietermaritzburg, where she was due to be married. It had come so close to disaster.

'Did you marry the man who made you so determined to take such a risk?'

'Guy. Oh yes, and it was well worth it. We never had any children but for damned near thirty years he gave me a good life. No regrets. The horses are my family.'

'What happened, if you don't mind me asking?'

'*Ingwe*. It had been stealing our chickens. Guy decided to trap it. He only had one arm, you see. Bitten off by a stallion,' she added in response to Dallas's questioning look. 'But that's another story. Something went wrong. He's buried here. Guy loved this place.'

'I'm sorry. And the leopard?'

'I shot it. Took me almost a week to get the bastard. Skin's inside.'

They both fell silent, each with their own thoughts.

'Jack never saw *Wakefield*, did he?'

'Not this farm. We moved here in eighty-three. My father – our father – died the year before, thirteen months after my mother.'

'So he must have told you that we were related?'

'No. I found out quite by chance. He'd kept letters. They're here; I'll show you later. Is Lady Pamela still alive?'

'Sadly, no. She died five years ago.' After a brief pause, Dallas went on: 'It's strange to think that for so long we've both known yet neither of us was aware of the other's knowledge.'

'The past is the past, Dallas. It's the future that matters.'

He nodded, deciding not to ask about her

cousin Sarah, the girl he had once been forced to marry. That too was the past.

'Tomorrow is another day,' Caroline said, banging the arms of her chair as she rose to her feet. Dallas started to get up too. 'Sit, sit,' she quickly admonished. 'You'll be staying the night at least, longer I hope. I'll have a room and bath made ready. Moses will bring in your saddlebags. He can take away anything that requires washing.'

Dallas was not sure what he was feeling as Caroline disappeared into the house. Idly he picked up the book she'd been reading, Mary Kingsley's *Travels in West Africa*, a heavy tome of more than seven hundred pages. Flicking through it he found a smudge of carelessly dropped ash and blew it out. Caroline's voice came from behind his shoulder. 'A remarkable woman and so young. She died of enteric fever while in Cape Town, nursing Boer prisoners of war at Simonstown. Such a waste.'

The early evening air had cooled; soon it would be too cold to sit outside. His gaze took in a view of snow-capped peaks standing sentinel over the distant mountains of Basutoland. Above and behind the house stood an imposing rock-strewn hill, the Inhluzan. *Cameron had been right*, Dallas thought. *It was just like Arthur's Seat in Edinburgh.*

When dinner was over – oxtail stew with dumplings – Caroline opened a bottle of South African port, which she said came from a place called Worcester in the Cape, to accompany home-made oatcakes, butter and cheese. The fortified wine was young but eminently drinkable. Sitting in front of a fine log fire, Dallas asked if he might smoke his pipe. He had noticed a rack of six or more above the fireplace. Guy's, most probably.

'That would be most agreeable,' Caroline said. 'It's an aroma I miss greatly.' She pulled two pins from her hair, leaned back and shook it free using the splayed fingers of both hands as combs to separate and straighten the twisted, shoulder-length strands. 'Mmm, much better.'

Conversation came easily, of immediate things more than distant memories. They would need time. Cameron had obviously told Caroline something of his family. How much she already knew remained unstated.

'Cameron mentioned that he has three brothers. Where are they?'

The lengthy silence from Dallas suggested she should not have asked. 'Sorry. Have I . . .?'

'You were not to know. Frazer, the youngest, was killed shortly before Cameron came here. At the time, he had no idea.' Dallas found he didn't mind talking about his son's death. Caroline was a good listener. He also told her about Torben and Duncan.

'This war is a terrible thing,' she said when Dallas fell silent. 'Guy wanted to go but because of his arm they wouldn't take him. Thank goodness it's nearly over. Tomorrow I'll show you round the farm.'

Dallas was woken by a gentle knocking at his door. The room remained dark and for a few seconds he had no idea where he was. The sound of a rooster welcoming another day told him it had to be close to dawn. Then he remembered finishing the bottle of wine.

'Come in.'

He heard the door open and a shadowy figure shuffled a tea-tray into the room, setting it down on his bedside table before moving to open the curtains. It was still too dark to see.

'*Ngi yabonga*,' he said, assuming it was a Zulu servant.

'Sun's up in fifteen minutes,' Caroline replied. 'The horses are saddled and waiting.' With that she was gone.

'We built *Wakefield* from nothing. You can see most of it from the next ridge.' Caroline dismounted, giving her horse an affectionate rub on the cheek. 'We'll walk them from here.'

They had climbed through a chill morning mist which served to make the silence around them even more noticeable. Occasionally something unseen dislodged a rock as it decided to remain anonymous and move away from the well-worn track their horses were following. Quite suddenly they emerged into a cloudless winter morning, the pale-blue sky stretching away as far as the eye could see. Dallas stopped to take in the view. There again were the snow-covered peaks of the Drakensberg, somehow closer than they had seemed the night before, rising from a blanket of white which filled every valley of the world below.

'It'll take a couple of hours to clear,' Caroline commented as she saw the expression of awe on Dallas's face. 'Not far now.'

She had said nothing about where they were going but the unmarked pile of rocks left no doubt that it was a grave. The track stopped there. 'Hello, Guy. I told you my brother would find me. Well, here he is.'

Dallas felt as if he were intruding. Caroline noticed his unease and laid a hand on his arm. It was the first time they had actually touched.

'We all have to go,' she said softly. 'So often it seems unfair, especially when those we love are taken tragically. Life is a journey. Some roads are longer than others. It's as simple as that. Guy could well have died after he lost his arm. He weathered the storm and carried on for another four years. In the end his heart let him down. In some ways they were the happiest years we had ever known.'

'You said last night that a horse was responsible. If you don't mind talking about it, what actually happened?'

'Not just a horse: a stallion. 'Bright Eyes' was his name. He was by far the best stud in our stable.' They were sitting on an outcrop of rock not yet warmed by the winter sun. 'It wasn't his fault, you know. Just one of those things.'

As she talked her mind drifted back to the day when Guy went to check that all was well with their brood mares and the stallion running with them. There had been a few stock losses in the district – put down to Bushmen from over the border in Basutoland, though no arrests were ever made. It only happened when times were tough in the mountains.

Guy was riding a gelding, Bright Eyes's brother, in fact. He had ridden right up to the mares when, without warning, the stallion lunged at his mount, jaws snapping and teeth bared. Missing his target he tried again, this time grabbing Guy by the forearm and pulling him from his saddle. The terrified gelding quickly made off, pursued by an unnecessarily jealous sibling. Once satisfied that the perceived threat to his harem had been taken care of, Bright Eyes returned and stood over Guy for a good ten minutes before losing interest and moving off to rejoin his ladies.

Caroline realised that something was wrong when Guy's horse came back without him. She found her husband stumbling home, one blood-soaked arm hanging useless, his hand twisted inwards at a peculiar angle. The bite had torn through muscle, severing tendons and nerves. She could see white worm-like things in the gaping wound.

After tying a tourniquet round his upper arm to staunch the flow of blood, Caroline and Moses made Guy as comfortable as they could in the pony trap and set off for the nearest hospital at Howick. Despite every effort to save Guy's arm, the wound turned gangrenous. After ten days the doctor had no option but to amputate it at the elbow. Even then it was uncertain that he would survive.

Caroline paused, picking up a stone and throwing it at nothing in particular. 'So you see, I was lucky. Sorry, correction. I am lucky. You're here, which is good in itself but if I'm not mistaken it also means that Cameron is interested in acquiring *Wakefield*?'

Dallas nodded. 'He is, though the lad seems to know precious little of what might be for sale.'

'Oh, it's for sale all right. Lock, stock and barrel. I just haven't told anybody else. My price is one guinea.'

Caroline's statement – delivered in the same matter-of-fact voice as the story she had just told – turned Dallas's attention from the rapidly dissipating mist to her penetrating blue eyes focused on his face. They told him that she meant it. 'Why?' was all he could think of to say.

'Cameron is my nephew. Family. He's young. Call it a wedding present, call it what you will. There are conditions, of course.'

Dallas could hardly believe what he was hearing.

She went on, 'This will always be my home. Cameron can have the main house but he must build another for me. Something simple. I'll show him where.'

Caroline's words sounded like a well-rehearsed speech. Dallas didn't interrupt.

'Popeti stays with me, as do Moses and his family. I'll pay them, even when I'm away.'

'Away? Away where? I thought you wanted to be here?'

'No. My home is here. One day I will die here. Before that day comes I intend to travel, to do things that have never been possible until now.' She laughed. It was a happy sound. 'I want to ride a camel, see the Sphinx in Egypt, go to Europe and climb that tower in Paris. Who knows? Watch the Derby at Epsom, spend a day at Royal Ascot. Might even try my hand at driving grouse in Scotland. I'm not a bad shot, Dallas. Oh, and one other thing. I want to shoot a lion.'

Although Dallas no longer saw the need to take life in the name of sport, he had once made his living from hunting. It had killed his one-time partner, Logan Burton. He remained silent.

'Cat got your tongue?' she said, smiling at her unintended pun.

'No, not at all. It's a most amazing offer and I only wish Cam himself could hear what you are saying. Are you sure that this is what you want to do?'

'Quite. Though there is one last thing.'

'Name it,' Dallas said.

'No matter what happens in the future, I want to be buried here. Where we are sitting now, beside Guy. Will you promise me that?'

'Of course.'

She stood up, extending her hand to Dallas. 'Then I do believe we have an understanding. I need you to give me a few details about Cameron but that can wait until this evening. Right now I should show you as much of the farm as I can.' Caroline pointed. 'You see where the river runs?'

362

Dallas turned back to look at the valley below. The mist had completely cleared.

The rest of the day was taken up exploring every corner of *Wakefield*. As it was winter, the mealie fields were bare, but Caroline explained her hopes for the extensive plantings of black wattle. 'These trees originally came from Australia. They're only a few years old but as you can see, they're quick growing and need virtually no attention. The bark yield should be around three hundredweight to the acre. We try to plant at least two hundred acres each year, so what's that?'

'Thirty tons annually,' Dallas replied. 'What will happen to it?'

'The raw bark has to be hung and dried before being bagged for export to Europe. It's used for tanning skins.'

'And the value?'

'The bark itself won't fetch much more than five or six pounds a ton but mature trees make excellent mine props and any smaller cuts can be sold as firewood. Nothing goes to waste and it needs no special machinery to plant or harvest so the return on capital employed should be better than any cash crop. That's the theory at least.'

Over a light lunch of cold meat and salad Dallas asked the question he had been putting off. 'Do you see anything of your cousin these days?'

Caroline looked at him before answering. 'Sarah's dead. I thought you knew?'

'No.'

'She was nursing at Intombi.'

'The hospital outside Ladysmith?'

'Yes.'

'What happened?'

'She took her own life. An overdose of morphine.'

'Why?'

'Nobody knows for certain but the coloured man they caught spying for the Boers was said to be her son. He was executed by firing squad.'

Dallas sat in silence for several minutes remembering the deceit that had forced him to marry Sarah, pregnant with another man's child – the Zulu wagon driver, Thulani. 'And her father?'

'He's still in Colenso. They made him mayor, so I heard.'

That afternoon they spent looking at the cattle. An Aberdeen Angus beef herd roamed the unfenced hills with two Zulu herd boys. Dallas spoke to them in their own language and learned that the disease which had decimated so much of Zululand a few years earlier had not reached here.

The river flats sustained half a dozen Friesian cows which they followed to the dairy for afternoon milking by a very large Zulu lady. 'We make our own butter and cheese,' Caroline said, dipping her finger in a bucket of frothing milk and tasting the warm liquid. 'Mmm.'

The pigsty had seen better days but the big blue boar had obviously been busy. Chickens roamed everywhere, scratching for anything that looked edible. They ate well, providing Caroline with a constant supply of tasty, dark-yolked eggs. Behind the house – fenced off from the chickens' attention – lay a neatly furrowed vegetable garden which produced a seasonal stream of fresh produce, enough for all on the farm, Caroline told him.

Finally they came to the horses. 'We're a bit depleted right now. The army wanted everything that was even barely rideable. They paid good money, though. Bright Eyes's blood line is still here. That's one.' Caroline pointed. 'Early Mist. She's done exceptionally well for us.'

Dallas noticed that with his half-sister nothing was ever 'I'.

'Give the girl another couple of seasons and then we'll find the right sire for her. That lot are all in foal.' She nodded towards a fenced field containing between fifteen and twenty fine-looking mares. 'It'll be three months at least before any of them drop. Only time will tell what they turn out like. Too late to become cannon fodder, thank goodness.'

They looked at the stables and next to them an enclosed area used for horse breaking and routine obedience training. A wizened little man of indeterminate age sat on one of the wooden rails chewing a stem of grass, his coal black eyes following their every move. 'That's Klipklop,' Caroline said, waving. 'He's from Basutoland. Part Bushman and the best damned horse trainer this side of Mokhotlong.'

Dallas hadn't the faintest idea where that was.

'Only problem is, he disappears from time to time.'

By five o'clock they were back at the house, where a tray of drinks had been set out on the verandah. Caroline excused herself, saying, 'Help yourself, Dallas. There's *nimbo paani* or whisky. Not much of a choice, I'm afraid. I wasn't expecting guests.'

'May I pour something for you?'

'Just my Popeti special, please – but don't let that stop you having something stronger.'

Dallas gave the lime juice a stir, making a whirlpool of the dissolving sugar and mint, then poured a glass for Caroline before splashing himself a good double dram of Scotch from a cut-glass decanter. The tumblers were just that, probably the same ones they had used the night before. No matter, he thought, savouring the peaty aroma of Glenlivet. It was not just any malt, but George Smith's original. The Glenlivet – a rare treat indeed.

Caroline returned with a pen, ink and some paper. Licking the nib before dipping it in a glass bottle marked 'Stephens', she turned to Dallas. 'There are just a couple of things I need to know about Cameron. First, his full name?' In less than five minutes Caroline had all the information she needed. 'Good. I'll set the wheels in motion. My solicitors are Hempson's in Maritzburg. There may be things that Cameron has to sign but I've no idea how long a transfer takes to register. I think that concludes a most satisfactory day.' She raised her glass. 'The future!'

'I'll drink to that,' Dallas responded '*Slanje*.'

'And by the way. Somebody owes me a guinea!'

Soon it became too cold to be outside. 'Supper is ready,' Popeti announced, confirming that it was time to go in. Their meal was simple but good – the previous night's stew to which had been added more vegetables and some stock, turning it into a rich and warming broth. They broke chunks of crusty bread, dipping them in the soup and wiping their plates clean.

Sitting by the log fire Dallas and Caroline stared into the flames, each only too aware that the last twenty-four hours had probably changed their lives forever. Their long silences were not awkward, as happens when people are at ease with one another. Dallas put down his pipe and laid an arm round Caroline's shoulder. She leaned her head against him. It was another world, one which had known its share of tragedy, even if untouched by the madness of war.

'It's getting late,' Caroline said, grimacing as stiff joints reacted to the effort of getting to her feet. 'I've put those letters by your bed.'

Dallas rose too. 'Thank you, Caroline. Thank you for everything.'

'Guy used to call me Caro.' She looked at him in the firelight. 'Would you find it strange if I asked you to do the same?'

Gently he held her arms, kissing her first on one cheek then the other. 'Not at all, little sister. Not at all.'

'Thank you. Goodnight, Dallas. Sleep well.'

'You too, Caro. Goodnight.'

The door of her bedroom stood open, the interior illuminated by a flickering candle. As Dallas passed he glanced inside and saw the leopard skin. It was stretched on the otherwise bare floor.

Going to his room Dallas found two bundles, each tied neatly with red ribbon. There must have been thirty letters at least. Taking them back to the fire, he threw on another log, lit his pipe and untied the first knot. In his mother's long and flowing handwriting he read *Jack Walsh*. The address was care of the general post office in Durban. Most of the postmarks were illegible but the earliest stamps depicted a very young Queen Victoria. He opened the first envelope. The letter was dated 16 February 1850 – the day Dallas had been born. *My darling Jonathan, We have a son.*

It took Dallas over three hours to work his way through the first bundle of letters. There was one a year, all written on his birthday, talking of little else but a boy's progress through life from the time he was born – at four-thirty in the afternoon, he discovered – through breastfeeding. There she digressed into a vivid personal memory of moments stolen by two people deeply in love, things he couldn't imagine Lady Pamela saying, and then wrote of his first steps. Dallas never knew that it took him fourteen months to stand upright. *Lazy fellow*, he thought; *Duncan was the slowest in our family and it only took him eleven.*

Nothing in the letters indicated that she had ever received a reply. Long forgotten incidents, some he didn't even remember, chronicled his early life with humour, pathos and sometimes concern. She described his physical characteristics and how they changed over the years, what he was good at and what he wasn't. A picture of twenty years painted in words.

The fire had burned low and so had his only candle. Dallas attended to both before going outside to relieve himself. Standing in the freezing cold he looked up at the Southern Cross. There was no moon and the heavens seemed so close you could reach up and touch the stars. He shivered. In the darkness a jackal called, its distinctive sound telling him it had found a kill. Dallas waited, expecting to hear others. There was only silence. For no apparent reason he realised that something was missing. Dogs. Caroline had no dogs. Nor cats, if it came to that.

Back beside the fire Dallas retied the first bundle and turned to the second. It was smaller, starting in February 1872. He had gone. His mother knew not where. She talked of the circumstances surrounding his enforced flight from Scotland and of the jewels she had given him, pieces Jonathan Fellowes left her when he too had fled his home and the woman he loved.

In her next letter Lady Pamela told Jack that Dallas was in Durban. To this he had obviously replied because the dates suddenly became random. She knew about their coincidental encounter above the Howick Falls. She knew too that Jack Walsh was married and had a daughter, Caroline.

Jack must have maintained his correspondence,

reversing the role previously played by Lady Pamela and keeping her advised of their son's fortunes. The letters went on through the Zulu War of 1879. His mother was aware that Jack had been wounded at Ulundi but she never found out how badly.

In October 1881, Dallas had returned to Scotland for a visit, taking Lorna and his family. While there, his mother had told him for the first time that his real father, Jonathan Fellowes, lived in Natal under the name Jack Walsh. She said nothing about her ongoing correspondence with him.

Dallas had told Lorna but, not wishing to embarrass Jack, never revealed his knowledge to him or his family. It was hardly surprising that in all those years his father also said nothing to his wife and daughter, though he continued writing to Dallas's mother.

In the last letter she commented on the first family visit back to Scotland and how thin she thought their son was looking. He read on. *At least he is happy now, Jonathan. I will always be grateful to you for giving me such a special son. Thank you for watching over him these last few years. Know that I love you more than life itself. Wait for me, my darling, for I shall not be far behind.*

Dallas sat by the dying fire, tears streaming down his face. Jack Walsh had died in 1882. Lady Pamela, his mother, thirteen years later. Life was so unfair. It had been a long wait but he had no doubt that they were together at last.

★

Dallas always enjoyed the element of surprise, though on this occasion his only other option would have been to spend a night at the Royal. He knew the address of Torben and Gerda's new residence, which was not far from the house Lorna had bought when she first arrived in Durban almost thirty years earlier. For a moment his mind wandered. How everything had changed since then – not only the city, but the people themselves. Somehow Musgrave Road seemed narrower. There were certainly many more houses, and grand ones at that.

The imposing wrought-iron gates were locked but Dallas could see what appeared to be a brand-new carriage drawn up in front of the house. At least somebody was home. A liveried servant – probably the driver – appeared and Dallas spoke to him in Zulu. The man's face broke into a huge tooth-flashing grin as he produced a key, opened the gate and snapped off a smart salute to the unexpected visitor. So much for security, Dallas thought, as the African led his horse up to the house, leaving the gate wide open.

Torben stood on the steps, hands on hips, looking every bit the successful businessman. 'Well, Father. This is indeed an unexpected honour. What brings you to our humble abode?'

His question was phrased in a way that invited comment on the recently acquired symbol of success. Dallas didn't rise to the bait. 'The opportunity to see my son and his family. Alice must be all of three months old by now and I haven't yet set eyes on her.'

As he dismounted, Gerda appeared in the doorway holding his granddaughter. 'Hello, Poppie. You look dreadful. So thin. We'll have to feed you up a bit.'

'Good day, Gerda. I won't say no to that. You're looking well.' If anything, Torben's Afrikaner wife was even larger than he remembered.

She turned one cheek for a kiss and thrust the blanket-wrapped baby into his arms. 'Don't you think she looks like Torben?'

Dallas looked down to see two inquisitive eyes staring up at him. 'I can see you both in her,' he said tactfully as a tiny hand stretched out and found the finger he was using to hold the blanket off her face.

'How long are you here for?' Torben asked, as if the visit was already an imposition.

'Only the one night. If that's convenient, of course.'

'Don't be silly, Poppie,' Gerda cut in. 'This is such a lovely surprise. Stay as long as you wish.'

'Thank you, but Lorna is expecting me tomorrow. Duncan should already be at *Morningside*. Tell me, are you two – sorry, three – coming to the wedding?'

'Wish we could, Father,' Torben replied, trying to look serious. 'Unfortunately, things are a bit busy right now. I've got a shipment arriving this week and, well . . . you know . . . business is business. I'm sure Duncan and Tanith will understand.'

Dallas nodded but said nothing.

Gerda looked sheepish and clutched at her

husband's arm. 'You said three. Actually, it's four, Poppie. I'm pregnant again.'

'And you're the first to know,' Torben said proudly.

Dallas handed Alice back, kissed Gerda again and extended a hand to his son. 'Congratulations. Both of you. This calls for a drink.' *More than one*, he thought to himself.

'Oh, it's so nice to have you here,' Gerda bubbled. 'I'll take you to your room – it's the blue one – then Torben can do the grand tour while I attend to Alice and arrange dinner.'

Dallas could see that drinks would have to wait.

The meal, served by the same man he had assumed was their driver, had a formality that was quite out of place, not to mention unnecessary. Dallas did not dress for dinner, using the excuse that he had nothing to wear. Torben and Gerda did, making the point that they always took the trouble even when it was just the two of them.

Though quick to show off his knowledge of commodities and investment opportunities, Torben would not be drawn on what exactly it was he did. 'Coal. Now that's one to watch, you mark my words.'

Gerda only talked about babies. 'Does Duncan know we'd like him to be Alice's godfather? He never replied to my letter. Ellie did. She's one of the godmothers. Ellie really wanted to deliver Alice but in the end it just wasn't possible. She and Lindsay have been so busy, you know. Will they be at the wedding?'

Dallas had no idea.

'When's Tanith due? We worked it out to be the end of October, didn't we, dearest?' Without waiting for an answer she went on. 'That's good. It won't be too hot then.'

Torben took up the rather one-sided conversation as if fearing a lull. 'Mother's fine. She wanted to do something special for the wedding but old man Taylor is making things difficult for everybody. What with that and keeping an eye on Meggie, she hasn't been to Durban in over a month.'

Dallas didn't pick up on the deliberate reference to his youngest daughter.

Torben let it pass. 'Do you see much of Cam? How is he?'

'Unfortunately not and to answer your second question, Ginnie probably knows more than I do. I'm only his father.' Dallas said nothing about his visit to Caroline Hammond.

'According to Mother, she never sees anything of Ginnie these days. Too busy running her parents' farm apparently.'

'Well, we'll soon find out.'

Conversation exhausted, Torben resumed his role as host. 'Port and cigars, then we'd best call it a night.'

Gerda took the hint and rose from the table. The two men stood and wished her goodnight. 'Don't be long, precious, you've got a busy day tomorrow.'

The alcohol had loosened Torben's tongue. 'See

all this, Father?' He waved an arm at nothing in particular. 'It's only the start. There may be a war on but both sides need my help. I'm neutral, if you see what I mean.' He tapped a forefinger on the side of his nose and nodded knowingly.

Dallas hadn't the faintest idea what his son was talking about. All he wanted to do was get some sleep. 'Torben, would you mind awfully if I sloped off to bed? It's been a long day and tomorrow will be the same.'

'Of course not, Father. I may miss you in the morning so go well and give my regards to everybody at home.'

As Dallas found sleep he wondered not about Torben but the unexplained comment concerning Meggie. It would have to wait.

Weary after the long ride from Durban, Dallas arrived at *Morningside* just on sunset. Mister David was waiting, watching the road which led south.

'I see you, *nkosi*,' he said, taking the reins of Dallas's horse.

'I see you, *umngane*,' Dallas replied, acknowledging his friend. 'How have things been since I was last home?'

'All is well.' Mister David nodded. 'But you forgot Madam Lorna's birthday.'

Dallas groaned. It was worse than he had expected. 'Should I ride back to my unit and get myself killed?' he joked.

Mister David's face broke into a huge grin. 'Better that than die here.' He had never understood why white people placed so much importance on the year of their birth. Women seemed to worry even more than men. He did not envy Dallas after such a serious oversight. The tired old lion was no match for the angry lioness!

Dismounting, Dallas stretched his weary limbs and looked towards the house. Lorna was waiting on the verandah. Even the dogs hadn't come out to welcome him. *Bad omen*, he thought, waving a greeting. 'Lorna, my love.' Dallas tried to hide his apprehension. 'It's been too long. I've missed you.'

Lorna was not fooled by her husband's uncharacteristic greeting but smiled to herself at the obvious guilt in his expression. All of the family had, in one way or another, passed on their birthday greetings. The only exception was Dallas, the one who should have reminded the others. Now he stood forlorn, like a schoolboy in trouble, waiting on the bottom step and looking up at her. The remorse written on his face melted Lorna's heart but she was woman enough to recognise her advantage.

'You are looking well, all things considered,' she said in a tone which made Dallas flinch. It was obvious that she was referring to the forgotten birthday. Should he mention their wedding anniversary, he wondered.

'You must have been doing so many important things in the last couple of months. The censors cut such a lot out of your letters!'

It was getting worse. Suza, lying at Lorna's feet, winked at him.

'My darling, I cannot tell you how bad I feel to have, well . . . missed your birthday.'

The admission – rather than an apology – was met by a stony stare from Lorna.

'I have no excuse. Can you forgive me?'

Her husband's plea was more than Lorna could bear. She knew him well enough to realise he had dropped all semblance of pride and was truly remorseful. Without more ado she fell into his waiting arms and kissed him full on the mouth. 'I forgive you, Dallas,' she said with tears in her eyes. 'Welcome home, my darling.' The only birthday gift she had wanted was to see him home, alive and well. All else was of no consequence – well, perhaps not quite, but forgetting her birthday was still just a niggle.

Dallas held Lorna as if he would die in the next few seconds, breathing in the scent of her. 'I love you, Lorna.'

Mister David shook his head as he led Dallas's army horse away to be brushed down and fed. All was as it should be.

Of Duncan and Meggie there was no sign.

That evening husband and wife sat on the verandah, sharing a bottle of well-rounded red wine from the western Cape, talking about family, the farm and Dallas's visit to the Drakensberg foothills. Lorna was stunned by what he had discovered and listened in awe as he spoke of finding his half-sister and reading the letters written by Lady Pamela to Jack Walsh, his father. When he told her of the tragedy in Caroline's life and her

377

decision to sell *Wakefield* to Cameron for one guinea, she could hardly believe her ears.

'That boy was born with a silver spoon in his mouth,' Lorna laughed. 'If Cam and Ginnie go there it also solves the problem of who takes over *Morningside.*'

Dallas nodded. 'Cam still knows nothing of this so best we don't mention it to Ginnie.'

'If we see her.' Lorna sounded serious for a moment. 'She's been so busy looking after her parents and their farm. Kevin has turned to the bottle, which is helping nobody.'

'But she'll be here for Duncan's wedding, surely?'

'We'll see, my darling, we'll see.'

At the news of Gerda's pregnancy Lorna just shook her head. She said nothing to Dallas about her suspicions concerning Meggie's feelings for Stanley King. After all, it was only a mother's intuition.

The evening was cool but, being so close to the coast, not cold. Eventually their conversation turned to the war, an unavoidable subject in such troubled times.

'What's this I hear about Kitchener taking Boer families from their farms and sending them to special camps?' Lorna asked. 'Is it true?'

Dallas rubbed his forehead. 'Unfortunately yes, and his orders also say we must set fire to whatever will burn and confiscate their animals. Lord Roberts knows that the Boer *komandos* rely on farms for food and shelter. He really has no choice but to do something about it. There's been a significant change in enemy strategy. The Boers know we've got the resources to wipe them out in conventional battles so they're using hit-and-run tactics to disrupt our lines of supply. Guerrilla warfare, they call it. The Spanish coined that term when they harassed Napoleon's armies on the Iberian Peninsula. Believe me, it's frustrating the hell out of our men in the field. And that's not all. There's a psychological effect as well. The British public get quite concerned when there are no great victories to read about in their morning papers.'

'So to keep them happy we wage war on innocent women and children?' Lorna's sudden sarcasm surprised Dallas.

'They're not innocent if they provide succour to the enemy,' he retaliated. 'What if a Boer *komando* killed Cameron or Duncan? Would you feel that way about a woman who baked the bread which gave them the freedom to do it?'

Lorna fell silent, staring out at the starry backbone of the winter night sky. How could she respond to such a question? Dallas, being a soldier, saw it only as a means to an end. She, on the other hand, empathised with the weak and helpless, those swept up in a war of greed and glory created by insensitive, stiff-necked men who used words like loyalty, duty and honour to justify whatever was needed to win. There was no answer.

'You may not agree with me,' Dallas interrupted Lorna's gloomy thoughts, 'but British behaviour is quite civilised and I know that Boer women and children will be well cared for in the concentration camps.'

'*Concentration camps*? Is that what they're calling them?' Lorna shook her head at how quickly the concept had been given a name.

'It simply means bringing scattered groups into areas where they can be watched – nothing else.'

'Well, I have a bad feeling that we are going to rue the day they came into being. If the tables were turned would we accept the "concentration" of our families into camps as a civilised means of waging war?'

Dallas shifted uncomfortably. He was no great supporter of the man charged with implementing Lord Roberts's strategy. Stories he had heard of the cold-hearted Kitchener did not bide well with him. However, he had to admire the man as a soldier.

When Dallas and Lorna retired for the night they did not make love. It was enough just being together, clinging to each other under the warm blankets. In the dark Dallas lay listening to the soft snores of his wife. Try as he might, he couldn't sleep. *If the damned Boers would just admit defeat all this worry would be over*, he thought. Cam could marry Ginnie and move to *Wakefield*, Duncan and Tanith could raise their imminent family and his baby daughter discover happiness with a good man. At least Ellie had found her soulmate in Lindsay Mayer. Family concerns filled his mind as he stared at the dark ceiling. War so often saw fathers burying sons rather than the other way around, as was expected in times of peace. Since being home he hadn't seen Duncan or Meggie. It was no secret where his son would be, but Dallas was sorry to have missed Meggie. The hospital was not unduly busy but she had drawn the four to midnight shift and wouldn't be home until the following morning.

August the fifteenth dawned clear with a grey-white smoke haze hanging low over the inland hills towards Eshowe and Nkwalini. *The Zulus would be burning off dry grass to promote a new season's growth*, Dallas thought as he waited.

Lorna burst onto the verandah, her blonde hair a sleep-tousled mess. She didn't care, though Suza got quite a fright at her sudden appearance and let them know in no uncertain manner.

'You sneaky old bugger,' she chided Dallas, not the dog, falling onto his lap and flinging her arms around his neck. In one hand Lorna held a small blue velvet box.

'Happy anniversary, my darling.'

'Oh, Dallas, and the same to you. What a lovely surprise. Thank you. You're a sentimental old idiot and I love you so very much.'

'Hope you like it. The choice in Durban was a bit limited.'

'Like it? It's superb.' She opened the box and stared at a twinkling two-carat diamond, claw set in gleaming rose gold.

'Here.' Dallas took Lorna's left hand, removed the ring from its box and gently placed his present beside the band that had been on his wife's finger for nineteen years.

Lorna dissolved into tears. 'You're not going to believe this.'

'What, my darling?'

'I forgot our anniversary!'

They looked at each other and both burst out laughing.

'What say you we take two horses, pack some lunch then spend the day away from everybody? We can ride down the beach towards Mtunzini – just you and me.'

'Oh yes, Dallas, yes please – but first there's something else I want to do. Come with me.' Lorna rose and took his hand, leading her husband towards their bedroom.

Dallas didn't complain.

When Torben had disappeared from Durban at the end of May, Gerda descended into a state of panic. The letter he left did little to alleviate her concern that her husband had run off with another woman. She decided to give him a week, then, if he hadn't returned, go to the police. Torben came back four days later. His distraught wife screamed her accusations at him until he could bear it no more. Secretly pleased, Torben confessed where he had been and why.

Ashen-faced, Gerda listened, only believing his far-fetched story when he produced the bank cheque. Carefully she fingered the paper, holding it up, looking for a watermark, hardly believing that the figures written on it were true. 'This is a fortune,' Gerda gasped, slumping into a chair to recover from her shock.

'You cannot say anything to anyone,' Torben warned. 'And you must promise – on the life of our baby – that you will not tell even your family, so help you God.'

Gerda had agreed, her stricken expression convincing Torben. That aside, he had been wise enough not to disclose everything, especially that his new master was the *Broederbond*.

Within a week the suitcase maker had clarified what Torben was to do. He had been instructed to invest a huge amount of money from an account in Germany through a broker in Durban who was dealing in low-ash, clinker-free steaming coal. The war had brought many ships to South Africa's ports. They and the railways were greedy for coal to drive the steam engines needed to carry men and supplies to a seemingly insatiable Lord Roberts. Those backing Torben were practical businessmen, quick to seize an opportunity even if it aided an apparent adversary. The investment would net them a fortune. So what if he committed some of his own money alongside that entrusted to him by the enemy? Torben quickly dismissed any idea of the Boers as enemies, reminding himself that true entrepreneurs recognised no national loyalties – just the need to make money. War was no more than an opportunity. Those he was working for could not possibly object to his parallel investment.

Torben had put in place a group of small companies which would be used to channel funds to and from his faceless partners. Ostensibly all were controlled by him. His was the only individual name to appear in company documents, other shares being held by various corporate entities, the owners of which were almost untraceable.

The broker turned out to be a German Jew. His was not a fancy office, the man himself as austere as his premises. 'It would be a good idea for you to invest also, Mister Petersen,' he said amicably. 'The companies you have registered on behalf of our silent partners seem to be in order. One more is neither here nor there and will be seen simply as a man of foresight showing confidence in the future of his country. Given time, I am confident that your personal investment will multiply many times over.'

Torben agreed, shook hands with the bespectacled broker and left his office. A month later he received his first commission, less the initial advance. Once again, it was paid by way of a bank cheque drawn on the Bank of England. Torben's unnamed benefactors were more than satisfied with his efforts. The time had come to acquire the best house in town and announce to the world – in particular, his family – that Torben Petersen was far from a failure. He had arrived, so to speak, and others would look up to him in the years ahead. Now he could keep his promise to Alice that one day she would wear diamonds and gold. Her wait had not been long.

That had been almost two months ago.

★

Tanith and Duncan's wedding day was a memorable one, if not completely what Lorna would have wished. The only guests were two old school friends of the bride, together with Doctor Parry and Matron Kelly from the hospital, who had agreed to give Tanith away. Nobody from her family deigned to put in even a token appearance. Ginnie didn't come either. Duncan and Dallas seemed quite unconcerned. Later in the day father and son would celebrate in a way nobody expected – least of all, Lorna.

The minister was a short, jovial fellow by the name of Jones who rejoiced in doing God's work and if a drink or two went with it, so much the better. He arrived a good hour before the midday ceremony was due to take place and after ensuring that all the house windows were open – apparently to allow his Lord and master ease of access – he made it clear that something alcoholic to wet his whistle wouldn't go astray. Lorna was horrified, especially when Duncan and Dallas decided to join him.

Family, friends and the minister waited inside with a slightly tipsy Duncan while farm employees lined the drive outside. Tanith and Matron Kelly, driven by Mister David in an open carriage, arrived at five past twelve. The bride wore a simple blue dress which she had made herself. Nothing fancy. Duncan thought she looked more beautiful than he had ever seen her.

The service was quick and straightforward. Afterwards, bride, groom and witnesses signed the register before moving to the verandah where Lorna had finger food set out and Champagne aplenty. She had not shed a single tear during the simple ceremony.

The fact that this was also Tanith's twentieth birthday made little difference to the small pile of wedding presents waiting to be opened on the parlour table. There were gifts from Cameron as well as Ellie and Lindsay, but nothing from Torben and Gerda. Nobody knew how one particular parcel had managed to get there – though Tanith recognised her mother's handwriting.

Dallas and Lorna gave the young couple money – a not inconsiderable amount – and some family jewellery. They had a more appropriate gift in mind but that would have to be discussed with Cam.

A faint mewing sound turned Tanith's head and she noticed Suza open an eye in response. The cat called again – from the far end of the verandah – and a supposedly deaf dog struggled to his feet. Nobody else had noticed so Tanith decided to follow and find out what was going on. Suza shuffled after the retreating cat, following it outside towards the stables.

Once both animals were out of sight, Tanith slipped across the garden and cautiously peeped into the tack room where they had disappeared. Suza, tail wagging, was staring into the open bottom drawer of an old chest of drawers, normally used for horsey bits and pieces, while a proud mother rubbed herself against his legs, turning and telling him what a clever girl she was. It now contained a litter of kittens, six in all. Suza turned his head one way then the other, examining the recent arrivals. Tanith must have made a slight noise of wonder for the cat heard, looked up and called her over.

Ten minutes later, Lorna found her brand new daughter-in-law sitting on the stable floor watching another mother suckle her young. 'Look at this,' she said quietly, 'aren't they adorable?'

The shot that shattered an otherwise peaceful afternoon caused understandable panic. Suza spun on the spot – fast for him – to face the stable door. The cat jumped up, shaking off her hangers-on but ready to defend them to the bitter end. Lorna and Tanith stared at each other in disbelief, listening. What they heard was a cheer, then another shot.

Lorna helped Tanith to her feet and with a look of fury on her face, marched back towards the house. Sitting on the front verandah, legs dangling over the edge, she found Dallas, Duncan and Father Jones. Another shot rang out as the minister took his turn. Lorna didn't believe what she was seeing. Three grown men trying to shoot the heads off her roses with a bloody great .455 Webley service revolver!

A cheer went up from the assembled audience as a flower tumbled to the ground. It was bad enough not being able to host the wedding she would have wished, but now this! 'What on earth do you three think you're doing?' she shouted. The answer was obvious. It didn't matter, Lorna was furious. 'Look at you. Talk about the antithesis of three wise monkeys!'

Nobody said a word.

Lorna realised that her reaction had a lot to do with the shock of hearing unexpected gunfire. She had been tense about the wedding but so too had Duncan and Dallas. They were only letting off steam and really doing no harm. What excuse Minister Jones had was anybody's guess.

The silence continued. All eyes were on her. She turned to Tanith and found her grinning at Duncan.

'Oh, bugger it,' Lorna said. 'Let's have a shot.'

Mister David's eldest son, Henry, now a powerful young man in his twentieth year of life, stood uncertainly before his father, who was preparing the family's midday meal. He entered the kitchen full of confidence but his courage failed when the person he had come to see made it clear the interruption was badly timed.

'I am going to join *nkosi* Cameron as a scout,' he announced. 'Here is his letter calling for me.' Henry tried to sound convincing but felt weak in the knees. He feared no man – except his father.

'When did this arrive?' Mister David said, his displeasure rumbling from deep within.

'It came yesterday.'

'So why did you not tell me then?' His father used the same tone, wiping flour from his hands on an apron, his dark eyes observing the son he loved, the one who would carry on his role at *Morningside* when he was gone.

'I . . .' Henry hesitated. 'I did not know how you would feel about me leaving home to fight for the British.'

Mister David sighed and rested his hands on the heavy wooden table. Outside he could hear things that were familiar to him – the laughter and chatter of female servants cleaning the house and gossiping about who was seeing whom at the kraal, a proud chicken announcing the arrival of another egg, the soft murmur of Lorna's voice from the verandah as she tried to console a tearful young wife worried by the infidelity of her husband. They were sounds of stability and peace in a country torn apart by the white man's war.

'Why is it that my firstborn son would leave when one day he must take my place here?' Mister David was clearly concerned that Henry wanted to follow such a dangerous path in life. He went on: 'This war between British and Boer does nothing for our people.' The enigmatic look which for an instant clouded his son's eyes was not lost on him.

'It will make me a warrior, as you once were,' Henry answered.

'I fought at the call of our king,' Mister David replied. 'Not a distant queen who knows nothing of our land.'

'And one day I too will fight for our people,' Henry said quietly. 'But first I must learn the ways of war.'

The simple statement made Mister David feel

quite uneasy. His sons had grown up alongside those of Lorna and Dallas. Henry was by far the smartest when it came to academic studies. Although exposed to European customs and education he had often expressed resentment that, despite the friendship he had with their employers, he could never be an equal. Standing face to face in the kitchen, Mister David detected something in his son that could prove much more dangerous than taking sides with the British. 'The Boers will kill you if you become their prisoner.' Mister David knew his warning was a feeble attempt to make his son stay at *Morningside*.

'I do not fear the Boers,' Henry replied. 'When this war is over we will still be strangers in our own land no matter who wins. The British are little better than the Boers.'

Mister David felt anger rise like an *assegai* ripping into the belly of an enemy, though deep in the young man's eyes lay a truth that he had never dared admit, even to himself. Times were changing and would go on doing so. In almost thirty years the man he worked for had been both friend and enemy. What Henry said was true. His people had been dispossessed, a once-proud nation having no choice but to do as instructed by those who had taken their land and traditions. If needs be, Mister David would die for Dallas, or any member of his family, without a second thought. But this was a new century, his son a young man with a European education and plenty of time to change the years that lay ahead.

Henry stood, waiting for the worst, and was more than surprised when his father turned back to knead a lump of leavened dough. 'Do you give your permission, *madala*?'

'Go with your friend,' Mister David said without looking up. 'And never forget that he is a brother, no matter the colour of his skin. If you seek a cause for the Zulu nation it can no longer come with the *assegai* but from that which the white man has given you.'

'They may not let me carry a rifle,' Henry said.

'I do not mean that,' his father replied with a weak smile. 'I mean with words. It is only by bringing understanding and forgiveness that we can truly become one people – Africans – not Zulu, British or Boers.'

At no other time in his life had the young man felt so much love for his father as he did at that moment, standing side by side in a Zululand kitchen. The older man had refused nothing, giving his blessing and guidance to pursue a course for the future. Progress might be made one step at a time but for the moment Henry believed that fighting alongside the British was a good place to start. All he had to do was learn and survive. Besides, being Zulu, war was in his blood. He would stand alongside his boyhood friend and together they would be men.

Without another word Henry turned and left the kitchen, his head held high.

TWENTY

The Boer farmer faced heaven in a spreading pool of blood. Beside him knelt an old woman, his wife of well over half a century, wailing her inconsolable grief for such a needless death. A few feet away lay his ancient flintlock. It wasn't even primed. Around him chickens resumed their ceaseless search for food, ever hopeful of finding seeds or small insects in the sunbaked dirt. Winter was gone from the land, replaced by the springtime promise of an early summer. There had been no rain for many months.

Duncan sat astride his mount staring numbly at the tragic scene. The Afrikaner had done no more than try to defend his home and the few mealies a lifetime of hardship had coaxed from the barren ground.

'Fuck,' Duncan heard Fairfax exclaim.

'It was either him or one of us.' The shaking voice came from behind him.

Duncan turned to see the youngest member of their patrol lowering his carbine. He had only ridden with them for a week, ever since Dallas had been taken sick and sent to hospital for observation. The boy was nineteen years old, a shipping clerk from Durban. His stricken expression reflected the feelings of most in the unit – this work was not to their taste. Many, including Fairy Fairfax, were farmers themselves. Unfortunately, their orders were clear and unquestionable.

It was only because of the public outcry in England that Lord Roberts had been forced to revise his scorched earth policy, limiting it to those occasions when troops were actually fired on, as a reprisal for damage to rail and telegraph lines or when providing a base for hostile operations. It sounded good but in practice made no difference whatsoever. The farm burning went on.

Fairfax and his scouts had been given the added responsibility of checking on farms and taking any action deemed necessary. Their leader felt the bile rise in his throat at the scene played out before them. The old man had been only too aware why the troop of armed soldiers came to check on his home and chose to die defending his meagre property. He appeared from the house cursing the intruders and bringing to bear an antiquated *bobbejaanboud* which had belonged to his father. The young man he aimed at reacted as any soldier would and fired first. His shot had been true, flinging the raggedly dressed Boer on his back as the steel-jacketed bullet found his heart.

'What now, sir?' Duncan asked, dreading the response.

'You know what to do,' Fairfax replied, wheeling

his horse towards a small kopje overlooking the farm and its buildings. He found it impossible to give the order that would cause a home and everything in it to be destroyed.

'Burn it,' Duncan said quietly, though loudly enough for his men to hear. 'House, barn, wagon, the lot. Sergeant Sims, have the boys round up any horses or cattle. We'll take them with us.'

The man turned his mount and trotted off, pleased not to have been given any other responsibility.

Duncan decided to look inside the house. He dismounted, drew his heavy Webley revolver and cautiously approached the open door. It was dark inside the tin-roofed building. Hot too. As his eyes adjusted after the glare outside he looked around. The single room was simply furnished with a bed, table, two chairs and, in one corner, a glass-fronted cabinet displaying a few family treasures. On the table beside an open bible stood a single photograph. It showed a middle-aged man flanked by two young boys of fourteen or fifteen. Twins, Duncan thought. All three stared seriously into the camera. Each carried a modern Mauser rifle, their chests crossed with belts of ammunition. Duncan picked up the sepia-toned image, gave it a quick dust with his sleeve, then walked outside and handed it to the woman he assumed was both their mother and grandmother. She looked up, eyes filled with tears. '*Dankie, meneer*,' was all she said.

'What about her?' one soldier asked. 'What do we do with the old woman?'

'Leave her be,' Duncan said. 'She's suffered enough.'

'Do you think she'll be all right?'

'I pray so,' Duncan answered softly, hoping that the smoke now rising straight up in the still air would summon help. Somewhere she had a family but her husband and home were no more.

Duncan joined Fairy on top of the hill and did not look back. He could smell the burning buildings and hear the crackle of flames as they consumed all before them. Try as he might, in the years to come Duncan would be unable to escape the image of the old woman in her long black dress and bonnet cradling the frail body of her dead husband. It was something that would haunt his dreams on many a restless night.

The war of armies facing each other on the field of battle was over, replaced by a policy designed to defeat a weary yet still-proud people regardless of the cost in human suffering. Duncan perceived this as a rape of the land and those who lived there – even if they were the enemy. Promoted since his return from leave he held a Queen's Commission and was sworn to carry out all orders issued by his superiors. In the last few weeks Duncan had become disillusioned and angry. Did not the fools in Whitehall realise the legacy their war would leave? How could those whose home was this land hope to pick up the pieces and live alongside their former enemies? The questions stayed with him as they rode away from the burning farm.

That was the moment when Duncan first realised he was African, not British. Mister David obviously was, but so too were the Boers, not to mention his own family and unborn child . . . even the Indians who had made this land their home. It was a radical thought, though one that carried with it a whisper of justice.

It had been almost six months since Meggie and Mister David took Stan King home to *Kingsway*. Six months in which he had not once made contact. *But then, why should he*, Meggie kept asking herself.

The time had passed quickly, what with one thing and another. Torben had become the proud father of a baby daughter, Alice. She was the apple of his eye and quite the sweetest little thing, even if Gerda insisted on referring to her sister-in-law as Auntie Margaret. It was well-meant but made Meggie feel positively old. In June she turned eighteen.

Duncan was married to her best friend – albeit a case of better late than never – though embarrassment over their daughter's condition had caused a serious rift with her parents. Tanith and her father were still not speaking.

Things at the hospital were quiet and on a Friday afternoon late in September Meggie decided to give life a little nudge. She could think of no believable excuse for making the journey to Nkwalini and for that reason had not lied to her mother. Lorna expressed fears for her daughter's safety but, when all was said and done, realised that she was more than capable of looking after herself. Taking her favourite palomino mare, Meggie carried both a Colt pocket pistol and Cameron's .44-40 Winchester saddle carbine. Her preparations soothed Lorna's fears, at least as far as four-legged predators were concerned.

Now she sat gazing at *Kingsway*, feeling more nervous than she ever had in all her short life. Mixed with the fear was a delicious anticipation of what might occur in the next few hours. Too many nights spent tossing and turning in her bed at *Morningside* had led Meggie back to the man she loved. The one they called *Ndlovu*.

One of the Zulus had informed him of the approaching visitor. 'Meggie?' She heard her name called and saw Stan standing in front of the house. Nothing had changed. 'Is that you?' he shouted, one hand shading his eyes from the sun. She urged her horse forwards to meet the huge bear of a man.

Meggie slid from the saddle and into his strong arms. 'I just wanted to see you,' she said when her feet were back on the ground. 'That's all.'

His bronzed face looked down at hers. 'The feeling is entirely mutual,' he said, a broad smile making Meggie's heart pound even faster. 'I assume you're staying.'

'Is that an invitation?' she asked.

They walked selfconsciously side by side, Stan leading Meggie's horse. Reaching the house, he unslung the saddlebags and swung them over one shoulder. She had forgotten his slightly bent arm.

Sliding the Winchester from its leather holder, he summoned a young *umfana* to come and take care of her horse.

As they went inside, Meggie's hand brushed the carbine causing a spark of static that shocked them both. Stan placed the things he was carrying on the table and turned to Meggie. Holding her by the shoulders, his lips found hers. Their kiss turned to fire and Meggie moaned with the heat it released in her. There, in the living room of Stan's rather austere home, both gave in to what until that moment had been unspoken between them. Any thoughts of others vanished as their bodies crushed together in a physical release of feelings held in check for far too long. The fact that he was twice her age never once occurred to either of them.

'I love you, Meggie,' Stan said into her curly black hair, breathing in the scent of this woman he had missed so much. 'God knows, I've wondered long enough if the vision that you are could ever see anything in a broken old man like me. I love you with all my heart and soul. Never have I loved another as I do you right now.'

Meggie had always wanted to hear those words from him but suddenly they frightened her. She was fully aware of the implications this moment would have for the rest of her life.

Stan felt Meggie tense and pulled back, finding fear in her eyes. Dropping his hands he looked away. 'I'm sorry, Meggie. Do please excuse my impulsiveness.'

She knew that he was about to walk away. 'No,

no.' Meggie clutched at his arm, seeing sorrow and pain replace the passion of only seconds before. 'I think you are the most wonderful man I have ever met.' She reached up to gently touch his unshaven face with long and delicate fingers. 'Until today I could never have been sure this moment would ever be.'

The gesture and her words caused Stan to bow his head. 'Then let me tell you that whatever happens from here, the opportunity to kiss and hold the only woman I will ever love has made me the happiest man on this earth.'

She smiled at the sincerity of his statement. It had come from the heart of this gentle giant, baring his very soul. 'Then your death would be such a waste for I love you, Stanley King. I think I have from the moment I first saw you at the hospital. Oh!' Meggie exclaimed, throwing both hands to her face and laughing as she remembered what had happened that day.

'What is it?' Stan smiled too, though surprised by the sudden change in her demeanour. 'Is it something I've done?'

Meggie shook her head. 'Far from it.' There was a mischievous look on her face. 'It's not important.' With that she threw her arms around his neck and kissed him hard on the mouth.

Stan bent and scooped her in his arms. With ease he carried Meggie towards the one room she had never been in, kicked open the door and sat her on his rumpled bed.

She did not protest although she was terrified

and at the same time excited by what was happening. Standing close he began to remove her clothing, unbuttoning the ruff-necked blouse and bodice beneath, peeling them clear of her slim shoulders to reveal small but firm breasts. He stooped, kissing each nipple in turn before pulling off his shirt, exposing the powerfully built torso scarred by so many adventures. Meggie had seen his body before, but the most recent wounds were now healed and somehow it seemed different. With one finger she traced a scar on his muscular chest, excitement surging from deep within her.

Stan guided her hands to the buckle of his belt and soon both boots and breeches lay in a heap on the floor. Slowly he eased Meggie back onto the bed and lowered himself to caress her milky white body. When his mouth found her most private places she held his head, moaning in exquisite pleasure as the fire from her loins became a raging inferno. Meggie could hardly remember him removing the split skirt she had worn for her ride over but was only too aware of the one word she cried out when at last, with a slow, smooth thrust, he entered her eager body. '*Ndlovu!*'

Now she lay secure in his arms, the setting sun leaving its shadows in every corner of the room. Time had lost all meaning and only now could she contemplate the beauty of what had occurred between them. Stan was dozing, his eyes closed, and she gazed at his face in wonder. No matter what her family might say or do – especially her father – she would never leave this man. As his wife she would bear him many children.

Meggie stayed only the one night, knowing she had to leave the next day if harmony were to be maintained at home. In the morning Stan showed her the pair of tusks belonging to Michael Duffy. They were huge indeed, and yellowed with age, the largest she had ever seen. After a breakfast of mealie meal and fresh milk they walked and talked, easy in each other's company. Lunch never happened. There were more important things to be done.

Reluctantly she kissed Stan goodbye and swung into the saddle. 'I've put some biltong in your saddlebag,' he said. 'Beside that little revolver.'

'A girl's got to protect herself.' Meggie laughed. 'Look what can happen!' With that she waved and was gone.

Lorna was sitting in the drawing room putting the finishing touches to an embroidered tea-cosy when Meggie stuck her head round the door and said, 'I'm home. Don't worry about dinner for me.'

Before she could retreat, her mother's voice cut back, the tone of authority unmistakable. 'In here, if you please.' Meggie hesitated then stepped into the room. Lorna went on: 'I believe we need to talk, young lady. That is, if our little secret is to be kept from your father.'

Meggie was momentarily stunned by her mother's perceptiveness and outward calm. 'How did you know?' she asked.

Sighing, Lorna patted the settee beside her,

indicating that her daughter should come and sit down. 'I am a woman, my dear, and despite what you children may think, I know what it is like to discover love and the intimacy that goes with it.'

Meggie was more than shocked at her mother's explicitness. 'What has this to do with me?' Still standing, Meggie attempted to avoid the conversation she could see coming. 'I should go and change.'

'Sit down,' Lorna said. This time it was a command. 'You and I need to understand each other before your father returns and finds out that you have been seeing a man twice your age.'

Meggie slumped into a chair opposite her mother. 'I have been seeing the man I am going to marry,' she said defiantly. 'So there is nothing to discuss.'

'I am not your enemy, darling.' Lorna spoke quietly. 'Your father and I love you dearly and it is no secret in the family that you are the apple of his eye. It would hurt him terribly if that were to change. For that reason it is important that you and I talk – woman to woman – about your infatuation with Stanley King.'

Meggie blushed. She had no idea how her mother could even have guessed at their relationship. Lorna's eyes had her fixed with a steely stare from which there was no escape. *Never lock eyes with a lion.* That was what her father once said. No doubt it applied to a lioness as well. 'It is not infatuation,' she said softly, bowing her head in submission. 'We love each other.' Meg heard her mother sigh, not knowing what it meant. Her next words spelled it out.

'Stanley King is a fine man, but don't you think he's just a little old for you?'

Meggie leapt to her feet and strode towards the door. 'It is no concern of yours whom I should choose to marry,' she shouted. 'Stan and I will wed and no-one – not you or Father or even the devil himself – can stop that from happening.'

With her daughter's angry words still echoing in the room, Lorna was left to ponder if she should break the news of Meggie's announcement to Dallas. How did you tell something like this to a man who still thought of his daughter as a baby? Her husband could be so blind at times. Lorna sighed. Meggie was a young woman who had obviously explored the forbidden fruit of a sexual encounter. But was it love? Lorna rose stiffly to her feet, none the wiser.

President Kruger was long gone, escaping into Portuguese East Africa on 11 September. In mid October he sailed for Holland to try to drum up European support for the Boer cause. Never again would he set foot in his beloved Transvaal.

Lord Roberts annexed the former Boer republic on 25 October, declaring it part of the British Empire. At long last the goldmines which Milner, Rhodes and Alfred Beit had coveted for so long became the property of Queen Victoria.

In Britain, the Secretary of State for the Colonies, Joseph Chamberlain, survived a profiteering scandal over his family's armaments business and the 'Khaki Election', as it had become known, returned a government which had been hard pressed by David Lloyd George's Liberals. In Africa, the white man's war went on.

October brought with it the promise of rain but no more than that. Clouds would build then disappear from whence they came, leaving only an early summer heat. Cameron rode with Henry at his side, well aware that some of the men did not approve of the bond that existed between their commanding officer and a Kaffir. Others, knowing Henry to be from their captain's family farm, saw it as no more than a master and servant relationship – an African always close at hand to cater for the other's needs.

Dust kicked up in small explosions from the horses' hooves as the patrol plodded wearily through the lowveld scrub north of Crocodile River. They were in the Sabi Game Reserve, an eighteen hundred square mile wildlife sanctuary created by President Kruger in 1898. Despite this, the evidence of recent poaching lay everywhere. It was also fly country and in the last week two of their unsalted horses had been lost to sleeping sickness.

Cameron's contingent had been caught up in Lord Roberts's overall reshuffle and was now spearheading the search for what was left of Louis Botha's Transvaal army. It had split up, moving north from Komatipoort after almost two thousand disillusioned and war-weary fighting men –

including many foreign mercenaries – surrendered to the neutral Portuguese authorities.

As he rode, Cameron was not thinking about the task at hand. Far from it. His mind dwelt on the contents of a letter he had received the day before when a bag of mail finally caught up with his troop. Thanks to their transfer from the Orange River Colony, it was over two months old. Cameron had been delighted to see Ginnie's familiar handwriting and sought the shade of a fever tree well away from his men, where he could devour her loving words in private. What he read brought only a cold, creeping fear.

I am sorry, my love, but I must be honest and find myself having to use words which I know will bring you great pain. I do not write this letter with ease, the more so as you are in constant danger. Better this than live a lie.

Kevin will never walk again and I have family at home who need me now more than ever. This is no life for you, dearest Cam, and it breaks my heart to say that we can never be husband and wife. Please do not hate me for my most difficult decision. You too must forget what might have been. I pray that one day you will find the love you deserve.

The letter continued with news of the farm and comment on the weather. Ginnie seemed to ignore the fact that she had changed his life forever.

Cameron sat stunned, reading her words over and over again, a sense of frustration and anger replacing the euphoria he had felt just minutes earlier. *If only I could go home and reason with her*, he raged inwardly. But that was impossible and Cameron knew it. All he could do for now was live with her words of rejection. At least he could sympathise with others who had received similar letters from wives or sweethearts. One young soldier had even shot himself. In those first few hours of grief, Cameron understood why – the thought also crossed his mind. In all the months of active service he had suffered the hardships knowing that when the war was finally over he had a wonderful woman waiting for him at home.

'Are you sick?' Henry asked, leading Cameron's gelding to where he sat alone under the yellow-barked fever tree. 'You look pale, even for a white man.'

Cameron looked up and grinned at his boyhood friend, forcing back the urge to weep. 'I'm fine,' he replied, but his words lacked conviction. 'Just a bit of bad news from home.' Seeing Henry's sudden look of alarm Cameron hurried to reassure him. 'Nothing's wrong at *Morningside*,' he added. 'Ginnie has decided not to marry me.'

Henry shook his head in sympathy. He knew of his friend's deep and longstanding love for Virginia. 'I am sorry,' the Zulu said. 'My heart is heavy for you.'

'Not your problem,' Cameron replied, rising to his feet and brushing the dust from his khaki uniform. '*C'est la vie*,' he added, feigning the attitude of one resigned to his loss.

Henry had not the faintest idea what Cameron had said but could see the agony written on his friend's face and realised such pain could easily become an all-consuming madness. He had seen it in others on the field of battle where they gave little thought to themselves or those around them. It was a pain that could so easily cause death.

That had been twenty-four hours earlier and still Cameron could not get the contents of Ginnie's letter out of his mind. The men noticed a change in him and it worried them too. Cameron had proved a capable leader and his sudden indifference was of considerable concern.

'Rider approaching,' Henry called. He was usually the first to notice any movement in the country around them. Certainly Cameron hadn't seen it. Beyond a flat plain of waving yellow grass the bush became quite thick where it followed the Sabie River. From it burst one of the forward scouts returning at the gallop. Halting the patrol, Cameron and Henry rode forwards to meet the African.

'There is a farmhouse about one mile beyond the river,' the scout reported. 'There are three men but maybe more inside. They are Boers.'

'Did you see if they are armed?' Cameron asked.

'I think they must be.'

Cameron dismissed the scout and sent Henry to summon Lieutenant Christison. He returned a few minutes later with the young officer Cameron had come to like and respect. 'Got a job for you,' he said, wasting no time. 'There's a farmhouse up ahead, a mile or so beyond the river. Take your section and search the place. Also ascertain the status of any occupants. There are at least three. No natives have been reported but take Henry with you in case an interpreter is needed. The rest of us will cross the river and wait in the trees. Have the scout tell you what to expect and let him act as your guide. Any questions?'

Grantley Christison thought for a second. 'No, sir,' he replied.

'Then you'd better get going. Good luck.' Cameron nodded at Henry and watched the two men as they rode off. A few minutes later he followed.

Sergeant-Major Mulligan went quietly about his duties ensuring that everybody was properly prepared. Weapons and ammunition were checked, saddle girths, even water canteens. Nothing was left to chance. The house up ahead could be an ambush. Mulligan glanced at his captain and wondered yet again what had changed him. The man he had ridden with for so long had suddenly become distant, as if his mind were somewhere else, and that worried the battle-hardened NCO.

After Lieutenant Christison led his men forwards, Cameron gave the order to follow. The river was shallow and once across it was not difficult for them to find a well-hidden spot from which to observe the farmhouse. Using binoculars, Cameron saw a big bearded individual appear at the front door and step into the sunlight, his hands in the air. Two others followed close behind.

'Much happening, sir?' Sergeant-Major Mulligan enquired softly.

'Take a look for yourself, Sarn't-Major,' Cameron replied, handing him the glasses.

Mulligan watched as three soldiers dismounted and cautiously entered the mud brick structure, weapons at the ready.

Without binoculars everything shimmered in the midday heat. The farmhouse sat on a grassy slope surrounded by fences that looked in dire need of repair, as did the building itself. Cameron suddenly started to feel uneasy about the situation. Taking the glasses back he carefully scanned the surrounding country, seeking out places that might conceal a body of men waiting to trap the unwary. There was a fold in the ground off to one side of the farmhouse which made it impossible to see what lay beyond. Cameron cursed himself for not being more thorough before sending his second in command to carry out the search. A hundred mounted men could be hidden there, he thought, realising that his mind was not on the job.

'Looks like the lieutenant is on his way back,' Mulligan said, shielding his eyes against the golden glare which lay between them and the farmhouse.

Cameron swung his glasses to watch Lieutenant Christison signalling his men to pull out. He was about to breathe a sigh of relief when the young officer pitched from his horse and fell to the ground. A shot rang out, then another and another as pandemonium broke loose. Someone next to Henry came down then a third man toppled forwards in the saddle, saving himself by grabbing the neck of his mount.

'God almighty,' Cameron swore. Through the glasses he could see at least one rifle barrel protruding from a front window of the building his men had so recently searched. 'The bastards have tricked them.' From the dead ground off to one side a group of horsemen burst into view, riding at full gallop towards the rear of the house. They were leading three saddled horses. Cameron's first instinct was to order an attack but he could see that they would never reach the farmhouse before the three Boers still firing from inside made good their escape.

'What do we do, sir?' Mulligan waited. 'Sir! What are your orders?'

Cameron could hear the frustration in his NCO's voice. Comrades and friends were being killed within sight of their position and he was doing nothing to help. For precious seconds Cameron wavered, unable to make a decision. He had forty men under his command and had failed them all.

'Sir?' Mulligan shouted it this time, a look of thunder on his face.

'We stay put, Sarn't-Major. Lay down cover for the incoming patrol. Fire at will. Get to it, man.' Cameron saw the look of disgust on Mulligan's face as he turned to relay the order. His men were straining their stirrup leathers waiting to charge the enemy.

The survivors were galloping at breakneck speed towards them, except for one. Henry had dismounted and was dragging Lieutenant Christison towards his horse, ignoring the unheard command to save himself.

All three men inside the house had stopped firing and were out of sight, probably mounting up at the back door. Cameron saw two of the Boers who had brought the horses break away and ride towards Henry. It was obvious they intended to thwart his attempted rescue of Lieutenant Christison.

'Target at twelve o'clock, two riders,' Cameron roared. 'Section fire, three rounds rapid . . . fire!' As one, the men held in reserve turned their attention to the horsemen bearing down on Henry and the wounded officer. The range was at least a thousand yards but section fire concentrated so many bullets on the target that one or two would hopefully find their mark. The shotgun effect worked. Cameron watched with satisfaction as one of the Boers was snatched from his saddle, the second reining away and racing to find safety beyond the ridge where his companions had already disappeared.

Henry was heaving and pushing the wounded officer onto his horse and with great difficulty managed to sling him over the saddle, his body hanging limp on either side. Finding a blood-soaked stirrup, the Zulu swung up behind him and headed for the river. A cheer rose from the watching soldiers as they acknowledged the act of sheer nerve and courage. Barring one presumed dead and two wounded, the patrol returned safely. They had been lucky and Cameron knew it.

Two soldiers helped Henry with Lieutenant Christison, placing him gently on the ground. Cameron slid from his horse and slapped his friend on the back. 'Well done, Henry, that was a brave thing you did out there.' The call was quickly echoed by others. He knelt beside the young officer whose eyes were open and staring.

'Had papers saying they'd signed the amnesty,' he blurted out, a terrible pain etched on his ghost-like face. 'Sorry, sir. They tricked us.' Blood soaked the wounded man's tunic and suddenly pink froth welled from his mouth, choking off any further report.

Cameron ripped open Christison's clothing. He had been shot in the back, the bullet ripping through his body and puncturing a lung. The exit wound was enormous. 'Dumdum,' Cameron muttered in disgust, aware that the practice of cutting bullets to make them expand on contact had been outlawed by the Hague Convention over a year ago. A bubbling gurgle ended the man's fight for life.

'Are we going to have a go at them murdering Dutchies?' Sergeant-Major Mulligan asked as he hovered over the tragic tableau. 'Give them a taste of their own medicine.'

'We will, Sarn't-Major,' Cameron replied. 'But only when I say so,' he added more firmly, fixing the man with a steely glare to establish his authority. 'Do you see that dead ground on the left, where the Boers disappeared?'

Mulligan squinted into the distance, looking at the barely discernible ridge Cameron had indicated. 'I do, sir. Just this side of the house and maybe two hundred yards out.'

'If you were their leader where would you position a pom-pom or machine gun?'

'Right there, sir. With a clear field of fire when we came in to rescue our wounded. In the open nobody would stand a chance.'

'Precisely,' Cameron said, knowing his NCO now understood why he had not issued an order to charge the farmhouse.

'Sorry, sir,' Mulligan said softly, trying to keep the exchange between the two of them. It was not his place to question a senior officer's orders but Irish blood remained Irish blood and sometimes it boiled over.

As if on cue, the sound of a fast-firing Maxim broke the silence and a hail of heavy bullets shredded the trees above their heads. 'Dismount and take cover,' Cameron bawled. His men needed no second bidding as the enemy gunner adjusted his range. He couldn't see his target but that hardly mattered. There was little shelter save for spindly tree trunks and a few rocks along the river. Cameron's horse whinnied in terror, collapsing as a shell smashed into its flank and exploded, shards of jagged metal finding the vital organs which until that moment had given it life.

'You were right,' Mulligan said unnecessarily as both men rolled behind the dead animal for protection. 'We would have been slaughtered.'

'True, but now they've trapped themselves – if we can act fast enough.' Cameron chanced a look at the far slope. Sure enough, the gun was positioned at one end of the distant depression. 'Smithy!' he called to one of his men, an ever-cheery Scot who crouched behind a tree a few yards away.

'Sur?'

'Ride like hell to the main column. Tell the artillery boys we've got a target for them. Here, take this map. Explain where we are then point out the enemy position. I believe there could be as many as thirty Boers up there with that pom–pom.' Cameron marked his map and thrust it into the waiting soldier's hand.

'Nay problem,' Smithy nodded, tucking it inside his tunic. Braving the more sporadic incoming fire, he swung into the saddle and splashed back across the river.

The main column was at least ten miles away and Cameron had his fingers crossed that guns could be brought up in time to prevent the enemy slipping away under cover of darkness. He turned to his NCO. 'This *komando* is probably low on ammunition and with any luck won't know our strength. All we have to do is keep them pinned down until the big boys get here.'

Mulligan reloaded his Lee Metford, leaned on the dead horse's saddle and took careful aim at the tiny target. 'Fire at will,' he shouted, squeezing the trigger.

Cameron sent Henry to ascertain the extent of their casualties while he kept watch on the enemy position, hoping the Boers would not try to break out. Whoever led the enemy would be a fool to keep them there. Their attempt to draw in the patrol had failed and under the unwritten laws of guerrilla warfare it was time to leave.

Henry returned to report two dead and three wounded. The horses had been hit hardest.

Cameron was relieved. Turning to the man he had grown up with he said, 'If you were a regular soldier, what you did out there today would have won you a Victoria Cross.'

'And white,' Henry added. 'My skin is the wrong colour, in case you hadn't noticed. Anyway, I didn't do it for a medal.'

'Then why risk your life for one of us?' Cameron queried, knowing that his boyhood friend harboured a deep resentment of the manner in which Europeans had treated the Zulu people.

Henry slapped a full magazine into the receiver under his rifle, pulled back the bolt and fed a live round into the chamber. 'I'm not sure,' he replied. 'Perhaps it was because I knew you would have done the same.'

It was three hours later when Cameron heard the sound of heavy artillery commencing its bombardment of the enemy position. They were firing from far back across the river, well beyond the effective range of a pom-pom. 'Here we go,' he called, raising his glasses and seeing the first shells come crashing down just behind the ridge. An

415

observer signalled the necessary corrections by heliograph and the next salvo fell slightly short. The gunners were bracketing their target. Seconds later came the combined fire of six 12-pounders dropping fused shrapnel shells into the depression itself.

As Cameron's patrol watched, they saw men and horses spill over the far rim in panicked flight. A cheer rang out along the river as the skilled observer signalled a slight change in trajectory, sending death and destruction to fleeing Boers. Solid steel balls indiscriminately ripped into both men and horses, tearing limbs from bodies, beheading some and disembowelling others.

It was a terrible sight but Cameron dispassionately watched the carnage. Through his field glasses he saw the dry grass changing colour. It had nothing to do with the rapidly setting sun. He felt no pity for the dead and dying – even the death of his young second in command had left him cold. *Had it been because he no longer cared*, Cameron wondered, realising that his hands were shaking uncontrollably. Never before had he lost any of his troops in action. The men were removing saddles and bridles from the dead horses, a bullet bringing peace to those that would be going no further.

Cameron looked around him. None of this would have happened if he was the leader his men had come to expect. He had let them down. It was something Cameron knew he would live with for the rest of his life. It was the stuff of nightmares.

'What do we do with the farmhouse?' Mulligan's voice cut through his thoughts.

'Burn it,' Cameron yelled. 'Burn the whole bloody lot.'

TWENTY-ONE

Adust devil swirled its way across the garden causing chickens to squawk and scatter in momentary panic. Lorna sat on the verandah, cooling herself with a finely decorated Chinese fan as she watched a sky boiling black with summer rain far out over the Indian Ocean. She could smell the distant storm. It would not be long before the dry ground turned to sticky, cloying mud.

Most days Lorna would spend the hour before dark reading, writing or just watching for anybody coming to the house. More specifically she watched and waited for any member of her family. That was how it had started but as the months passed her vigil became little more than routine: a time to relax and think.

At least letters came but Lorna was often worried by what she read between the lines. Duncan's words were becoming more and more pessimistic. He wrote of winning the war only to create a legacy of hate in those who were defeated. She understood why her son should be so concerned. Duncan had always spoken out about what he believed, quick to condemn injustice in any shape or form. The burning of Boer farms was a practice he would not condone.

Cameron caused Lorna the greatest concern. Since the war started his letters had been bright with optimism and full of praise for the British. About a month earlier, something had happened which changed that completely. The last letter Lorna received was so brusque she sensed only bitterness and anger. He gave no explanation. As a mother, Lorna knew she could do nothing to help either of her boys until they were home where they belonged.

Only Ellie's letters brought any glimmer of hope for the future. She wrote that casualty numbers had dropped off considerably and married life with Lindsay was a joy.

Lorna did not expect to receive word from Dallas as he had never been one to sit down with pen and paper. It was Duncan who kept her up to date with his well-being, ending every letter, *Father is well and sends you all his love*. She always smiled at that, knowing full well that Dallas would not even have been consulted. The paucity of letters from her husband had nothing to do with a lack of love. Lorna accepted that. In his mind she was with him always and nothing had changed. *And a fat lot of good that does*, she mused, placing Duncan's letter to one side and watching a rider coming towards the house.

It was Meggie, returning from one of her now quite regular visits to *Kingsway*. She no longer sought permission as nothing her mother could say or do would deter her from seeing the man she loved and intended to marry. Lorna was only too aware that if she tried to stop Meggie visiting Stanley King her daughter would probably leave home and alienate herself from the family forever – something Lorna could not bear even to think of. Their relationship remained strained, but on the surface both pretended that Stan King was not an issue between them. Dallas still knew nothing of the situation and Lorna prayed that he would soon come home and put an end to the matter once and for all. Meggie was her father's darling, while she adored and respected him. He was the only person their headstrong daughter might listen to.

It had not taken Lorna long to realise that the attraction Stanley King held for Meggie had a lot to do with his being very much like Dallas. Both were older men who had led fascinating, often dangerous lives. Was it not said that sons often marry mirror images of their mothers; and daughters, those of their fathers?

Meggie was covered in dust. She waved a cheery greeting to her mother. Dismounting, she patted herself down, removed the short Winchester from its leather boot and called a servant to take care of her horse. Wearily she climbed the steps, said hello to the dogs and slumped into a cane chair beside her mother.

'You're home sooner than I expected, young lady. Problems in paradise?' Lorna hadn't intended sarcasm but the words were out before she could stop them.

'No, Mother.' Meggie raised her eyebrows in unstated annoyance. 'Stan had to go to Durban and I didn't want to stay there on my own.' She saw the letter lying on a *riempie* stool between them and recognised Duncan's handwriting. 'I stopped off to see Tanith on the way home. She's enormous.'

'The poor wee lamb's a week overdue,' Lorna pointed out, putting aside her resentment of Meggie and Stan's relationship.

'Duncan must be panicking,' Meggie said. 'I hope it's a girl – they're so cuddly. Boys do nothing but kick and squirm all the time.'

Lorna laughed. 'I'll go over tomorrow and see if I can be of any help.'

Meggie read her brother's letter while Lorna's mind drifted. This would be her first real grandchild. Somehow she had not been able to accept Torben and Gerda's daughter as one – though, of course, her feelings on the matter remained unstated. Duncan and Tanith's child would be family by blood and Lorna found herself wondering what she could do to welcome their baby into the world. She had followed the pregnancy closely and was slightly concerned that it had gone beyond term.

'In fact,' Lorna suggested, 'we should both go and see Tanith in the morning.'

'That would be grand,' Meggie replied brightly, sensing a return of their mother and daughter closeness in the shared anticipation of a new family member.

If only Dallas and Duncan could be here too, Lorna

thought with sadness. They would be missing the start of a new Granger–Acheson generation.

Torben found himself sleeping less and less each night. There was no doubt he was being followed to and from his plush office at the cemetery end of West Street. Those who shadowed his every move were white, but he had been unable to determine any more than that. When Torben finally summoned enough courage to confront one of them, he did so armed with an umbrella and his two–shot derringer pistol. The fellow simply turned away and disappeared into an area crowded with Indian traders pedalling their exotic wares from a labyrinth of makeshift stalls. Torben decided not to follow. Feeling frustrated, he resumed his walk home.

Even in the leafy street off Musgrave Road where his house, more like a mansion, stood secure behind an eight foot high wrought–iron fence, he could still feel their eyes watching him. It was not a case of being paranoid. Those who hounded him were highly organised, having the resources to draw on so many people that not one face stood out in his mind.

Torben closed the front door behind him, passing his umbrella to a uniformed African maid who had been taught to curtsey when accepting a task from the master or mistress of the house. He found Gerda in the drawing room.

'Is all well, dearest? You look very pale.'

'It is nothing.' Torben shook his head, attempting

to avoid any further questions from his rather observant wife. 'Just the heat.'

'You really should take the carriage, poppet. This weather is far too hot for you to be walking.'

Mumbling an excuse, Torben left the room and went upstairs to his study. Sitting behind his desk he stared at the wall opposite, reflecting on what had happened since leaving his office. *Whoever that man was, he wanted to remain anonymous*, Torben thought. At least it confirmed his suspicion that he was under observation. Not knowing why or by whom frightened him more than anything else. Could it be that the *Broederbond* were keeping an eye on him? Torben struggled to find an answer that made any sense. Were his employers making sure that their agent was doing what they paid him to do? He doubted it. Anyway, these people seemed young, clean-cut and fit looking – more like policemen. That thought really frightened him. What if the British authorities were wise to his double dealings? Although the day was warm, Torben felt a sudden chill in the room. He could be hanged for what he was doing. Adding to his personal wealth was one thing, helping finance the enemy's war effort quite another.

Torben decided that the risk was worth taking. It would not be long before he was able to assume his rightful place in Durban society, and why stop at Durban? He would be welcomed in exclusive establishments and prestigious colonial clubs from Cape Town to Kimberley, rubbing shoulders with the empire builders of Africa. Money bought respectability and opened doors. Even wealthy Jews were accepted, despite their religion or climb to the top, often from the most humble beginnings. *Yes, any risk was small compared with the potential rewards*, he thought. Rising, he poured himself a generous measure of the most expensive malt whisky he had been able to purchase in Durban. Already two cases of Scotland's finest were on order, most of which would be used as gifts to favoured business associates, impressing them with his wealth and taste.

A sharp rapping on the door downstairs and the sound of a loud commanding voice snapped Torben out of his growing complacency. For a second he froze in absolute terror, powerless to move. How had he got past the gates? That stupid Kaffir must have left them open again! He could hear the maid arguing with their unexpected visitor. Whoever it was had no intention of going away. Downing the contents of his glass in a single swig, Torben stepped out onto the landing. Gerda was already there, protectively clutching Alice to her ample bosom.

'What's going on? Who are those men?' she asked fearfully.

So there were more than one – that, he hadn't anticipated. 'I am about to find out,' Torben replied calmly. 'Do not worry, my dearest. The last time strangers came to our door we ended up making a lot of money.' He laid a reassuring hand on Gerda's arm and smiled. Inside, his stomach was churning. 'You put Alice to bed and I'll see to our visitors.'

Torben descended to the entrance hall where the maid was still holding the strangers at bay. There were three of them, all dressed in ill-fitting dark suits and wearing bowler hats. They looked quite ridiculous and he knew without a second glance that these were no businessmen. 'Thank you, Sixpence,' he said. 'I'll deal with this.' The maid needed no second bidding.

'Mister Torben Petersen?' one of the men asked. He was in his mid forties and spoke with a London accent. His companions were younger. Torben thought them to be in their late twenties and tough-looking. *Bullyboys*, he decided.

'I am he,' Torben replied with a dignity and coolness that surprised even himself, especially as fear was causing his legs to tremble. 'And who, may I ask, are you, sir?'

'Inspector Wild, Durban City Police.' The man showed no identification and gruffly pushed past Torben, the two subordinates hot on his heels. They stood in the hallway taking in everything around them. 'Who else lives in this house?'

'My wife, daughter and four servants,' Torben answered, a note of anger rising in his voice at the attempted intimidation by a man claiming to be a police officer. The others started opening doors, one moving towards the stairs. Their unauthorised intrusion enraged Torben. 'Do you realise who I am, Inspector?' he queried, his voice quivering with indignation.

'I thought we'd established that, sir.'

Ignoring the facetious reply, Torben went on,

'And I have given no permission for you or your bullyboys to go poking about in my private house.'

The policeman turned to Torben, an icy expression in his cold blue eyes. 'They are only doing their job, Mister Petersen. I am sure you have nothing to hide.'

Torben had no idea what the man meant. 'I think you should state your reason for this unwarranted intrusion and then leave before I place this matter in the hands of my solicitor.'

'I am sure you know only too well why we are here,' Wild said, picking up a hand-painted porcelain vase and examining it with no real knowledge of its rarity or value.

'Then I am sorry to disappoint you,' Torben fumed, glaring at the intruder into his home and life. If this had something to do with his recent dealings with the Boers, why was he being questioned by the police and not military intelligence? 'So I will ask you one more time to please leave. If you have any more questions then I suggest we meet at my solicitor's office in the morning.'

'Fair enough,' the Inspector replied, placing the small vase carefully on its stand. 'Despite the war an Englishman's home is his castle. Isn't that so, Mister Petersen?'

The two others returned to the hall and shook their heads in answer to a questioning glance from Inspector Wild. 'Very well,' he said. 'We will meet with you tomorrow. Shall we say ten o'clock,

Mister Petersen? No need to give us the address. Good evening to you, sir.'

With that the three men were gone, leaving behind a seriously shaken Torben, who turned to the living room in search of another drink. 'Damn them,' he muttered, seizing the cut-glass decanter.

Gerda joined him. She had obviously been crying, her make-up smudged, eyes red and moist. 'What have you done, Torben, to bring such fear into our home?'

'Nothing,' he said, though there was little conviction in his words. 'My solicitor will clear it up in the morning.'

'One of them even came into Alice's room,' Gerda said, suppressing a sob and wiping a wet cheek with the back of a podgy hand. 'It was horrible. He just stood there looking around without saying a word. I was so frightened.'

'Well, they're gone now.' Torben's mind was somewhere else. *What in the world could they have been looking for,* he puzzled to himself, suddenly annoyed at having to wait until the morning to find out. He decided to go and blast that lazy Kaffir for not locking the gates as he had been instructed.

Little did either of them realise that their lives were about to change forever.

Tanith Granger-Acheson alternated between screaming and breathing short explosive bursts of air as she hung on to the brass bedhead, her knees drawn up, legs spread wide.

'Push,' Lorna encouraged her daughter-in-law. 'It won't be long now, you are doing fine.'

Lorna and Meggie had arrived only an hour earlier to find the highly distressed young woman, wide eyed and terrified. They were greeted with the words: 'My waters have broken. Caliph has gone to fetch the midwife and tell my mother. I think they're going to be too late.'

Lorna had realised there was no time to waste and immediately took charge, barking instructions at Meggie. If necessary they would deliver the baby themselves. It was something Lorna had never done but having had six children of her own, not to mention plenty of practice helping with animals on the farm, she didn't hesitate. With repeated words of encouragement, she kept a close watch on Tanith's condition while Meggie mopped her friend's perspiration-soaked face with a cool damp cloth.

'Oh, Duncan, where are you?' Tanith cried. 'Bloody war,' she spat out between gasps for air, struggling to sit up in a desperate attempt to relieve her pain. 'The bloody war did this.'

Lorna smiled. 'More likely my son, I think.'

Tanith was beyond explaining what she meant and fell back exhausted. Meggie turned to her mother in wide-eyed fear and for a moment irrationally hated Duncan for causing so much pain and suffering. The thought quickly passed when she accepted what was taking place – the miracle of new life.

After the longest hours in Tanith's life, Frazer

Dalrymple screamed his way into the world, one of those squirmy, uncuddly things – Meggie's first nephew.

The district midwife had been delayed by another delivery – one which sadly ended in tragedy – but she arrived in time to cut the umbilical cord and examine her more fortunate patient for any signs of postnatal haemorrhage. A gaunt woman in her late fifties, silver-white hair drawn back into a bun and a face pinched by time and worry, she nodded her approval of the work Lorna and Meggie had done, declaring the newborn as healthy as a baby could be.

Of Tanith's mother or other family members there was no sign.

'He's so beautiful,' Meggie said dreamily, leaning over Tanith and looking down at the blanket-wrapped bundle cradled in her arms, his tiny face screwed up, a mask of apparent indignation at the strange world he had entered. Tanith smiled sadly but said nothing. Her only wish was that Duncan could have been there to see his son.

'Nine pounds four ounces is bloody big,' Lorna said, as she hovered behind Meggie and tried to catch a glimpse of her grandson. She was bursting to hold the baby in her arms. Not for many years would Frazer Dalrymple Granger-Acheson have so many women clamouring for his body, but at this moment in time neither he, nor his mother, grandmother or aunt had any idea of what lay ahead.

Come evening Lorna was well satisfied that

Frazer and her daughter-in-law would both be fine. Meggie had gone back to *Morningside* to see if Mister David's daughter, Aminta, could act as Tanith's personal nurse until she was on her feet again.

Waiting for them to return, Lorna sat holding her grandson, rocking him in her arms as she had done so often with a different Frazer. Sitting beside the bed she hummed quietly as Tanith snatched some much-needed sleep. Lorna looked down into Frazer's face with both joy and sadness. She firmly believed that this innocent child bore the spirit of his namesake – her youngest son – lost so tragically to the unfairness of war. *How long must this madness continue*, she wondered. *When would the family be together again?*

Early the following morning the horrified scream which shattered a quiet cul-de-sac on the Berea in Durban caused Torben to leap from his bed, grab a dressing gown and rush from the room he shared with his wife.

'What . . . what is it?' Gerda slurred, waking more slowly than her husband, who was already gone. In a few steps he reached the nursery, where the sound had originated. Alice's African nanny, Hilda, was standing beside the cot, hands waving uncontrollably in the air, her face a mask of wide-eyed panic.

Torben pushed the woman aside and, heart pounding, stared down into an empty cot. Where his precious daughter should have been sleeping he saw only an envelope. On it, written in red ink, was his name. 'Oh God,' he gasped. 'God, not her, not Alice. They've taken my baby!'

Gerda, who had hurried after her husband, stood at his shoulder and started to scream hysterically as soon as she saw the empty cot. Unable to think, Torben turned and slapped his wife across the face, hard. It had the desired effect. 'Alice is not dead,' he said, feeling a moment of guilt. 'I have no idea why she has been taken or by whom, but I promise you this, my love, we will soon have her back safe and well.'

'How soon?' Gerda fell against him, sobbing quietly.

Torben walked his wife back to bed, had her take a sedative, then went to question the nanny. She had not seen or heard anything. Going to his study he slumped into the leather chair and stared at the envelope left by whoever had abducted Alice. With trepidation he tore it open and read:

Your daughter is safe and well looked after. She is our insurance that you do not betray the trust we have placed in you. When the time is right, she will be returned. Under no circumstances speak with the police or . . .

The threat was left open ended.

Torben sat back deep in thought. The eyes and ears belonged to the *Broederbond*, of that there was now no doubt. Only yesterday the police had spoken to him and he told them nothing. But had they been police? The unanswered question only added to his concern, lengthening the shadow that had fallen over his life. There was only one way to find out. Getting his daughter back was all that mattered. Suddenly, wealth meant very little – it had cost him his baby.

He could hear Hilda ululating, a sound which would do little to console Gerda. Hopefully the laudanum he had given her was working. That morning Torben had no choice but to let the servants look after his wife. His priority was to start the search for Alice. He had no idea where to begin. Why on earth would he betray the Brotherhood? To do that would be admitting to treason. Could it be that he was no longer needed? If that were the case then the people he worked for were more ruthless than he had ever imagined. The thought terrified him.

His mind still in turmoil, Torben went to his dressing room then downstairs where he told Sixpence to keep an eye on Gerda while he was out. The carriage was ready and waiting. He would not be walking today.

Pacing the floor at his solicitor's office was frustrating in the extreme but he quickly established that no meeting had been arranged for ten o'clock. At ten-thirty Torben thanked the lawyer for his indulgence and hurried home.

Gerda slept fitfully under the alcoholic tincture of opium. What to do next? Torben frantically tried to think how he could persuade his employers he would never betray them. Their action made no sense to him. It wasn't a question of money – his freedom was already at stake, possibly even his life.

No matter what options Torben considered, he

could not decide where to start. The one word that kept coming back was 'family' – his own as well as the one he had grown up in, that of Lorna and Dallas Granger-Acheson. Suddenly, with crystal clarity, Torben realised that they were the only people he could truly trust. More now than ever before he needed his father. If anybody could help him rescue Alice from the *Broederbond*, it was Dallas. He couldn't leave Durban, at least not yet, but Torben knew he had to find out where his father was and arrange to meet him.

Dallas was not a man who took kindly to sickness in any shape or form – especially when his was the case in point. After three weeks of enforced rest and tests, which had done little for his health or humour, Dallas decided enough was enough, discharged himself and rejoined the Fairfax Scouts. He realised all was not well – the nagging cough told him that – but believed fresh air and exercise would put the malaise behind him. Besides, he also knew that Tanith must have had her baby and wanted to hear from Duncan whether it was a boy or a girl. When told by a proud father that his first grandson had been named Frazer Dalrymple, Dallas felt a surge of emotion – a new life for an old, and all was well.

It was now late November and the war had settled into a monotony of frustrating and usually long days in the saddle trying to find an army which had, quite simply, vanished. Farm burnings continued and it was rumoured that President

Steyn and Louis Botha were planning to strike in the Cape Colony and Natal where the same deterrent could not be used against them.

Duncan had noticed that his father often appeared listless and taciturn. The change worried him and one evening as they made camp he saw Dallas having trouble lifting the saddle from his horse. Quickly Duncan strode over.

'Can I help you, Father?' he asked, expecting a sharp rebuke.

Instead, Dallas turned a fevered gaze to his son. He was perspiring profusely. 'Thanks,' he mumbled, leaning against the horse. 'I'll be fine in a minute.' With that the saddle slipped from his grip.

Duncan dived forwards and steadied him, lowering his father gently to the warm earth. 'Why didn't you say something? You've got a raging fever and shouldn't even be here.' Dallas did not respond. He felt weaker than he could ever remember and was beyond caring. Duncan laid him on his back, using the saddle as a pillow. 'Stay here while I fetch Fairy.'

'Hadn't planned on going anywhere.' Dallas coughed and his attempt to wave off Duncan's concern failed. He had trouble lifting his arm.

Fairy Fairfax knelt beside his friend and didn't waste words. 'Ambulance wagon for you, old son.' Turning to Duncan he added, 'Sooner he's out of here the better. Don't know why the stubborn old bugger came back before they found out what was wrong with him. Told him so but he wouldn't listen. Anyway, at his age he shouldn't be out here wandering all over the veld.'

Dallas wanted to sit up and show his commanding officer that he was perfectly able to ride and fight with the best of them, but knew he didn't have the strength to protest.

Duncan and Sergeant Sims lifted Dallas onto a litter and carried him to the covered ambulance wagon. In it already lay one of the troop who had ignored a supposedly insignificant wound until it turned septic. He stank, his body poisoned by gangrene. The man was delirious and rambling. 'Burn it, burn it,' he kept repeating to the ghosts of darkness. Dallas could see them too as he fell into a strange world between the living and the dead.

There was no moon, making it too dark to travel until the following day. Duncan sat with his father all night but by morning he was no better. Just before dawn the horse-drawn wagon, a big red cross splashed on each side of its canvas cover, trundled away towards the nearest hospital.

'It's for the best,' Fairy said as he and Duncan watched it go. 'Look at it like this, he's the lucky one. Your father might well be back at *Morningside* in time for Christmas.'

Duncan heard the words but was far from convinced. Never before had he seen Dallas so sick and helpless. Typhoid, cholera and dysentery seemed to be taking a far greater toll than Boer bullets. He turned away, silently praying that his father would survive. It was wrong to think the worst but, apart from his own concern, Duncan could not face the possibility of having to tell his mother more bad news – she had suffered enough as it was.

Lorna stood staring from the kitchen window at precisely the time Dallas was being lifted into the wagon. Meggie was there too and turned just in time to see her mother swaying unsteadily before buckling at the knees in a sudden swoon.

'Mother!' she shouted, rushing to catch her.

'Sorry, darling.' Lorna shook her head as if to clear it.

'Let's get you sitting down.' Meggie helped her to a chair. 'I wonder what brought that on? Nothing nasty, I hope.'

'Probably my change of life,' Lorna volunteered, not believing it for one minute. She said nothing of the terrible dread that had suddenly overwhelmed her.

Meggie looked at her mother's drawn face and suggested bed was a better idea than sitting in the kitchen. Lorna readily agreed. She needed to be alone.

'I'll fetch you some water,' Meggie said, once her mother was lying down. 'Drink as much as you can.'

'Thank you, dear.' Lorna closed her eyes. *What had happened*, she questioned herself. It was nothing to do with her body showing its age. It was more like a vision, something inexplicable. A feeling of dread descended on her and she could hear a voice repeating two words over and over: 'burn it, burn it'. In that moment the answer came to her. One that she loved was in mortal danger. It was not something Lorna could explain, even to Meggie. Intuition or not, the message was clear and she fought back an overpowering need to cry out. One of the people in her life was teetering on the edge of death and she had no idea which one – not that it made any difference.

Meggie returned with the water to find tears streaming down her mother's deathly pale face. She placed the tray on a bedside table then brought a chair close and sat, taking one of Lorna's hands in hers. A slight squeeze acknowledged her presence but no more. If there was no improvement by morning she would send for Doctor Parry.

Somehow Meggie sensed that her mother's condition was more emotional than physical. A baby boy had been born into the family and the men who should have been there to welcome him were hundreds of miles away in a world of death and destruction. Their place was at home, working the land and being the husbands God had intended them to be.

Lorna drifted into a sleep haunted by nightmares. Meggie remained at her mother's side giving strength when the dreams came. It was a long night and often she dozed off. Through the mists of sleep Meggie heard a jackal howling into the night. It was not a welcome sound.

The ambulance wagon made slow progress along a track rutted by rain and the never-ending supply columns which fed an army Lord Roberts was about to leave in the hands of his Chief-of-Staff, General the Right Honourable Horatio Herbert Lord Kitchener, 1st Baron of Khartoum. When it finally halted outside a solid, stone-built hospital, the orderly who looked inside shook his head in frustration. One of the men was dead.

'Get this chap to the examination room.' He gave his instructions and two Sikh doolie-bearers lifted the surviving soldier's stretcher. 'The doctor is on duty. He'll want to have a look at him.'

The unconscious man was carried into a white-tiled room where they had to wait while a nurse finished washing fresh blood from the metal table. The smell of carbolic acid stung their eyes. Lindsay Mayer stood by the sink, cleaning his hands after completing an emergency appendix operation on a naval gunner brought in earlier that morning. He turned to the new arrival and his jaw dropped in disbelief. It was his father-in-law.

'Dallas?' Lindsay needed to know if he was conscious but received no response. The man was hardly breathing and sweating profusely. He coughed, a harsh sound which had Lindsay start his examination by listening to the patient's lungs. Methodically he carried out further tests, each new finding moving him closer to making a diagnosis. The nurse hovered and helped where she could.

At last he was finished. 'Get this man into a ward,' Lindsay said to the stretcher-bearers. 'Nurse, please make sure he has a bed bath and is given something more appropriate to wear. What he's got on can go to the laundry.'

Or the incinerator, the nurse thought to herself.

'After that, please find my wife and ask her to meet me in the office.'

Ellie was conducting her afternoon rounds when she received the message from Lindsay. 'Thank you, nurse. Tell him I'll be there as soon as I can.'

It took her another fifteen minutes. 'They've brought in your father,' Lindsay said, wasting no time on preliminaries.

Ellie's hand flew to her mouth. 'Is . . . is he . . .?' She had turned ashen, eyes wide and staring behind her glasses.

'He's not wounded. I'm fairly certain that he has advanced pneumonia. If you feel up to it I would appreciate your opinion.'

'Of course. Where is he?'

Lindsay told her then added, 'And I think you should send a telegram to your mother saying what has happened.'

Ellie nodded and left. She had not become hysterical, simply efficient in her response to his devastating news. Both knew only too well that pneumonia was usually fatal when contracted in the warmer months. Little could be done other than to let the infection run its course and pray that Dallas could summon the strength to come through it alive. Helplessness was often the worst part of their chosen profession. Physical injuries could be treated with surgery and splints but pneumonia or infectious diseases caused by conditions lacking even the most basic sanitation were another matter altogether. Ellie realised that she might be seeing her father for the last time.

Lindsay sighed and tried to stretch away the tension. He had deliberately let his wife go alone. The Granger-Achesons were a tough lot and if anyone had a hope in hell of surviving it was Dallas.

When Lorna received the telegram concerning her husband's condition and whereabouts she didn't waste a second. She had been expecting it.

Mister David prepared the carriage for the trip to the Thukela railhead while she packed a few essentials and made sure everybody knew what had to be done in her absence. A distraught Meggie was told to contact Cameron and Torben, then, with Mister David's help, hold the fort at *Morningside* until her mother returned with Dallas. That did not include visits to *Kingsway*.

Lorna had no idea how long she would be gone. What went without question was that she would bring her husband home, no matter who or what stood in her way. If the worst were to happen then Dallas would die in her arms on the land they had tamed together.

The slow train journey back to *Morningside* gave Lorna a long-awaited opportunity to catch up with her eldest daughter and, in particular, find out about married life with Lindsay. Ellie was as efficient as ever and Lorna gladly let her take charge of their travelling arrangements while she kept a watchful eye on Dallas. Ellie had organised places for all three of them on one of the hospital trains carrying wounded to the coast.

'I don't know how I would have managed all this without your help, dear. It was quite stupid of me to think I could do it all on my own.'

'Nonsense, Mother. If I hadn't been here you would have coped perfectly well. You always do.'

Lorna smiled. 'Does Lindsay mind your coming home with us? I didn't even think to ask the poor man.'

'Of course not. This is family.'

'So is he, Missus Mayer, or should I say "Doctor Mayer"?' Other than in letters, it was the first time Lorna had used her daughter's married name and title.

Ellie laughed. 'That sounds so strange coming from you, Mother.'

'And how is married life?'

'In many ways no different, but there is so much more I can't put my finger on. How do I explain it? It's as if a huge part of me was missing and I didn't know it. Mother, I've never been happier in my life. Lindsay feels the same.'

'I'm so very pleased for you both. Do you realise, there hasn't been one wedding in this family which has allowed your father and me to either give away a daughter or provide a proper reception?'

'You're quite right. I hadn't thought of it like that. There's still time, though. Cam's wedding can't be far off and don't forget Meggie.'

Lorna hadn't intended to say anything about

her youngest daughter's affair with Stan King but realised Ellie was probably the only person she could confide in. When all was said and done, the situation sounded a lot less serious than Lorna had previously thought.

'So Father has no idea?'

'Absolutely not.'

'Will you tell him or leave that to Meggie?'

'I can't keep it from him.'

'No. But first let me speak to my sister. This is not a matter of taking sides. For better or worse, it's Meggie's life we're talking about.'

There was no point in going over the same ground time and time again, so Ellie changed the subject. 'Have you heard anything from Cecily and Stephen?'

'No, not a word and I have no idea how to contact them.'

'Neither have I. If there's time while we're in Durban I'll check the house. Failing that I can do it on my way back.'

'How long will you be able to stay, dear?'

'That rather depends on Father. A week. Ten days at the most.'

'So no Christmas at home?'

'Sorry, Mother. Next year – with Lindsay. We might even let you arrange a belated reception for us – unless there's something else to celebrate, of course!'

Lorna smiled. 'Of course.'

They sat in silence for a while, both keeping an eye on their unconscious patient. It didn't last long.

'Do you ever see Torben and Gerda?' Lorna asked.

'Last time was a month or so after Alice was born. They made me a godmother, you know.'

'Yes, and Duncan godfather.'

'Right now it's Frazer I can't wait to see. God, how strange that sounds. How is he doing?'

'Fine. He and Tanith are both well. Aminta seems to have become his full-time nanny. She carries him everywhere, wrapped in a blanket on her back. When they come to *Morningside* his favourite place is under the cassia tree, beside Katie and his namesake. He and Aminta sit there for hours. Suza usually joins them, as if he's keeping guard. It's quite strange.'

'And Tanith's family? What's the story there?'

'As you know, they didn't come to the wedding. Her mother has seen Frazer but that's not common knowledge. Mister Taylor is being as pigheaded as ever and the boys just do as they're told.'

Ellie shook her head. 'Let's hope he comes to his senses. Life is too short to stand in the way of other people's happiness.'

Lorna found herself thinking about Meggie and Stan rather than Tanith and Duncan. *Had Ellie intended that*, she wondered.

Dallas moaned, which usually meant he needed water. The two women turned quickly to their patient.

TWENTY-TWO

Captain Cameron Granger-Acheson sat in his canvas tent baking in the early December heat. Both end flaps were open but even the air was too hot to move. Eye-stinging sweat trickled down his face as he looked at the papers spread out on his folding table. The immediate problem was to think of some credible reason why one of his troop had lost two of Her Majesty's rifle magazines. Although he and his men had been brought in from the field for a short break and long overdue refit, life around camp lacked the excitement and dangers they had become used to. Then there was the paperwork.

'Bugger,' he swore as a great blob of sweat dropped from his nose causing part of the report to form a blue-black sea of spreading ink. Administration was an officer's duty but it was not one that Cameron took on with any enthusiasm.

'Beats being out in the bush, wouldn't you say?' Captain Sam Snelling asked cheerily, filling the tent with a bright smile and his huge bulk. 'Three meals a day and the officers' mess to drink yourself stupid. Can't be bad, eh? Got time for one?'

Cameron looked up at the quartermaster whose reputation for being among the last to leave the mess each night was legendary. A regular soldier, he was horribly overweight, preferring the sedentary life of base camps where a supply of good food and drink was never far from his place of work. Being cheerful by nature, as well as unusually generous with regimental supplies, made him popular with both men and officers from the field.

'No can do, I'm afraid. Got to finish this ridiculous report, all for the sake of two bloody magazines,' Cameron responded irritably. 'Then I've got to take a weapons inspection.'

'Forget the report,' the quartermaster offered. 'I'll write them off and issue your man a couple more.'

'Much appreciated.' Cameron crumpled up the sheet he had been working on. 'I still have to do the parade but since you've saved me a lot of damned paperwork the least I can do is buy you a drink or two this evening.'

'Sounds good to me, old boy,' Snelling grinned. 'Roast beef and Yorkshire pud in the mess tonight. Better get in early before it's all gone.'

Cameron smiled, shaking his head as the big soldier went on his way. Rising to stretch legs stiff from sitting he stepped outside and stared at the row upon row of white tents pitched in neat lines as far as the eye could see. He could hear the bawled orders of NCOs drilling their men, a blacksmith's hammer clanging his anvil as he shod a seemingly endless stream of horses. Turning back

Cameron glanced around the tent that was both his office and sleeping quarters, noting – not for the first time – the complete lack of personal belongings. One folding table, one canvas chair, a camp stretcher and paraffin lamp – all carefully itemised and none of them his. A blanket bedroll, mirror, spare uniform and the holstered army issue Webley revolver which hung from a nail also belonged to Queen Victoria. They at least went with him while he was protecting her empire, patrolling a vast land nobody seemed to control. *Heaven help him*, he thought, *if anything should go missing*.

The letter from Virginia still haunted him but he had told nobody – save for Henry – and had been able to bury himself in a world of kill or be killed. It was the nights, when she came uninvited into his dreams, that were the worst. Christmas was not far off and Cameron hoped he might wangle enough leave to go home. That would be the time to confront Ginnie and plead his case for their future.

'Captain, sir?' A familiar voice jolted him back to reality.

Cameron glanced up from the last of his report-writing to see Sergeant-Major Mulligan standing at the entrance to his tent. 'Yes, Sarn't-Major?'

'They want to see you up at the ops room, sir.'

'Any idea what it's about?'

'No, sir.'

Glad of a diversion and the possibility of action, Cameron grabbed his hat and tunic, strapped on the revolver and walked briskly to the tent that served as communications and administration headquarters for his company. There he was met by the regiment's adjutant, a captain like himself.

'Ah, Cameron.' He stepped outside to get away from the chattering telegraph. Behind him sat two soldiers whose job it was to sort the mounds of paperwork the army ran on. 'I am afraid there's some bad news for you.'

Cameron had not been expecting the adjutant's words and immediately feared the worst. Someone in the family was dead or dying. He said nothing, though the colour drained from his face.

The regiment's senior captain continued, 'There seems to have been a bit of a delay – can't think why – but we have just received word that your father is seriously ill. Not wounded, if that's any consolation: pneumonia, apparently. It seems your mother doesn't trust military hospitals and intends taking him home to be looked after. That was some days ago. The CO has approved your immediate leave.'

'Thanks, Tom. Not your fault.' Despite his words, Cameron felt a sense of frustration. 'Have you any idea how bad he is?'

'Sorry, old chap. Your pass is valid until midnight on New Year's Day. Don't worry about the troop. I'll organise for a replacement officer to stand in while you're away.'

Cameron took the all-important piece of paper and walked back to his tent, stunned by the hand life had dealt him. He had hoped to be home for Christmas but not under these circumstances. The family could lose – Lord knows, they may already have lost – the person who stood out as a rock in the sand dunes of their lives.

The man had called himself Inspector Wild when he introduced himself to Torben. He was in fact a well-educated Dutchman by the name of Klaas. Brought up in England, his London accent came easily, though it was those years of enforced exile that made him a passionate supporter of the Afrikaner cause. Klaas saw his role in the war as that of a liaison officer. More correctly, he was both a spy and a member of the *Broederbond*. Now he stood in the single room of a Boer farmhouse, a tiny bundle in his arms. 'The baby's name is Alice Petersen,' he said. 'You will be her mother until it is decided otherwise.'

The woman was middle-aged, her face pinched by hardship and worry. Gently she took the living bundle from him. Heidi van der Merwe had lost a child some months before and now her husband was away, riding the veld with Jan Smuts. The death of her own offspring had been almost beyond bearing when Klaas made contact, saying he had a task that she would be paid for – to look after a six month old baby girl. Heidi would have done it without the money. Anything to fill the vacuum of loss and loneliness that had become her life. She peered down into the blankets to see a smiling face staring back. 'She is truly beautiful,' Heidi whispered in awe. 'And she is mine.'

'Only for as long as I say so,' Klaas reminded

her. 'Until then you will be well paid to care for the child.'

Heidi looked sharply at the man she suspected of belonging to the secretive organisation she had heard referred to as the *Broederbond*. It was not a woman's place to ask questions, though she knew her husband was a member. She had met this man Klaas a year earlier when her husband had brought the stranger home for a night. Heidi did not like him then and did not like him now. He stank of treachery and deceit. 'Until you say otherwise,' she agreed in words – but not in her heart.

Alice Petersen was at least in good hands, even if that happened to be more than two hundred miles from her home in Durban.

Klaas placed a small bag of coins on the table, picked up his hat and left without saying another word. Heidi stood rocking the baby and crooning the only song she knew, 'Sarie Marais'.

Lorna sat by the bed she and Dallas had shared for so many years. At times her husband was almost lucid, his breathing noticeably easier after leaving the highveld. They had spent a night at Addington hospital in Durban and Ellie had managed to send a telegram telling Meggie when to expect them at the Thukela railhead. There had been no time to check Cecily and Stephen's house or to contact Torben. The journey from Durban took two full days.

Meggie was horrified by her father's appearance. He looked haggard – having lost over a stone in weight it was hardly surprising – and did not seem to recognise her.

Ellie had a hard job convincing Mister David that rest and plenty of liquid would do more for Dallas than his *muthi*. However, when they finally got him into his own bed she was not surprised to find a small and very old square of snakeskin lying on his chest. It had strange scratch marks on it and Ellie decided to leave it. The magic charm could do no harm; it might even be helping. She realised how precious the talisman must be to Mister David and how lucky her father was to have such a friend.

'My love,' Dallas croaked through parched lips. 'Why don't you get some sleep?'

Lorna was dozing and snapped awake at the sound of her husband's voice. They had been home for nearly three days and these were the first coherent words he had spoken. She gripped his hand in hers. 'I'm fine, my darling. I was sleeping in the chair.'

'You should be in bed, not sitting here.'

'I am where I want to be,' Lorna said, smiling. 'Beside you and nowhere else.'

As she stood and brought a glass of water to his lips, Dallas looked up at the familiar face hovering over him. 'My angel,' he sighed. 'Where have you been?'

'Here, my darling. Right here.'

As if on cue, both his daughters tiptoed into the room. Dallas held up an arm and weakly beckoned them forward. Each hugged their father in a way that took him back to when they were children. Tears flowed freely.

'Hey, steady on. I'm not going to die,' he reassured his women. 'I'll be back on my feet and keeping an eye on Duncan before you know it.'

'Over my dead body,' Lorna snapped. 'Your war is over, my boy, so get used to it. I need you here.'

Dallas winced at his wife's commanding tone. He knew she was right. For a moment he actually found himself wondering what jobs might need his attention around the farm. God willing, the war would soon be over and, as the bible said, swords could be turned into ploughshares. They had lost a son and two others were still at risk. It was enough. More than enough.

A mist seemed to lift from his mind as Dallas realised he also had a grandchild that he had not yet seen. Frazer, Duncan's son.

Outside, a dog barked. Saba. Cameron's dog never barked unless . . .?

'Cam!' Lorna shouted. In seconds she was rushing down the steps and breaking into a run to meet her firstborn son. Saba was already by his horse's side. 'What a wonderful surprise, darling. We weren't sure if you would be coming. Does Ginnie know?'

'Mother,' Cameron said, ignoring the question and leaning down to kiss her on the cheek. 'How is Father?' Dismounting he continued their conversation while squatting to greet his exuberant dog, the boxer's docked tail wagging back and forth like an overwound metronome.

'He's going to be fine, dear. Your timing could not have been better. The fever has broken and he's talking again. Meggie and Ellie are with him inside.'

'Who else is here?'

'Nobody.'

'I thought Torben and Gerda might be.'

'No. We haven't seen them or Alice in ages.'

Cameron shrugged. 'That must be a relief.'

Lorna ignored the comment. 'Wait till you see little Frazer. Actually, he's not little, he's huge. Have you heard from Duncan?' she babbled, walking beside Cameron as he led his horse towards a shy *umfana* who waited to take it from him.

'Not recently. Fairfax could be anywhere.'

When Lorna looked up into her son's face she was startled to see a coldness in his steely blue eyes that hadn't been there before. It gave him a distant, haunted look. *The war*, she thought sadly, *it has changed all of us*. 'I can't wait to catch up on your news.' Lorna was determined to remain positive but a mother's intuition told her all was not well.

'There's not much to catch up on.' Cameron shrugged, removing his saddlebags and sliding a military carbine from the leather bucket strapped to his saddle. 'You can take my horse,' he said to the young Zulu. 'Make sure he is well rubbed down and fed.'

'*Yebo, nkosi*.' The boy led the tired animal towards the stables, leaving Lorna, Cameron and slobbering Saba standing in front of the house. Meggie and Ellie were waiting on the verandah.

Before Cameron could say hello he was swamped with hugs and kisses.

Mister David hung back respectfully, a huge grin on his gleaming black face. 'I see you, *nkosi*,' he said.

'And I you, *madala*. Your son is well and sends greetings.'

Mister David nodded and nearly fell over Suza, who had actually moved to see what all the fuss was about.

'Come and see Father,' Ellie said, taking one of her brother's arms.

'I'm sure he feels quite deserted,' Meggie added, seizing the other.

Later that evening, Lorna looked at her husband and burst into tears. It was going to be a good Christmas.

That night the rain came, falling in torrents on the tin roof. It was a sound Dallas had all but forgotten. One that said he was home.

Cameron had never replied to Ginnie's letter. He carried it in the pocket of his tunic, next to the heart she had broken. Its contents he could repeat word for word but that did little more than bring back the memories. Today he would find out if the woman he loved could say the same things to his face.

She had always been there and when childhood friendship turned into something more, Ginnie gave him the time he needed to work some of the wildness out of his system. If anything, it made him love her all the more. They had never actually made love, though that was due more to him. Virginia Waring-Jones was the woman he would spend the rest of his life with and respect for her virginity was his way of telling her so.

Ginnie understood him better even than his parents. Cameron remembered how the two of them would talk for hours of a family, the farm and plans for their future together. How God must have laughed at that, he thought to himself. Then the war came. It shouldn't have changed anything but when Kevin was wounded it changed everything. Cameron sometimes wished he were the one who would never walk again.

Apparently, Ginnie hadn't called at *Morningside* since before Duncan and Tanith's wedding in August. That had been four months ago. Her letter reached him in October. Had he left it too long?

It was Ginnie's father who answered the door and invited Cameron into the living room. He was surprised at how much the man had aged. Of Kevin or any of the women there was no sign.

'I'll call Virginia,' he said, obviously embarrassed by Cameron's unexpected arrival.

When she appeared a few minutes later Cam froze. He had intended sweeping her up in his arms, smothering the woman he loved with kisses and making everything good again, but her reserved demeanour instantly dispelled any thoughts of doing that. Instead, he stood awkwardly – hat in hands – while she took a seat and carefully gathered in the long dark dress she was wearing.

'Please, Cameron, won't you sit down?' she invited, almost formally. 'You are looking well. Are you home for Christmas? How is the family?' The words came tumbling out, as if from someone he barely knew.

'My darling, these past weeks have been the worst hell I have ever known. How could you suddenly say that you no longer love me? It isn't possible.'

Ginnie's hands were clasped in her lap, knuckles white with strain as she unconsciously wrung her hands together. There was a ring on her engagement finger which she kept turning. Not his.

'It was not a good idea to come here,' she replied softly. 'My intention was never to hurt you. I had no choice.'

'Choice? Ginnie, you love me. How in God's name can you use a word like "choice"?'

'You've seen Father. Kevin is, let us say, having a little sleep. I cannot desert my family. Somebody has to run this place. They need me more than you do.'

'We can work something out,' Cameron replied, pacing the room. 'Your family is important but I do not believe your feelings for me have changed. Our love is built on a lifetime of knowing each other. Something like that doesn't just stop.'

'Cameron, I really would prefer it if you sat down,' Virginia said gently. 'You are working yourself into a temper.'

'A temper?' Cameron repeated the word in

exasperation. 'I've been stuck out in the bloody veld fighting to give this country a future and all you can say is that I'm working myself into a temper? Well, so what!'

'Sit down,' Ginnie said again, more forcefully this time. 'There is something you have to hear which will hurt you even further. I must tell you all the same.'

'What could hurt more than refusing to admit that you still love me?' Cameron fell into a chair opposite Ginnie. 'There can be nothing in this world worse than that.'

'I do not think that you should come here again,' Ginnie said, her head bowed. 'I am to be wed in three months.'

The statement hit Cameron harder than a Boer dumdum bullet. For a moment he was unable to comprehend what Ginnie had just told him. 'Who?' he finally asked, his voice little more than a whisper.

'Paul Norman,' she replied, still unable to look him in the eye.

'Norman!' Cameron exploded, leaping to his feet. 'You can't mean it. That little weasel from next door?'

'I knew you would not understand. Paul has asked me for my hand in marriage and I have accepted. That's all there is to it.'

'When did all this take place?' Cameron asked, standing over Ginnie.

She didn't answer. 'Paul has been very kind to us. We might even join the two farms.'

'Look me in the eye and say that you love him,' Cameron demanded. 'Or is this no more than a marriage of convenience?'

'I do love Paul,' Ginnie said, although her voice was not as convincing as she had intended. 'I am sorry, Cameron,' she went on. 'The wedding date has been set so I would rather you say no more and leave this house.'

'The only thing that kept me going out there was the knowledge of our love.' Cameron nearly choked on the words, forcing himself not to burst into tears. 'Every night I told myself we were one day closer to being together. Then your letter arrived. I wanted to desert my men and be back here with you. You were all I could think about. Ginnie, I will not – no, cannot – accept that there is another you love more than me.'

'What's done is done,' Ginnie said, holding out the ring he had given her. 'Take this and know that there was no other way.'

Cameron stepped back, his face contorted with anguish and anger. 'Keep it. Call the bloody thing a wedding present. I hope you find happiness.' With that, he stormed out of the house.

Outside he seized the reins of his horse and swung into the saddle. Turning its head Cameron kicked it into a canter and rode away without once looking back. Tears flowed and he ignored them. It was over.

Ginnie hadn't moved. She sat in the chair crying uncontrollably, her mind in turmoil. How could her life have become so complicated? How was it that she had found solace in another man's arms and yet her heart could not let go of Cameron? She had thought she was over him until he appeared and stood in front of her. 'Oh, Cam,' she sobbed, knowing full well that if it were not for the war their future could have been all they had planned. Life was so unfair.

When Cameron returned to *Morningside* the fury on his face made it plain no questions would be tolerated. All knew where he had been. Even Saba, sensing something was seriously wrong, decided that it might be best to give her master a wide berth.

Sitting in his favourite chair on the verandah and looking down towards the lush green of cane plantings along the Mhlathuze River, Dallas reflected on how close he had come to dying. There had been many times in his life he had stood toe to toe with death but more often than not the instinctive decision which kept him alive was his own. Pneumonia had been a different matter altogether. The insidious disease was something over which he had had no control. All he had to fight with was his will to survive and the knowledge that his family needed him, Lorna in particular.

No, he would not be returning to active service. The medical report submitted by Doctor Parry and Ellie would see to that. In many ways Dallas was glad. He had done his bit for Queen and country and now it was time to think of the future – even admit a few mistakes.

This was not cattle country. Dallas accepted that, though he had persevered and been more successful than most. Sugar was, without doubt, the way things were moving and Zululand yields were far better than anything in the rest of Natal. It was only a matter of time, two or three years at most, before the rail line from Durban reached Empangeni. Another mill would be needed by then. What if it were on his doorstep? The thought called for a family discussion. But with Christmas just a week away, it would have to wait. Anyway, Ellie had already gone and Cameron had other matters on his mind.

There was nothing anybody could do about his break-up with Ginnie. Even the news that Caroline Hammond was giving him her farm, *Wakefield*, met with a snapped response: 'And what am I supposed to do with the place – become a bloody hermit?' Nobody could talk to him. Tanith had tried – introducing Frazer – but that only added to his depression. Mister David tried, seeking news of Henry. Cameron did at least take the time to tell him of his son's bravery, swelling the Zulu's heart with pride.

Saba had shadowed her master's every move. Cam would take a rifle and they would be gone for hours, disappearing into the swampy reed beds round the Mhlathuze Lagoon. Dallas suspected that an old croc who lived there was the challenge but the wily old fellow was well protected by an early warning system provided by the plovers he allowed to feed in and around his giant jaws.

Dallas remembered when his friend and mentor, John Dunn, had shot a twenty-two footer on the lagoon. *Man-eater it might have been but monsters like that are a thing of the past*, he thought, before his mind snapped back to the present.

At least some of the family would be home for Christmas. Cameron, Meggie, of course, Tanith and Frazer – the grandson he had only just met. Torben and Gerda were expected, though they hadn't bothered to confirm they were coming. Dallas looked forward to seeing the changes in Alice, though he realised that their visit would also mean having to put up with Gerda's perceptions of the important things in life. From what he had seen for himself, Torben's growing wealth was no figment of his imagination. His son's business was doing well and he had done it on his own with no calls for help.

'Penny for your thoughts?' Lorna said, joining her husband and laying an affectionate hand on his shoulder.

'I was just thinking about this place and our rather special family,' he replied, reaching up to touch her. 'They may cause us concern from time to time but when all is said and done we are so very fortunate.'

Lorna sank into a chair beside him. 'Even with the tragedies that have befallen us?' she asked, though it was not really meant as a question.

'God has plans that we are not privy to,' Dallas responded, bringing a faint smile of surprise to her face.

'That is not in doubt, my darling, but I have never heard you admit it. Don't tell me age and maturity have brought on a bout of religious fervour in my normally pagan husband?'

Dallas looked uncomfortable. 'I don't think so,' he replied seriously, 'though somehow it makes it easier to accept what we have lost in our lives.'

Lorna nodded and fell silent.

Dallas had come to know every nuance of her manner and felt she had more to say. 'You seem a bit distant. Is something wrong?'

Lorna looked up at the sky before replying. 'There is something I think you should know,' she said. 'But first you must promise not to overreact and get angry.'

'How can you expect me to do that when I have no idea what I should not get angry about?' Dallas had a pained expression on his face. 'Give me a hint. That's only fair.'

'It concerns Meggie,' Lorna said. 'And I still need your word.'

Dallas felt immediate alarm at the mention of his youngest daughter, the person who had a place in his heart second only to Lorna. He always tried not to differentiate between any of his children but Meggie had always been special. Lorna knew that and accepted their closeness, so whatever was on her mind had to be bad news. She left him no choice. 'You have my word that I will not display anger at anything you have to tell me.'

'Meggie is seeing Stanley King.'

'She's what?!'

'Remember your promise, dear,' Lorna hurried to remind him.

'Stan King,' Dallas roared. 'He's an old man. He's my age!'

'No he isn't,' Lorna said, placing a restraining hand on her husband's arm to prevent him leaping to his feet and striding up and down the verandah as he was prone to do when he needed to think. 'Keeping it from you is breaking Meggie's heart. She can't bear the thought of hurting you.'

Lorna's well-chosen words eased Dallas's anger. 'Who else knows?' he asked.

'Only Ellie. She tried to talk Meggie into telling you but couldn't convince her.'

'At least that explains why she seems to have been avoiding me.' Dallas was calming down, though he couldn't accept the thought of his little girl in the arms of a man twice her age. Perhaps when his strength returned, he would ride out to *Kingsway* with a *sjambok* and teach the old lecher a lesson or two . . . 'I think I should have a chat with our Meggie,' was what he said. 'Explain to her that it cannot work.'

'Why?' Lorna asked, taking him completely by surprise.

Dallas looked at her in disbelief. 'Why? I would have thought that was obvious.'

'This may come as a bit of a shock to you, my husband, but your little girl – the one you used to carry around on your shoulders and tuck into bed with a story – has grown up. She is a young woman ready to leave our house in search of her own life.

Don't look so surprised. I have been thinking that Stan King is a man very much like yourself in more ways than you would dare admit. Meggie might not realise it but to some extent she's paying you an enormous compliment.'

Lorna's outburst stunned Dallas. 'I don't care,' he said. 'All I know is that she is far too young to be running around with any man – young or old. Meggie's still a child.'

'In your eyes she will always be the baby girl who played rough and tumble games with her brothers and sisters one minute and dolls' houses the next. Those days are gone, Dallas. Our family has grown up. Letting our little girl lead her own life is just as painful for me as it is for you, but I have realised this – even greater sadness will follow if you confront our daughter and attempt to stop her seeing the man she loves. She will dig in her heels and the character you so admire will do the rest.'

'She will listen to me,' Dallas growled. 'I am her father.'

'Think about it.' Lorna laughed bitterly. 'I did the same thing for the man I love. Our daughter sees in Stan King the same strengths she sees in you.'

Lorna could sense Dallas's reaction and recognised his shock. 'It is perfectly normal,' she soothed. 'We women often look at the first real love in our lives and find our fathers. It's from them we learned what it is like to be sheltered from harm, to find comfort in their strength and protection in their arms. Is it so surprising, then, to unconsciously seek another who will provide us with the same sense of well-being and love? I think Meggie has found that and more in Stan King.'

Dallas listened to Lorna's logical explanation but still could not accept that his little girl had turned to another. No-one was good enough to take Meggie from him, though he grudgingly had to admit – to himself if nobody else – that no matter what man had appeared in his daughter's life he would have found some fault with him. In the case of Stan King, age was the only shortcoming he could think of. Damn it, he had always liked and respected the man – until now.

'Dallas?'

'What?'

'Go to your daughter and let her know you are still the loving father she has always known.'

'How can you expect me to condone what she is doing?' he asked quietly.

'I don't. But you have to recognise that Meggie is no longer a little girl and one day soon she will start a family of her own. Dallas, love is not about possession, it's about giving. Perhaps that is what makes it so difficult.'

Dallas turned to Lorna, hearing the wisdom in her words. His undying love for this woman who herself had given up so much to be by his side in a strange and often dangerous land had never been stronger. 'I will still have to sit the bounder down and have a fatherly chat with him.' He smiled weakly. 'Won't that be fun!'

Lorna leaned across and rested her head against his shoulder. 'Sometimes I wonder why I love such a stiff-necked old goat,' she said, tears welling in her eyes. 'But I do, my darling, and I am not alone in my love for you. The same applies to our children, and now there's a whole new generation coming into the family who will grow up loving their grumpy old grandfather. One day there may even be great-grandchildren.'

Dallas hoped his wife didn't notice his own tears. Yes, it was time to accept that Meggie had become a woman but it would not stop him telling Stan King what he expected of him – that was a father's duty.

TWENTY-THREE

Gerda hardly ever left her bed anymore and seemed to have no interest in anything, including her own pregnancy. Torben had promised to find their daughter and bring her safely home but that was proving easier said than done. He couldn't leave Durban and had no choice other than to do as instructed and hope their nightmare would soon be over.

Torben had taken one chance. Realising that the servants knew what had happened and that they could not do without them, he explained that the *Broederbond* had been responsible for Alice's abduction and offered a reward for any information leading to her safe return. It had been a very clever move and one which was unlikely to be discovered. Blacks talked to blacks but seldom to whites – especially members of a secret Afrikaner society which saw them as little more than a source of slave labour.

This was a test and Torben knew he must pass it if they were to have any hope of seeing Alice again. It had already been more than six weeks and he had received no word from her abductors. Under no circumstances would he entertain the idea his daughter might be dead – that was impossible.

Without mentioning anything to Gerda, Torben had also made it known to her brother that there would be a substantial reward for any information concerning Alice's welfare or whereabouts. It was a risk, he told himself, but Mark was Afrikaans-speaking and mixed with many unsavoury characters who might, from time to time, be called on to undertake special contracts for the Brother-hood. To date he had heard nothing.

Torben continued working, waiting and hop-ing, trying to keep some semblance of sanity in his everyday business life. Even casual acquaintances noticed a change in him. He no longer frequented any of his favourite clubs and Gerda had with-drawn from the social life of Durban. Gossip at the tea parties held by those with nothing better to do was that her baby had died of some ailment caught from the African nanny. There were tut-tuts of sympathy but nobody actually called on the Petersens, who lived in splendid isolation except for the regular house calls of a well-paid physician Torben had sworn to secrecy. Although he main-tained the supply of laudanum which kept Gerda calm and in her bed, the doctor had warned that continued use of the drug might affect her preg-nancy. Torben reduced the amount he administered but that was all.

On the leather-inlaid desk, letters for the past week – delivered to the house by messenger from his office in West Street – lay unanswered. Having made sure there was nothing in the mail which concerned Alice, Torben quickly lost interest in everyday business correspondence. One envelope was still sealed. It displayed the fine copperplate hand of Olaf Petersen, the banker brother of his long dead Danish mother, Jette. Olaf was his business partner, a financial wizard who handled the European end of their highly lucrative armaments business and various other dealings from his office in Copenhagen.

Torben picked up a silver letter opener and carefully slit one edge of the envelope. He was not in the mood to read his uncle's letter, which would undoubtedly contain the usual analysis of projects concluded and new ventures to be explored. For a second Torben had a fleeting memory of another Christmas, one he had spent in Denmark with Olaf's family. There had been sleigh rides, snow falling gently, happiness and smiles of welcome and, oh, how they loved their food. '*Tak for mad,*' the Danes would say – thank you for the food, everything from *smørrebrød* and *frikadellers* to pork stuffed with apples and prunes or flaky butter pastry covered in melted sugar and slivered almonds. It was certainly far removed from the pain and suffering with which he now lived. Perhaps he could send Gerda to Kobenhavn, Torben thought. She would be well looked after and the sea voyage might do her good. Then he remembered that his wife was nearly six months pregnant. A trip to Europe would require three months at the very least. His mind was wandering as he slid a single sheet of paper from the envelope.

'God in heaven!' Torben exploded at the words he read, the hand holding the letter shaking uncontrollably. *How long had it lain on his desk*, he questioned himself. Days. It had been there for days and he hadn't bothered to open it. Olaf's scrawled handwriting gave Torben his first glimmer of hope that he might soon find his daughter:

. . . and for this reason I do not agree with the methods that have been employed by certain colleagues of mine with regard to their recent actions concerning a member of your family. I therefore deem it my duty to impart information which may assist in bringing this matter to a satisfactory conclusion.

Torben continued to read, hanging on to every word. The note concluded: *Should you reveal the source of these facts I have no doubt that it would result in the most dire consequences. I therefore urge you to proceed with the utmost caution.* It was unsigned.

Sitting back, he placed the piece of paper on his desk and stared despairingly at the heavily draped window. God, the world was so small. A miracle had occurred but Torben knew he would need help to follow up on what Olaf had told him. It was not something he could do on his own. Some weeks earlier he had received a telegram from Meggie saying that their father had been taken ill and was going home. Since then, the annual invitation to spend Christmas at *Morningside* had arrived and with it a note saying that Dallas was recovering but would not be returning to active duties. Torben had not replied. There were other things on his mind and acceptance would have meant telling the family about Alice. Suddenly that had all changed. It was time to travel again.

Come Christmas Day Dallas had still said nothing to Meggie about Stan King. He hoped his daughter would tell him of her own free will. Lorna had promised not to interfere but that didn't mean a hint or two would not be dropped to let Meggie know the groundwork had been done.

Cameron's decision to leave *Morningside* two days before had come as a complete surprise to Lorna and Dallas. Admittedly, his mood and need to be alone made him almost impossible to talk to – so much so that the opportunity never arose to discuss the idea of Duncan and Tanith building a place of their own on the farm. Without Cameron's approval as the eldest son, there was no point in even hinting at the possibility.

Tanith lived in a house she was looking after while the owners spent a year in Europe. They had left her one servant, Caliph, who did any heavy work, and after Frazer was born Mister David's daughter Aminta had moved in to act as nanny for the new baby. Lorna respected her daughter-in-law's independence but was sorry she had turned down an offer to use the guest accommodation at *Morningside*. Of course, the invitation had nothing to do with being closer to what was then an impending grandchild! At least the problem of finding a suitable wedding present had been solved. The gift of a pony and trap had given Tanith mobility and meant that she and Frazer could come to the farm without waiting to be collected.

Tanith, Frazer and Aminta arrived a little before midday on Christmas Day, bringing a sense of family to the house. Lorna and Meggie jostled to hold or amuse the robust and highly vocal Frazer, whose still-unseen father was many hundreds of miles away. Dallas didn't see it quite like that. Here he was surrounded by women and not one of them was paying him the slightest attention!

Although places had been set for Torben and Gerda – just in case they did arrive – only four of the family sat down to a Christmas meal that year. As always, Mister David had excelled himself. The dining-room table had not been extended to take the extra leaves which allowed it to seat twelve at full stretch, but nevertheless it displayed the sparkling family silver and a fine selection of festive fare. Rich guinea-fowl soup was served and Dallas said grace, blessing the food they were about to eat. He also took the opportunity to ask their maker to watch over those who could not be with them and thanked him for his own recovery. For Dallas and Lorna, an African Christmas in the blazing heat of December never quite compared with the more traditional setting they had grown up with in Scotland – snow, and a roaring fire to keep out the cold – but it was still special. A time for family.

Dallas checked the carving knife and expertly honed its already razor sharp edge on the steel before addressing a succulent haunch of well-hung *nyala* which had been marinating in red wine for the last three days. It needed no pressure to slice the tender meat. There was well-cooked roast pork with crackling and apple sauce for those who preferred something milder, various vegetables, even cold ham, brawn and ox tongue, all home prepared. A spicy beef curry and yellow saffron rice waited for the adventurous with crisp, wafer-thin poppadoms and an array of sweet and savoury sambals.

'Goodness gracious,' Tanith exclaimed. 'This would feed an army.' She hadn't intended the reference and nobody picked her up on it. For the moment, war was a long way from their lives.

Dallas poured wine for everybody and proposed a toast: 'Absent friends.' The response came back: 'Absent friends.' It brought a tear to Lorna's eye which she quickly dabbed away with her napkin.

Fresh fruit salad and cream concluded the feast, followed by demitasse cups of black Turkish coffee. Everybody was replete. They had done justice to a magnificent meal.

Tanith excused herself to feed Frazer while Lorna went to the kitchen where she made sure the staff also had a share of the food.

Arm in arm Dallas and Meggie walked out to the verandah where a decanter of port had been placed beside his chair. Dallas searched for his pipe.

'No smoking, please, Father. Not until those lungs of yours have had a chance to recover.'

'If you insist. Then walk with me instead.'

Meggie hesitated but Dallas took her arm and

together they stepped out into the afternoon sun. Lorna and Tanith were sitting on the grass under the cassia tree which gave shade to two simple graves. Fresh flowers lay on both. Tanith fed Frazer without any hint of embarrassment and made no attempt to cover herself when Dallas and Meggie approached. Each had their own thoughts and they stayed there in silence, sharing them with spirits from the past.

'Don't you Grangers give a girl any warning before you drop in?' She used the name her half-brother Dallas had adopted when he first arrived in South Africa.

'Sorry. Father told me about what you want to do with *Wakefield* and I came to say don't. Ginnie and I are no longer engaged.'

'And to do that I suppose you decided to forego a family Christmas? That wasn't very sensible.' Caroline Hammond looked up at the unsmiling face and saw nothing but sadness. 'I assume you're staying, so now you're here might I suggest you get off that old nag and go catch us some supper. There's precious little in the larder.'

'Thank you. If you don't mind I'll see to my horse first. He can be a bit temperamental with strangers.' Cameron swung a leg over the saddle and slid to the ground.

Klipklop was squatting a few yards away, his eyes focused on those of the bay gelding. Slowly he rose and moved forwards, muttering something unintelligible, never once breaking visual contact. The horse lowered its head and seemed to be listening. Still talking, the little Bushman turned and walked away. Cameron watched in disbelief as his horse meekly followed.

'I don't think you need worry about him,' Caroline said.

Cameron looked towards the distant peaks – it was impossible not to – then turned to gaze up at the rock-strewn slope of the Inhluzan. He had the strangest feeling of being watched. Caroline had started towards the house when his eye was caught by a lone bateleur eagle, soaring in effortless circles against the cumulus clouds of the midsummer sky. When he caught up with her, Caroline was lifting down a ten-foot, split-cane fly rod from two wooden pegs where it hung on the wall outside.

'I used it only last week,' she said, handing it to him.

The hexagonal rod was feather light, its waxed cotton line wound onto a reel made by Alex Martin of Edinburgh. *Only the best*, Cameron thought. A rather drab fly had been hooked into the special loop bound and laquered to the varnished wood just in front of a cork handle.

'That's a March Brown,' Caroline said. 'You might do better with a Zulu or a Coachman. Try it and see.' She handed him a flat, rather battered tin of assorted flies. 'Don't go any larger than a twelve. There's quite a bit of water coming down but the river was stocked last year. Rainbow and brown. Put back anything under ten inches.' She laughed. 'Here endeth the lesson.'

'Where should I try?'

'That's up to you, my boy. The river is my boundary – sorry, your boundary. Have fun, I've got things to do.' She passed him a landing net. 'Not least, tidy myself up a bit. You'd best get going, it's a fair walk. See you later.' Caroline turned and disappeared inside. From behind a lace curtain, she watched him walk away – the man who now owned *Wakefield*. She hadn't told him in so many words but the transfer had been registered. *God*, she thought, *he looks just like my father*.

It was summer though the air seemed thin and bracing with none of the sticky heat he had left behind at *Morningside*. Christmas Eve, Cameron reflected, realising that his thoughts were not with the family but here, setting off to try to outwit a wily trout or two in a Drakensberg mountain stream. Not having much experience of fly-fishing, he was glad to be alone where nobody could watch his attempts at deceiving a distinctly canny quarry.

The river was swollen and mud brown, not crystal clear as he had expected. It swirled and sucked, rippling round large rocks which protected deep pools of surprising tranquillity. Cam found what he thought would be an ideal spot and drew off line to lie in a tangle-free pile at his feet. He flicked the rod back, keeping its tip high, held it there for a fraction of a second while the line straightened out behind him, then brought it forwards, releasing some of the pile which he controlled with his left hand. *So far so good*, he thought. Back again then forwards. Nothing. The fly had dropped and caught in the grass. He released it and started again. Better. But he wasn't getting the distance he wanted. His father could keep a fly in the air effortlessly, singing back and forth in an ever-lengthening loop until he decided where it would touch the water.

Cameron's line hit first, followed by the fly. Splash! That was not the way to do it but the current quickly carried it downstream. With his left hand he retrieved line into the pile, shortening what was out in the water until he could raise it with the rod and try again. A few more casts and Cameron was becoming more confident. *Why weren't the fish biting*, he wondered. The water must be too murky. Another cast. Perhaps a different fly, something a bit brighter?

Wham! The fly had drifted downstream, close to the bank. Cam had been on the point of retrieving the line and flicking it into another cast. Suddenly the rod came alive in his hand. It bent, jumping furiously and almost touching the water. He lifted the tip, keeping tension on the line. Give a bit, take a bit, slowly. Keep calm, he told himself. It felt like a monster. *Damn*. The landing net was out of reach. Cameron didn't have enough hands and nearly lost his footing trying to get it. Tension. Keep the tension. His right hand he held high, the net at full stretch in his left. In seconds it was caught. A spangled rainbow, all of six inches long.

Cameron carefully removed the fly and released the fish, one of many he would catch in that mountain stream. Now he had to do something about supper.

Returning to the house three hours later he presented Caroline with two fine trout, each well over a pound in weight and which had his full admiration as worthy adversaries. He and Caroline cooked them in a pan with lemon and butter, outside over a glowing bed of coals. It was the best Christmas Eve dinner Cameron could remember.

'How are things on the front?' Caroline asked, sipping a cup of sweet tea.

'Boers are on the run but that doesn't stop them making fools of us.'

She stayed silent.

'The faster we burn the bastards out and pack their families off to camps, the better.'

'That's not the answer,' Caroline said quietly. 'We have to live alongside each other when this conflict is over. Waging war on innocent women and children won't help.'

Cameron swung on his host. 'Are you some kind of Boer lover?' he asked, chin jutting forward in challenge. 'Those *Boere meises* are no more innocent than their menfolk. They keep the *komandos* in the field and that costs us lives. Don't feed me your liberal rubbish.'

Caroline looked at him. She had sensed from the moment Cameron arrived that he was on the point of cracking. What she didn't know was why.

For a while he remained silent. Caroline waited patiently.

'My brother was killed by the Boers.'

'I know. This is war.'

Finally he sighed and fumbled in the pocket of his tunic. 'Read this,' Cameron said, passing her the crumpled note.

'I'd rather you talked about it.'

Cameron let his hand fall and the words came, spilling over each other while Caroline listened in silence. He told her everything, dredging secrets from the dark recesses of his soul until eventually there was no more. 'My mind was somewhere else. Others died because I felt sorry for myself – men who had trusted me.'

In that moment she realised that Cameron was angrier with himself and his own lack of control than with anybody else – even Ginnie. 'I said this to your father and I'll say it to you. Losing yourself in the past is often easier than facing the future. Memories are the milestones in our lives but if we stop moving, life loses its interest. The road ahead may not be easy but at least it's going in the right direction. Where it leads is something we mere mortals will never know.'

Cameron looked at her in the firelight as she rearranged the coals and threw on another log. Sparks flew up then settled.

'Sorry about my outburst. You could have taken offence but you didn't. Strangely, I feel much more relaxed. Thank you.'

'For what? It's Christmas. Oh, and by the way, the transfer has gone through. *Wakefield* is now yours.'

Cameron's jaw dropped.

'Don't look so surprised. It doesn't mean you have to live here.'

'But Ginnie and I are no longer getting married.'

'Who's Ginnie? I thought the world was bigger than that. Anyway, you do what you want. Right now there's a bottle of bubbly to open. Care to do the honours?'

'Milestones,' he muttered. 'You're an amazing woman.' Cameron dropped the note into the coals, watching it blacken then burst into flames.

'See? You've got it. Milestones.'

They both smiled.

Sitting under the stars sharing a bottle of Bollinger seemed so natural.

'Father explained that you are his half-sister. I can't believe it. That makes you my aunt. Do I still call you Caroline?'

'Certainly, though I prefer Caro. Did Dallas also tell you about my lion?'

'Funnily enough, he did.'

They talked easily, as friends do, of everything and nothing.

'Oh, and one other thing. I have to go and see Guy in the morning so please make yourself at home. Popeti is in Durban for Christmas and Moses won't be back until Boxing Day.'

Cam looked at her staring into the fire. 'Thank you, Caro, for everything.'

As the embers turned grey and died they walked arm in arm into the house. Candles burned in two rooms which opened off the simple living room. 'Sleep well,' Caro said, giving Cameron a peck on the cheek before turning in to one of them.

Cam lay in the darkness, more at peace than he had felt in months. The silence was so deep it had a sound all of its own. He didn't hear her come to him but suddenly she was there. 'Nobody should be alone on Christmas Eve,' Caro said.

Meggie saw him first, riding slowly towards the house, his face shaded by a wide-brimmed if slightly battered hat. There was no disguising the size of their surprise visitor.

'Stanley King, if I'm not mistaken.' Dallas let the name hang in the air. 'I wonder what brings him here on Christmas Day?'

Lorna was quickly on her feet and gave Meggie's arm a reassuring squeeze. Tanith had finished feeding Frazer and stayed sitting, expecting the worst. Meggie didn't move; her heart was in her mouth. Everybody knew what was going on between her and Stan but Dallas had been waiting for his daughter to tell him. She had come close that afternoon, trying to summon the courage. Ellie and her mother both said that she was the one who had to tell her father. There were two men in her life that she could never hurt. Dallas was one of them. Now the other had appeared before her as well. It was too late.

Although Meggie's father had never mentioned her relationship with his old friend she knew, from little things said by her mother, that he was aware of it. Stan dismounted at the house, greeted Mister

David – who was setting out afternoon tea on the verandah – then turned and walked purposefully towards the cassia tree. There was a quiet confidence in his stride as he approached, hat in hand, his face and bare arms burnt brown by the sun.

'Good afternoon, Dallas,' he said when close enough not to shout. 'Ladies,' Stan acknowledged the others. 'A merry Christmas to you, one and all.'

'Turn around and ride home, Stan,' Dallas said firmly. 'You are not welcome here.'

Meggie's worst nightmares had been realised. She glanced desperately at her mother, seeking support. None was forthcoming. This was a matter between her father and the man Meggie wanted to share her life with.

'Hello, Meggie,' Stan said, ignoring Dallas and turning towards her. 'I wanted to see your father.'

'Well, here I am.' Dallas stepped forwards to challenge him. The two men stood toe to toe while a hushed audience took in the David and Goliath confrontation.

'Dallas,' the larger man said in a tired voice. 'We have been friends for too many years for me not to be honest with you. I have come here to ask permission for your daughter's hand in marriage.'

'Then you have a hide thicker than a Cape buffalo,' Dallas replied, looking up at the composed Englishman. 'You also have about ten seconds to get on your horse and leave.'

Stan didn't move. 'Go ahead, Dallas,' he said. 'If it makes you feel better, put one on my jaw. I am not leaving without Meggie's answer to my proposal.'

Despite Dallas's weakened condition, the blow came from nowhere – fast and hard – causing Stan's head to snap sideways. Meggie screamed, hands flying to her mouth, but nobody intervened. Lorna grabbed her daughter's arm before she could rush forwards to Stan, now slumped on the grass holding his jaw. Slowly he rose to his feet and again stood in front of Dallas, who had obviously hurt his arm and knuckles.

'You can keep on doing that if it makes you feel better,' Stan said. 'I love your daughter. I may be older than she is but I can't help how I feel about Meggie – any more than you can control your determination to look after her. I swear to you, Dallas, on this most holy of days, that I will love and protect this woman as no other ever could. I would die before letting anything bad happen to Meggie.'

Dallas stared back at his unrepentant friend, knowing he had meant every word.

Stan braced himself for another stinging blow. It never came. Anger faded from Dallas's eyes and he shook his head. 'You know I had to do that,' he said quietly. 'I may not be pleased with what is going on between you and my daughter, but I do believe you are a brave and honest man who is true to his word. I cannot ask more than that – though I will certainly find it difficult to think of you as my son-in-law.' Dallas held out his right hand and Stan took it, gratitude and relief written in his expression. 'I suppose you should first ask Meggie if she wants to marry you.'

Stan grinned and winced, at the same time massaging his jaw. 'I hope she hasn't inherited her father's left jab,' he said.

'No,' Dallas replied with a wry grin. 'Meggie is more like her mother. She prefers a right hook.'

Both men smiled. It was probably true.

Stan turned to Meggie and dropped to one knee. 'Margaret Maud Granger-Acheson, will you do me the honour of consenting to become my wife?'

'Yes, you dear sweet fool. Yes, yes, yes.' Although her answer did not actually require words as Meggie flew into his waiting arms and smothered him with kisses.

When they stood up, Lorna added her congratulations then introduced Tanith and Frazer. By this time even Mister David had joined them, a grin splitting his face from ear to ear.

Meggie disentangled herself and stood in front of Dallas. She threw her arms around his neck and tears of joy flowed freely. 'Thank you, Father. I will always love you.'

Dallas hugged his little girl close to his chest. Entrusting his youngest daughter to another was in many ways as hard as losing a son to the war.

Stan King had been accepted. Tea was forgotten when Lorna produced one of Ellie's bottles of Moët. 'I'm sure your big sister wouldn't mind,' she said, passing the Champagne to Dallas for him to open.

Tanith, Frazer and Aminta left the house around six, heading north to Empangeni. Before the sun set on Christmas Day 1900, another unexpected visitor would arrive at *Morningside*. Tired and dusty, Torben Petersen appeared just after seven o'clock.

Grim-faced and disbelieving, Lorna and Dallas sat in the study listening to Torben recount the events surrounding the abduction of his daughter over seven weeks earlier and what he had since learned from his Uncle Olaf in Denmark. He did not produce the letter itself – or tell the full truth. Torben dared not confess his part in helping to fund the military and political aims of his Afrikaner employers. Instead, he implied that the reason was to do with his role in supplying artillery pieces to the British. An act of revenge by the *Broederbond*.

Christmas Day or not, Torben had left Gerda at home in Durban. Her sister Lanice, who knew about Alice's disappearance, welcomed any excuse to visit the big house on the Berea and as this was the first time she had actually been asked to stay, accepted the invitation without hesitation.

'So it all comes down to finding this fellow Klaas,' Torben ended his revelation, head bowed.

'The man who posed as a policeman in your house,' Dallas said reflectively.

'Why on earth did you not tell us all this before?' Lorna gently reprimanded her stepson.

A red-eyed Torben looked up. 'I was too frightened. The Brotherhood said I should speak to nobody. They've got eyes and ears everywhere, even in Durban. I wouldn't be surprised if the local police really were involved in Alice's disappearance.'

'Well, there's no two ways about it,' Lorna said forcefully. 'We get my granddaughter back – whatever it takes.'

For the first time in weeks, Torben felt a wave of relief. The fact that his stepmother had referred to Alice as her granddaughter was only part of it. There were times he had felt like a stranger in the family – an outsider even – despite the fact that he had grown up alongside those who had always seen him as their brother.

'Would you mind if Stan King hears of this?' Dallas asked unexpectedly. 'After all, he is practically family.'

Torben nodded his agreement, having learned earlier in the evening about Meggie's engagement. 'Finding Klaas may not be as difficult as I first feared,' he said. 'It's no secret that the war is practically over.'

'Don't believe all you hear,' Dallas corrected his son. 'That's nothing more than politicians' talk. The Boers are far from being beaten. Not even Kitchener understands what he's dealing with. Botha, de Wet, Smuts and the others know they can't win but their *komandos* can keep this thing going until the British public get fed up with it and start to question why the war is not over. It's politics, pure and simple. The Boers are becoming damned good at playing the game.'

'I tend to agree,' Lorna backed her husband. 'This war could drag on for years.'

Dallas continued, 'Look, your uncle has told you that Klaas is a Boer sympathiser – a spy, to put it bluntly – who spends a lot of his time in Pretoria. Did he say why?'

'Because it gives him access to Portuguese East. It's neutral territory. A way of keeping in contact with agents from outside Africa,' Torben answered. 'He is actually a Dutch citizen.'

Lorna said what her husband had been thinking. 'Duncan has applied for a posting to military intelligence in Pretoria. He wants nothing more to do with the farm burning. Perhaps he could help us find this man?'

'Depends on what else he's doing,' Dallas pointed out. 'If necessary I can go to Pretoria myself.'

'Leave it to Duncan,' Lorna protested. 'You are needed here.'

'And you are the one who said we must get Alice back, whatever it takes. Besides, I'm not without contacts in that part of the world. First I will write to Duncan.'

Lorna did not pursue the subject. If the need arose her husband would go to the Transvaal capital. She could not stop him. His health was improving, though he was far from being at full strength.

'I could come with,' Torben added.

'No,' Dallas countered. 'It would be better if you return to Durban. Gerda needs you there, especially in her current condition. Besides, we don't want to take any unnecessary risks. If you are seen to be threatening this Klaas fellow, the Brotherhood may decide to do something drastic with

Alice. Go home and look after your business. It seems to be going extremely well.'

Torben saw the wisdom of his father's advice – and also the irony.

There was nothing more they could do that night so Lorna retired. It had been a long day. Dallas offered Torben a cigar, which he accepted. Meggie wasn't about so Dallas poured them both a brandy then selected a pipe from the rack on his desk. 'We'll find her, son,' he said. 'Have no fear of that.'

Stan stayed overnight at Morningside, sleeping in Cameron's room. Torben slept in the guest suite.

Over the breakfast table, Dallas told Stan and Meggie all that had been discussed the night before. Stan realised the significance of being included and offered any help he could. Torben instinctively liked him – though he couldn't work out why the man wore a bracelet.

After spending Boxing Day at *Morningside*, Torben took his father's advice and returned to Gerda in Durban. Surprisingly, he was sorry to leave, expressing genuine disappointment at not seeing Tanith and Frazer. Lorna promised to pass on his good wishes.

Hogmanay didn't hold its usual appeal. Dallas sat up to see the New Year in but his thoughts kept going back to Alice, wondering whether or not they would be able to find her. He had already written to Duncan, setting out everything that Torben had told them. Would it be enough?

Lorna found herself worrying more and more about Cameron, hoping time was easing the pain he carried in his heart. When he left she had seen in his face the look of a man who no longer cared if he lived or died. Where he was going, that could be fatal. There was nothing she could do but wait.

Lorna also sensed her husband's restlessness at seemingly doing nothing while Alice remained at risk. He had poured himself into the planning of new ground for cane planting, laying out blocks and supervising the digging of irrigation channels, but that was not enough. He might be a farmer but his family came first. Waiting for word from Duncan was not his idea of doing something positive.

Each day Dallas returned from the fields filthy. Before washing and changing into clean clothes he would go directly to the table hoping mail had arrived. It was their only contact with the world beyond *Morningside*.

The letters did come, mainly from Ellie. One written soon after her return to the hospital told them that she had found Cecily and Stephen's house in Durban empty, with no sign that they were back from Bechuanaland. She made mention of the train breaking down at Dargle Road, where they waited six hours for a replacement locomotive. Dallas remembered the small station and thought of his half-sister, wondering what she had done for Christmas.

Being alone couldn't have been much fun for Caro. *They should have invited her to Morningside*, he thought. Next year perhaps.

At last, word came from Duncan confirming his posting to staff headquarters in Pretoria. He had received Dallas's letter telling him the terrible news about his goddaughter and promised to do everything he could to find Klaas. He also said that Cam had been promoted to major and was with a new unit hunting down Boer *komandos*. Apparently, they had an unenviable reputation for doing their job with ruthless efficiency, showing little or no compassion for those they drove from their homes.

There had been no word from Cameron himself.

Already it was late March. Dallas made his usual beeline for the table, to find a letter addressed to him in an unfamiliar sloping hand. Curious, he tore open the envelope.

'Who is it from?' Lorna asked, joining him and trying to peek. 'It's obviously a woman's writing.'

'Caro,' Dallas said, surprised as he read its contents. 'She reminds me of something I said to her last year.'

'Oh yes?' Lorna's tone invited more of an explanation.

'I promised to help her shoot a lion,' he replied, shrugging his shoulders in a gesture which said 'so what?'. 'This really isn't the right time. It will have to wait. I'll write and tell her.'

'Good,' Lorna said. 'Does she say anything about giving *Wakefield* to Cam as a . . .' Her question tapered off. There would be no wedding, she thought sadly, knowing the pain and anger her son carried with him was for that very reason.

'No. But I doubt Caro would have changed her mind. Cam is a favourite of hers.'

Dallas didn't say anything but a thought niggled at the back of his mind. How had his half-sister known he would be at *Morningside*?

The Fairfax Scouts seemed to be spending more and more time following orders to round up women and children – even African servants – then burning their homes. Duncan's posting to staff headquarters in Pretoria brought with it promotion to the rank of captain and took him away from actions he saw as completely unjustified. His new duties related to field intelligence. Although the endless meetings and paperwork soon became tedious, Duncan was well placed to try to trace the elusive *Meneer* Klaas.

The officers' mess was a solid sandstone building not far from parliament house. It was there that Duncan had met Major Scott, commander of the military intelligence division charged with determining who in the predominantly Boer population could be trusted and who could not.

Major John Scott was a lean, arrogant Englishman with few friends – a problem largely of his own making. His often offhand manner didn't seem to bother the young colonial captain who had sought his assistance on one matter in particular.

'Got word of that chap Klaas today,' Scott said one lunchtime when he found Duncan sitting in a worse-for-wear leather chair reading a month-old copy of *The Times*. 'Seems your man is back on our patch.'

Duncan lowered the paper and looked up with interest at the senior officer standing over him, a large gin and tonic clutched in one hand. 'You've just made my day, John. Is the information reliable?' Duncan tried to hide his excitement. It was the first he had heard of the man since receiving his father's letter in January. Until that moment Duncan had doubted the claims made by Torben's uncle in Denmark.

'Sixty percent,' the major said, slumping into an empty chair beside Duncan. 'It appears Klaas is of interest to us as well,' he continued, watching his fellow officer's reaction. 'He's on our list of most wanted foreign nationals working for the Boers. Quite a tricky individual, it would seem. Keeps slipping in and out of the country through Portuguese territory. Word has it he's thick as thieves with the German Kaiser's agents.'

'You haven't said where I might find him,' Duncan pushed, only to receive a sideways look from the intelligence officer.

'And I have no idea why this man Klaas is of interest to you,' Scott said.

'It's a family matter,' Duncan replied. 'Something I would rather not discuss.'

'Would it make any difference if the man were dead or alive?' the major asked.

'It would,' Duncan told him. 'Dead men can't answer questions.'

Scott nodded. 'True. Though I cannot promise

to keep him that way if we catch him. It would be better for us if Klaas simply disappeared. That way he won't become a political issue with the Dutch or German governments. We are having enough trouble with them already, bleating about how we are treating their nationals. These Uitlanders are a real pain in the arse. Klaas would claim neutrality if we tried to keep him in prison. Do you get my drift, old chap?'

Duncan understood exactly what the British major was alluding to. 'All I ask is a few minutes with him.'

'I see no reason why that wouldn't be possible. First we have to catch the blighter. The man has been seen twice in the last forty-eight hours. Here, in Pretoria, though that doesn't mean he hasn't left by now.'

It was all Duncan needed to know. He would be seeing Cam that evening and even if his brother couldn't help, Henry sometimes came up with surprising snippets of information. It was worth a try.

TWENTY-FOUR

Duncan was rightly nervous about visiting the shantytown outside the capital, a place of dispossessed Africans – too poor or unwilling to return home – mixed with the dregs of European and native intercourse. He left his horse at a trading store near the outskirts and promised the uninterested owner a penny or two for keeping an eye on it whilst he went on foot to try to make contact with a man Henry had told him was well informed when it came to matters concerning people coming and going in Pretoria's shadowy world of criminal activity.

Dressed in cast-off civilian clothing and an old army greatcoat – something which made him far too hot – Duncan looked like any other down-and-out Uitlander. However, he carried his Webley service revolver in one of its deep pockets. Although asking questions could prove dangerous, Duncan selected a Zulu and spoke to him in his own language, saying that he needed to find a Portuguese person known simply as Ramos. The unemployed mine labourer considered his request then nodded, offering to show him a grog shop the man frequented. Duncan dropped a couple of coins into an outstretched hand to seal the bargain, then followed the Zulu's broad back to a flimsy structure made of corrugated iron and old hessian bags.

Pushing through the tiny doorway, Duncan found himself in a smoky, unlit room where men sat on crude benches or leaned against the wall drinking warm millet and sorghum beer or *witblits* – white lightning – from bottles and a variety of other containers. The clientele were mainly black or coloured but there were some white faces, bearded or otherwise, as well as African prostitutes who would provide sex for the price of a drink. It was a world largely frequented by those who had lost hope.

'That is the man you seek,' the Zulu said quietly in a resonant voice, indicating with a nod rather than pointing.

All eyes seemed to be on him, Duncan felt, as he made his way to one of the few tables where a swarthy individual with a shaved head watched his approach with indifference. He wore a gold earring and, unlike most others in the place, appeared to be reasonably well dressed. Duncan put the man at about thirty years of age. The scars on his face told him he had not had an easy life.

'Ramos?' Duncan asked, standing over the man who sat with an African woman, a half-finished bottle on the table in front of him.

'Who wants to know?' The man had tensed, noticing that Duncan's hand was still in his coat pocket.

'I am a friend of the Zulu you know as Henry – from *Morningside*, in Natal.'

'And what does this friend of Henry from *Morningside* want of me?'

'Just some information,' Duncan replied. He had not been offered the empty chair vacated by the prostitute. 'About a Dutchman by the name of Klaas who comes and goes from Pretoria.'

'I am very thirsty, my friend,' Ramos said, producing a large knife which he had been holding under the table. 'I trust that hand in your pocket has the money to buy me a drink?'

Duncan removed it, placing an 'old head' half-sovereign on the table in front of Ramos. The man's face showed contempt. Duncan took the hint and doubled the amount.

'This one you speak of is here now,' Ramos said, pocketing the money. 'But it would be dangerous taking you to where he is.'

'You could tell me how to find the place,' Duncan suggested.

'Do you know what he looks like?' Ramos asked, and Duncan frowned. 'I thought not,' he continued. 'So you must pay me more if I am to take you to him.'

'It seems I have little choice. How much more?'

'The same again, my friend,' Ramos answered.

Duncan counted out another half-sovereign, in smaller coins this time. 'I will pay you the balance on delivery,' he said.

Ramos nodded and swept up the money. 'Come back at four o'clock tomorrow morning and I will take you to him. Meet me at the big tree out on the road.'

'Why not now?' Duncan sounded suspicious.

'Because I have other matters to conclude,' Ramos replied. 'That is why.'

Duncan sighed in frustration at the delay but realised that the man sitting at the table was probably his only hope of finding Klaas before the military police tracked him down. 'I will be there,' Duncan said.

'Make sure you bring the rest of my money,' Ramos laughed, swigging from his bottle.

As Duncan was about to leave the shebeen a familiar voice behind him said quietly, 'Do not trust the man. Ramos has no loyalty to anything.' He turned to acknowledge the warning but the Zulu was already melting away into the smoky atmosphere of sweat, stale beer and unwashed bodies.

He walked back into the welcome daylight and after taking a couple of wrong turns to make sure nobody was following, retrieved his horse and paid the storekeeper as promised. It was probably more than the man had made all day. Swinging himself into the saddle, Duncan glanced over his shoulder at the shantytown and wondered what the future held for its inhabitants.

Finding the big tree for his rendezvous with Ramos was easy. Whether he liked it or not, he had to trust the Portuguese.

Duncan waited. The pre-dawn shantytown emitted none of the noises of Africa, only the discordant squabbling of two women – probably drunk, he thought – dogs barking and a bawling child.

Ramos made no apology for being late and didn't waste words on a greeting. 'The man you seek is staying at a boarding house in town,' he said. 'Follow me.'

Duncan rode behind his informant to the outskirts of Pretoria, where he followed him to a large and rambling house in one of the less wealthy areas of the Transvaal capital.

'Your man is staying here,' Ramos said quietly. 'Room three. Klaas is tall, in his mid forties, with no beard and a bit more hair than me.' He rubbed his bald head, seeming to find it funny. 'And an English accent. Now, my money if you please.'

'First, take me to his room,' Duncan said firmly.

Ramos withdrew his outstretched hand. 'This was not in our arrangement.'

Duncan slipped the revolver from his pocket.

'As you wish,' Ramos said, shrugging and sliding from his horse.

Duncan dismounted and after hitching his reins to the broken-down fence followed the man through an overgrown garden onto the verandah. Treading carefully, they came to a window which was open at the top.

'Room three,' Ramos hissed, easing the bottom wide enough for a person to enter.

Duncan stepped forwards and listened. There was no sound from inside. Cautiously he peered into the unlit room. He could see nothing. Suddenly the razor-sharp edge of a knife blade touched his neck.

He froze. It had come from behind.

'I see him,' a voice said softly from inside the room. 'Give Ramos the gun, unless you want your throat cut. It's such a messy way of dying.'

Duncan let him take the Webley.

'Won't you come in,' the unseen man invited. The East End London accent told Duncan it had to be Klaas. He clambered through the window as a match flared and in seconds the room was illuminated by a paraffin lamp. Ramos climbed through after him and shut the window.

Klaas was fully dressed and held a silver-plated Smith & Wesson revolver. 'Who are you and why do you seek me?' he asked, the gun pointed unwaveringly at Duncan's chest.

'Mister Klaas, if I'm not mistaken.'

'That is hardly surprising since you were foolish enough to seek me in such a clumsy manner. Now. Must I repeat my question?'

'My name is Duncan Granger-Acheson. I am a captain at British staff headquarters.'

'Granger-Acheson.' Klaas nodded in understanding. 'And what brings you here at such an anti-social hour?'

'I believe you know the whereabouts of something which was taken from my brother some months ago. Tell me where it is and I have no further quarrel with you.'

'Your family is well known to me. You are related to Torben Petersen, are you not?'

'Correct,' Duncan replied. 'So you also know why I have been seeking you.'

'At this very minute, I am more interested in who gave you my name.' Klaas smiled questioningly.

'Tell me where my niece is and I will be gone,' Duncan replied with a dry mouth.

'I wish that were possible,' Klaas said sadly. 'You know as well as I do that I am wanted by your people. Having found me, I really don't think you can be allowed to leave.'

Duncan felt the first pangs of fear turning to cold terror. He was not likely to leave the room alive and wished he had paid more heed to the Zulu who had warned him about Ramos. Stupidly, he had not told anyone of his mission. It was unlikely that his body would ever be found should Klaas choose to kill him. Worst of all was the thought of never seeing his infant son. 'I will give my word as an officer and a gentleman not to betray you to the authorities,' Duncan said, attempting to remain calm and in control of his emotions. Instinct told him that he had to keep the man talking and play for time if there were to be even the slightest chance of survival.

'I am sorry, Captain,' Klaas said. 'This is not the time for idle chatter.'

Duncan noticed the Dutchman nod and instantly Ramos's hand clamped around his mouth and nose, forcing his head back. With all the strength and speed Duncan could muster, he reached up and grabbed the man's wrist, turning and lashing out as he felt cold steel come in contact with his neck. A well-aimed kick found the glass-covered lamp, smashing it against the wall. The sudden darkness lasted less than a second as yellow flames surged up the paraffin-soaked curtains.

His unexpected resistance took both attackers by surprise. No gunshot followed. Duncan had guessed correctly that the Dutchman would want to kill him as silently as possible. Attention was something the man could do without. Duncan spun on his heel but failed to avoid a savage blow from Klaas, who slammed his revolver against the back of his head, knocking him to the floor.

'Enough,' he heard Klaas say, as if from a great distance. 'The fire and your handiwork will take care of him. Leave quickly, by the window.'

Duncan lay in a semiconscious state and wondered what they were talking about. He opened his eyes to find flames spreading rapidly through the room, creeping across the carpet, licking hungrily at the dry wooden walls. A numbness in his throat told him that the fire was not his only problem. His hand sought the cause and came away covered in blood as it welled from a deep slash in his neck. He fought to stay awake, groggily gaining his feet and staggering towards the door. It was locked, but the key was still there. Duncan managed to turn it and fell out into the passage beyond.

Already the acrid fumes and crackling flames had alerted others and the cry 'Fire! Fire!' brought half-dressed residents spilling out of their rooms in panic. Someone caught Duncan under the arms, dragging him outside into the fresh air as the tinder-dry building became a billowing furnace of fire and dense black smoke.

'You all right, mate?' Duncan heard what he thought was an Australian accent. 'Strewth, this fella's had his bleedin' throat cut.'

So that was it, Duncan thought as he passed into oblivion.

'You were damned lucky, little brother,' Cameron said, standing by the hospital bed.

Duncan looked distinctly mournful. The person who had pulled him from the boarding house was an out-of-work grain bag sewer. After checking to make sure the wound was only superficial, he had used the tools of his trade to quickly and carefully stitch it up. Fortunately for Duncan, the man used a curved sewing needle and not the broad-tipped sailmaker's variety normally needed for heavy hessian bags. According to the army doctor who later examined the wounded captain and dressed the nasty gash to his head, the work was excellent. Duncan would be on his feet in a day or two. He had been more than just lucky.

'You can tell Henry that his information about Ramos was quite right. He led me straight to Klaas but only because that Dutch bastard wanted to know where I got his name from. Fortunately, he's none the wiser. He probably thinks I'm dead by now so at least Alice is in no greater danger.'

'It may not be that simple,' Cameron warned. 'When you're on your feet there's bound to be an enquiry. The powers that be will want to know why an officer from staff HQ was pulled from a burning building with his throat cut.'

'I'll think of something. Our immediate problem is still Klaas. I almost had him, Cam,' Duncan rasped, struggling to sit up. 'Now he and Ramos are probably halfway to Portuguese East.'

'What makes you say that?' Cameron asked.

'Stands to reason,' Duncan said. 'They took both the horses and Klaas knows he's wanted by military intelligence. That fire at the boarding house will have drawn a lot of attention. If I were him, I would get out of the country until things quieten down.'

'You could well be right,' Cameron agreed. 'The border is patrolled by Steinacker's Horse but it's a bloody big area. My latest orders are to go in and give old "Stinky" a hand.'

Duncan had heard of the self-styled Baron – Colonel Ludwig Steinacker – who had become a legend in the eastern Transvaal. 'So he may not have given us the slip after all. May you have better luck than me.' Settling back against the pillows, he sighed. 'Be careful, Cam. That man is much more dangerous than Torben and Father realise – especially if Ramos is travelling with him.'

'Then you'd better tell me all you know.' Cameron sat on the bed and listened until a not-to-be-meddled-with matron came and chased the tough-looking major from his brother's side.

Still mulling over what he had learned, Cameron rejoined his new troop outside Pretoria and was met by Sergeant-Major Mulligan.

'All stores and men accounted for, sir,' he reported smartly.

'Thank you, Sarn't-Major.' Cameron glanced around the cluster of white canvas tents and noticed Henry, currycombing his horse on the picket line. 'Please inform the officers that there will be a briefing in my tent at 1700 hours.'

'Sah!' the senior noncommissioned officer acknowledged with a salute. They were not in the field so he considered such a gesture appropriate.

Cameron watched his NCO stride away to inform those necessary that group orders were scheduled for later that afternoon. He often wondered why Mulligan chose to stay as a sergeant major under his command when the man could so easily have secured a more senior posting with their previous unit. The Irishman was not one to talk much – let alone explain his feelings – but the simple act of refusing promotion in favour of staying with Cameron said more than words could about loyalty and respect. It was a gesture which had touched Cameron very much – one which had helped him come to terms with past mistakes.

Henry glanced up, coming stiffly to attention as military protocol dictated.

'I see you, my friend,' Cameron said in Zulu – the language they used with each other in private conversations. 'I have just returned from visiting Duncan in hospital. The man you recommended to him as a source of information tried to cut his throat.'

The Zulu turned a shade of grey. 'What happened? Is he badly hurt?'

'His injuries are not serious.' Cameron went on

to tell him what he had learned from Duncan, then said, 'Now, I need to know more about this man who tried to kill my brother. Come with me.'

Henry followed Cameron to his tent where he spread a map on the folding table. 'Have you any idea where we might find Ramos?' he asked.

After a brief examination, Henry's finger followed the railway line to where it stopped at Pietersburg, well to the north of Pretoria. 'He has a woman here,' Henry said. 'I have heard that he often visits her.'

Cameron studied the map, considering the options open to Klaas. It made sense that he and Ramos would not take a direct route to the border. There were too many troops and checkpoints to the east of Pretoria whereas further north, above the Olifant's River, British influence all but ceased to exist.

'Who is this man Klaas?' Henry asked, realising that his friend was holding something back.

'The man we really want,' Cameron replied. 'You and I have to find him.'

Henry scowled. 'Why did you not tell me this?' he asked. 'Do you not trust me?'

Cameron was taken aback by the rebuke and, after pausing for a few seconds, decided to tell his friend the full story.

Henry listened in silence. Until that afternoon he had known nothing of Alice's abduction. He was both hurt and angry. Even Duncan had hidden the real reason for seeking Ramos as a contact.

'My brother told me in January, after he

received a letter from Father. He has been looking for Klaas ever since,' Cameron concluded. 'I am sorry, we should have said something sooner.'

'You do not have to apologise,' Henry replied coldly. 'I am only an African,' he snarled, not waiting for permission before leaving Cameron to reflect on the parting words of a man he had grown up with. There had been no reason to keep the matter a secret from Henry but the damage was done.

Barking dogs alerted Heidi van der Merwe to the fact that she had visitors. Tucking Alice into her crib, she hurried to the front door to see who it was. What she saw sent a shiver of fear through her. A mounted patrol with an open, horse-drawn wagon was approaching the farmhouse.

'*Kak*,' she swore softly as they spread out to encircle the somewhat dilapidated building. Defiantly, Heidi stepped from the doorway to confront the officer in charge. He was accompanied by a civilian interpreter with a long black beard. Heidi could not remember his name but knew him as one of the burghers who had traitorously signed away his allegiance to the Boer cause.

'Heidi van der Merwe,' he said, speaking in Afrikaans though he knew she could understand English, 'you are to gather up only those personal possessions that you can carry and come with us in the wagon.'

'What is this about, traitor?' she spat in the same language. 'Do you wage war against helpless women and children? There are no menfolk here.'

'It is not my decision, woman,' the Boer said. 'I only do what I am told.'

Heidi thought about the baby and realised that she and she alone was responsible for its safety. Resistance would be futile. With shoulders slumped she went back inside to gather up a few clothes and mementos – as well as Alice. Even before she returned to the front door, she could hear the bellowing of her cows as they were herded from the milking shed.

With Alice in her arms, Heidi stepped out into the sunlight.

'Whose baby is that?' the Boer asked. 'It is well known that you lost your only child.'

For a moment, Heidi felt a sense of panic. No matter the real reason for this baby being here, she had grown to love little Alice as her own. 'It belongs to my sister,' she lied.

The Boer shrugged. It was of no great matter to him. He spoke to the mounted officer beside him then turned to Heidi and said, 'Get in the wagon. Both of you.'

Heidi obeyed. She could not face any further questions concerning Alice. 'Where are you taking us?' she asked the African driver.

'*Ek veet nie*' – I don't know – he replied in Afrikaans.

The bearded burgher overheard, taking pity on the woman and child. 'You will be taken to Middelburg camp in the Transvaal,' he told Heidi. 'That is what they tell me.'

She had heard of the place but could not remember why. Heidi had no idea how far it was from her home in what, to her, was still the Orange Free State.

'Is it a long way?' she asked.

'I have no idea,' the man answered. 'I have never been to the Transvaal.'

Sitting and holding Alice, Heidi watched as flames burst from the roof of her home. She closed her eyes and tried not to cry. The life she had known since coming to this farm as a young bride was being taken from her. If her husband was still alive, she thought, how would he ever find her? All she had now was the tiny infant peacefully asleep in her arms. What lay ahead was nothing but despair.

TWENTY-FIVE

Major Granger-Acheson's newly formed unit remained independent of Steinacker's Horse, which operated mainly to the south, between Komatipoort and their base at Sabi Bridge – country Cameron knew of old. His task now was to patrol the flat, flood-prone veld further north towards the Olifant's River. West lay the northern Drakensberg while to the east the Lebombo Hills formed a natural border with the neutral territory of Portuguese East Africa. It was fever country, where unsalted horses normally lasted no more than a couple of weeks before feeding the scavengers of Africa. Though the stifling heat of summer was past, months of heavy rain meant that malaria remained rife.

Cameron's men were mostly born on African soil. Some, like Sergeant-Major Mulligan and Henry, came from his old troop, but there were new faces too: colonial volunteers – Canadians, New Zealanders and Australians in the main – tough and battle hardened, used to living in the saddle and coping with the adversities of nature.

Boer *komandos* ranged this land at will,

unhindered as yet by the blockhouses and barbed wire that Kitchener would soon use to restrict their freedom of movement throughout the Transvaal and Orange River Colony. Cattle raiding and minor skirmishes were frequent but of little concern to Cameron, whose orders were to deny the enemy access to the outside world.

If Klaas and Ramos had done what Duncan suspected, he would be ideally placed to try to prevent their escape. There were a lot of ifs and buts, though no better ideas. Only Henry knew anything of Cameron's personal agenda. He had calmed down and apologised since storming from the tent outside Pretoria and now seemed just as determined as his old friend to do anything which would help find Alice. Zulus did not make war on women or children and to him those who had taken Torben and Gerda's baby were not fit to be called men.

Cameron pushed his troop hard. It had taken them three days, riding north-east from dawn to dusk, before they reached the Olifant's and followed it down from the Drakensberg into the sticky heat of flat knobthorn and mophane veld. Camp was established above a gorge close to the confluence with a second river which joined it from further north. Their slight elevation gave them the benefit of any breeze and an opportunity to observe the surrounding country. Portuguese East Africa was little more than five miles distant.

Although their primary mission was to establish picket points along the border, the fact that Klaas was wanted by military intelligence in Pretoria gave Cameron a legitimate excuse to be making enquires about him. Nevertheless, he briefed Henry in private. 'I want you to accompany young Pickstone. Try to avoid Boer *komandos* but try to find word of any white men who are strangers in the area. One of those we seek has an English accent, the other, as you know, is Portuguese.'

'What if we find them?' Henry asked.

'Under no circumstances is Klaas to be harmed. I want him here, alive.' Cameron was deadly serious. 'Should something happen to Ramos, that cannot be helped. I am placing my trust in you, old friend.'

Henry understood what was being asked of him. 'Thank you, Cam,' he said. 'It is a responsibility I undertake on behalf of your family. It is also my family.'

Cameron stretched out his hand and Henry accepted the firm clasp. 'It is I who thank you, Henry,' Cameron spoke in Zulu. 'For we are brothers despite the colour of our skin.'

It was a rare moment between two people of different rank and race. Henry had no doubt that this hard man with a reputation for acting alone truly accepted him as an equal. *If only such a thing were possible in times of peace*, Henry thought to himself as he left the tent.

Finding Klaas would be like looking for a needle in a haystack. As his horse drank from the muddy river, Henry scanned the bush, looking for anything out of the ordinary – any shape or movement that didn't belong. Eyes, in turn, watched him. A hippo yawned, baring curved tusks and long pointed incisors. Another in the group of half a dozen or so sounded his distinctive grunting bellow. Henry had seen many of these mighty beasts in the Mhlathuze – eaten their meat too. Otherwise, there was silence. Henry looked again. A rock had appeared where moments before there had been nothing. Elephant, the grey ghosts of Africa which his father and Cameron's had hunted for their ivory before he was even born. The rock moved again, duplicating itself as if by magic. As he watched in awe, one turned to the side, the late afternoon sun showing off two sweeping tusks that seemed to scrape the ground as he moved. They were the first elephants Henry had ever seen. The same day had shown him another new animal. Lion.

'See anything?' a voice asked at his elbow, breaking the mood of that moment.

'No, sir,' Henry replied to Lieutenant Pick-stone's question. 'Just Africa.'

'I know what you mean,' the other man said with a smile. 'When I was a boy I read a book by Frederick Selous. *A Hunter's Wanderings in Africa*, it was called. Those were the days. Never thought I'd see all this for myself.'

Henry glanced at the young officer who came from Cape Town. His revelation did not surprise Henry. They had both been born in this land but until now neither had experienced the wild beauty that could capture a man's soul.

'Sir, over there.' One of the mounted soldiers pointed, drawing the lieutenant's attention to a thin plume of smoke rising from trees to the east of their position.

'Let's have a look-see,' Pickstone said.

Cautiously the five-man patrol approached what was obviously a hunters' camp where they were met by a bearded white man casually cradling a large double rifle. It pointed at nothing in particular but the officer noticed that both hammers were cocked and ready for instant use. A number of Africans armed with a mixture of Martini-Henry rifles and old muzzle-loaders eyed the soldiers suspiciously.

Pickstone had assumed they were Boer poachers but as they came closer, Henry broke into a broad grin and turned to the lieutenant. 'I know this man. His name is Will Green.'

'Mister Green, I presume?' the soldier greeted him without explaining his choice of words.

Will simply stared, taken completely by surprise at being recognised in the middle of nowhere. He certainly did not know the soldier who had spoken – though the Zulu at his side seemed familiar. 'By God, I do believe it's young Henry, son of that old scoundrel Mister David. What brings you here, boy?'

'No more than takes you so far from Swaziland, *madala*.'

'How do you know this man?' Pickstone asked.

'He is the major's godfather and an old friend of his family,' Henry replied, dismounting as Will eased off the hammers on his Rawbone 8-bore. The two men greeted each other warmly, not in the least surprised at how small Africa could seem.

'What in hell are you doing here?' Will asked in Zulu. 'Last I heard you were at *Morningside* keeping an eye on that father of yours.'

'I am now a scout with *nkosi* Cameron,' Henry replied proudly. 'He is not so far from this place. My father told me that you were back at Nsoko.'

'That was a long time ago. At least, it seems that way now.'

'We are looking for an *umlungu* they call Klaas. Have you heard of this white man?'

'Sorry, Henry,' Will answered. 'That name means nothing to me.'

'He might be travelling with a Portuguese called Ramos.'

'That one I do know,' Will spat. 'We are old enemies. He passed this camp less than a day ago. I can't say who was more surprised, him or me. There was another man with him but they didn't stop long enough for introductions – if you get my meaning. Pasty-faced fellow with not much hair. Could that be him?'

'This sounds like the one we seek. Do you know where they were going?'

'Across the border most likely, but there's not much over there until you get further south.'

Lieutenant Pickstone had not the faintest idea what the two men were talking about though he recognised names in their conversation. What Henry had discovered was obviously important, so he sent one of the men back to find their commanding officer. The needle had been found.

When Cameron received the news he burst out laughing. There is a God, he admitted – aware that Will was well out of earshot. It took them less than an hour to reach his hunting camp.

Will greeted his godson with genuine affection. 'How is your father?' he asked as they stood clasping each other in a bear hug which neither man wanted to break. 'Is he still fighting for Queen and country?'

'Not anymore. He got pneumonia and damned near died. Mother and Ellie probably saved his life. He's back at *Morningside* throwing himself into new sugar planting. What about you? Last time I saw you, Buller was still waiting to move north.'

'I stayed with him through the Transvaal. When Roberts decided he was no longer needed that was it for me too.'

'So you went back to Swaziland?'

'For a while. If you want my advice, never get married. I've got seven wives and life at home is one problem after another.'

Cameron laughed but didn't comment. His hurt at losing Ginnie was under control, though he had no intention of talking about it. A fleeting image of another woman and a farm far to the south flashed through his mind. He had told nobody where he spent those few days. 'Then you left again?'

'Spent some time chasing gold up near Piggs

Peak but that was a waste of time. White gold is easier to come by.' Will gestured to the camelthorn fire where a blackened pot steamed on a bed of glowing coals. 'There's enough for you and Henry to join me.'

While Will told the Africans what was going on, Cameron made sure his men had all that they needed. He didn't comment on the pile of tusks stacked beside a wagon which had seen better days.

That night they enjoyed a spicy stew of indeterminate origin, soaked up with hand-worked balls of mealie meal and washed down with some excellent Portuguese red wine.

'This is a damned sight better than that tobacco-coloured muck the mess calls rum,' Cameron enthused.

Lions were not far off. Ever hopeful of finding a meal, their throaty calls carried far in the warm night air. The talk was mainly about home. Dallas and Lorna. Duncan, Tanith and little Frazer – the son his brother had not yet seen. Ellie and Lindsay – the former very special to Will. Meggie. And when Cameron could avoid it no more, his own broken engagement to Ginnie. Strangely, he could talk about it as if she no longer existed. Finally they returned to the matter Henry had raised when they first arrived. Cameron told Will why they were seeking Klaas.

The old trader had known nothing about Alice's abduction or the near death of Duncan in Pretoria. When all was said he knocked the ash out of his pipe and spat into the fire. 'Your man could cross the border anywhere. Ramos has plenty of contacts on the other side but to get somewhere they will have to go south.'

'I feared that,' Cameron said, staring into the hypnotic flames. 'We have to find them.'

'Chasing white men – one a Portuguese citizen – in neutral territory is not such a good idea.' Will shook his head. 'If you were caught they would lock you up and throw away the key.'

'That might apply to a soldier but what about as a civilian? Correct me if I'm wrong but people seem to come and go across the border as they please. Nobody knows where it actually is.'

'And how would you resign your commission out here with all these fine lads depending on you?' Will chuckled. He could see what the eldest son of his old friend and partner was thinking. 'You would have to be bloody careful.'

'Not if I were with an old poacher who knew the lay of the land,' Cam continued their round-about conversation.

'Someone who just happened to have with him the best bloody tracker in this part of Africa,' Will went on. 'Who is also one of my sons.'

Cameron wondered what other family the old rogue had fathered. Although Will was his god-father, the most time they had ever spent together had been during the Natal campaign. Even then he found out little about the children of a man who, by his own choice, led a largely tribal life and was ostracised by others because of it. Will couldn't have cared less. 'Would you be prepared to take me through Portuguese territory on your way back to Swaziland?' Cameron asked, swirling the contents of his metal mug. 'I would pay you.'

The old man looked momentarily offended. 'I will help but not for money,' he bridled. 'Call it a favour to your father.'

'Then I suggest we leave at first light. If Klaas and Ramos reach Delagoa Bay we'll never find them.'

Will scratched his beard and sniffed. 'Just like the old days,' he said, breaking into a near-toothless grin.

Cameron called a briefing with his officers and Sergeant-Major Mulligan. Lieutenant Pickstone would take command, leading the patrol south and setting up picket points at any border crossing where there was evidence of recent activity. They agreed coordinates for a rendezvous three days later. It was all the time Cameron could afford to be away from his official duties.

'What will you be doing, sir?' Lieutenant Pickstone asked when the others had gone.

'That I am not at liberty to tell you,' Cameron answered, folding a map which lay on the ground illuminated by the flickering fire. 'Suffice it to say I have received information of interest to military intelligence. Henry will be coming with me. We leave at first light under the guise of a civilian hunting party.'

Lieutenant Pickstone saw no reason to question Cameron's orders. He knew that he was more than capable of taking command in the absence of his senior officer.

★

Dawn came quickly to the African veld, the sky clear and cloudless, rapidly changing colour as both man and beast faced a new day. Sounds of a camp already awake took over from those of nocturnal hunters returning to sleep.

Breakfast was brief, only biscuits and coffee. Will had his men moving out before the sun came up, dew still wet on the grass. Cameron had discarded his khaki uniform, leaving it and a Lee Metford carbine with Lieutenant Pickstone. His horse and army saddle he could do nothing about. Wearing the garb of a man at home in the bush, he carried a percussion 'Cape' gun borrowed from Will – one barrel a .577 rifle, the other a 12-bore shotgun loaded with sixteen SSG pellets.

Henry carried a single shot .450 lever action Martini, heavy enough for most eventualities. He rode at Cameron's side, appearing to those they might encounter as his gunbearer.

Will's son, Eli – a quiet mixed-race boy of around fifteen – easily picked up tracks of the two men and packhorse that had recently called at their camp. 'They are in no hurry,' he said to his father, distinguishing the faintest marks of shod horses from the otherwise confusing mass of game trails.

Cam turned to Will. 'If you were these men and wanted to reach Lourenço Marques, would you go to the coast then south to the port or stay inland and make for the railway?'

'No question in my mind,' he answered. 'I'd head for Ressano Garcia.'

'Across the border from Komatipoort. Inland it

is then,' Cameron nodded, pleased that his thoughts had been confirmed.

The hours passed slowly and largely in silence as they pressed on. 'How far ahead do you think they are now?' Henry asked their young tracker.

'Perhaps half a day,' Eli replied, chewing reflectively on a blade of grass. 'But we are no longer gaining on them.'

Cameron heard the conversation and realised that Will's wagon was slowing them down. He reined round and rode back to speak with his godfather.

'Do I sense a problem?' Will asked.

'Your son is doing you proud,' Cameron replied. 'But we are not closing the gap.'

'Then Eli must go ahead with you,' Will said immediately. 'Even on foot he will be faster than those you follow.'

It was what Cameron had hoped to hear.

'I shall go on to Swaziland. Look after my son, Cam, and Godspeed.'

They made their farewells and left Will trundling slowly south. Cameron, Henry and Eli pushed on at a fast pace with Will's son leading like a good bird dog at point. He was extremely fit, his half-run, half-walk devouring the miles until, just before sunset, a shot rang out, bringing him to a dead stop.

Heidi and Alice, along with dozens of women and children suffering a similar plight, had travelled in an open freight train from Standerton to Pretoria.

There they were joined by many others and herded into different carriages to continue the journey. Their destination displayed a sign marking it as Middelburg. She remembered the name now: it was the place where Louis Botha and that evil man Kitchener had spoken of peace. That had only been a few weeks ago, before Milner and the British government made new demands causing the talks to collapse. Since then the farm burning and forced removals that brought them to this strange and terrible place had increased in intensity.

The cheese and bread Heidi had packed with her meagre possessions were long gone. British soldiers had supplied water at some of their frequent stops but no food. From the railway station, the frightened and confused passengers either walked or were taken in horse wagons to a bare patch of old farmland where conical tents and white-painted rocks defined the salient features of Middelburg concentration camp. Dust drifted over the grassless veld and the stench of open-pit latrines caused Heidi to gag as they stood in the sun awaiting registration. Wherever she looked, people wore shabby working clothes which had seen better days. The uninterested faces of existing detainees stared at those waiting in line – not because they sought something, but because they had nothing else to do. There were no smiles of greeting, only sullen expressions of defeat and apathy. Heidi felt a sense of panic and held Alice closer.

Registration completed, a bored British doctor

gave Heidi and Alice a cursory examination before handing them on to one of the Boer trustees, who took them to a tent, telling the exhausted 'mother' that this would be their new home. Before leaving, he briefed Heidi on the do's and don'ts of the camp.

Holding Alice to her breast, Heidi slumped down on the canvas bed which all but filled a space devoid of anything else except two neatly folded and well-worn blankets. 'Shh,' she whispered, rocking Alice, who grizzled in her arms from lack of a meal. 'Help will come, my little one. The Lord will provide.' Heidi had no idea why she had said that. *What hope was there for them*, she thought. They were prisoners, far from the home which lay in charred ruins two days' journey away.

In that moment of despair Heidi wanted to lie down and die but knew she could not. The infant she held needed her to live. During the last months she had all but forgotten her own child and had no idea if a husband who still knew nothing of Alice had also been lost to the unforgiving land she so loved. Somewhere out there, he and his two brothers were fighting for what they believed. For this, strangers had destroyed their home and brought her to this desolate plain in what might as well have been a foreign land. Heidi rocked the baby in her arms and hummed the familiar strains of 'Sarie Marais'. Alice responded by dribbling and closing her eyes. Keeping up the rhythm she wondered where their next meal would be coming from. Staring at the sleeping face she realised that nothing had changed. Life would always be a fight for survival.

'You have just arrived?' a woman's voice asked from the tent flap, causing her to jump. 'Do you have extra food that I might buy?'

Heidi stared at the stranger and was immediately struck by her gaunt appearance. She was probably near to her own age but unknown horrors made her look much older. 'I am sorry. We have nothing,' Heidi replied. 'Surely they feed us here?' she asked. 'They must!'

The woman stepped into the tent and gazed down at Alice. 'How old is your baby?' she asked in a tired voice.

'She is eleven months.' Heidi was more or less correct.

'And quite beautiful,' the woman said, a tear springing to her eye. 'I prey to God that she has a happy life.'

Startled, Heidi laid Alice on the bed and tucked a blanket round her. 'Why do you say such a thing?' she asked, standing up.

The woman did not reply. Shaking her head she started to walk out of the tent, then stopped and looked back. 'This is a place of death for those so young. I lost a child only last week.' With that she put her head down and hurried away, leaving Heidi with a feeling of dread. She had been in the same place and knew what grief could do to a person's mind. At least now she had Alice.

TWENTY-SIX

A dozen or so skittish buck burst from the bush ahead then stopped, looking back in the direction from which they had come. Guinea-fowl rattled their distinctive alarm call as they sought refuge in the trees. Eli spoke quietly. 'The ones you seek are not far ahead and have shot one of those impala to eat. It is good. They do not know we are here.'

'What do we do?' Henry asked.

Cameron looked at the lengthening shadows. 'It will soon be dark,' he said softly. 'Let them settle down for the night. We'll hit them at dawn while they're still half asleep.'

Henry nodded. He liked the plan.

Eli had done his job and done it well. In the morning he would leave to rejoin his father. The matter with Klaas and Ramos was no concern of his.

From a saddlebag Cameron produced three sticks of the biltong Will had given him before they left the wagon. The dark sun-dried meat, soaked in vinegar, salt and spices, was still raw in the centre. Having eaten nothing since before dawn it took the edge off their hunger.

Henry hobbled the two horses, removing both guns and placing them within easy reach. Despite the ever-present danger of lions, a fire was too risky. Eli would take the first watch, followed by Henry then Cameron. As darkness closed in, a distant glow pinpointed the position of Klaas and Ramos. Later, they heard raised voices and laughter. Sounds carried far in the African night.

An hour before sunrise, Cameron thanked Eli and wished him a safe return to his father. Will's son carried no weapon other than a knife as he disappeared into the pre-dawn darkness. 'Time to go,' Cam spoke quietly to Henry, who rubbed his eyes and flung back a dew-covered blanket.

The grass was wet underfoot and not a breath of wind ruffled the awakening bush. Somewhere in the distance a lion announced to all that he had eaten well. Moving warily they approached the still-burning fire which had been further away than Cameron expected. They were close now. Near enough to make out two blanket-covered bundles stretched beside it. The Dutchman had not worried about keeping watch, relying on a huge blaze to ward off any prowlers. *It had done exactly the opposite*, Cameron thought as they slipped closer.

A horse suddenly snorted, its nervous whinny causing the sleeping men to sit up in alarm. Beyond the fire they could see nothing but both had snatched up weapons. Klaas pointed what looked like a .38 revolver while Ramos worked the lever of a Winchester .44-40 then waved it back and forth in the darkness.

'Who is it?' Klaas shouted in Afrikaans.

'Drop the guns!' Cameron called back in English.

'Or die where you sit,' a second voice said from somewhere else.

Not knowing how many men were out there, Klaas and Ramos realised they had little choice and did as instructed. Cameron stepped forwards, the twin muzzles of his 'Cape' gun pointing ominously at the man who had spoken. Henry moved in from beyond the fire, keeping Ramos covered.

'Who the hell are you?' Klaas switched to English. 'And what do you want with us?'

'It matters not who we are,' Cameron replied. 'What we want is a simple answer to a simple question. Give us that and you can be on your way.'

'You are not Portuguese,' Klaas said. 'If this has to do with what goes on across the border then you are contravening the neutrality of this territory. Not even the Boers would risk doing that.'

'As I said,' Cameron repeated, 'all I want is the answer to one simple question.'

Puzzled, the Dutchman stared up at the tough-looking figure standing over him. 'What is it you wish to know?' he asked.

'The whereabouts of a baby girl taken from my brother in Durban.' Cameron's tone made it clear he meant it. 'You were responsible for her abduction.'

For a moment Klaas appeared confused by the question. It seemed so out of place here, in the middle of nowhere. 'Petersen's child,' he said after a long delay. 'And if I tell you where she is how will you know it is the truth?'

Cameron saw he had a point. 'Because if you have lied my brother and I will find you again and there will be no second chance.'

Light dawned in the Dutchman's eyes as he realised Duncan had not been killed in the boarding-house blaze.

'I am rapidly running out of patience,' Cameron said. 'Tell me now or by God I'll take you back to military intelligence in Pretoria. They would love to have a cosy little chat with you.'

Everything happened so fast that Cameron was caught completely off-guard. Ramos had recog-nised Henry and noticed him switch his attention momentarily to Klaas. It was all the time he needed. Slipping a pistol from his boot he raised it and fired in one fluid motion, missing his target by the merest fraction of an inch. Cameron turned in time to see Ramos flung back against his blanket. Henry only had one shot but it hit Ramos in the centre of his chest. Sensing danger he swung back to Klaas. The man was lunging at him with a wicked-looking knife. Instinctively, Cameron fired from the hip.

The explosion which followed was deafening, tearing the gun from his grasp and flinging him to the ground. Cameron had not checked the bor-rowed weapon and when he squeezed the back trigger the bullet slammed into a dried hornet's nest in the left barrel, tearing it apart like a tin opener and sending a shard of jagged metal into his groin, another furrowing its way across his face and almost taking off an ear.

Lying stunned on the ground, Cameron was vaguely aware that Henry had swung his empty rifle, smashing it into the side of Klaas's head. The Dutchman crumpled and fell heavily on top of Cameron. Henry hauled the limp body aside, kicking his knife well out of reach. Before checking on Cameron he gathered up both handguns and the Winchester, discarding his Martini in favour of the eleven-shot carbine.

Cameron could feel the pain coming in waves. Something seemed to be wrong with his hearing as well. Henry was kneeling over him, tending to his wounds. The wounds on his cheek and ear had stopped bleeding and were not life threatening but the metal splinter lodged close to his stomach was much more serious. 'Klaas?' he asked through gritted teeth.

Henry shook his head. His blow had killed the man.

Cameron rolled his eyes in frustration. He had taken a risk going after the Dutchman in Portuguese territory. Now the only hope they had of finding his half-brother's baby was gone and his own chances of survival were not worth putting money on. Another wave of pain caused him to cry out.

Dawn was breaking and time had no intention of standing still. Henry rummaged through the things Klaas and Ramos had been carrying but found little of use. He fabricated a bandage of sorts then announced. 'I am going to make a litter.'

Finding the right trees was far from easy but by

using Klaas's knife, blankets and leather reins, Henry was able to construct something that he hoped would work. Once satisfied, he took one of the horses and rode back to recover their own mounts and equipment. When he returned, Cameron had passed out.

It took Henry another hour – by which time the sun was high in the sky – before he was ready to move out. He had turned loose the horses they didn't need and left everything else as it was. Vultures were spiralling high above. Hopefully, Africa would take care of the two bodies, neither of which had died of natural causes. He had no idea where they were going, but it made sense to turn west and try to get back across the border.

Henry looked critically at Cameron, whose well-tanned face had a dirty-grey pallor. He wondered if his friend could survive. Without medical help he would be unlikely to see another sunrise. 'Just sip,' he said, bending down and trickling water between his parched lips.

'How long have we been going?' Cameron asked weakly, as Henry checked the litter and its occupant.

'Half a day,' he said. 'We are making good progress.'

'You don't need to pretend. The hand of death is near and I must ask something of you before it's too late. It is a matter of great importance. I have a farm near Dargle, below the Inhluzan . . .'

Henry was not listening. He had seen a column of mounted men coming towards them through the shimmering afternoon heat. There were ten of them at least, armed and wearing the uniform of Portuguese soldiers. Cameron could make out the rhythm of their horses' hooves. At least his hearing had improved.

'I think we may have a problem,' Henry said.

As they approached, the horsemen adopted a crescent formation and advanced at walking pace, carbines drawn and ready for use. A man wearing the gaudy uniform of an officer rode forwards towards Henry and Cameron. He spoke but neither of them understood what he had said.

'No speak Portuguese,' Cameron looked up from the litter and shook his head.

'English?' the officer asked.

Cameron nodded.

'I speak some. What do you do here?'

'Hunting,' Cameron lied. 'Had an accident.'

'Do you have permits?' Without waiting for an answer, the officer gracefully dismounted and removed his riding gloves. He was surprisingly young, with fine dark looks and a pencil moustache. Carefully he examined the bloody swab of makeshift bandages. 'You need a doctor,' he announced. 'It is fortunate that we have one close at hand. Tell your boy to follow.'

Henry glanced at Cameron, who said in Zulu the equivalent of 'So far, so good'.

The Portuguese soldier swung into the saddle and with a short hand signal formed up his patrol and moved out. Henry trailed along in the rear, leading Cameron's horse and the litter behind his own. A little over an hour later they arrived at their destination. From the number of tents, wagons and horse lines, Henry realised that the camp housed a regiment-sized cavalry unit. In the heat of the still afternoon the Portuguese flag hung limply from a white-painted pole.

Fewer than ten minutes later, Cameron lay on a table in an open-sided tent, the sloping roof of which displayed an internationally recognised red cross. A short, white-coated man with a bald head and thick spectacles carefully probed the wound in his abdomen. As the doctor, who reeked of garlic, placed a cloth over Cameron's nose and mouth, he recognised the pungent scent of chloroform. Within seconds his world faded into oblivion. The young officer stood outside, watching the proceedings with undisguised interest.

When Cameron regained consciousness he found himself on a camp stretcher in a tent lit by a single spluttering lamp. Henry sat beside the bed, head drooping and breathing heavily as he slept.

'*Amanzi*,' Cameron croaked, bringing the Zulu awake.

Henry picked up a pitcher, pouring some of its contents into an enamel mug and holding it to Cameron's mouth. The tepid water trickled slowly between his cracked lips.

'Better,' Cameron said, once he had quenched his raging thirst. 'How am I doing?'

Henry gently lowered his friend's head to the pillow. 'The doctor removed this.' He held up a two-inch piece of jagged metal. 'And has done what he could to improve your ugly white face.'

Cameron gave what he thought was a grin.

'I think that without his skills you would not be here,' Henry went on.

'It is also thanks to you.' Cameron had no doubt that Henry had saved his life.

An armed guard stood outside the tent. Henry leaned forwards and spoke softly into Cameron's ear. 'We are now prisoners of the Portuguese. It seems they have found our two friends.'

Cameron swore under his breath, wondering if they hung those found guilty of murder. 'The good doctor may not have done me such a favour if we are accused of killing them. Let's not forget, Ramos was Portuguese.'

'And he tried to kill us,' Henry said, attempting to remain positive. 'You are alive and that is what matters.'

Cameron had no idea if this confidence could be justified. He stared up at the canvas above him, aware of the tightly pulled stitches as pain pushed back through the morphine which had been administered when he first arrived. Henry's presence was somehow soothing. It was probably the first time in his life that Cameron really thought about the Zulu as a person. Henry had simply been there – for as long as he could remember. His friend, yes. Colour didn't come into it but he was from a different class, a servant. This man had just saved his life and sought nothing in return. Truly, that made them equal.

Not so many miles from the Portuguese camp,

Will Green poked at his fire with a stick and tried to think. He had just learned all that had happened since before dawn that morning.

Not long after leaving Cameron and Henry, Eli had heard what sounded like three shots. He shrugged and continued north for perhaps an hour before realising that his father would want to know what had happened. There was no option but to go back.

Something had died. The vultures told him that. The two bodies had been partly devoured but Eli could see that only one had been shot. Both were white and neither was the one called Cameron. Looking around he found his father's 'Cape' gun and realised the damage it must have done to whoever fired it. What he did not know was whether that person had also been shot. Other evidence told him that two horses – one dragging a stretcher – had set off towards the border. Eli had almost caught up with them when he saw the approaching soldiers. Keeping hidden he had followed the patrol to their camp.

'This does not sound good,' Will said as he watched a scorpion, which had been hiding in a log trying to escape the flames. 'And you're sure it's Cam that's hurt?'

'Certain, Father.'

Will shook his head as the scorpion lost its battle for life. 'If he says he was hunting without a permit, no problem. He can grease a few palms and walk away. That's not what worries me.' Will was trying to come up with some way of helping his godson but only one thought kept coming back. *If those bloody Portuguese discover two dead bodies, Cam could find himself swinging at the end of a rope.*

The chill of a new dawn brought dew to the tents and pushed tiny pepper ticks high in the grass, waiting for the first rays of morning sun. No sentries had been posted and Eli scanned the sleeping camp with the all-seeing eyes of a serval cat – his tribal totem. One tent was guarded by a blanket-wrapped soldier who sat on a stool outside the entrance. He appeared to be sleeping. It had to be the one where they were holding the major and Henry. Carefully Eli circled the camp until he was only yards behind it. He paused, listening for any sound which might indicate danger. There was only a rhythmic snoring from further down the line. Taking a knife from his belt, Will's son stepped forwards and slit the canvas.

Henry awoke with somebody's hand resting lightly on his mouth. In the dim pre-dawn light he could just make out a shadowy figure standing over him, a finger indicating the need for absolute silence. He nodded and rose, stepping across to Cameron's stretcher. Waking him gently he whispered that help had arrived. With Henry's arm round his back, Cameron managed to sit up. Eli slipped a pair of soft leather *veldschoons* onto his bare feet and without a word both men helped him through the back of the tent and into the bush beyond.

The pain in Cameron's stomach was a dull ache

as they followed game trails through the bush that no horse could hope to follow. Each step seemed to twist and stretch the army doctor's handiwork but Cam gritted his teeth and, with Henry's help, kept going. Progress was slow and it took them until almost midday to reach a camp which looked as if it had been there for days instead of only hours. All traces of wagon tracks had been carefully obliterated.

Will welcomed them with obvious relief.

As expected, it was not long before a Portuguese patrol of at least thirty men – led by the officer who spoke English – found the camp.

Will shuffled forwards to meet them, waving as if to attract attention. 'Am I pleased to see you,' he blurted out, stumbling and shaking convincingly. 'I need quinine and phenacetin urgently. How far is your camp? Is there a doctor?'

The young soldier pranced his horse forwards, not sure what to do next. Duty prevailed. 'We are looking for escaped prisoners, senhor. One white and one black. I will have to search your wagon.'

'By all means, Colonel,' Will said, flattering the man with a rank higher than he owned. 'Most of my boys are down with blackwater. Two died this morning. There's a dead horse in the bloody river and we've been drinking from it for a week. Just hurry up and get me some *muthi*. I need whisky too.'

The officer looked down suspiciously. 'Do you have papers, senhor?'

Will rummaged in a pocket and produced a

well-worn permit authorising him to trade in Portuguese territory. With a shaking hand he offered it up.

'This seems to be in order Senhor Green, but I must insist on carrying out a search.'

'Then for the love of God, Colonel, please hurry.'

He rode forwards but reined in his horse at the sight of such a disgusting camp. There was mess everywhere. Apart from the chaos, three sweat-soaked Africans lay beside the open wagon, moaning and calling for water. Another – a coloured – appeared to be dead. Two graves had recently been dug, the mounds displaying crude wooden crosses. The young man made the sign of a crucifix on his chest. He didn't hear Will come up behind him.

'You can see why we need help. I cannot leave here. Please, Colonel, you are our only hope.'

Shaking his head he reined round to distance himself from the scene. 'I will send the items you have requested. There is no need to trouble you further. Good day, Senhor Green.' With that he kicked his horse into a canter and rejoined his column.

'Tell them to make it quick,' Will called shakily to the departing cavalry officer. Once the troops were out of sight, he wiped the nervous sweat from his brow and shouted, 'Right, lads, let's get the hell out of here.'

Immediately, Eli and the apparently sick Africans jumped to their feet, quickly clearing soil from the two graves. Where there should have been a corpse the ground moved and Henry sat up, spitting a hollow reed from his mouth. Cameron, they had to help.

'Bloody close,' Will muttered, walking back towards the wagon. 'I'm getting too old for this kind of game.'

'Thanks, Will,' Cameron said. 'We owe you and Eli our lives.'

'Well, best you get back over the border before we have to come up with something else. All this excitement is no good for my heart.'

'That's exactly what we intend to do,' Cameron said, shaking Will's hand. 'I don't need your death on my conscience.'

His godfather grinned. 'Pity about Klaas and that other fellow, though. What happens next? You're no closer to finding Torben's daughter.'

'I don't know, Will. I honestly don't know.'

TWENTY-SEVEN

Acutting wind blew incessantly, covering everything in a layer of fine dust. The tent provided little protection as Heidi did what she could to keep Alice clean. Water was strictly rationed and there was no guarantee it had not been contaminated by the totally inadequate sanitary arrangements which affected everybody in the camp. The child was grizzling. Heidi felt helpless.

There had been two burials that morning, presided over by a bearded *predikant* of the Dutch-derived *Nederduits Gereformeede Kerk*, or NGK as it was better known. He wore a tattered black suit and hat, his powerful voice promising that the wrath of God would strike down those responsible. Heidi wondered why he was taking so long to do it.

One of those they mourned was the child of a woman Heidi had befriended. Like her, Marie Burger had nothing else in the world save for her infant daughter. Now she did not even have that. The camp doctor had diagnosed measles but there was nothing he could do to save the little girl.

Heidi sat by the cot she had fabricated from an

old packing case and tried to soothe the young child. Alice's temperature seemed higher than normal and it worried her – not that she was feeling much better herself. When Heidi had woken that morning she experienced a strange pain in her stomach and felt feverish. These soon passed and she prayed the symptoms had meant nothing serious. Her greatest fear was that something might happen to her, leaving little Alice alone and unloved.

Lifting her from the wooden box, Heidi made sure the threadbare blanket gave as much protection as possible. Carrying Alice tight against her she sought out Marie's tent and found her friend sitting inside, clutching a framed photograph. She was weeping and did not look up as Heidi entered.

'Can I do anything for you?' she asked, feeling the woman's pain.

Red-eyed, Marie looked up. Although she was only twenty years old she had aged considerably in the short time Heidi had known her.

Placing Alice on the bed, she wrapped her arms around the younger woman. 'She is with God,' Heidi offered lamely. 'In a better place than this.' The photograph showed a husband and wife with a tiny baby. The proud parents were probably wearing their best clothes, the child a long christening gown. It brought tears to Heidi's eyes as well. Marie began sobbing again. 'We must remain strong,' Heidi said, tightening her grip. 'God and our menfolk expect it.'

'My baby did no harm to the British.' Marie

stated a simple fact. 'So why has God chosen to take her away?'

Heidi did not have an answer. She suddenly felt quite sick as a new wave of fever hit her.

Will Green's wagon trundled towards the border. Cameron lay in the back surrounded by skins, tusks and a clutter of other bits and pieces. Henry rode beside the Zulu driver, a man who knew his father and had once worked at *Morningside*.

'Soldiers coming!' Eli shouted a warning to Will, who swung round in his saddle and saw that they were being followed. He could not see long distances but the dust left no doubt.

'How many?' he called to his son.

'I think it is the same ones who came yesterday.'

Will felt sick in the stomach. Having passed through the Lebombo Hills he was sure they must have crossed the ill-defined border between Portuguese East Africa and the Transvaal. Where it actually ran was a moot point when you were outnumbered by at least three to one. Even if Cameron and Henry could be hidden, Will had no doubt that the Portuguese would find the rapid recovery of his men more than a little suspicious. They had come so close to evading capture but with a heavily loaded wagon there was no hope of outrunning the rapidly approaching horsemen. Reluctantly, he held up a hand, indicating to his driver that they should wait for the Portuguese patrol to catch up. Eli had been correct – it was the young officer they had fooled the day before.

'I see that miracles are still possible, senhor,' he said sarcastically, a faint smile on his face. 'And I also notice that you have gained an extra employee. Perhaps there is yet another in your wagon?'

Will's heart was pounding. 'We picked him up a few miles back.' He hoped that one African looked much like another to the aristocratic soldier.

'Then, senhor, I can only assume that you are aiding this man's escape from justice. I am forced to arrest you and all those in your company. Please, I would like to look in the wagon.'

'Capitano!' The cry came from one of the Portuguese patrol.

He looked at where the man was pointing and was genuinely startled to see a column of raggedly dressed individuals coming towards them from the west. Will looked up and assumed it was a Boer *komando*. What would happen next was anybody's guess. Thankfully, there was no evidence that Cameron and Henry were in any way associated with the British armed forces.

They moved with practised precision, fanning out to confront the mounted Portuguese. Will counted about twenty of them. One came forwards to address the soldiers. The man was tiny – even on horseback – with a huge handlebar moustache, bushy eyebrows and piercing black eyes. When he spoke it was in heavily accented English, revealing a mouth devoid of teeth save for a few yellowed stumps. 'Vot do you men tink you are doing in British territory? Do any of you dagoes speak English?'

The army officer smarted at both the question and the insult. He did, however, admire the man's knee-length leather boots and hand-crafted silver spurs. 'I do, senhor. And who are you to question my authority on Portuguese soil?'

'I am Colonel Ludwig Steinacker,' he answered. 'Who de pluddy hell are you?'

'Captain Ferdinand da Gama. On behalf of His Majesty King Carlos of Portugal, I must insist that you and your men submit to my authority.'

'Cheeky also. It is de other way round. You haf invaded de Empire of His Majesty King Edward de seventh of Great Britain. I can prove it if you so vish.'

'And how would you do that?'

'Vit a map and compass – assuming they teach you to use such tings.'

Da Gama ignored the barbed remark. 'Agreed. I have a map. Do you have the compass?'

'I do,' Steinacker said, swinging from his horse.

The Portuguese officer also dismounted, producing a map from inside his tunic and spreading it on the ground. Their men waited, watching each other for any signs of aggression.

Steinacker looked around then pointed at three readily identifiable geographic features. 'Vood you agree those three hills are these ones?' His finger stabbed at the map.

Da Gama studied both and unconsciously bit down on his bottom lip. 'I would.'

Producing his compass, Steinacker orientated the map with true north, then called a bearing, which the captain recorded. This was done twice more to give a triangular reference on their position. The lines put them almost exactly on the border – too close to say whose territory it was.

'It vood appear ve are both right and wrong,' Steinacker said as the two men rose to their feet. 'If ve are to avoid an international incident it vood be best if ve both vitdraw.'

'Agreed, Colonel. But I will take my prisoners with me.'

'And I disagree,' the wiry little man said, looking up at Captain da Gama. 'Since neither of us can be certain vere ve are, might I suggest that these men be allowed to go their own way?'

The Portuguese officer stared hard at Will. He knew the men he sought had left him two British army horses. There was no sign of the one whose life he had most definitely saved. The African on the wagon looked familiar but he couldn't be certain. Without further ado he shrugged his shoulders in a gesture of acceptance. 'So be it,' he said cheerfully. 'I have done my duty.'

'Tank you, Captain.' Steinacker thrust out his hand. 'I appreciate your gesture of goodvill.'

Da Gama took the hand. 'If all disputes could be settled between reasonable men there would be no cause for war.'

'A good point, Captain. A good point. I bid you good day, sir.'

The young officer saluted smartly and Steinacker returned the gesture. On command, the

Portuguese column wheeled and rode back in the direction from which it had come.

Will climbed stiffly from his horse and introduced himself.

'I haf heard of you, Mister Green,' Steinacker said. 'Tell me, in your recent travels haf you perhaps encountered a British major?'

'Funny you should ask that,' Will grinned. 'I happen to have one by the name of Granger-Acheson in my wagon. Seems he had a bit of an accident on the wrong side of the border.'

'I see. Then it is fortunate for him a certain Lieutenant Pickstone told me de major and an African scout ver doing a little detour through Portuguese territory. That cavalry camp is quite new so ven they did not return as planned a little look-see vas called for. Ve ver very lucky.'

'I agree. It wouldn't do to start a rumour that the major had deserted.'

'Vitch vay are you going, Mister Green?'

'South. To Swaziland.'

'Then ve vill make a *machila* for de major so ve can carry him. His men are no more than ten miles to de vest of here. I trust de mission vas a success.'

Will shook his head. 'British intelligence may think so but the major had a personal reason for being there. From that point of view, I'm afraid it was a failure.'

In the flickering yellow lamplight, Marie Burger muttered words of prayer and dabbed Heidi's forehead with a sweat-soaked cloth. The fever was intense, her mind flipping through uninvited memories as if she were watching a magic lantern show. There was nothing more the camp's English doctor could do and that night Marie saw the signs of death in her friend.

In a blanket-covered wooden box beside the bed where Heidi lay in her delirium, Alice grizzled and cried with hunger.

'My baby's name is Alice Petersen,' Heidi said in a moment of absolute lucidity. 'Her family is from Durban.'

Marie was startled by the statement but dismissed the words as another fevered rambling. Suddenly Heidi gripped her wrist and tried to sit up. Staring eyes, burning with the flame of fever and frustration, bored into hers.

'She is not mine,' Heidi said fiercely. 'The *Broederbond*. They took Alice from her true mother. You must promise to return her if . . .' Letting go of Marie's wrist, Heidi sighed and sank back against the sweat-soaked blanket. 'Promise me!' she demanded. 'You are her only hope.'

'I promise,' Marie said half heartedly, if only to placate the dying woman. 'Petersen – in Durban. I will remember that.'

Before the sun rose Heidi van der Merwe died of typhoid. Marie gently lifted Alice from her improvised cot and cradled her in her arms. She still had milk from the child she had so recently lost and placed Alice on a nipple already leaking in anticipation. The sensation flooded Marie with maternal instincts as she realised her own need to be a mother had been given a second chance at fulfilment. *The Lord worked in strange ways*, she thought to herself and began to hum.

Lieutenant Pickstone completed the task of setting up border pickets between latitudes twenty-four and twenty-five degrees south while Cameron remained at Sabi Bridge, too ill to move. Henry sat with him day and night, encouraging his friend to stay alive while the fevers came and went.

The infection had been bad but by introducing maggots to devour any dead flesh the wound was kept clean and at last started to heal. Eventually he was well enough to travel and 'Stinky' Steinacker made arrangements for his transfer by rail from Komatipoort to Pretoria.

Duncan was the first person to visit him in the military hospital. Cameron told his brother all that had transpired. There was no news of Alice and they had to accept that the trail had run cold. He learned that Major John Scott had fronted for Duncan at the boarding-house fire enquiry, saying it was a matter of military intelligence and thus classified. He would at least welcome the news that Klaas was no longer a worry. Duncan's wound – which had healed to an interesting scar – would one day make a fine story for his children. He hadn't told Tanith.

Lindsay had been expecting Cameron's arrival at the hospital and gave him a full examination before contacting Ellie to say that all was well. She promised to get there as soon as possible but in the meantime sent a telegram to *Morningside*.

Within weeks Cameron was able to leave his bed and walk with the aid of a stick in the hospital grounds. Winter had come early to the highveld and most days were too cold for him to remain outside for long. He was still unfit for military service so Lindsay provided a medical certificate which would allow him to recuperate at *Morningside*.

Cameron thought about leaving the train at Dargle Road but decided against it. Duncan had sent Torben a telegram and his half-brother met him at Durban station. When Torben first saw him he could hardly believe how much Cameron had changed. The soldier who stepped slowly onto the platform was a shadow of the man he had known all his life. Torben had already heard how Cameron had risked his life to try to stop Klaas from escaping. The fact that the Dutchman had been killed before saying anything which might have helped them find Alice was just as painful to Cameron as were his wounds.

Neither man knew what to say. Cameron had not seen Torben or Gerda since before Alice was born. He had never actually met his niece. When he had heard Gerda had miscarried, losing a baby boy, Cameron had been so caught up in his own life that he didn't even write.

'I'm sorry, Torben,' he said. 'For everything.' The two men stood on the platform, their arms around each other, not ashamed of the tears that flowed.

Cameron spent that night at the house off Musgrave Road. Gerda hardly spoke. Her sister Lanice was there too, so that Torben and Cameron could make an early start for Zululand the following morning.

Lorna, Dallas and Mister David watched the carriage as it wound its way up to the house. Saba was gone from the verandah long before it stopped.

At first, Lorna was shocked at the sight of her eldest son. A livid scar ran up one side of his face to where a scab had formed round the base of his ear. He was far from his usual healthy weight and walked slightly stooped, leaning on a walking stick. She switched her attention to Cameron's eyes, searching for that only a mother could understand. With relief she saw that the bitterness was no longer there. His anger had gone too – only sadness remained. It was time to heal that as well.

Dallas greeted both his boys. The time for talk would come later.

Foregoing the usual greeting, Cameron looked up at Mister David. 'Henry saved my life,' was all he said. Saba looked pleased that someone had.

There was an awkward moment when Meggie returned early in the evening. Both brothers knew of her engagement to Stan King but up until then Cam hadn't commented. He could hardly believe the change in his little sister. Overnight, it seemed, she had grown into a vibrant woman.

Quickly he broke the ice, hugging Meggie and saying, 'Let's see the ring, then.' He remembered he had told Ginnie to keep the one he had given her. He smiled. 'I hope you and Stan will be very happy.'

Tanith was keen for first-hand news of Duncan and over dinner on his second night home Cameron accidentally let slip that a man called Ramos had nearly slit his brother's throat. Lorna and Tanith were horrified but Dallas came to the rescue, saying knowledgeably that it was nothing more than a scratch and he hadn't wanted to worry them. The peace held.

Torben stayed for three days before he went back to Durban. Despite everything, they were the happiest days he could remember.

Time passed quickly and soon Cameron was back on a horse, talking about returning to take command of his unit.

'Why don't you get out on medical grounds and come back to farming?' Dallas asked as he showed off his new cane plantings. 'You have done enough for your country.'

Cameron could hardly believe the changes his father had made. 'I would be deserting my men if I did that,' he replied quietly. 'I have to go back.'

'You know,' Dallas said, 'if you stick your hand in a bucket of water the level rises. When you take it out, it goes back to where it was.'

'You sound just like Mister David,' Cameron smiled. 'Or are you going mad in your old age?'

Lorna had seen her husband relax since their eldest son returned home. Cameron was recovering from his wounds and the war no longer dictated his life. Although he never spoke of Ginnie, the pain of losing her seemed to have subsided.

'It's about time you and I took a trip to *Wakefield*,'

Dallas said one evening after dinner. 'I think that might change your mind about going back to the army. After all, Kitchener has enough troops over here to sink the whole of Africa. One man more or less won't make the slightest difference to the eventual outcome of this war but a visit to my half-sister might change your life forever.'

Cameron looked quizzically at Dallas. How could he tell his father that she already had?

TWENTY-EIGHT

Duncan was only too aware that the following day would be the first birthday of a son he had never seen. He wrote to Tanith at least once a week, sometimes more. As a present for Frazer, he had his photograph taken in full uniform, hat under one arm, head turned and smiling into the camera. It was an excellent likeness, carefully composed to hide the stitched scar on his neck. Tanith's and Duncan's mothers had separately sought more information about his injury and he had lied to both, saying it was little more than a scratch. The photograph for Frazer would prove it to them. He signed it, *To Frazer, with your father's love. November 1901*. After having it mounted in a silver frame, Duncan lovingly packed the picture in a straw-filled box which he addressed to his son and despatched by recorded delivery.

There was no longer a front line as such and reports reached Duncan's desk from all over the country. It was his job to summarise these and keep High Command appraised of progress with the war. This included the construction of fortified blockhouses which were being built to protect

Lord Kitchener's highly vulnerable lines of communication and supply.

Beside the reams of reports lay an open copy of *The Spectator*, in which Britain's Commander-in-Chief confidently predicted that the war would be over by April 1902. His forecast was based on the fact that Boer *komandos* relied heavily on the veld itself to feed their horses. Come winter the grass would die, denying them the fodder they needed to remain in the field. As Kitchener knew, the enemy had no hay or grain to fall back on. His predecessor's ruthlessly implemented scorched earth policy had seen to that.

Duncan sat behind his paper-swamped desk and listened to the *clack-clack* of hobnailed boots in the marbled corridors of staff HQ. Other than the jarring man-made sound, the afternoon was unusually quiet. He looked up from the neatly stacked piles of paper, his mind somewhere out on the never-ending veld – a warm wind blowing – listening to the swishing sound of long grass parted by horses and the slap of metal on leather. Duncan missed the Fairfax Scouts, their banter in the field, the frantic *chrr-r-r-r* of panicked francolin as a covey of terrified *i-Swempie* burst into flight from right at your feet.

He was daydreaming and unread reports lay on the desk in front of him. Snapping himself out of the pleasant memories he sighed and reached out. His hand picked up the newspaper instead. An article caught his eye condemning the way in which Kitchener was conducting the war. Somebody who had probably never set foot in South Africa – let alone during the war – was objecting to the way he intended to extend the existing blockhouse system. It quoted sources within the Royal Engineers, saying that up to eight thousand were to be built throughout the Orange River Colony and the Transvaal – some even in the Cape. Each housing at least ten men, they would be sited along existing roads an average of a thousand yards apart and joined together with barbed wire. In effect, the whole country was to be broken up into more manageable areas. 'Farming people', as the article put it, before suggesting that Kitchener should be sacked.

Not only were the blockhouses under attack, earlier in the year a Miss Emily Hobhouse had visited a number of the so-called concentration camps. Her damning reports in the British press had been seized on by the Liberal Party, who used a public outcry to force the War Office in Whitehall to establish a commission of enquiry. All things considered, Lord Kitchener was not having an easy time of things.

'Are you in, old boy?' Duncan looked up from his reading as he heard the familiar voice of Major John Scott from the doorway.

'Come in,' Duncan beckoned, rising from the chair and stretching his back. 'What can I do for you, sir, or is this a social visit?'

'More like what I can do for you,' he replied, hanging his hat on the stand just inside the door and pushing back a curl of sandy hair which had flopped forwards. 'I've just come from the POW compound where my chaps have been interrogating a couple of recent arrivals. Something cropped up about that fellow Klaas who your brother kindly dealt with for us. We were most grateful to him so this is by way of thanks. Are you still pursuing that family matter?'

'Indeed we are,' Duncan answered with interest.

'Would I be correct in thinking it concerns a missing child?'

'You would. Even my father's contacts have come up with nothing. Her name is Alice Petersen.'

'I know. And her father is your half-brother. The man we've been chatting to worked with Klaas when he was in Durban. He says that the baby was taken to a woman called Heidi van der Merwe on a farm somewhere near Standerton just inside the old Free State border. Apparently, she was paid to look after the child. It seems the *Broederbond* are involved but don't ask me why. Our man told us everything he knows, of that I'm certain.'

Duncan couldn't believe his ears. 'I can't thank you enough, John,' he said, thrusting out a hand to his friend from military intelligence. 'I'll send a telegram to Torben right away, then see if there's anything on record about a person of that name.'

'Glad to be of service, dear boy,' the major said, leaning across the desk. 'You can buy me a drink in the mess when you've finished pushing all this paper around.'

The reports will have to wait, Duncan thought,

when his unexpected visitor had gone. He turned to a large map which took up most of one wall and his finger found the place he was looking for. It lay where the railway line from Natal crossed the Vaal River. A shaded area told him that most farms in the area had been cleared. However, that meant there would be records of any people transferred to camps. It was what Duncan had hoped for. At last he had something positive to tell Torben.

Within twenty-four hours his half-brother had received the telegram. Torben stood in the study and reread Duncan's words, hardly daring to believe that there was suddenly another chance of finding Alice. His first instinct was to tell Gerda the news but he stopped himself. Since their second child had died she seemed to have lost interest in life itself. Gerda never admitted that the baby's deformities could have been caused by her growing dependence on laudanum. It didn't matter. Gerda had convinced herself it was God's will that she would never have a family. She remained in the house and spent hours seeking salvation in a huge leather-bound bible.

Torben knew that finding Alice and bringing her back was the only thing that might save his wife's sanity. *What if Duncan's information turned out to be false*, he questioned himself. To raise her hopes then dash them would be cruel. He had no choice but to make up some excuse and go to Standerton himself. Torben placed the telegram in his pocket and went to the nursery that had once been Alice's room. More than a year had passed since his daughter had been taken from them. He opened the door and stared at the empty cot, wondering if it would be too small when he brought her home.

The following day, Torben took a train from Durban. His destination lay almost two hundred and fifty miles distant in the southern Transvaal. It seemed to take forever as they climbed from the coast into the Natal midlands, stopping and starting for reasons which were quite beyond him. He thought of his last journey inland, remembering it as having been much faster.

Stepping onto the platform Torben welcomed the opportunity to stretch his legs. A warm wind ruffled his hair, the total lack of humidity in stark contrast to what he was used to at home. Since crossing the border, blockhouses and barbed wire had followed the track. That too was new. British soldiers were directing dozens of Africans as they struggled to offload an open wagon containing bales of wire, iron sheets and other building materials. Looking around, the faces that stared back at him reflected nothing but apathy. Standerton was a town that had lost its soul.

Torben wasn't sure where to begin his search so he booked into the only hotel and started asking questions. Time and again he was faced with the blank stares of people who claimed not to speak English or were simply unwilling to help a person they viewed as the enemy. The fact that he was a civilian made no difference whatsoever.

Cursing his own stupidity for not thinking of it sooner, Torben realised he would probably have more success speaking to whoever was in charge of the British garrison. It was not long before some name-dropping paid off and he found himself talking to a corporal who had records of absolutely everything and was only too happy to prove that his system worked.

The farm Heidi van der Merwe came from lay not in the Transvaal but slightly to the south-west, in the Orange River Colony. Hardly able to contain his excitement, Torben asked how he could get there.

'Not much point in doing that, sir,' the army officer said as he produced yet another ledger. 'We cleared out that area more than six months ago.'

Torben's heart sank.

'Let's see now.' The soldier ran a tobacco-stained finger down one page after another. 'You might have chosen a less common name,' he complained. His finger stopped. 'Here we are – van der Merwe, H., with one female infant. That must be them. They were sent to one of the camps.'

'Which one?' Torben asked eagerly.

'According to my records they were taken by rail to Middelburg. That's all I can tell you.'

'That's enough,' Torben said. 'You have been most helpful.'

There would be no train until the following day so Torben returned to the hotel deep in thought. It was no secret that some camps were worse than others. He had read the damning newspaper reports of Emily Hobhouse. Middelburg was a familiar name but that didn't mean much. There were so many camps where malnutrition and disease were rife. 'Please, God,' he heard himself mutter, 'protect my little angel.'

Dallas and Lorna sat on either side of the dining table in Durban, listening to Torben pour out his plea for help. They had come at his request, dropping everything to help find Alice. Gerda had no idea of the real reason for their visit and after putting in a brief appearance for dinner – during which she did little more than push food around her plate – retired early. She had not dressed specially and seemed completely uninterested in news of the family.

'The authorities at Middelburg were uncooperative, to say the least,' Torben told them. 'Even Duncan has not been able to find out anything concerning this van der Merwe woman, save that she died some time ago. When he asked them about the baby she had with her they claimed to know nothing about any child.' Torben shook his head. 'They are either absolutely incompetent or deliberately lying to hide what's going on there.'

Dallas leaned back in his chair and let out a deep sigh. 'We are too close to be beaten by British bureaucracy,' he said. 'Did they say why you were refused access to the camp?'

'Not in so many words. They said it was a restricted area – whatever that may mean – and I had no authority to be there.'

'Surely you told them of the circumstances?' Lorna queried.

Torben turned to his stepmother and was surprised to see the intensity of anger and frustration burning in her eyes. 'The bastards couldn't have cared less,' he replied, grateful for her concern.

'Well, they had bloody well better get interested,' Dallas growled. 'This is my granddaughter we're talking about.'

'Our granddaughter,' Lorna corrected him, reminding her husband that Alice was kin to both of them.

Dallas took the point and shook his head. 'Sorry, that's what I meant.'

Torben hadn't been listening. 'Is there some way we can turn things in our favour and use the system to get us into that camp?' he asked. 'If anyone can come up with an answer it has to be you, Father.'

Dallas thought about it for a second then leaned forwards over the table. Looking at Lorna he said, 'Ellie and Lindsay have a new posting. How far is it from Middelburg?'

She picked up on what her husband was thinking. 'By train, no distance at all. They're near Jo'burg and as doctors in the army medical corps would probably have access to the camp.'

Torben looked at Lorna and saw the determination written on her face. She was not his mother but had always been there, as had all the family. None had wavered in helping him search for Alice, though it had come so close to claiming the lives of Duncan and Cameron. His clandestine collusion with the *Broederbond* haunted him and Torben wished, not for the first time, that he had never encountered the faceless body which seemed to control every facet of his life. Greed had dictated his choice, then for some unknown reason those he served had taken from him something no amount of money could ever replace – his daughter. Torben had long since decided that if he could get her back, if he could hold Alice in his arms again, he would somehow sever all links with the Brotherhood – even if that meant leaving Africa forever and taking his family to live in Denmark.

'Then Torben and I must leave as soon as possible,' Dallas said. 'We'll go to Johannesburg and contact Ellie.'

'I think this matter is best left to me,' Lorna quietly interjected. 'I'm the one who should travel with Torben.'

Both men looked at her as if she had gone quite mad.

'Give me one good reason why not,' Lorna went on. 'There's nothing your father can do that I can't. It's about time I did something constructive to bring this family together and, besides, I would like to see Ellie and Lindsay, not to mention a son I probably won't even recognise!'

When Torben looked to his father for comment, Dallas merely shrugged. 'Then I suggest we leave in the morning,' he said to Lorna. The matter was settled.

Lorna was horrified by the sights she saw on their journey from Durban to Johannesburg. Natal showed evidence of the war but the real devastation came when they crossed into the Transvaal, where blockhouses and barbed wire lined the track as they travelled north, through mile upon mile of once-prosperous farmland now devoid of crops and cattle. Here and there burnt-out homes stood as gaunt testimony to the times. The towns they passed through were little better. Beggars, black and white, called up to those in the carriages, their pleading faces sullen, seeking no more than a means of survival. Everywhere she looked, Lorna saw the drab khaki of military uniforms. She had not expected anything like this. It was another world, not the Africa she knew and loved.

As if reading her thoughts, Torben commented, 'This war has caused so much suffering. Tell me one good thing that has come of it.'

Lorna turned to him. 'You seem to have made a lot of money,' she said.

It was the truth, though her observation caused Torben to feel quite uncomfortable. 'So will you when Father's new cane plantings are cut,' he countered in his own defence. 'In war there are always those who will make money. Even governments do it. Is that something to be ashamed of?'

'I did not mean to imply that you have been anything other than honourable in your business dealings,' Lorna replied. 'It was merely an observation.'

'Sorry.' Torben realised he had overreacted and offered a partial explanation: 'There are things I'm not proud of when it comes to the money I've made.'

Lorna reached over and squeezed his hand reassuringly. 'And I'm sorry for putting you in a position where you thought I was questioning your integrity.'

'Mother, I –' Torben started to say something then stopped.

Lorna looked at her stepson with some surprise. He had used a word she had not heard from him since he was very much younger. His estrangement had increased as he grew older, but suddenly, for no apparent reason, he was once again the insecure little boy Dallas had introduced to the family so long ago.

'What is it?' she asked gently, worried by the anguish that clouded his face.

'There's something I want you to know,' he said, turning away to compose himself before looking her in the eyes. It was then that Torben bared his soul, telling her of his links with the *Broederbond* and how it had led to the abduction of his daughter.

Lorna listened without interrupting. When he finally fell silent she simply patted his hand and said, 'What you have just told me is a matter between us. There is no reason why it should go any further.'

Torben impulsively gave her a hug, something else he had not done in years. His burden had suddenly eased. At least one member of the family knew the truth and had not judged him. It was a beginning. Now they needed to trace Alice.

Finding lodgings in a city crowded with military personnel was not easy but Torben used his money and influence to pull strings. Once they had booked into a hotel, Lorna sent word to Ellie at the hospital where she now worked. It was not the messenger who came back but Ellie herself.

Lorna hadn't seen her daughter in almost a year, not since they brought Dallas back to *Morningside*. For Torben it had been even longer. Both of them commented on how gaunt and tired Ellie looked. She put it down to the fact that the 'bloody camps', as she called them, were causing more problems than the war itself.

'To give you an example,' Ellie said as they sat in the hotel lounge, 'before the Fawcett Commission forced Milner to assume control of the camps and improve conditions, infant mortality was running at over six hundred out of every thousand – mainly due to measles. Lindsay has been lobbying for change. He spends more time with politicians than patients these days.'

Torben swallowed, dreading that Alice might be part of Ellie's startling statistic. Lorna was not surprised and listened as Torben told Ellie what had brought them to Johannesburg.

'So you believe that my goddaughter might be at Middelburg?' Her tone sought more information.

'From what I have been told, this woman van der Merwe came to the camp with a female infant,' Torben went on. 'She died of enteric fever and the authorities refuse to say what happened to her baby. All the evidence I have points to that child being Alice.'

'Then we had better go and fetch her,' Ellie said, making it sound so simple.

'Torben has tried but was fobbed off,' Lorna said. 'We felt that you, as a doctor, might stand a better chance of getting into the camp.'

'I will still need authority from the army,' Ellie said, thinking out loud. 'Duncan should be able to come up with some piece of official paper. Fancy a trip to Pretoria tomorrow?'

Lorna and Torben nodded their agreement. This was family.

The knock on Duncan's door at staff headquarters interrupted his concentration and Lorna could hear the frustration in her son's voice.

'Come!'

He looked up from another boring report to find three familiar faces grinning at him from the doorway. The scowl turned to a smile as Duncan shook his head in disbelief and jumped up to greet them. 'Mother, Torben, what a wonderful surprise. Hello, Ellie.' He hesitated. 'Is something wrong? What brings you all to Pretoria?' The smile had gone.

'Everybody is fine, dear,' Lorna assured him as she held out her arms.

Duncan seized his mother in a huge hug then shook Torben's hand and kissed Ellie on each cheek.

'Let's have a look at you,' Lorna said, holding him at arm's length and examining the scar on his neck. 'Tanith and Frazer loved the photograph, though I can see why you turned your head sideways!'

'It's nothing, Mother. How's Tat? I've put in for leave but she doesn't know. You mustn't say anything; I want to surprise her. She says Frazer is growing so fast.'

Lorna opened her handbag. 'I've brought a letter for you – here.'

Duncan held out his hand. 'And Father, how's he? What about Cam?' He turned to Torben. 'Is there any news of Alice? Was my information of any help?'

'She is why we are here,' he said.

Duncan found chairs for his mother and sister then listened as Ellie explained.

'Then let's see what we can do.' He pressed a button on his desk and in seconds an adjutant appeared. Duncan told him what was needed and the man soon returned with a triplicate pad of the form he had requested – a security clearance applicable to any military installation. Although Duncan did not have the authority to sign such a document he shrugged and completed one each for Ellie and himself, stamping them and adding a scrawled signature. 'I'm afraid Ellie and I will have to do this on our own,' Duncan explained. 'We are both in uniform and know how the system works.' He laughed. 'Though I don't expect anybody will query our credentials.'

Ellie picked up one of the passes and smiled. It was signed with a single name – 'Kitchener'. 'Aren't you taking a bit of a risk?' she asked.

'I've only signed the originals,' Duncan grinned. 'We can lose them if we have to. The copies are blank.'

His sister shook her head. It was just like Duncan to bend the rules.

Lorna and Torben returned to Johannesburg. Duncan had been right: their civilian presence in a military establishment – especially one under close scrutiny – could only arouse suspicion.

Citing 'family reasons' Duncan was able to obtain forty-eight hours' leave. He also spoke to John Scott and told him what had transpired. The intelligence officer gave him a name to ask for and promised to help if he could.

Duncan and Ellie travelled the eighty-odd miles to Middelburg on an overcrowded passenger train, reaching their destination late that afternoon. They had no difficulty finding accommodation and after a meal best forgotten, both retired early. What Duncan did learn from his sister over dinner was that she and Lindsay had put their names forward for missionary work in Bechuanaland. Ellie made him promise that he would say nothing to their parents.

The next day dawned hot and dusty. Deciding to go without breakfast, Duncan managed to hire a pony and trap from the hotel for their visit to the camp. They were there before eight o'clock, met at the gate by a bored-looking corporal who did at least salute at the sight of Duncan's rank. Their passes were of no interest to him.

'I am looking for a Major Donovan,' Duncan said, staring icily at the soldier.

'Over there, sah,' the corporal replied, pointing to a corrugated iron structure with a makeshift wooden verandah.

Duncan urged their unwilling horse forwards and secured the reins to a spindly roof support before extending a hand to his sister. He knocked on the door and was bid enter. Ellie did so first, stepping into a single room with one window which looked across what appeared to be a parade ground. The major rose from his chair, not expecting a woman.

'I heard you were coming,' Major Donovan said after Duncan introduced his sister as Doctor Mayer and then himself. 'What can we do for you, Captain?'

Duncan sensed a note of hostility in the commandant's question. He was a burly man in his mid forties, overweight and uncomfortable in an ill-fitting uniform. Despite that, the ribbons on his chest provided an impressive record of service in many campaigns. 'The C-in-C has instructed me to accompany Doctor Mayer on a fact-finding mission to this camp. She is compiling a report on all children under five years of age.'

'Bloody politics,' the major sneered. 'I keep submitting requests for better rations and medical supplies but the answer from staff HQ never changes. Refugees are low priority. Now that Milner is putting Kitchener under pressure, he needs to find scapegoats.'

Duncan nodded in sympathy with the observation.

'Well, Doctor,' the major said, turning to Ellie, 'we have nothing to hide; be my guest. I will introduce you to our resident medical officer, Doctor Kelly. He can confirm what I have just told you.'

Duncan sensed that the officer's hostility was directed more towards Lord Kitchener than himself or Ellie. It was obvious the major was a caring man, frustrated by a system which had him looking after women and children rather than facing the real enemy.

The major escorted Ellie and Duncan along a path lined with white-painted rocks until they reached a long, low structure displaying a large red cross on the wall. Despite the relatively early hour, it was hotter within the corrugated iron structure than it was outside. Tightly made beds of starched linen ran from one end to the other. They were all empty.

A thin, bespectacled officer wearing a white smock over his army uniform stood up from the single desk where he had been reading a *Rand Daily Mail* and saluted smartly. Major Donovan introduced him as Doctor Kelly, confirming that he would answer any questions Ellie might wish to ask.

She nodded her thanks to the major. 'Where are your patients?' she asked, seizing the initiative. 'Considering the number of people in this camp, I find it most surprising that the hospital is empty.'

'Those who fall sick prefer to stay in their tents,'

Kelly replied. 'I'm afraid these Boers are a very backward people who would rather put their trust in God than modern medicine and a British doctor. You can see that for yourself if you don't believe me.'

'I don't doubt what you say,' Ellie smiled sweetly. 'I certainly wish to speak with your patients but don't be alarmed. My mission concerns children, especially those too young to take care of themselves. I need to know how many have died since this camp was established in February and how many are held here now. Infants under three I would like to see for myself. This is no witch hunt, Doctor Kelly. The purpose is to provide information, not criticise or comment on how well you are doing your job.'

The doctor looked visibly relieved and suggested they examine the records while his staff made arrangements to have all children under the age nominated by Ellie brought to the hospital.

Major Donovan excused himself, saying he had a mountain of paperwork to catch up on. Duncan thanked him and promised they would report to his office before leaving.

Ellie sat at the desk studying a meticulously maintained journal which turned names into numbers, analysing camp inmates from their date of arrival at Middelburg. Neatly drawn columns separated adults from children under fifteen, listing both by sex. Every page was totalled and ruled off, each month carefully summarised. Arrivals, births and deaths – even marriages – were recorded.

They had no idea if Alice was alive or not. Ellie scanned the hospital records for an hour, making copious notes. She was stunned to find close on a thousand deaths of children under fifteen. *No wonder they want to keep this secret*, she thought. Suddenly her face lit up. She had found an arrival listed as 'van der Merwe, H'. The columns showed a single female with one child, also female. It corresponded with Duncan's information. A red ink entry in the right-hand column read 'died enteric March 31st 1901'. It did not say what had become of the child. The system had its flaws. Ellie could only hope that she was still in the camp. Certainly the deaths from disease were far fewer than they had been earlier in the year.

'This is not going to be as easy as we thought,' Duncan muttered in Ellie's ear. 'There are so many. If Alice is here, how on earth will we recognise her?'

Ellie had no easy answer. They were looking for a little girl between eighteen months and two years old, looked after by a woman who was not her mother. It was hardly a lot to work with but it was all they had.

A line of women nursing babies or holding the hands of infants had assembled outside the hospital. They stared with suspicion at the staff, including Ellie and Duncan.

'Better get started then,' Ellie said, looking up at Doctor Kelly. 'How many have we got?'

'Seventy-eight mothers with children under three,' he told her. 'Will you require an interpreter?'

'That will not be necessary,' Duncan replied. 'I suppose you speak the *Taal*, Doctor?'

'Unfortunately not,' he admitted. 'Nor do any of my nurses.'

Duncan was pleased. His own knowledge of Afrikaans was limited to say the least but Ellie spoke it fluently and would be able to converse freely without being understood by the doctor or his staff.

Doctor Kelly consulted a clipboard and called out a name. A woman reluctantly stepped forwards holding the hand of a little boy aged about three.

Ellie looked into his mother's eyes. 'I am a doctor, not your enemy,' she said in Afrikaans. 'I am here to examine your little boy and arrange medicine if he needs it.' The mother looked surprised at an English doctor's use of her home tongue. Ellie could see that it had defused the Boer woman's initial hostility.

Name after name was called as the day wore on. Ellie talked to mothers and carried out a thorough examination of each young child or baby, prescribing treatment or medicine where warranted. Doctor Kelly recorded everything Ellie translated for him. When they took a short break for lunch he spoke up. 'What you are doing for these people is all very well but we simply do not have half the items you are prescribing.'

'Things are improving, Doctor,' she smiled at him. 'I can see that from your records. Lord Kitchener has realised he extended the camps without providing adequate medical facilities. Redressing that situation has been one of Sir Ian Hamilton's priorities since he took over as the General's Chief-of-Staff. Put in a requisition and see what happens. I'm sure you will be pleasantly surprised.' Ellie glanced at her brother, who shifted uncomfortably but looked suitably serious.

It took the rest of the morning and all of the afternoon to conclude the examinations. At the end of the day Ellie had a list of eight little girls within the right age group. She had asked each mother a series of questions and paid particular attention to their replies and reactions. Not one gave any indication that the children were anything other than their own.

With no more people to see, Ellie turned to Doctor Kelly. 'Is that it?' she asked, her voice sounding weary.

He checked his list of names and found a couple with no ticks against them. 'Two did not report as instructed,' he said. 'If you wish to see them we can go to their tents.'

A nurse came and said something to the doctor. It was obviously important.

Ellie turned and spoke quietly to Duncan. 'We may have seen Alice and not known it but all my instincts tell me that is not the case.'

'We know there is a possibility that she has died,' her brother pointed out.

'Somehow I can't believe that,' Ellie said, removing her glasses and running a hand through her short blonde hair. 'Our search is not over yet.'

She turned back to Doctor Kelly, who waited

patiently, having dealt with the nurse's emergency. 'The two mothers we have not seen, what children do they have?'

Kelly consulted his clipboard. 'One has a boy of three.' He ran his index finger down the list. 'The other a girl of around eighteen months – sometimes we don't have an exact age.'

Ellie nodded. 'We will see the baby girl first,' she said in a tired voice. 'What is the woman's name?'

'Burger. Marie Burger,' the doctor replied. 'According to my records it is not her own child. She is acting as foster mother to the orphan of a woman who died some months ago.'

'Her name?' Ellie asked.

'Van der Merwe,' the doctor said without consulting his notes.

Ellie felt her heart miss a beat. Everything fitted.

Duncan looked sharply at his sister and a smile passed between them, wiping away any feelings of weariness. It seemed that the search was over.

Marie Burger had always known the day must come when some stranger would take away her reason for living. It was why she hadn't gone to the hospital. The English doctor didn't need to be told her child's name and seemed better informed about Alice than she was. It was the beginning of the end.

Two days later Major John Scott arrived at the camp with a letter ironically signed by Sir Alfred Milner himself, now Baron Milner of St James's and Cape Town, the skilled politician whose backing of Cecil Rhodes and Alfred Beit had been largely to blame for starting the war in South Africa. With the officer from military intelligence were two civilians who, he explained, had come to collect the toddler being looked after by Marie Burger. He introduced them as the child's real father, Mister Petersen, and his mother from Natal.

Knowing Major Scott and being satisfied that the paperwork was in order, the handover of a confused and tearful Alice was a mere formality, nothing more than another statistic. Nobody gave a moment's thought to Marie Burger, who later that day was found hanging from the pole in her tent. Middelburg camp records showed her death as accidental. Only the numbers had to tally.

Torben would never learn that the woman who had been a mother to his daughter for the last eight months had taken her own life.

TWENTY-NINE

Dallas had been in a sultry Durban for five days and it was driving him mad. There was still no word from Lorna or Torben, and although he had promised to stay at the Berea house until their return, time was beginning to drag.

Gerda kept very much to herself, which was probably a good thing. She thought Torben had gone on another of his business trips and didn't seem to find it strange that Lorna went with him. Lanice came to the house every day, which meant that Dallas could at least get out and attend to other matters. He had never met the woman before, though the rumours of her past life were well known to him. Dallas instinctively liked Lanice, who was genuinely concerned for Gerda, and by keeping her occupied had managed to reduce her sister's dependence on drugs to almost nothing. They would play cribbage, crochet, cut and arrange flowers, even just talk. As long as Gerda had somebody with her and something to do, she was fine.

Dallas's business meetings did not take nearly as long as he had expected. For some time there had been talk of new land releases by the government for those willing to plant sugar cane. The scheme was still some way off and Dallas couldn't help but wonder who gave anybody other than the Zulus the right to dictate what happened to their land. Times were certainly changing and, for the Zulus, not for the better.

Sir Liege Hulett was talking sugar production in the foreseeable future of thirty thousand tons from Zululand alone. Almost fifteen tons of cane had to be processed to yield one ton of sugar so at thirty tons to the acre – high in comparison with Natal – that would mean planting over fifteen thousand acres. Dallas had applied for new cane quotas, which he was surprised to find had been approved without the usual bureaucratic delays and conditions.

Sitting in the Durban Club he scanned the *Natal Mercury* for news of the war. Even that seemed to have gone quiet, though he noticed that the blockhouse line from Kroonstad to Lindley was due for completion by the year's end. Mention of Lindley started him thinking about Frazer, who had been killed not far from there. It all seemed so long ago. Dallas could picture the place and recalled his promise to Lorna that he would bring their son home. Somehow it was no longer important. He was with them always. *Would Lorna see it the same way*, he asked himself.

Dallas had no plans for the afternoon and was wondering what to do when he remembered Cecily and Stephen. Were they back from

Bechuanaland? Only one way to find out, he decided, freshening himself up in the cloakroom and letting an Indian valet polish his shoes while he waited for Torben's carriage and driver.

A Zulu Dallas didn't recognise answered the door and asked him to wait while he found out if visitors were being received. The fact that somebody was home lifted Dallas's spirits as he stood in the hall, hat in hand, looking around. They must have returned very recently, he realised, noticing still-drawn curtains and dust covers on some of the furniture. It was dark and, thank goodness, quite a lot cooler than outside, where the weather was building to an afternoon thunderstorm. The servant returned and bid him follow.

Stephen Holgate was only two years younger than Dallas but the stick-thin figure who greeted him was not the man he knew. 'Hello, Dallas, what a pleasant surprise,' he said. 'Sorry about the shambles, old chap. New staff and all that. Must get round to doing something about it.'

Dallas realised he was staring. 'Stephen, good to see you. When did you get back? Where's Cecily?' Somehow he knew the answer.

Stephen shrugged and opened his hands, palms up and fingers splayed in a gesture which clearly said *not here*. 'Last week, to answer your first question. Afraid you've caught me at a bad time.'

Stephen had first met Dallas nearly thirty years earlier. It was Lorna who had introduced him to a woman fifteen years his senior – Cecily Jerome – first cousin of the late Randolph Churchill's wife,

Jennie. They fell in love but never married, their liaison frowned on by many. Cecily and Stephen couldn't have cared less, becoming close friends with Dallas and Lorna, whose circumstances were equally unconventional. Ellie had developed a particularly close relationship with Cecily, who was both her godmother and mentor. As she stayed at the couple's house in Durban while studying to become a doctor, it became her home away from home.

Dallas moved to the almost closed curtains. 'May I?' he asked, before opening them.

Stephen nodded and screwed up his eyes as light flooded into the room.

There was so much Dallas had to tell his old friend – Frazer's death, Ellie and Duncan both having married, his grandchildren, the abduction of Alice. Now was not the time.

Lightning flashed and a peal of thunder crashed close behind, rattling the window. In seconds the heavens opened, pounding the glass with driving rain.

'It's the most beautiful place, Dallas,' Stephen said over the noise from outside, his mind miles away. 'There are animals the like of which we had never seen. Gemsbuck – *Ko*, the Bushmen call them – with straight, needle-sharp four-foot horns. *Nakong*, or sitatunga, strange antelope which seemed to walk on the water but would submerge and hide if danger threatened. Our camp was at Totin beside Lake Ngami. It fills from the Okavango, which floods south-east down the

Botletle towards Lake Xau. The water is crystal clear and in October, before the rains, all manner of beasts arrive in their thousands. We would lie under the stars at night and listen to the lions. Sometimes their footprints passed right through our camp.' He hesitated. 'That's where she is, not far from a village called Xhumaga. I watched her die, Dallas, and there was nothing I could do.'

Dallas laid a hand on his friend's shoulder.

Stephen was staring at the rain as it ran down the window. 'The fever came first. We assumed malaria and thought it would run its course. It didn't. She just got weaker and weaker. When the tremors started I held her, held a woman who was wasting away before my very eyes. Do you know, Dallas, Cecily felt more afraid for me than she did for herself? "*Tsamaya sentle*, Stephen". Those were her last words. Her journey was longer than mine and she lived every mile of it.' He reached up and touched the hand resting on his shoulder. 'It's fate that brought you here today, Dallas.'

They talked for hours, well beyond the storm and into a warm summer evening. Dallas did tell Stephen why he was in Durban, as well as all that had transpired since they last met. He promised to come back with Lorna as soon as she and Torben returned from Johannesburg – no matter what the outcome of their mission. Stephen agreed to spend Christmas at *Morningside*.

By the time Dallas got back to the Berea, Gerda had retired for the night. On a table in the hall he found a telegram with his name on it. The message was cryptic and brief: 'MISSION ACCOMPLISHED RETURNING TOMORROW'. It was signed 'TORBEN'.

Cameron knew that Ginnie's marriage to Paul Norman had been postponed – twice, apparently – but he hadn't once been to see her. The dream of a life together was part of the past. Only the future mattered.

Cameron had promised to hold the fort at *Morningside* while Dallas and Lorna were away. As it turned out there wasn't a great deal to be done. Meggie was not there most of the time and one visit to Tanith and Frazer had been more than enough. Cam was very fond of his sister-in-law but they had little in common and when Frazer decided to regurgitate an entire meal all over him, the opportunity to go home and change was most welcome.

He and Saba spent many hours trying to outwit the old saurian of Mhlathuze lagoon. Although Cameron saw him on a number of occasions, that was as close as he ever got. Mister David had told him that *ngwenya* grew about one foot a year for the first five or six years of their lives then slowed right down and only increased in length by an inch or so every twelve months. The old fellow in the lagoon was all of eighteen feet long – maybe more. Which meant that he had been born a good fifty years before the birth of Shaka, founder of the Zulu nation, who had been just over forty when he was murdered in 1828. The calculation occupied Cameron's mind as he sat waiting for the crocodile to surface.

Almost an hour had passed and there was still no sign of the ancient monster. He found himself thinking of Caro and the farm she had given him. It had been almost a year since . . . Suddenly there were two eyes watching him from the water, a snout breaking the surface two feet in front of them. The *click-click* as he cocked the hammers of his father's .577 sounded loud and out of place. Although he remained totally focused on the crocodile, it slipped back below the surface and was gone.

To hell with this. The day was coming to an end and the mosquitoes were getting hungry – not to mention the leeches on his legs. *There would be none of these bloody things at Wakefield*, he thought, carefully removing another. Cameron decided to go there as soon as his parents returned. He would go by himself, not with his father.

It was another five days before Dallas and Lorna returned to *Morningside* with the news that Alice had been found and was back with her parents in Durban. Apparently, the change in Gerda had been quite unbelievable.

Alice hadn't recognised them and at first seemed quite confused by the sudden change in daily routine. To everyone's delight, her tiny mind adapted fast as sights and sounds not seen or heard in over a year awoke dormant memories. A mother's scent, the unchanged nursery, Hilda's bulk and toothless grin. Perhaps even the humidity. It was only when Gerda tried to sing 'Sarie Marais' that Alice cried.

Lorna had been so elated when she returned to Durban with Torben and Alice; the news of Cecily's death from sleeping sickness hit her hard. She and Dallas spent two days trying to help Stephen pick up the pieces of his life and make him realise that there was a future – no matter how bleak it looked. He refused their immediate invitation to *Morningside* but confirmed he would be there for Christmas.

Dallas was not sorry when Cameron said that he intended going to *Wakefield* by himself. There were a thousand and one things to do at home. 'Perhaps Caro would like to come for Christmas. Why don't you ask her?' Dallas said, holding Saba's collar to stop her following Cam's horse.

In strictest confidence, Lorna had told Dallas that Duncan had been granted leave and planned to surprise his wife and family. That it would be, he had thought, especially since Cameron considered it an excellent idea that Duncan and Tanith build their own house on the farm.

The Petersens would be coming too.

Cameron broke his journey in Durban to meet a very special young lady, his niece. He was amazed at the size of Alice, who understood not one word of English but would happily respond when Gerda spoke to her in Afrikaans. Torben laughed. 'Good thing for the future, I suppose.' Cam had never seen his half-brother so relaxed and felt closer to him than at any time he could remember.

Torben knew about his father's half-sister giving Cameron her farm. Dallas had told him. Instead of the usual display of jealousy he was genuinely pleased. 'If you need a hand catching some of those trout, just give me a shout.'

'It's about bloody time you turned up,' Caro called, hands on hips.

The wide-brimmed hat still shaded Cameron's face.

'Can't hang around here waiting for you. I've got better things to do.' She noticed a stiffness as he dismounted and secured his horse.

'At least I wrote, which is more than some people I could mention,' Cameron responded, removing his hat.

'My God,' Caro exclaimed, a hand flying to her mouth before she jumped down from the verandah for a closer inspection. 'What happened? Your letters said nothing.'

Cameron wasn't sure how he should greet his aunt, who had reached up to touch the scars. 'It's a long story,' he said, kissing her cheek. 'I have also resigned my commission.'

'On medical grounds, I suppose, judging by the limp and the mess your face is in. How's your father?'

'Fully recovered, thank you. He and Mother would like you to spend Christmas at *Morningside*.'

'That's kind of them. What about you, Cameron?'

He hesitated. 'I would rather be here but not if you are there. What's the point?'

'Being with family sounds like a good reason to me. We'll talk about it later. Now, let Klipklop see to your horse.'

An Indian woman had appeared from inside with a tray of drinks. 'Ah, Popeti, there you are. You remember my brother's son, Cameron? As you are aware, he now owns *Wakefield*.'

After putting down the tray, Popeti studied the blond-haired young man with the scarred face before bringing her palms together and leaning slightly forwards. '*Namaste*.'

'Nice to see you again,' Cameron replied.

'Popeti, please make sure the spare room is made up,' Caro instructed. 'Cameron will be staying for a few days. I hope.'

'And how are you, Caro?' Cameron asked, smiling at his aunt.

'*Nimbo paani* or Scotch?' she answered.

Cameron did most of the talking, telling her of Duncan's near-death experience with Messrs Klaas and Ramos and how they had both been killed in Portuguese East Africa. It was almost embarrassing to reveal that his own wounds were caused by an accident.

Caro was delighted to learn that Alice had been found and reunited with her parents. Meggie's engagement to Stan meant little to her. She had never met either of them, though she remembered how Dallas had a special affinity with his youngest daughter. Ellie and Lindsay were just names to her as well.

That evening they ate corned beef with boiled potatoes, cauliflower and a white sauce. 'All home-produced,' Caro said, dabbing at her mouth with a napkin. 'Hope you don't mind Moses slaughtering one of your beasts?' she added, more as a statement than a question.

They ate on the verandah by lamplight then turned it off to watch the stars. Caro produced a bottle of Portuguese red wine. Cameron felt completely at home and relaxed.

'Tomorrow we must talk about you taking over this place. I'm getting itchy feet.'

'What about the lion?'

'On the list of things to do but it can wait.'

'Father has this theory that it's safer to approach lions on all fours.'

Caro looked incredulous. 'Crawling, you mean?'

'Yes. He says they find you less threatening like that.'

'Well, tell your father he's mad. You and I will have to get that lion on our own. I refuse to be responsible for my half-brother's death!'

The evening disappeared. Time didn't matter. They opened another bottle. When that too was gone the time came to call it a night.

'Your room,' Caro pointed to one of two candlelit doorways.

'My room,' Cameron agreed.

'I enjoyed this evening, Cam. Christmas at *Morningside* would be wonderful.'

They kissed goodnight and she was gone.

He blew out the candle on his bedside table and in seconds was fast asleep.

★

Cameron had no idea where he was when the fire woke him. The room had filled with acrid, eye-watering fumes but beyond the open door was a raging inferno. 'Caro!' he screamed. There was no reply.

Flames licked hungrily at the thatch over his head. The only way out was through the window. He had to find Caro. No sooner had his bare feet touched the ground outside than the room behind him burst into flames. With a crackling sigh the whole roof collapsed, sending a spark-filled shower of burning thatch spiralling into the night sky. There was no possibility of going back inside. 'Caro,' he called again, hoping beyond hope that she had managed to escape. The heat drove him further back.

He ran round the house, calling her name. Suddenly a black figure burst from the flames dragging something behind him. The man seemed to be on fire himself. Cameron rushed forwards to help and found his hands sticking to raw flesh. Sweeping the African into his arms he carried him clear of the house and laid him gently on the ground.

Klipklop and others had appeared with buckets of water but it was too late. Cameron looked around in desperation. Popeti, in her dressing gown, long black hair hanging to her waist, covered Moses with the thing he had salvaged from the house. It was a leopard skin.

'Madam Caroline is gone,' she said simply. 'Moses will take care of her.'

There was no option but to let the fire burn

itself out. By morning, the house was nothing more than a smoking pile of ashes atop a rectangular plinth of scorched rocks. A couple of charred roof poles miraculously remained standing, otherwise it had all gone.

Cameron knew what he had to do. A milking pail was all that he could find. Klipklop brought the other things he had asked for.

The twisted metal frame of the double bed told him he was in the right place. Everything else turned to ash as the shovel touched it. He half filled the bucket and carried it to where the little Bushman waited with his horse.

It took Cameron an hour to find Guy's grave. When he left that place – high on the Inhluzan – there were two piles of rocks, not just one.

Cameron was in a state of shock. There could be little doubt that the tragedy had been accidental – probably caused by the candle in Caro's bedroom – but the police would have to be notified. Telling his father would be the worst thing.

Returning to the still-smoking rubble Cameron discovered that Moses's body was missing. He knew from past experience that the Zulus took care of their own, so it was one less thing requiring his attention. Before doing anything else, Cameron made sure the farm's labourers understood that their employment was safe and that the day-to-day running of the farm would continue as normal. He learned that Moses had a son and put him in charge of everybody except Popeti. She would return to her family in Durban and spend Christmas there, coming back early in the new year. What she would find on her return remained to be seen.

Cameron's efficiency was his way of dealing with loss. He had been there before.

The police in Howick recorded that Cameron Keith Adair Kingholm, the owner of a farm called *Wakefield*, near Dargle, had reported an accidental house fire in which his widowed aunt, Caroline Hammond, had died. Her next of kin was listed as Dallas Granger-Acheson of the farm *Morningside* in Zululand. There were no suspicious circumstances.

As he had expected, they had no interest in the Zulu who had died trying to save her.

Saba had been lying on the eastern corner of the verandah. Her eyes appeared to be shut but she saw him long before anybody else, gave one bark and was gone.

Lorna looked up from her book and took off the glasses she used for reading. She could see a lone rider coming up towards the house, slouched in the saddle and in no particular hurry. Cameron wasn't due back for another couple of days, but Saba was in no doubt about her master's return.

He didn't dismount. 'Hello, Mother. Is Father inside?'

Something was wrong; she could sense it. Duncan? Alice? What had happened? 'He's at the workshop. They're building cane trucks.' Should she ask?

'It's Caro. She's dead.'

Lorna's hand flew to her mouth as Cam wheeled away to find his father.

Dallas was just as surprised as Lorna to see Cam back so soon but less sensitive, not noticing something was wrong.

'Well, well, look who's here,' he said, wiping grease from his hands and smiling a welcome. 'Come back to give me a hand?'

There was no easy way to tell him. Cam knew that when he did the emotion he had held in check for almost three days would burst like a dam flooded with summer rain. He swung down and stepped close to his father. Words wouldn't come but the dam broke and he clung to him. They stood like that until the flow eased.

'What's happened to Caro?' Dallas asked quietly. He held his son close, dreading the answer and trying to be strong.

In fits and starts, Cameron told him and for the first time in his life their roles reversed.

When he could talk, Dallas asked. 'Was everything lost?'

'Moses managed to save the leopard skin,' Cam replied, before he remembered last seeing it covering the dead Zulu's body.

Dallas said nothing about his mother's letters to Jack Walsh, the long-dead father he shared with Caro. 'That was where you spent last Christmas, wasn't it?'

Cam nodded but said no more. Dallas had found out how Caro had known he was back at *Morningside*.

'I'm going to rebuild it, Father. Hermit or not, *Wakefield* will be my home.'

The dam had found its new level.

THIRTY

Cameron and Dallas travelled to *Wakefield* in mid December 1901. Torben went too, leaving Lanice with Gerda and Alice. All three of the men needed to move on from things that Caro might have called 'milestones' in their lives.

Moses's son, Nelson, greeted them and took great pride in showing Cameron that he had everything well in hand. Outwardly he displayed no emotion over the death of his father.

Cameron paid all the employees – giving each person a special *bonsella* for Christmas – then told Nelson that he wanted the rock plinth cleared and enlarged so that they could start rebuilding the house early in the new year. He paced out the shape he wanted and marked it with wooden pegs.

Dallas's horse followed the faint track that climbed high above the farm. Caro had been the last remaining link with his father and he was sorry that he had not known her better. One day soon he would bring Lorna to this place. She had never met his half-sister but was well aware of what her husband had lost.

Cam had done a good job. He would, Dallas thought, though he added more stones to the new mound before sitting and fumbling in a pocket for his pipe. Caro liked the aroma of tobacco.

Torben helped Cam wherever he could and the two brothers found themselves talking easily.

'I'll be moving up here after Christmas,' Cam told him. 'The house will take some time but if you don't mind roughing it a bit, bring Gerda and Alice up for a few days. We can always make a plan.'

'I would like that, Cam, very much indeed.'

They slept under the stars that night, not near the burnt-out house but beside a bend in the river where Cam managed to guddle two trout for supper. Dallas had no luck, then Torben made it three. It was the first fish he had ever caught.

In the hour just before dawn, Dallas could have sworn he heard a lion. *Strange*, he thought, knowing that there had been none in that part of the country for probably a hundred years.

When the three men returned to Durban, it was to find Duncan at the Berea house. He had arrived earlier that afternoon, hoping to see Alice and spend the night before completing his journey to Empangeni.

Gerda had welcomed her old flame with open arms but Lanice showed more restraint in greeting a man wearing the uniform of a British army captain. Alice soon broke the ice and by the time the others arrived all three were taking tea in the garden, watching the curly-haired cherub as she played contentedly on a patchwork quilt her mother had made. Duncan had changed into civilian clothes and nobody spoke about the war.

He had not seen his father in over a year, not since he had been invalided out of the Fairfax Scouts. 'You are carrying a bit more weight than the last time I saw you,' Duncan smiled as they embraced.

'Good to see you, son, this is a surprise.' He held him at arm's length to look at the scar. 'You were bloody lucky – then, you always were.'

'The person who stitched it can do my sewing any time!' Gerda added.

They all laughed.

The next morning, Torben lent Duncan a horse and watched as his father and two brothers set off for Zululand. He and his family would follow by train in a few days' time. There was still something to be done before Christmas.

Duncan did not take the turn-off to *Morningside*: he had other things on his mind.

Aminta saw him arrive and went to find Tanith. 'Madam, there is a person at the door who wants to see you.'

'Who is it, Aminta?' she asked, looking up from spoon-feeding a bowl of mealie meal to Frazer.

'A man in uniform, madam.'

Tanith sounded irritated by the interruption. 'Here, finish feeding him while I see what he wants.'

Mister David's daughter sat beside the little boy and whispered in his ear. 'Your father is home.'

Frazer actually jumped when he heard his mother's sudden scream of delight. 'Duncan! Why didn't you give us any warning? Look at me – I'm a mess.'

'I'm looking at you, Tat, and you look fine to me. Come here.'

Tanith needed no second bidding.

Mister David took the pony trap to collect Torben and his family from the Thukela railhead. It was the second time he had made the trip in three days, the last being to pick up Ellie and Lindsay, who were accompanied by Stephen Holgate.

Even with such a full house, Lorna had managed to juggle the accommodation to suit everybody – with the possible exception of Meggie. Stan was expected that evening and would sleep in Torben's old room, now refurbished for use by visitors. Ellie and Lindsay had Ellie's old room while Stephen was in Duncan's. Torben, Gerda and Alice would be using the guest suite. Duncan, Tanith and 'Little Frazer', as Lorna called him, were only due on Christmas morning and would leave again that same afternoon.

Dallas and Cameron steered clear of Lorna's domestic arrangements and simply did what they were told. That way, everybody was happy. They were sitting on the verandah working on Cameron's plans for *Wakefield* when Dallas spotted a lone rider. At first glance he thought it must be Stan, but looking again he realised the build was wrong.

'Bloody eyes,' he said, picking up his old stalking spyglass from the table beside him and focusing on the distant horseman. A man, it certainly wasn't.

Cameron had been concentrating on some figures – not his strong point – and wasn't paying much attention to anything else. Saba stood up and made a whining noise in the back of her throat which she kept repeating until her master realised that she was trying to tell him something. He turned to see what the dog was staring at, dropped his pencil and stood up in stunned surprise. It was Ginnie. Riding right up to the house, she did not dismount.

As he stepped forwards, Cam heard her sharp intake of breath. Selfconsciously he raised a hand and felt the scar on his face. 'It's better than it was,' he said curtly.

'Cameron, I have no right to be here but –'

'You can say that again,' he interrupted.

'Cam.' The voice came from behind him. 'Might I suggest that you give Ginnie a chance to say what has brought her here?' Dallas paused, then added: 'As Mister David might say, "an ostrich cannot see far while its head is buried in the sand".' He stood up and nodded at Ginnie. 'It took some guts coming here today. I apologise for my son's lack of courtesy.'

Suitably rebuked, Cameron saw that his father was right. Mumbling an apology of his own, he stepped from the verandah and helped Ginnie dismount. She was trembling and suddenly, more than anything else, all he wanted to do was hold her.

The reins slipped from his fingers as she fell sobbing into his arms.

'Oh, Cam, I hurt you so much, my darling. Can you ever forgive me?'

He was not over her. Cam had always known that and now it was Ginnie who came to him. 'I love you, Ginnie. I have never stopped loving you.'

'Nor I you, my dearest. God, I was such a fool.'

When Dallas went inside he quickly found Lorna and told her what was going on. They couldn't resist a quick peep from behind the curtain. Lorna even had her fingers crossed. 'Leave them,' she whispered, feeling as if they were intruding. She didn't say it but thought April or May would be a good time for a wedding. She would make damned sure this one was at *Morningside*.

Cameron poured Ginnie a cool drink and they sat on the verandah, her hand in his as she told him what had happened.

'Paul knew I didn't love him. He's a very sweet man, Cam. He bought the farm from my parents and has given Kevin a job as his bookkeeper.'

Cameron looked decidedly dubious. 'I thought he . . . well . . . do you think he can do it?'

'With the drinking, you mean?' She understood exactly what he had meant. 'That had a lot to do with feeling sorry for himself. Paul has shown confidence in Kevin and as you may or may not know, my brother is a real wizard with figures. Cam, already he's a different man.'

'And your parents? What happens to them?'

'Paul doesn't need the house. It's his, but for as

long as Mother and Father are alive it will remain their home. Kevin and his family will live there too.'

Cam shook his head at the apparent simplicity of it all. 'I've got some news for you too.'

'I'm all ears.' Ginnie drained her glass and added: 'Mmm, that drink was delicious. What was it?'

'*Nimbo paani*,' Cameron replied.

Ginnie did not stay that night and left with enough daylight remaining to get home before dark. She was wearing a ring Cameron had not forgotten, one that Caroline's father had given to his grandmother.

Earlier in the evening, Torben and his family had arrived, closely followed by Stan King.

Over a late dinner, Ellie and Lindsay announced their intention to see out the war then go to Bechuanaland as missionary doctors. Lorna was not surprised. The loss of Cecily had touched her daughter deeply. When the meal was over, she slipped away for a quiet word with Frazer and Katie. Lorna detected the aroma of cigar smoke before she saw Torben.

'I thought you might come out here,' he said, putting an arm around his stepmother. 'The matter we discussed has been dealt with. A man called van Deventer came to my office the day before yesterday. It was most strange, really. He apologised for what he described as "matters getting out of hand" and said he quite understood my wanting nothing more to do with his organisation.'

'The *Broederbond*, you mean?' Lorna asked.

'Precisely. He said that arrangements had been made for my shareholding in our various joint ventures to be taken over by another party.'

'Did he say who that would be?' she queried.

'As a matter of fact, he did. De Beers.'

Lorna just nodded. The wheels of politics and power would go on turning no matter who governed the country or how many had to suffer in order to satisfy the demands and ambitions of so few. Damn it, she thought, I could probably count them on the fingers of one hand.

Torben took Lorna's silence as a sign she wanted to be alone. 'I'll see you in the morning, Mother.'

She leaned her head against him. 'Sorry, dear, I was just woolgathering. It's funny how things that once appeared to be so important can become quite the opposite.'

He was not altogether sure what Lorna was referring to. 'If you mean the business, that will be fine. My own investment in the coal industry is looking most promising and Olaf has identified a number of new opportunities. We're looking at shipping. How does "The Petersen Line" sound to you?'

Lorna smiled. 'I like it.'

'The ships will be mainly cargo with a few first-class cabins for passengers. If you and Father were to make another trip to Europe, the owner's cabin would always be at your disposal.'

'That's a very kind thought, dear. Thank you. Now it's late, so may I suggest you check on Gerda and my granddaughter then get some sleep. Tomorrow will be a big day.'

Torben gave his stepmother a squeeze and kissed her on both cheeks. 'I'm looking forward to it.'

Alone under the cassia tree Lorna laid a hand on the black marble of Katie's gravestone. It would soon be ten years since they had lost their daughter and already more than two had passed since Frazer had been killed. It was time that she had been referring to. Its passing was one of the few things mere mortals could not influence. *Time moves at its own pace*, she thought, *bringing change whether we are ready for it or not.*

'I need to talk to the two of you,' she said quietly. 'How do I tell your father you are both here? Will he understand that the body Frazer used in another life is no longer of any use to him and should stay where it is?'

From the tree above, a wood owl called softly and Lorna looked up. *Weh, mameh – weh, mameh*, it seemed to be saying. She recognised the Zulu for 'Oh, my mother – oh, my mother.'

But another voice also spoke from the darkness behind her. 'There is no need, my love, he has told me already.' Dallas put his arms around her. 'Happy Christmas, my darling.'

At that moment Lorna experienced a sense of peace and contentment she had all but forgotten. *Time*, she thought to herself. *It's time to move on.*

That night Cameron lay in his bed staring into the darkness. He was still alone on Christmas Eve.

★

Thanks to unexpected visitors, Duncan, Tanith and 'Little Frazer' were late arriving for Christmas lunch. It had been a year and a half since Tanith had seen her family, so nobody complained.

Although Aminta came with them, Mister David had hoped for news from Henry. He was not surprised at his son's silence. After all, he knew it was not only a white man's war.

Author's Note

Lord Kitchener's prophecy proved to be correct and on 31 May 1902 the Treaty of Vereeniging brought to an end a period of African history during which both sides, Boer and British, lost almost three times the numbers killed in action to inadequate medical facilities and the ravages of disease.

Over twenty thousand, mainly women and children, died in concentration camps.

There are no accurate records of African deaths but the figure lies somewhere between fifteen and twenty thousand. The peace signed in Pretoria did little to recognise such a sacrifice and denied the country's African population any say in the future of South Africa.

Over four hundred thousand horses, mules and donkeys were either worked to death or fell foul of conditions for which they were ill prepared.

Britain's scorched earth policy certainly deprived the Boer *komandos* of essential supplies in the field but it also devastated the country's rural economy. An estimated seven million cattle, sheep and horses were either killed or removed from their rightful owners.

After the war, Dallas and Duncan developed *Morningside* into one of the biggest cane-growing estates in Zululand. Will Green became a regular visitor, mainly to get away from his wives. Duncan and Tanith built their house and before too long, 'Little Frazer' had a sister, Gwen. Lorna established a clinic on the farm and started a school for Zulu children of their employees.

Ginnie and Cameron were married at *Morningside* in May 1902. The new house at *Wakefield* was completed later that same year. They had no children and the horses became their family. Klipklop came and went, though Popeti lived with them until her death in 1924.

Torben and Gerda had another daughter. They called her Marie, for no particular reason. Perhaps they just liked the name. The coal industry flourished and with it, Torben's business. Every two years they took a family holiday in Denmark.

Ellie and Lindsay spent two years in Bechuanaland before moving further north and joining a Scottish missionary group based near Blantryre in what was then British Central Africa. They had one child, a boy. His name was David.

Stephen Holgate disappeared while swimming in the Indian Ocean. He had been staying with Dallas and Lorna at their beach cottage near Umdhloti. His body was never found.

Lorna had a third family wedding at the farm. In September 1904 Meggie and Stan married. She was twenty-two, he forty, and they were as much in love as ever – more so if that were possible.

Stan bought most of the cattle from *Morningside* and trekked them to *Kingsway*. The farm was flourishing and with the rail line now through to Empangeni a lot of their earlier transport difficulties were solved. Colin was born to Meggie and Stan in July 1905 and Robert – Bob, as they called him, except when he was naughty – the following year. Noel arrived in February 1908. That was supposed to be it. Unfortunately, it wasn't: Meggie had a *laat lamajie* in August 1913. His name was Joe. Bringing him into the world cost Meggie her life. She was thirty-one. Stan never remarried. He died in 1935, aged seventy-five. Two of their four sons were killed during the Second World War.

Mister David? He was taken by a crocodile in the Mhlathuze lagoon. It was never proved but that's what they say. Henry never returned to *Morningside*.

And on Christmas Eve 1902, Cameron shot a lion near Lindley.

Beverley Harper
Shadows in the Grass

*Enraged screams filled his head. Deadly shapes
bore down. Animal and man driven by one single
thought. Kill or be killed. Neither wanted to die.*

Falsely accused of a terrible crime, impetuous
young aristocrat Lord Dallas Acheson is forced to
flee his native Scotland, leaving behind the only
woman he has ever loved – Lady Lorna de Iongh.
From that day onwards, he must learn to live a
different life in a land where danger is an ever-
present partner.

Fate takes him to southern Africa and the emerging
seaport of Durban, from where he sets off to trade
and hunt, seeking his fortune in the little-travelled
midlands of Natal and the wilds of Zululand. Tested
to the limit, Dallas discovers more than he could
have imagined.

Married to a woman he doesn't love, he yearns to
abandon the restraints of nineteenth-century society
to be with Lorna. And when the Zulu war breaks
out, finds himself torn between old and new
loyalties, required to be an enemy of the land that is
now his true home.

Brimming with the trademark qualities of evocative
storytelling and accurate research brought to vivid
life, Beverley Harper, author of *Jackal's Dance*, is
indeed 'Australia's answer to Wilbur Smith'.
AUSTRALIAN GOOD TASTE

Beverley Harper
Jackal's Dance

Agony exploded in her knee. She staggered, tried to keep going, then nearly fell as a shocking pain rushed up her leg. Confusion and fear swamped her senses, escape suddenly essential. The tuskless cow turned and hobbled away, each step agonising torture. Her front right knee joint had been shattered by the single copper-jacketed bullet.

Man, her hated enemy, had just handed out a death sentence.

As the rangers and staff of a luxury lodge in Etosha National Park, Namibia welcome the last guests of the season, thoughts are predominantly on the three-month break ahead. Except for Sean, who is fighting his growing attraction for the manager's wife, Thea.

Camping in the park nearby, Professor Eben Kruger has his work cut out keeping the attention of the university students in his charge on the behavioural habits of the cunning jackal.

None of them could ever be prepared for the horrendous events about to take place. Each will be pushed to breaking point as the quest for survival becomes the only thing that matters.

Shocking, gripping, breathtaking. Beverley Harper's outstanding new novel is a guaranteed bestseller.

Beverley Harper
The Forgotten Sea

Not a pretty sight. Certainly not one the authorities on Mauritius, that gem of a tourist destination in a trio of idyllic islands once known as the Mascarenes, would like to become public knowledge. Their carefully nurtured image was of sparkling blue sea, emerald green palm fringes haphazardly angled along pure white beaches . . . This was ugly, messy.

When Australian journalist Holly Jones flies to Mauritius to cover playboy adventurer Connor Maguire's search for buried ancestral treasure, it promises to be a relaxing two weeks in an exotic island paradise. What she hasn't planned on is an infuriating, reluctant subject with a hidden agenda. Or one who stirs the fires in a heart grown cold. But can she trust him . . .

After the body of a young woman is washed up on a beach, Holly finds herself caught in a deadly murder investigation and the island's darkest secrets.

A compelling, passionate tale from Beverley Harper, author of the bestselling *People of Heaven*, *Echo of an Angry God*, *Edge of the Rain* and *Storms Over Africa*.

'We have our own Wilbur Smith in the making here in Australia'
SUN HERALD

Beverley Harper
People of Heaven

*The poacher didn't shoot her. Bullets cost money and
a shot might alert the rangers . . . On the third night,
after enduring more agony than any man or beast
should ever have to face, the rhinoceros took one last
shuddering breath, heaved her flanks painfully, and
sought refuge in the silky blackness of death.*

In 1945 two returning soldiers meet on a train
bound for Zululand. They have nothing in common;
Joe King is a British–South African landowner,
Wilson Mpande a Zulu tribesman. Yet destiny will
link them for generations.

Michael King and Dyson Mpande, the sons of
enemies, share a precious friendship that defies
race and colour. But as the realities of apartheid
transform an angry South Africa, the fate of the Zulu
nation is as precarious as that of the endangered
black rhinoceros, hunted for its horn. Each must
fight for what he loves most.

And a great evil between their families will test their
friendship beyond imaginable limits.

Passionate, suspenseful, evocative, Beverley
Harper's fourth novel is a worthy successor to her
previous bestsellers, *Echo of an Angry God*, *Edge
of the Rain* and *Storms Over Africa*.

'Harper is Australia's answer to Wilbur Smith'
AUSTRALIAN GOOD TASTE

Beverley Harper
Echo of an Angry God

Likoma Island in Lake Malawi is renowned throughout Africa for its exotic and treacherous beauty – and its secret history of human sacrifice, hidden treasure and unspeakable horror. A history that cannot be hidden forever.

Lana Devereaux travels to Malawi seeking the truth behind her father's disappearance near Likoma Island fifteen years ago. But Lana soon finds herself caught in a web of deceit, passion and black magic that stretches back over two hundred years and has ramifications that reach well beyond the shores of Lake Malawi.

Beverley Harper is fast becoming one of Australia's most popular storytellers. *Echo of an Angry God* is her most thrilling adventure yet and follows the enormous success of her previous novels, *Storms Over Africa* and *Edge of the Rain*.

'a fast paced yet affecting thriller with . . . compelling authenticity'
WHO WEEKLY

'a terrific adventure'
GOLD COAST BULLETIN

Beverley Harper
Edge of the Rain

The blood scent was fresh. Hunger ached in her belly . . . the lioness slid forward as close as she dared. The little boy seconds away from death was two, maybe three years old. He was lost in the vast, heat-soaked sand that was the Kalahari desert.

Toddler Alex Theron is miraculously rescued by a passing clan of Kalahari Bushmen. Over the ensuing years the desert draws him back, for it hides a beautiful secret . . . diamonds.

But nothing comes easily from within this turbulent continent and before Alex can even hope to realise his dreams he will lose his mind to love and fight a bitter enemy who will stop at nothing to destroy him . . .

From the author of *Storms Over Africa* comes a novel of courage and an unforgettable journey into the beating heart of Africa.

Beverley Harper
Storms Over Africa

Richard Dunn has made Africa his home. But his Africa is in crisis.

Ancient rivalries have ignited modern political ambitions. Desperate poachers stalk the dwindling populations of the game parks. For those of the old Africa, the old ways, nothing is certain.

But for Richard – a man used to getting his own way – the stakes are even higher. Into his world has come the compelling and beautiful Steve Hayes. A woman he swears he will never give up. A woman struggling to guard her own dreadful secret.

Richard has no choice. He must face the consequences of the past and fight for the future. To lose now is to lose everything . . .